He opened the bril... the vision.

As she gazed into .... heart raced; her bearings were lost. In the depths of his eyes, she glimpsed a fountain in a forest. The turquoise waters of the ocean. An underground well encased by sacred stones. She, the forest fairy, was immersed in the blue waters of the warrior's eyes, the waves emanating from him flowing through her, cleansing her. Beckoning her.

In Tristan's eyes, Issylte glimpsed a black bird—a sea raven—soaring over an open sea, hovering now before her. A small dove fluttered in her breast, called forth from her soul. White wings unfurled as she took flight, rising into the azure sky alongside the black seabird—-floating together through the diaphanous clouds scattered across the vast ocean.

In the breadth of an instant, Issylte was bound to this warrior, the Blue Knight of Cornwall, as if fate had indeed entwined them. Through the windows of his eyes, she peered into his soul, her own blending with his, as if they were the forest and the ocean, encircled now within the three layers of protective stones, the holy trinity of sacred elements of the Goddess.

The Wild Rose and the Sea Raven

by

Jennifer Ivy Walker

The Wild Rose and the Sea Raven,
Book 1

The Wild Rose and the Sea Raven

Cover Art by *Rae Monet, Inc.*

The Wild Rose Press, Inc.
PO Box 708
Adams Basin, NY 14410-0708
Visit us at www.thewildrosepress.com

Publishing History
First Edition, 2022
Trade Paperback ISBN 978-1-5092-
Digital ISBN 978-1-5092-

The Wild Rose and the Sea Raven, Book 1
Published in the United States of America

Dedication

To Tara
For nurturing my firstborn novel with the same love
that I nurtured you as my firstborn child

Chapter 1

The Emerald Princess

This was torture, being forced to sit still while her attendants yanked her hair into tight braids as they tried their best to transform her into a proper princess.

Issylte yearned to be astride her horse, galloping towards the forest, the chilly wind whipping her hair and stinging her cheeks with glorious freedom.

Instead, she had to endure the agony of her long blonde hair being plaited with ribbons of emerald silk and sparkly gold thread. Because her father's betrothed was arriving today with an entourage of royal courtiers and servants. And Issylte had to appear perfect when presented to the woman who would become her stepmother and queen.

She shuddered at the thought.

The entire castle was ablaze with activity in preparation for the upcoming royal wedding between Issylte's father, King Donnchadh of Ireland, and Princess Morag of Scotland. The royal marriage would create an alliance between the two kingdoms and bring an end to the twelve long years of her father's solitude since the death of his wife, Queen Liadan, during Issylte's birth.

Father deserves to be happy, Issylte thought begrudgingly, flinching as her ladies in waiting stuffed her into an elaborate, elegant, dark green gown.

She glanced over at the seamstresses who were meticulously sewing the crystals and gemstones to the gauzy creation that she would have to wear to the wedding. It looked like a ridiculous cake. And extremely uncomfortable. She rolled her eyes in exasperation.

There would be hundreds of lords and ladies in all their finery. Sumptuous feasts, stifling etiquette. Issylte was terrified that her father intended to select her future husband from among the royal wedding guests.

The thought of putting her sweat-drenched palm into the polished hand of some *dashing* prince made her stomach turn. And he would probably whisper into her deaf ear.

She would have to pull away from him, turn her head completely around so that he could speak into her good ear, and look like a total idiot. She'd die of humiliation.

Or pretend that she'd heard whatever charming, witty thing he'd said. Search for clues in his facial expressions and mimic them, as if she thought he were oh, so clever. By the Goddess, she hated being a princess!

Brangien's voice interrupted her disquieting reverie.

"You are positively *radiant*, sweetheart. These silk ribbons really enhance the color of your gown. And the golden threads in your hair. They sparkle and shimmer in the light."

Issylte sighed audibly. She plopped down onto her vanity stool, pouting at the sight of the intricate braids on either side of her pinched face. She glowered at her reflection in the mirror. By the Goddess, she wanted to gallop away from all the madness of royal wedding preparations! But Brangien absolutely loved it.

Her nurse came up behind her to place a delicate golden coronet, adorned with emeralds, upon her head. Brangien kissed Issylte's cheek and gave her an affectionate squeeze. "You're sure to please your father and attract the eye of many a fine lord as well!"

Issylte rolled her eyes. She would soon reach the marriageable age of fourteen, and Brangien positively reveled in playing the role of royal matchmaker. But Issylte had no desire whatsoever to attract a potential suitor. Or to be a *proper princess,* for that matter.

Brangien stroked her golden hair—unbound in the style of *young maidens*—and beamed at Issylte's reflection in the mirror. "I know that you, my dearest, stubborn princess, would rather be cleaning your horse's stall instead of donning these exquisite gowns." She gestured to the expansive, royal armoires that her father always kept generously filled. "But tonight, you will behave as the Emerald Princess of Ireland and make your father proud. And this gown is *perfect* for the occasion."

Brangien kissed her cheek again. Issylte exhaled, slumped her shoulders, and reluctantly accepted defeat.

Her nurse lovingly stroked one of the slender braids. From the obvious contentment on her face, Issylte knew that Brangien approved of the dark green gathered velvet bodice of her gown, the fancy braids, the golden crown of emeralds glinting upon her head.

"Darkest green, like the forest you love so well," her nurse whispered into her left ear as she squeezed Issylte's shoulder. Brangien gently wiped a tear from her eye, basking Issylte in the golden glow of her generous grin. "My Emerald Princess."

Issylte couldn't help but return a loving smile.

Although her nurse frequently drove her crazy with the endless matchmaking attempts, she absolutely adored her *Gigi.*

A blare of trumpets sounded, heralding the arrival of Princess Morag and her royal procession from Scotland. Brangien took Issylte's hand, urging her towards the door.

"Come, let's go quickly. Your father the king will wish us to be there to greet his betrothed."

Exiting Issylte's royal chamber, Brangien led her down the long corridor to the stone staircase, which led to the Great Hall below.

The Castle of Connaught was sumptuously decorated for the royal wedding, with evergreen and ivy garlands embedded with roses and peonies in full bloom. Huge bouquets of spring flowers in elegant vases graced every tabletop. The tapestries on the castle walls were clean and fresh, and the wooden furniture was fragrant with the scent of pine oil. Gleaming marble floors and crystal chandeliers glistened in the morning sun as Issylte, Brangien, and two attendants proceeded to the Great Hall to meet King Donnchadh and his royal guests.

The entrance doors were opened wide, flanked by members of the royal guard, dressed in their finest livery. Her father's banner—a great white hawk with outstretched wings against a dark forest green background—welcomed her, the Emerald Princess, to the Great Hall.

At Issylte's approach, a trumpet sounded once again, announcing her arrival. The sight of hundreds of elegantly attired courtiers and royal guests assembled in the Great Hall made Issylte's heart flutter wildly.

"Her Majesty, the Princess Issylte!"

Royal servants ushered Issylte to her father, who was resplendent in his dark green tunic, his cloak of white ermine, and his golden crown embedded with the same emeralds and diamonds that embellished her own coronet. He sat regally upon on his throne amidst an array of courtiers whose gowns and tunics were adorned with fine silks and emblazoned with the various coats of arms of their respective territories. All eyes were upon her as she executed a wobbly curtsey before the bemused and twinkling eyes of her royal father.

"Greetings, daughter. I am most pleased to have you here with me as we welcome my betrothed."

King Donnchadh's hazel eyes shone with approval as Issylte took her place at his right side. *Brangien must be bursting with pride*, Issylte thought, for her father seemed pleased with her appearance—and performance. She breathed a sigh of relief upon her small throne, wiping her drenched palms along the sides of her gown, grateful that the dark green color would hide the sweat.

The trumpets blared once again as the herald announced the arrival of the royal court of Scotland.

"His Majesty, King Griogair of Scotland, and her Royal Highness, the Princess Morag."

Issylte's stomach lurched, and her mouth went dry, as the royal family of Scotland regally entered the reception hall, bowing their heads in deference to King Donnchadh of Ireland.

Judging by his silver hair and beard, and the age lines which creased his craggy face, Issylte guessed that King Griogair was about twenty years older than her father. He was rather stout, yet tall, and addressed her father warmly.

"Greetings, King Donnchadh! It has been many

years since I have been to Castle Connaught. You look well, Donnchadh. Your palace has been lavishly decorated for the wedding of my daughter. I am most pleased."

King Griogair bowed his head to Issylte's father, clasping his arm in greeting. He straightened, offering his hand to the dark-haired beauty behind him.

"Allow me to present my daughter, the Princess Morag."

Her father's face beamed in admiration as he beheld the exquisite beauty of his betrothed. A bitter wave of jealousy washed over Issylte at the unmasked joy upon his face, as if all that mattered was his utterly beguiling bride.

She couldn't deny that her future stepmother was beautiful. Princess Morag was tall and slender, with lustrous, long black hair that graced her slim waist. Her eyes were like black obsidian, a stark contrast from her porcelain complexion. Issylte watched in morbid fascination as her future stepmother dipped into a low, regal bow before her intended husband, humbling him with her rare beauty as she humbled herself before the handsome king of Ireland. A waft of fresh lavender perfumed the air.

"I am most honored to meet you, King Donnchadh. I hope you find me worthy of becoming your queen."

His cheeks reddened with pleasure, her father greedily accepted the hand of his betrothed. Raising his intended to a stand, he fervently kissed Princess Morag's hand and spoke, his voice breathless as an eager adolescent.

"Welcome to Castle Connaught, my queen." Her father's voice quavered with glee.

As if suddenly remembering he had a daughter, he turned to Issylte and offered his palm.

Her legs trembled; hundreds of butterflies fluttered in her chest. It was time. He now expected her to perform like a proper princess and gracefully curtsey before the future queen. In front of *hundreds* of royal spectators examining her every move. Issylte held her breath and swallowed the lump in her throat. Sweat trickled down her palms.

"May I present my daughter, the Princess Issylte, whom the people of Ireland affectionately call '*The Emerald Princess*'."

At her father's gesture, Issylte rose unsteadily from her throne, smoothed her green velvet gown, and reluctantly placed her drenched palm into his hand. She approached her future stepmother, dutifully bowed her head, and lowered herself into a deep curtsey, all the while praying that she would not stumble and humiliate herself at this most crucial moment. She could feel the judgmental eyes of countless aristocrats and courtiers assessing the regal quality of her *princessly* grace. Or lack thereof.

"It is an immense honor and great pleasure to meet you, Your Majesty," Issylte stammered, her voice quavering as much as her roiling stomach. She prayed she would not vomit on the future queen's magnificent, sapphire-blue gown.

"Greetings, Princess Issylte," the dark-haired beauty crooned. "You are indeed as lovely as I have been told. I trust that you will come to love me as your future stepmother. And *queen*."

The glacial, imperial voice seeped into Issylte's bones like a winter chill.

Her father's betrothed displayed her elegant hand for Issylte to kiss.

Issylte brushed her lips against the icy hand of her future stepmother. An unpleasant shiver crept up her spine at the frigid touch. As the queen's skeletal fingers tightly gripped her own, a tingling numbness inched up Issylte's arm, as if her strength were being absorbed.

Issylte recoiled, withdrawing her hand as if frostbitten. She rose unsteadily to her feet on weakened legs.

The queen's black eyes fixed upon her with the stark gaze of a predator. Exposed and vulnerable, her limbs quivering and her mouth dry, Issylte returned, shaken, to her father's side.

Brangien flashed her a reassuring smile that did not reach her troubled eyes.

King Donnchadh escorted his magnificent bride to his left side as the King of Scotland completed his royal introductions.

"And now, allow me to present my daughter's personal guard and duly sworn knight, the *Morholt.*"

An enormous warrior emerged from the entourage of heavily armed knights surrounding her father's bride. Issylte had never seen such a giant of a man, who stood a whole head taller than the rest of the guards, his heavily muscled arms as large as the trunks of a tree. Fiery red hair extended well past his shoulders, braided in peaks like the pointed horns of a dragon. The Morholt's bushy red beard was also braided—two giant fangs protruding from his gruesome mouth.

Issylte stared, transfixed with terror, at the Morholt.

He wore a knight's armor—with metal chest plate, gauntlets, and greaves—all magnificently detailed in gold, with intricate engravings of dragon scales upon a background of deepest black. His plumed helmet, which he held in his hand, was also black—adorned with a golden dragon emblazoned across the forehead. Serpents slithered up each side of the headpiece, to a crested peak where an elaborate black ostrich feather magnificently unfurled.

The massive Morholt bowed and—placing his right fist over his heart in a gesture of fealty—thundered in a deep baritone voice that shook the room.

"King Donnchadh of Ireland, it is my greatest honor to serve you, as my princess becomes your *queen*." Rising to his feet, the Black Knight locked eyes with Issylte's father. "May you always find me worthy, my king."

The Morholt bowed majestically and stepped back into precise formation among the royal guards of Scotland.

Issylte's father nodded his head gravely, his royal regard assessing the formidable Black Knight. "I accept with gratitude your pledge of fealty, Morholt. As the greatest warrior in your land, and as my bride's sworn protector, your worth will be immeasurable in your service to Ireland."

Her father seemed unnerved by the encounter, for he hesitated, somewhat flustered, before finally beckoning his royal guests to enjoy the sumptuous feast which awaited.

"Let us celebrate the arrival of my betrothed, the future queen of Ireland. Royal guests, lords, and ladies—Everyone. Let us eat, drink, and be merry!"

The lively procession burst cheerfully into the vast, gaily decorated banquet hall. Enormous trestle tables and chairs had been strategically placed so that spectators could enjoy the musicians, jugglers, dancers, and troubadours who were performing in the center of the floor. Lively music was playing, and servants were pouring goblets of wine and ale as the guests filled the opulent ballroom.

Seated beside her father and his honored guests at the royal table, Issylte was enthralled as the bejeweled dancers in exotic bright silks performed with the troubadours, *jongleurs* and *trouvères*.

Royal courtiers laughed joyfully at the spectacular entertainment. Platters of stuffed pheasant and peacock, roast venison and boar soon filled the tables, perfuming the air with delicious aroma. Issylte devoured the sweet pastries and candied fruits, savoring the delicious cherry flavor of her favorite *tartelette aux cerises*.

She spotted Brangien at a nearby table. Her nurse was obviously enjoying the fine French wine, from the flush in her cheeks and the sparkle in her eyes as she beheld Issylte's gaze.

The final courses were at last finished and the dishes cleared away. Now, the royal musicians began to play the lively, enticing *carole*. Guests raced to the center of the banquet hall to form a circle of exuberant, energetic dancing. Joining fingers, couples paired off to perform in the center of the ring, returning to their places as others took turns dancing in the middle, each pair attempting to outdo all the others with impressive, daring finesse.

Issylte was frustrated that she was too young to participate. She bobbed and bounced in her chair, leaning from side to side with the beckoning rhythm of the music. She longed to dance breathlessly amid the bright colors of the ladies' silk dresses, the glittering gold thread of the lords' tunics, the gaiety of the guests and jovial ambiance of the betrothal feast.

Brangien spoke gently into her good ear. "It is time for us to retire now, my princess. You have your equestrian lessons in the morning. I am certain your father the king will want his beautiful daughter to be well rested and at her best for the upcoming wedding. Come now. Say goodnight and let us return to your chamber."

Issylte pretended not to hear, her eyes fixed on the dazzling display on the dance floor.

Brangien insisted quietly but firmly. "Issylte." Her tone brokered no refusal.

She rose reluctantly from her chair, the magic of the night suddenly dispelled. The music called to her, the dancing and revelry intoxicating and inviting.

She forced herself to curtsey dutifully before King Griogair and Princess Morag, bidding them goodnight. She kissed her father on the cheek and whispered, "Good night, Father," into the shell of his ear.

His eyes shone with love, but Issylte was unsure if that emotion was for her as his daughter or for the haughty, exquisite beauty at his side who laughed seductively as she clutched his arm, drawing his attention back to her. Issylte swallowed a lump in her throat.

She exited the vibrant ballroom, casting a brief glance back at her father, whose eyes never left the enticing brunette at his side. The festivities continued in full splendor as she followed Brangien down the long, lonely corridor, up the empty stone staircase, and back to the silence of her royal bedroom.

Her attendants removed her jeweled crown and unbraided the ribbons from her hair. They removed her luxurious emerald velvet dress and helped her into a soft white cotton nightgown. Brangien tucked her in amongst the fluffy pillows and embroidered linens of the glorious, canopied bed, bestowing a goodnight kiss upon her cheek as she prepared to leave.

"Gigi," Issylte sniffled, addressing her beloved nurse by the name she'd given her as a toddler. "I wish my father wouldn't marry her. She frightens me."

Tears flowed down her cheeks. Her father would have little time for her now, with his beautiful new bride who wanted him all for herself. A deep, heavy ache gripped her heart.

Brangien sat down on the bed beside Issylte, caressing her hair to soothe her. "Shhh…" she whispered, stroking Issylte's cheek. "It's only normal that you should feel resentful. You've had your father's attention your whole life, and now he plans to remarry. Of course you'd prefer it if he didn't."

Issylte loved the comfort of her Gigi's touch. It always managed to ease her fears, to make her feel safe. And loved.

"Don't you fret now," Gigi whispered into her left ear as she tucked the covers snugly around Issylte. "Even if your stepmother is cold and uncaring, you'll *always* have me."

Gigi hugged her tightly, cocooning her in the maternal warmth of loving arms.

"Now, no more unpleasant thoughts. Think about riding Luna tomorrow morning. Galloping through the forest that you love so much. That will give you pleasant dreams, my princess. Goodnight, sweetheart. I love you."

"I love you, too, Gigi."

Issylte kissed her nurse, who extinguished the candle on the bedside table and gave her one last reassuring smile as she closed the bedroom door behind her.

Issylte closed her eyes, anticipating the joy of riding her dappled gray mare in the morning. There was nothing she loved more. She smiled with delight, pulling the blankets under her chin, burrowing her head deep into the soft pillow.

Without warning, her fingers remembered the queen's icy cold touch. Her hand once again felt drained, with the same disturbing sensation of her energy being leeched. A frisson of dread shivered through her, despite the warmth of the blankets. Issylte rubbed her arm vigorously, as if to remove the unpleasant, numbing chill.

When she finally did fall asleep in the luxurious canopied bed, Issylte dozed fitfully, haunted by vivid nightmares of cold, black eyes watching in the darkness, a malevolence lurking in shadows, biding its time.

Chapter 2

The Blue Knight of Cornwall

Tristan clenched his sword and positioned his feet, preparing for another attack. Despite the mild winter sun, he was drenched from the brutal training session. Sweat poured from his matted hair, stinging his eyes. His opponent was circling, sizing him up, searching for a weakness.

His rival feinted left, lunged right with a swift downward strike. Tristan deftly blocked the powerful blow and parried, redirecting the offensive force into a counterattack that caused his adversary to step back. He had him now. With a savage flurry of strikes, Tristan disarmed his opponent and pointed the tip of his victorious sword just under the vanquished knight's chin.

"Yield!" Connor bellowed, gritting his teeth in a furious grin. "You bastard. I'll never hear the end of this now. Vaughan will never let me forget it."

Tristan lowered his sword and swiped his arm across his sweaty brow. He grinned from ear to ear. Connor was twenty, two years older than Tristan. And he'd beaten him. Again. Three times in a row now. Damn, it felt good.

"Until tomorrow, Tristan of Lyonesse," Connor muttered, shaking his hand and slapping him on the shoulder in congratulations. The knight sauntered off the training field with Vaughan, who launched a series of jibes at the unfortunate victim.

At least Connor had a decent sense of humor. Tristan could hear him laughing as his two friends trudged towards the knights' lodge, every bit as exhausted as Tristan himself after today's strenuous battles. Their mentor, Gorvenal—the First Knight of Tintagel—showed no mercy.

Gorvenal now approached Tristan in the center of the training field. A giant of a man, the Master of Arms was one of the very few taller than Tristan, carrying more bulk and brute strength as well. With his dark brown hair, enormous height, and muscular build, Gorvenal could pass for Tristan's older brother. And the ferocity of his character made the similarities all the more striking.

"Well done, Tristan! You fought well against Connor. I've been observing your horsemanship. Your skill with the bow and arrow. And especially the way you handle the sword. All are exceptional. I'm most impressed."

Tristan grinned despite himself. Never one to enjoy praise, he nevertheless was pleased with Gorvenal's approval.

"Your uncle the king has asked for you. I've spoken to him of your potential in becoming his champion. He would speak to you, so get cleaned up, and I'll come to your room in half an hour. We'll go together to see the king."

As he walked back to the castle, Tristan glanced across the courtyard where Gorvenal and the other men at arms supervised the training of approximately 100 knights such as Tristan himself. Riders were charging with lances at suspended dummies—the quintains—while trying to avoid being struck by the outstretched, wooden arms. Other knights were engaged in mock combat with wooden swords and shields. Several groups were scaling walls, maneuvering siege ladders and battering rams. Archers fired at targets and trained with both crossbows and longbows. It was thrilling, exhausting, and merciless. Tristan loved it. It was the only way to assuage the guilt that choked him.

He'd come to Tintagel ten years ago, after witnessing the brutal slaughter of his family in an attack by Viking invaders when he was eight years old. Tristan had seen the burning and pillaging of his village while the invading warriors raped the local women, butchered the men, and took as slaves the people whom he had grown to love.

Orphaned, consumed with guilt and rage, Tristan had been sent to live with his uncle, King Marke of Cornwall, in this fortress built high upon the craggy Atlantic coast of southwestern Britain. First as a squire, now as a knight, Tristan fueled his anger into the training with Gorvenal. The weapons master understood his need, demanding that Tristan forge his fury and brute strength into the might of his sword. A sword that had become quite mighty indeed.

For nearly a decade now, King Marke of Cornwall had provided for Tristan, whose mother Blanchefleur had been the beloved younger sister of his good-hearted uncle. Since Marke had never married, and had no heirs of his own, Tristan was destined to inherit not only his parents' kingdom of Lyonesse—including the myriad Islands of Scilly, stretching as far south as France —but also the kingdom of Cornwall, from his uncle.

Tristan now returned to his room in the castle, where a page helped him remove his armor and soiled tunic. Tristan washed, donned a clean tunic, and belted his sword at the hip for the meeting with King Marke.

A knock summoned the page to open the door. Gorvenal entered. "All set?"

Tristan nodded, and the two men set off for Marke's royal chambers.

The castle guards escorted Gorvenal and Tristan into the royal antechamber. King Marke was seated in a chair which served as an informal throne in this reception area where he welcomed invited guests and dignitaries. This afternoon, the setting sun shone through the western windows, and Tristan glimpsed the turbulent sea in the inlet far below the cliff upon which Tintagel had been built.

He regarded Marke, whom he loved and respected not only as king, but as a man more like a father than uncle. Tristan gazed into the familiar twinkling blue eyes, taking in the still powerful build that had defended Cornwall in many a battle.

Tristan knelt with Gorvenal before his uncle in tribute, then stood at the king's gesture to rise.

"Tristan, my nephew, how good it is to see you!" Marke heartily exclaimed, embracing him warmly. "Gorvenal has informed me of your exceptional skill with the sword and the lance. Come, both of you, seat yourselves here beside me. Servants, bring food and wine for my guests!"

Platters bearing goblets of wine, assorted cheeses, and fresh fruit quickly appeared. The delicious aroma of roasted meats made Tristan's mouth water. The three men dug in, their lips smacking with the savory goodness. Marke grinned at his nephew, nodding to his First Knight as he wiped his mouth on a linen napkin.

"Gorvenal, inform Tristan of your proposed plan. I find it a splendid idea and give it my wholehearted approval. Please, enlighten him."

Intrigued, Tristan searched the familiar scarred face of the knight whom he served. The warrior responsible for all the tests of physical endurance, the strength training, the mock battles. The mentor who had helped him hone his rage into exceptional skill with the sword. The man whom Tristan loved like a brother.

"Tristan, the High King of Britain, Arthur Pendragon, is seeking new candidates to train as Knights of the Round Table in his castle of Camelot. To determine which ten knights of Cornwall will earn this prestigious honor, I have proposed to King Marke that we host here at Tintagel a *Tournament of Champions*. A three-day competition among the young warriors of the entire kingdom of Cornwall."

Gorvenal gulped a hearty swallow of wine from his goblet and wiped his mouth with his sleeve. He turned to face Tristan, his eyes full of challenge. "The tournament will include archery, jousting, and a battle of swords. The top ten winners will earn the privilege of training with King Arthur's champion, the First Knight of Camelot— the legendary Lancelot of the Lake."

Gorvenal grinned, his eyes ablaze with the same fire that Tristan had only seen in the heat of battle. His mentor's enthusiasm was contagious. Tristan leaned forward to the edge of his seat, his foot bouncing rapidly against the marble floor. Adrenaline thrummed in his veins.

King Marke leaned back upon his informal throne,

locking eyes with him. Tristan's heart was in his throat. His mouth was parched. He considered reaching for his goblet to quench his thirst, but he dared not turn away from his uncle's direct gaze. He swallowed forcefully, his heartbeat thundering in his ears.

"As my sister's son, blood of my blood, you are the presumptive heir to my kingdom of Cornwall."

The king took a long pull of wine from his silver chalice, eyeing his nephew over the rim. Tristan could barely stand the tension. He was an arrow, nocked in a tightly drawn bow string, ready to take flight.

"Gorvenal informs me that you are the top warrior here at Tintagel. That you stand a very good chance of qualifying in—perhaps even winning—the competition."

Marke motioned to a servant, who approached, carrying a tray which held a small, jeweled box. The king picked up the box and offered it to Tristan. "Open it," Marke commanded. Tristan complied.

Inside the jeweled box was a shield-shaped golden ring, bearing the profile of the royal bird of Cornwall— the *chough*, or sea raven. The eye of the black bird was a large blue topaz gemstone, glinting in the afternoon sunlight. The outer perimeter of the ring was encased by fifteen small golden coins, which Tristan recognized as *bezants*.

"Cornwall is your heritage as it is mine, Tristan," Marke explained. "Your mother's birthright was the kingdom of Lyonesse, on the southwestern tip of Cornwall. The region called *Land's End*, with the hundreds of Islands of Scilly that extend all the way to Brittany."

Marke gestured to the ring in Tristan's hand.

"This ring symbolizes your destiny. The shield represents the kingdom you defend for me. The *chough,* or sea raven—the royal bird of Cornwall—signifies your heritage as my heir, and the kingdom of Lyonesse, your birthright. The blue topaz stone I have chosen to represent you, Tristan. Should you qualify as one of the ten winners of the *Tournament of Champions*, I will dub you the *Blue Knight of Cornwall*. My blood, my champion—and my heir."

Tristan placed the ring on his finger. His throat constricted with emotion, Tristan knelt in gratitude and humility before his uncle.

King Marke stood and placed his hand on Tristan's bowed head. "May this ring grant you good fortune not only in the upcoming *Tournament of Champions*, but throughout your entire life. Wear it with the pride and honor my sister would have felt had she lived to see the man you have become. Go now, knowing that you bear the symbol of love and blessing of your king." Helping Tristan to his feet, Marke gripped his shoulder and chuckled, "I am certain that Gorvenal has even more intensive training in mind for you and the warriors of Cornwall. The tournament begins in two months' time. Prepare well, and make me proud, Tristan."

Tristan thanked his uncle profusely, assuring him that he would settle for nothing less than qualifying for the opportunity to train in Camelot.

He retreated shakily from the royal reception area with a still-smiling Gorvenal, who slapped him on the back with a hearty grin. "*The fuckin' Blue Knight of Cornwall!* Hell, yeah! Congratulations, Tristan. Now, we *train*!"

Chapter 3

The New Queen

Morag scrutinized her reflection in the oval mirror of her royal chambers. Her lustrous black hair—scented with rosewater—was unbound, cascading down her back, the way he liked it. The corset of her deep crimson gown was tightly laced, emphasizing the fullness of her breasts, all the more enticing with the snugly gathered velvet bodice, so soft to the touch. A sumptuous bouquet of red roses stood on the bedside table under the sunny window, the ruby color subtly enhancing her scarlet gown. And the bed was scented with lavender, to arouse passion. She tugged her neckline a bit lower at the sound of the expected knock upon her door.

A stern nod sent her royal attendants scurrying from the room, leaving her alone with King Donnchadh. As her husband entered the fragrant chamber, his ardent eyes locked with hers, fixing on the sumptuous swell of her bustline. Morag smiled coyly at him, content with his obvious lust. She'd learned long ago that, in a world ruled by men, her striking beauty and seductive wiles gave her tremendous power over them. And she needed to wield every bit of it today.

"My husband, please, come sit with me. Let us share this fine wine." She poured two goblets of rich burgundy. The same color as her gown. She glanced at him from lowered, intoxicating lashes.

With an impatient grin, the king unstrapped his sword and placed it on the floor. His eyes lingered on the plush bed before he seated himself at the small table at her side. She handed him the goblet and watched as he took a large swallow, his eyes never leaving her *décolletage*. She leaned forward to give him a better view as she feigned adjusting the tablecloth.

When he placed his goblet down, she lowered herself slowly onto his lap, brushing her breasts against him as she nestled her soft bottom against his loins. She smiled inwardly at the immediate response. She needed to act quickly, while he was entranced.

She brushed a lock of auburn hair from his eager face, placing her full mouth close to his. "My love, I wish to discuss something with you that has been troubling me lately."

Donnchadh kissed her swanlike neck, his hands clutching at her waist, pulling her more firmly against his lap.

"I would like to develop a closer relationship with Issylte. As her new stepmother, I'd like to supervise her lessons myself. Teach her more proper, courtly behavior. The eloquence and etiquette more becoming to a princess."

The king wasn't really listening. Just as Morag had planned.

"It is time for her to be married. I propose that we wed her to King Marke of Tintagel. A royal wedding would create a profitable alliance between Ireland and Cornwall, much like our marriage has strengthened the ties between our two kingdoms. Don't you agree, my love?"

She kissed the shell of his ear, offering him the full view of her creamy white breasts.

"Mmmm," he murmured. "A splendid idea." He leaned her back in his arms, smothering her neck and shoulders with passionate kisses. "And I have another idea," he growled, easing the neckline of her gown down over her shoulders as he ravished her breasts with greedy lips.

Morag rose from his lap, unlaced her corset seductively before him and dropped her gown to the floor. She sauntered across the room, swaying her slender nude hips, as Donnchadh quickly threw off his royal tunic, breeches and boots and followed the bewitching temptress, a moth drawn to the flame.

****

Several weeks later, King Donnchadh departed with his Marshal and Seneschal to finalize plans for the construction of additional lodging for the hundreds of knights that the Morholt insisted were necessary to bolster Ireland's military might. Queen Morag had been patiently waiting for this planned excursion. And now, with the king gone for at least a fortnight, she planned to take full advantage of his absence.

As she proceeded into her antechamber to await the arrival of the Morholt, whom she'd summoned, the queen did not notice Brangien, who was seated in the adjacent servants' room, embroidering under the opened window in a quiet corner.

Queen Morag dismissed her attendants as the burly Viking entered her antechamber. The Black Knight was not clad in his usual intricately detailed armor, having donned instead a more casual tunic and breeches for today's private, intimate meeting. But his magnificent sword gleamed at his hip, ever ready to defend his beloved queen.

"My queen," he said, his voice deep and rich, as he knelt to kiss her extended hand.

She gazed down upon his thick, russet hair. He smelled of leather, horses, and pine. Her body stirred in response.

The Morholt rose to his feet to await her command. Morag turned, wandering over to the open window where the drapes fluttered in the morning sunlight and the fragrant pine scent of the lush forest wafted in upon the summer breeze.

She gazed out across the grassy plains which led to the thick, dense woods surrounding the castle. The very, very, dense woods.

"I have given our plan careful consideration. There is one outcome I had not considered."

She turned to face him. To her delight, his bold eyes were piqued with interest. And lust.

"If Donnchadh and I marry the Princess Issylte to King Marke of Tintagel, she could very well bear him a son. The heir to the throne of Cornwall." She locked her eyes upon his. "As you well know, I have not been able to conceive a child. In the two long years since my marriage, despite the futile amorous attempts of my hapless husband."

Morag floated across the room, her dreamy dress a soft blue like the endless sky.

She ran her white hands up the front of his massive chest, her slender fingers stroking the thick, dark hair at the base of his throat. "Or the ardent, frequent lovemaking of my lusty, virile knight." She kissed his neck, tracing a circle with her dainty tongue. She smiled contentedly at his guttural moan.

"Although I have no desire whatsoever to bear a bawling brat, it would be disastrous if Issylte were to produce an heir. For if I remain childless, her son would inherit not only the throne of King Marke of Cornwall, but the entire kingdom of Ireland as well."

She tugged the front of his tunic, pulling his chest against hers.

"Princess Issylte is the greatest threat to my throne." She shared her breath with him.

He lowered his mouth to devour hers, moving to assault her swanlike neck. His face flushed with desire, he raised his head and snarled, "Then she must die."

Morag wrapped her slender arms around his thickly corded neck and pulled his face down to hers. She teased his lips with her own, rubbing her hips against his in a provocative dance of seduction. Taking him by the hand, she led him most willingly into her adjacent chambers, to the inviting, enticing, lavender-scented bed.

A short while later, after he had left, the queen was recovering from the amorous assault of her beloved Black Knight. Her limbs were still quavering with pleasure, her loins smoldering like glowing embers, when there was a sudden, urgent knock at her door.

The queen, who had dismissed her attendants for the intimate tryst, quickly donned her hastily discarded blue gown and smoothed her sex-tousled hair. Inhaling deeply, she rose to her full regal stature and opened the door to find one of her royal guards standing before her, visibly distressed.

He knelt at her feet, his head bowed in homage. Morag's heart leapt to her throat. Had someone seen? Or heard? She had practically screamed, lost in the throes of pleasure. The Morholt knew all the ways to drive her wild.

"Rise, Sir Knial. What is it? What is wrong?" She tried to calm her racing heart.

The knight was obviously flustered. He rocked from side to side, shifting his weight from one foot to the other. By the Goddess, what was wrong?

"I just saw the Lady Brangien leave the servants' quarters, my queen. The room beside your royal chambers."

He stammered, beside himself with agitation.

"I did not realize she was there, Your Majesty. You gave explicit orders that no one was to be in the vicinity. I did not see her, my queen. But I did notice her leave, just a few moments ago. She raced down the hall and took the stairs to the kitchen. I did not know of her presence in the servants' quarters, Your Majesty. I have failed in my duty."

He dropped to his knees, his head lowered in shame.

Morag's mind raced. She needed to react quickly. What had Brangien overheard? She couldn't take a chance. She had to act decisively. And immediately.

Fortunately, she'd already spoken to her husband about having a more direct influence on Issylte's upbringing. This would work to her advantage now.

"Fetch the Lady Brangien. Bring her to me in the throne room. Go quickly."

The knight rushed to obey. Queen Morag summoned four of her remaining guards. She gave them quiet, explicit instructions. All four gravely nodded their heads and left to follow orders.

Her heart pounded with adrenaline. It was exhilarating, this new power as queen. With her husband away, the timing was perfect. And with Issylte gone from the castle on her daily equestrian lesson—which would keep her away for the remainder of the morning—it was downright ideal.

Queen Morag sent for her attendants and ordered them to assemble the castle servants in the throne room and to await her there. As they scampered off, eager to please, she returned to her private chambers to gather her wits and polish her regal appearance.

She brushed her jet-black hair and plaited it in a thick braid, which she tossed down her back. Upon her head she placed a silver coronet, adorned with icy aquamarine gemstones, which perfectly complemented her shimmery blue gown. To put a rosy glow into her nervous pallor, she pinched her cheeks and bit her lips to give them a hint of blush. With one last glance in the mirror, she smoothed the folds of her dress, held her head high, and proceeded to the throne room, followed by the two remaining royal guards who had been waiting at attention just outside her bedroom door.

The eastern wall of ogival windows bathed the glorious throne room in brilliant morning sunlight. Graceful white stone columns held the curved arches along the length of the vast room, where two green velvet tufted thrones were centered upon a raised wooden dais, flanked by the royal standard of King Donnchadh—the great white hawk upon the dark green background. The throng of servants apprehensively awaited her, their new queen.

Murmurs rippled through the crowd assembled on either side of the long carpet which covered the stone floor and extended from the entrance to the rich walnut dais. At the sight of the queen and her royal guards, the throng fell silent as Morag purposefully strode into the room and claimed her seat upon the throne. Brangien stood uneasily before the dais, Sir Knial the escort at her side.

"Dear Brangien," the queen began, her voice commanding and cold despite the fondness of the term with which she addressed Issylte's governess. "You have been a most loyal servant for many years, for which King Donnchadh and I are most grateful."

She smiled insincerely at the woman who appeared terrified to have been summoned to the throne room. Morag exulted in the thrill of power. Her pulse thrummed with excitement.

Motioning for the steward, Lord Lugaid, to approach, she handed him a black velvet pouch and ordered him to give it to Brangien. The nurse accepted it hesitantly, her fearful eyes fixed on the queen.

"Please accept this as compensation for your excellent service to the Castle of Connaught. However, since I plan to personally assume the responsibility of educating the Princess Issylte from now on, you are henceforth dismissed from your duties as her nursemaid."

Gasps of shock reverberated through the crowd of servants.

Queen Morag nodded to the four guards who had received the explicit orders just outside her royal antechamber.

"My royal guards will escort you to your room so that you may pack your belongings. You are to depart at once, before the princess returns from her equestrian lessons."

Brangien emitted a guttural moan and dropped to

her knees.

Morag impassively smoothed the folds of her elegant gown and lifted her haughty chin to glare at Brangien. "I wish to avoid a most unpleasant scene. You will depart immediately. Thank you for your service, dear Brangien. You are hereby dismissed."

The four royal guards escorted the distraught nurse from the throne room.

As the servants bowed before her, Queen Morag gracefully stepped down from the gleaming dais and glided up the carpeted path, followed by a trail of simpering royal attendants.

A few moments later, a small crowd gathered at the front of the castle and bid goodbye to Brangien, who rode off into the forest with the queen's four loyal guards. Morag smiled in wicked delight.

****

Issylte returned from her riding lesson, her cheeks windburned, her hair a tangled mess, her spirit still soaring. She led Luna into the stable, where she removed the horse's saddle, storing it upon the wooden stand. She brushed and groomed the dappled gray mare, who was now munching on the sweet-smelling hay that she'd placed on the floor of the stall. At the sound of footsteps, Issylte looked up and spotted her two attendants, Roisin and Aislinn. They seemed upset, their eyes puffy and red, as if they'd been crying. Issylte's heart pounded. Something was terribly wrong.

"What is it?" she gasped, dreading the response.

Neither one of her ladies in waiting seemed willing to respond. They glanced at each other in desperation, both avoiding her imploring eyes.

"Please, Roisin, tell me! What has happened?"

Issylte took hold of her attendant's trembling hands.

Roisin gulped, as if finding the courage to speak. Finally, she whispered, her voice cracking with emotion, "The queen dismissed Gigi! She ordered her to leave at once. And now, Your Majesty... Gigi's gone!"

Issylte couldn't believe what she was hearing. *Gigi was gone?* She turned to Aislinn, who nodded, her eyes downcast, her lip quivering.

She didn't know what to do. Her mind raced. She was terrified of the stepmother who haunted her every move, always lurking in the shadows. She certainly could not run to the frightful queen with soulless eyes and icy hands. Father was gone, for at least another week.

She could jump on Luna and gallop after them!

"Where did they go?"

Her eyes darted to the saddle. She had ridden hard today, but Luna had rested for about an hour. She might still be able to catch them...

"I don't know. She rode off with four of the queen's guards. Some of the women in the kitchen were talking about a sister in southern Ireland. Perhaps Gigi was sent home to her?"

A sister? Gigi had never mentioned a sister. Surely, if she'd had family, she would have shared that with Issylte. They always shared everything.

The enormity of loss hit her like a physical blow. Issylte dropped to the floor, her legs unable to support her weight. She couldn't breathe. Her temples pounded; her stomach clenched. She lowered her head to her knees and wrapped her arms tightly around them. She wailed, long and slow—the pitiful, plaintive bellow of a wounded animal.

Memories flooded her. Gigi holding her hand as they strolled through the woods. Collecting acorns to make pretend cakes. The countless stories of forest fairies who inhabited the thick woods. The woodland creatures who would protect their beloved Emerald Princess. Gigi's enormous brown eyes, so full of love...

The pain was suffocating. Issylte sobbed, gasping for breath. The pressure on her chest was so intense, she couldn't breathe.

Roisin wrapped her arms around her. "Please don't cry, Your Majesty. Perhaps when your father the king returns, you could ask him to bring Gigi back."

Issylte raised her face, her heart alit with the slightest glimmer of hope.

I can speak to Father! He comes home in a week. I can plead with him. Tell him how much I need Gigi. Yes, Father can bring her back!

She threw her arms around Roisin, rocking back and forth to mend her shattered soul.

"And, even if he doesn't agree to bring her back as your governess, he can surely send for Gigi to come for a visit. Perhaps for Yuletide. Wouldn't that be lovely, Your Highness?" Aislinn raised her brows, empathy shining in her pale blue eyes.

Issylte smiled gratefully, fragile hope blossoming in her tender heart.

Roisin extended her hand to help Issylte to a stand. Brushing the hay from her riding gown, she lost herself in Luna's soulful eyes. The tears started anew. Issylte hugged her horse, sobbing into the long, dark mane. The warmth of Luna's coat was comforting, her familiar scent reassuring. Luna nickered in response, nudging Issylte with her wet muzzle.

After a few moments, bolstered by the hope of speaking to her father upon his return, fortified by the solid strength of her beloved mare, and accompanied by her supportive attendants, Issylte returned to the castle. And ran right into her wretched stepmother.

"Ah, there you are, Issylte. I was beginning to wonder what had detained you." The queen glared at Roisin and Aislinn. The two attendants cast their gaze to the floor.

"I am certain your two servants informed you of my decision to dismiss Brangien."

At the sound of Gigi's name, Issylte nearly melted. But she did not want to give her stepmother the satisfaction of seeing her despair. She stared at her boots instead. She bit her lip to stop it from quivering.

"You are fourteen years old now. You no longer have need of a nursemaid. I, as your stepmother, shall assume the responsibility of your education from now on."

The queen glowered at Issylte, in apparent disapproval of her *unprincesslike* appearance.

"Go to your room so that your attendants may bathe and properly attire you. I shall have the kitchen send up a platter of food. You'll be delighted to know that I have engaged a new Latin tutor, and your first lesson is this afternoon. Go now. I shall send for you as soon as he arrives."

Issylte curtseyed, as required, before the heartless queen and escaped to the sanctuary of her private room. She threw herself onto the plush bed, burying her face in the downy softness. She could feel Gigi tucking the blankets around her, dispelling her childhood fears.

Her throat constricted, and she sobbed into her

pillow.

Roisin stroked her hair. Aislinn sent servants to fetch hot water for her bath.

When her porcelain tub was ready, Issylte's attendants helped her disrobe. She slid into the steaming comfort, sighing contentedly as Roisin lathered her hair with lavender soap, washing away the grief with her gentle touch.

And so, to survive the unbearable pain of loss, Issylte clutched tightly to the fragile thread of hope.

Father returns in a week. I must hang on until then. He'll make things right. I know he will. He always does.

Chapter 4

The Tournament of Champions

The castle of Tintagel was hosting the *Tournament of Champions,* a challenging three-day event where ten winners would earn the prestigious distinction of becoming Knights of the Round Table for Arthur Pendragon, the High King of Britain. Nearly three hundred candidates from the entire kingdom of Cornwall had arrived at the castle for the thrilling competition, which was set to begin today.

Along one side of the castle grounds, approximately one hundred tents had been pitched to provide housing for the competing warriors, who were now rushing about, donning their chain mail armor, preparing for today's joust. The sizzling aroma of sausages roasting over the cooks' campfires and the tang of sweat filled the air. Horses neighed as grooms saddled them, leading the first group of coursers to the fields where the event would take place.

Although many privileged guests enjoyed the luxury of lodging within the castle itself, additional tents had been set up along the opposite side of the field for the hundreds of royal spectators who planned to stay for the duration of the tournament. Brightly colored banners of various noble houses fluttered in the crisp spring breeze. Fluffy clouds scattered across the bright blue sky as jubilant lords and ladies filled the grandstands, the preferred viewing granted to the highest ranks of nobility. The thrum of excitement rippled through the crowd.

Today's joust, the *Running of the Rings*, would take place on two fields, with each contestant allotted two runs. Atop the courser provided by the masters of horse, each knight would charge at a fixed, wooden target containing three circles in its center. A lance striking the outer ring would score one point, with three for the inner ring and five for the center circle. Since every candidate would have two jousting runs, the maximum possible score was ten points. Any competitor thrown from his horse would be disqualified and eliminated from the tournament; the top one hundred of the highest-scoring candidates would advance to the second day's archery event, to be held tomorrow.

The competitors had been divided into groups of ten, with half competing on each field. Tristan, Vaughan, and Connor had arrived at the preparation area together. The first two groups had already run, with several contestants eliminated. Connor was up next.

A rush of adrenaline hit Tristan as he watched his friend settle into the saddle and position his lance, preparing to charge.

The bright red flag dropped, and the courser flew towards the target, clumps of mud churned up as thundering hooves pummeled the grassy field.

His lance secured to his body, his horse speeding towards the target, Connor hit the outer ring on his first run, scoring one point. He rode back to the starting position where the master of horse steadied his mount, awaiting the next drop of the flag. Under his breath,

Tristan whispered a fervent prayer to the Goddess to grant his friend better luck.

The flag dropped again. Connor surged towards the target, gaining speed and momentum, his enormous lance held tight against his body. The earth shook under the courser's pounding hooves.

This time, Connor struck the inner circle. Tristan heaved a sigh of relief. Four points. He prayed it would be enough.

Tristan was next. The stable hand approached him, leading the courser which he would ride. Adrenaline thrummed in his veins as he climbed into the saddle and adjusted his helmet.

His heart raced; power surged through him as the groom led his horse to the starting position to await the signal of the judge's flag. He spotted Vaughan, who would be competing in the next group, standing in the crowd to cheer him on. Vaughan flashed him a hearty grin.

The flag dropped, and Tristan flew like an arrow, his thighs gripping the horse's powerful flanks as he bolted down the field towards the triple circle of rings. Gripping his lance tightly with his arm and shoulder, preparing to pummel the target, his courser suddenly reared—as if in pain—nearly throwing Tristan from the saddle. Although he recovered quickly, and managed to stay on his horse, he missed the target entirely. Fear clenched his stomach in a tight fist.

He returned to the starting position to prepare for his second run. His mouth was parched, his body quivering with adrenaline and fury. If he did not hit the inner circle on this run, he would be eliminated from the competition. That couldn't happen. He'd promised his uncle Marke that he would qualify.

He remembered the ring his uncle had given him. Perhaps it was superstition, but Tristan felt compelled to gaze into the eye of the sea raven. Sliding his hand out of the protective metal gauntlet, he quickly kissed the blue topaz stone for good luck. Bolstered now with courage, he slipped his hand back into the glove, gripped his lance, and leaned forward in the saddle. His heart thumped wildly in his chest.

From the corner of his eye, he saw the vibrant flash of color as the flag dropped.

Like a furious gale of wind, he blew off the starting post, storming at the target with the force of a tempest. He could feel his courser's strength and speed, swift and sure, as he focused his entire being on the center of the target.

The impact of his lance striking the center ring reverberated through his bones. The thrill of victory shivered up his spine.

Five points. Pray the Goddess it would be enough.

Connor threw an arm around his shoulder, a huge grin plastered across his face, as he congratulated Tristan. The two friends watched from the sidelines as Vaughan executed two stellar runs, hitting the inner circle each time, for a total score of six points.

The trio headed back to their shared tent, where pages helped them remove and store their armor. Grooms watered the horses and returned the magnificent animals to Tintagel's royal stables. The cooks had something delicious roasting over the fire, and Tristan's stomach growled in response. *I'm heading there next,* he decided, ravenous after the morning's exertion.

He removed his sweaty tunic and dumped a bucket

of cold water over his head. As he shook out his hair, droplets splattered from his dark brown locks. Connor chuckled from the stump where he was seated, picking the mud from his boots with the tip of his knife.

Vaughan grinned as he approached, a goblet of ale in each hand. Tristan accepted the offered mug and gulped greedily, quenching his thirst. The adrenaline from the joust had parched his throat, and the ale slid down smoothly.

"I saw Indulf startle your horse in the first run."

Vaughan took a large gulp from his goblet, wiped the froth with his sleeve, and locked eyes with Tristan.

"He blew a stone from some sort of pipe. It struck your horse's rump, and that's why he reared. Keep your eyes on him, Tristan. He has no honor. He cheats. I hope one of us goes up against him in the battle of swords. I, for one, would love to wipe that fucking smirk off his bloody face."

Tristan kicked the dirt in disgust. He'd very nearly been disqualified by Indulf's deceit.

A loud commotion drew his attention. Hearty shouts echoed across the tents.

Near the cooks' campsite, competitors were gathering around a tree to see the list of names of those who had qualified for the second day of the tournament. Candidates were shoving each other, trying to read the list. Others celebrated with cheers and mugs of ale. Some were slinking away, their faces grim in obvious defeat.

Connor, who had run ahead to see the list, came bounding back to join Tristan and Vaughan. His joyous grin stretched from ear to ear.

"We made it! All three of us! The Goddess be praised!"

The trio of knights clapped each other on the backs, exuberant in victory, thrilled for tomorrow's archery event.

The enticing aromas emanating from the cooks' fire were too tempting for Tristan to resist.

"Come on, let's grab something to eat. I'm starved!"

The roast boar was salty and sweet, dripping with honey. Tristan devoured the baked beans and roasted corn, soaking up every drop on his plate with his loaf of crusty fresh bread, courtesy of the castle kitchens. The yeasty flavor melted in his mouth, the delightful taste lingering on his palate.

Now that his stomach was full, and he'd rested a bit with Vaughan and Connor, the thought of tomorrow's archery competition brought a renewed rush of adrenaline.

"We have a couple hours before dark," he said to his two friends, lazing in the grass a few feet from the campfire. "We can shoot a few arrows to practice for tomorrow. Sound good?"

Connor and Vaughan exchanged glances. Vaughan nodded and stood, stretching his back by reaching his arms high over his head. The three friends headed back to the tent to retrieve their bowstrings and quivers of arrows, spending the rest of the afternoon in the designated area where targets had been set up for practice.

Later that evening, Tristan sat near the campfire with Vaughan and Connor, eating the roast venison and vegetable stew that the cooks had prepared. He took a hearty pull from his goblet of ale, gazing into the fire as he listened to descriptions of the day's jousts, sharing the excitement of qualifying for tomorrow's event.

Indulf was seated among them. His blond hair was tied back, revealing his pockmarked face. A long, curved nose gave him the appearance of a hawk. As the third son of the Count of Hame in eastern Cornwall, Indulf would never inherit a title of nobility. Tristan suspected that Indulf hated him for being the nephew and presumptive heir to King Marke's throne. He sensed the jealous stare of the knight who had tried to disqualify him in the morning joust.

Tossing a twig into the fire, Indulf taunted Tristan.

"You were very nearly thrown from your horse in the first run, Tristan. How fortunate that you hit the center circle on your second, else you would not have qualified. The Goddess herself smiled upon you today," he smirked, glaring at Vaughan.

"The Goddess, and my ring," Tristan mused, eyeing the black *chough* with the gleaming blue topaz eye. He held it up for Indulf to see.

"A gift for luck, from my uncle Marke. Seems it brought me good fortune today, wouldn't you say?" Tristan shot Indulf a lupine grin.

"Indeed," the knight huffed, rising from his seat near the fire.

"We'll see if you are so fortunate tomorrow," he scoffed, slithering off to his tent. Tristan watched Indulf's retreating form, his face contorted with disgust.

The other competitors rose, wished one another good luck in the morning's event, and headed off to their respective tents. Tristan, Vaughan, and Connor returned to theirs.

Lying on his bedroll, Tristan imagined facing Indulf in the final event. The battle of swords. Adrenaline coursed through his veins. When elusive sleep finally found him, he slept fitfully, dreaming of revenge.

The morning dawned cool and bright, with just a hint of the warmth that summer would soon bring. Tristan, Vaughan, and Connor finished their breakfast of porridge, meat, and ale, returning to their tent to fetch their weapons for the archery competition.

Tristan was a fine archer, but he knew his best event would be tomorrow's challenge of the sword. It was essential for him to place today, for only the top twenty would advance to the final day's competition in the Tournament of Champions.

The archery competition was divided into two areas with three targets spaced at increasing distances of 30, 50 and 70 yards. An arrow landing in the outermost circle would earn one point, with three for the inner ring and five for the bull's eye in the dead center. One arrow would be fired at each target.

The competitors were lined up, awaiting their turn, with Tristan, Vaughan, and Connor in the queue. Among the three, Vaughan was by far the most skilled, having grown up hunting with his father in the woods of the Kennall Vale in western Cornwall.

"All right, lads, watch how it's done!" he boasted as he approached the first target. Nocking his arrow, drawing his bow tightly, Vaughan released a bull's eye at each of the three targets for a total score of fifteen points. He was sure to place among the top twenty qualifiers to advance in the competition.

Vaughan removed his arrows from the three targets and returned to his companions' side, grinning ear to ear. Tristan approached the starting point and positioned himself before the first target.

His first arrow hit the inner circle. Three points. His

second shot scored three more. It might be enough, but he had to be sure. This last shot was crucial. His legs shook with adrenaline.

At the seventy-yard target, he positioned his feet, nocked his arrow, and drew the bow tightly. Just as he was about to shoot, a loud cough startled him, shattering his concentration.

Tristan turned to see Indulf grinning. Of course. *The bastard!*

Tristan rolled his shoulders. A trickle of sweat ran down the side of his face. His stomach clenched in fear at the thought of losing. The humiliation of facing his uncle in shame. No, he refused to let Indulf rattle him. He needed to focus. To concentrate. He shook his head to clear his thoughts.

He stared into the eye of the sea raven. He kissed the blue topaz stone, praying the Goddess would guide his arrow straight and sure.

He positioned himself perpendicular to the target. Lowered his bow and nocked the arrow. Raised the bow and drew the string tightly back as he took aim. His uncle's words came back to him. *Make me proud, Tristan.*

All the summers hunting in Kennall Vale, all of Vaughan's lessons, the first buck he'd taken so many years ago. Tristan channeled it all into a perfect release, watching with bated breath as his arrow thwacked the dead center of the target. Bull's eye. Five points. A total score of eleven. He prayed it would be enough to advance to tomorrow's final event.

As he retrieved his arrows, he spotted Indulf, leaning against a tree, his arms crossed over his chest. One side of his mouth was drawn up in a smirk. He snickered as Tristan walked by. Fuming silently, his fury as taut as a bowstring, it was all Tristan could do to restrain himself. He joined Connor and Vaughan, who wisely said nothing as the trio returned to the tent.

That evening, huddled around the campfire, the competitors anxiously awaited the results of the archery event. Gorvenal finally posted the list of those who had advanced to the final competition.

Tristan, Vaughan, Connor, and Indulf had all qualified.

Twenty contestants now remained in the *Tournament of Champions*, and the stakes were high.

Only the ten victors of the final event would be knighted by King Marke in the throne room of Tintagel to embark upon the journey to Camelot. Only the ten victors would earn the privilege of training under the legendary Sir Lancelot of the Lake, First Knight of King Arthur Pendragon. And only the ten victors would be dubbed Knights of the Round Table of Camelot.

Everyone fighting tomorrow seemed edgy and jumpy. Some competitors burned off steam with wooden swords on the dummies that had been set up on the practice field. Tristan, Vaughan, and Connor ran a few miles in the surrounding woods, and returned to enormous vats of steaming seafood and fresh fish cooked over an open fire.

Tristan ate his fill of haddock, crab, and scallops, then sat alone in quiet contemplation, mentally preparing for the final event. After a while, he and his companions retired to their tent, anxiously awaiting the dawn.

****

The salty tang of ocean spray and the pine scent of the surrounding forest perfumed the air as Tristan entered the field to compete. The sun blazed overhead, and under the heavy chain mail, he began to sweat. His muscles quivered with tension, begging for release.

He clutched his wooden sword and shield, his hands drenched inside the leather gloves. He shook out his legs to keep them limber. He had to win this fight. Too much was at stake.

His heart raced wildly. He was a child again, standing in the woods near his father's castle in Lyonesse.

The enormous Viking with the horned helmet and the long red beard forced his bloodied, battered father to his knees. The massive arm raised the savage sword, ready to drop. He was too young, too weak to fight. He could do nothing to stop the lethal blade from slicing off his father's head before his very eyes. Impotent rage and guilt were smothering him. His chest was too tight; he couldn't breathe. His mouth was so dry…

A sharp, fierce croak rang out through the sky. Disoriented, Tristan looked up, momentarily blinded by the sun. A magnificent sea raven soared overhead, his wings unfurled in glorious grace.

Tristan remembered. He removed his glove, wiped the sweat from his brow, and kissed the brilliant blue eye of the sacred *chough* on his ring. He took a deep breath, then blew it out from billowed cheeks, the bellows over a forge.

His opponent entered the field. Tristan was sorely disappointed to see that it was not Indulf, but a warrior named Donzel from the region of Camborne.

They circled each other, searching for weakness. Strategizing.

Tristan waited, tensely coiled, ready to attack.

Donzel lunged; Tristan blocked and parried. His opponent lunged again wildly, and Tristan saw his opportunity.

He blocked the blow and reversed the attack, cutting upwards from his right. He brought his sword around in a tight circle, launching a series of blows which disarmed and toppled Donzel to the ground.

Tristan held the tip of his wooden sword against his opponent's exposed throat and placed his foot on Donzel's stomach.

The crowd erupted in cheers.

Vaughan and Connor rushed to Tristan, congratulating him with slaps on the back, dragging him off the field to celebrate their combined victories.

"By the Goddess, Tristan, you're a beast!" Vaughan roared, his arm wrapped tightly around Tristan's neck.

They laughed and stumbled all the way back to their tent. With the help of their pages, they removed the heavy chain mail, then washed the sweat from their faces in buckets of icy water. Sporting fresh tunics and hearty grins, mugs of ale in hand, they proceeded to the area designated for the *champions.*

Gorvenal and the masters-at-arms announced the names of the ten finalists who had qualified for the voyage to Camelot. Tristan was thrilled to hear the names of his friends and dismayed—but not surprised— to hear Indulf's as well.

Cheers of victory resounded though the woods. The ten champions would soon be knighted by King Marke in an official dubbing ceremony, complete with a royal feast. They would embark on a journey to Camelot, to train with Sir Lancelot, and become Knights of the Round Table of King Arthur himself.

Holding up his mug of ale, Tristan proposed a toast to his two brothers in arms.

"To us, three champions from Cornwall! To King Marke, King Arthur, and Sir Lancelot!"

As the three friends gulped the ale from their goblets, wiping the foam from their lips, Vaughan shouted triumphantly,

"To Camelot!"

Chapter 5

The Queen's Huntsmen

Issylte was heartbroken when King Donnchadh sent word that he wouldn't be returning for at least two more weeks. She needed to speak to him, to beg him to bring Gigi back. She struggled to maintain hope, but it was so hard, for her stepmother's haunting black eyes followed her everywhere. Issylte was tense and frightened all the time. The queen was a coiled serpent, ready to strike.

The only highlight in her life was horseback riding. The Master of Horse, Lord Liam, certainly played a large role in her enthusiasm for all things equestrian. Not only was he attractive—tall and muscular, with long blond hair that he wore pulled back in a leather cord—but his gentleness with Luna melted her heart.

His eager smile lit up his handsome face. Issylte was thrilled whenever he flashed her a friendly grin. She loved the way Liam handled the horses, the kindness and patience he showed her in their daily equestrian lessons. He'd taught her to care for Luna herself, and Issylte treasured the time they spent together—whether riding through the forest, galloping across the plains, or mucking out the stalls. Lord Liam was the only one who didn't seem to mind her *unprincesslike* behavior.

Liam arranged riding lessons for Issylte each day, always accompanied by at least six of her royal guards.

47

As they rode through the verdant forest, the wind whipping her hair, the fragrance of pine needles filling the air, Issylte was gloriously free, far from the menacing eyes of her wicked stepmother, the handsome Liam at her side.

Today, Issylte's handmaidens had accompanied her to the stables, where the royal guards were already mounted and prepared for her daily ride. Yet, Issylte did not recognize any of the faces of her knights. A surge of panic washed through her.

Perhaps they are in training, thought Issylte, trying to calm her racing pulse.

Liam helped her into the saddle. He stroked Luna's mane and crooned into the mare's ear.

"Good girl, Luna. Good girl."

Liam's horse was not saddled. *Where was Golnar, his stallion?*

"Lord Liam, aren't you riding with me today?"

She couldn't shake the feeling that something was terribly wrong. The leather reins shook in her wet hands.

The Master of Horse seemed troubled, preoccupied.

"Not today, Your Highness. I've been informed that Lords Cian and Bolduc will accompany you in my stead." Lord Liam gestured to two of the six royal guards already mounted in their saddles.

Upon these words, the dark-haired Lord Cian addressed her. With his grisly beard, brooding eyes, and gruff voice, he seemed like a bear. Issylte did not want to go riding with him.

"Yes, Your Highness. Queen Morag suggested that perhaps you tire of the monotony of the same trail each day."

He nodded to the clean-shaven huntsman beside

him. "Lord Bolduc and I shall show you a different route—one that leads to the sea."

The two huntsmen exchanged glances. Issylte didn't like the menace in their eyes. Something was very wrong. She could feel a thrum from the forest. A warning.

"Indeed, Your Highness, it is most beautiful. I have no doubt you will enjoy it immensely. And now, Princess Issylte, we shall proceed. Lord Bolduc and I—and these fine royal guards—are all at your service."

Lord Cian bowed his head, tugged his horse's reins, and headed towards the forest. Lord Bolduc and several of the royal guards followed his lead. Issylte glanced back at Lord Liam. He was standing there, watching her go. She had the sudden urge to race back to him.

"This way, Your Highness. To the sea." Lord Cian kicked his horse and led her into the dense woods. The remaining wo knights filed in behind her. Preventing her retreat. Issylte's mouth went dry, and her hands shook as she clutched the reins tightly.

They rode deep into the foreboding forest, where the earthy scent of rich loam mingled with the rot of decaying leaves from ancient oaks. The woodland trail was unfamiliar, the gnarled branches and roots making the journey increasingly treacherous.

She struggled to keep up with Lords Cian and Bolduc.

The two huntsmen were quickening their pace, turning this way and that, along the sinuous path that required her constant attention, for Luna could easily be injured. The thick canopy of oak and beech trees blocked nearly all the sunlight. It was becoming nearly impossible to follow the dangerous serpentine trail.

Urging their horses to quicken their speed, the huntsmen delved deeper and deeper into the forest with Issylte desperate to keep up. She didn't know these woods and would never be able to return to the castle on her own.

Her hands trembled so much, she could hardly ride. Her pulse pounded; her stomach clenched in a knot.

Flustered and frightened, she realized with dread that the other guards were no longer behind her and that she was alone with two strange men. The forest itself was warning her of imminent danger.

Cian halted abruptly.

Bolduc stopped his horse in front of Luna, blocking Issylte's path.

Cian flew out of his saddle and yanked Luna's reins out of her hand. Issylte couldn't breathe.

Bolduc dismounted and pulled Issylte brusquely from her saddle. He grabbed her forearm, restraining her at his side. Her legs were shaking so badly she could barely stand. Her heart was in her throat. What were they going to do?

Cian led Luna away from her, tying the mare to a tree. He tethered the other two horses nearby. Bolduc clenched her arm.

Her body quivered. Fear tightened her stomach, and a wave of nausea rose to her throat.

She couldn't outrun two grown men, nor could she untie Luna and leap onto her back without being captured again. She was at the mercy of these two huntsmen. Perhaps if she screamed, the other guards might hear…

As if sensing her thoughts, Cian barked, "No sense calling for the royal guards, Your Majesty. The queen made sure her own loyal knights would be posted today. We obey her orders."

The queen replaced the guards? That's why Liam didn't come. Dear Goddess, what is happening?

Rustling leaves sounded from the forest behind them. Issylte whirled around, certain that wolves had tracked them.

Bolduc released her arm, then quickly withdrew his bow from his back. In rapid succession, with deadly accuracy, he nocked and fired two lethal arrows.

Issylte sensed the thud as the body of a stag fell to the ground before them. Bolduc's arrows had found their mark. One was embedded in the deer's eye socket and the other in its neck. The magnificent beast lay lifeless at her feet.

The queen's huntsmen exchanged a meaningful glance. Cian nodded.

Bolduc withdrew his dagger and began to carve up the stag. Bewildered and terrified, Issylte could not comprehend what was happening, nor could she control the tremors in her legs.

The burly, dark Lord Cian removed his hat from his head and placed it across his chest. He knelt before her, his dark eyes filled with regret.

"Your Majesty, we cannot obey. The queen sent us here today with orders to kill you. To make it appear as if there'd been an accident. She told us to say that we'd taken you along the coastline to show you the sea. That your horse had reared—frightened by crumbling rocks along the cliff. That you were thrown from your palfrey, cast into the sea, and despite hours of frantic search, we had been unable to find your body."

He took hold of Issylte's ice cold hand and kissed it.

Still on his knees, he looked up at her, shaking his head in shame. "The queen demanded that we take you deep into the forest, cut out your heart, and bring it back to her as proof that we'd obeyed. She said your riderless horse would return to the castle, and King Donnchadh would hear of the tragic death of his only child. Soon, word would spread throughout the land that Princess Issylte had perished in a terrible accident." He kissed her hand again. "But...Your Highness, we cannot obey."

Issylte collapsed to her knees, her mouth trembling uncontrollably. She turned first to Cian, then to Bolduc, who was still carving the corpse of the deer.

The stark realization hit her like a blow to the stomach.

Her stepmother had ordered her death. They had brought her here to kill her.

To cut out her heart!

Issylte vomited into the decaying leaves. When she finally finished retching, she wiped her mouth with the cloth that Cian offered.

Overcome with emotion, she covered her face with her hands and sobbed.

Cian's deep voice was soothing. "Your Majesty, we simply cannot kill you, but neither can we return to the queen empty-handed. Bolduc is cutting out the heart of this stag. We'll offer it to the queen as proof that we obeyed."

Bolduc strode over, the stag's heart in his hand. He took a cloth from his pouch, wrapped the heart in it, and placed it in his saddlebag. Issylte was still on her knees, disheveled, shaking, and crying.

"You must never return to the castle, Your Highness. The queen will believe that you are dead, but you must stay hidden, so she will never discover the truth. If she were to learn that yet you live, she would have you hunted down and killed, and execute both Cian and myself." Bolduc knelt beside Cian, the two huntsmen humbled before her.

Issylte lifted her tear-stained face. "But…what can I do? I can't return to the castle. Where can I possibly go?"

Cian rose to his feet and extended his hand to help raise Issylte as well. Bolduc stood up beside them.

She smoothed her tangled hair, brushing leaves and twigs off her gown. She wiped her eyes and looked imploringly at Cian. He gestured to a stream which flowed through the forest nearby.

"See this stream, Princess? It leads through the forest to a stone cottage which is well hidden in the woods. An old woman lives there. Some call her a witch; others, the queen of the fairies. She has a good heart and is a gifted healer." He removed a ring from his finger and unsheathed his dagger. With a tremulous smile, he gave them to Issylte. "Take this ring to the fairy witch. When she greets you at the door, offer it to her as payment for your shelter. It is solid gold, which she can sell in the local village for the provisions you will need. Tell her how the queen tried to have you killed. The fairy witch will shelter you, not just because she has a kind heart, but because you are the king's only child. The rightful heir to the throne. There will come a time when you'll claim your birthright. In the meantime, you must keep your identity hidden. Queen Morag must never learn the truth."

Issylte strapped Cian's gifted dagger to her ankle and placed the gold ring in the bodice of her gown. She gazed into the kind eyes of the two noble huntsmen.

"I cannot thank you enough for your courage and kindness. I will never forget your act of bravery, Lords Cian and Bolduc. Someday, somehow, I will find a way to reward you. You have my solemn word."

Cian and Bolduc each kissed her hand. They placed their right fists over their hearts in fealty and bowed their heads in homage.

Pointing once again to the stream, Cian urged Issylte to hurry.

"Follow the stream, Your Majesty. Go quickly, and use the dagger to defend yourself if necessary. The fairy witch's cottage lies deep in the Hazelwood Forest. It's sheltered in a grove of trees, hidden by branches covered with vines and briar. Go now, and may the Goddess be with you, Emerald Princess."

Issylte stumbled away, following the stream deeper into the forest. She heard the loud slap and shout of "HAH!" as Bolduc frightened her beloved mare. Tears stung her eyes and she staggered, nearly tripping over her dress.

She would never see or ride Luna again. She would never see her father, would never have the chance to beg him to bring Gigi back. She'd never see Gigi again. Ever. Her throat was so tight she couldn't breathe.

She couldn't go home. She'd never see the handsome Lord Liam again. Or Roisin and Aislin. Sharp branches cut her cheeks, the copper tang of blood filling her nostrils.

King Donnchadh's gentle face floated before her, and Issylte nearly choked. He was lost to her now, just like Gigi. Her father would be heartbroken to learn of her "death", and Issylte would long for the feel of his arms around her and the loving gaze of his twinkling, merry eyes.

Suddenly, her fingers sensed the icy pull of her stepmother's touch. A shiver crept up her spine. Could the queen see her? Did someone follow her? She began to run. She stumbled through the forest, following the stream. The cottage was hidden in the woods. A witch fairy lived there. A kind one, Lord Cian had said.

The temperature was dropping. She had to hurry. Soon, it would be dark, and the predators would come out of the woods. There were wolves…

Hungry, frightened, and alone, Issylte sensed she was being watched and followed. She searched the forest but could see nothing in the dimming twilight. She withdrew the dagger that Cian had given her. At least she had some protection. She heard a rustling in the woods. But, with her deaf ear, she couldn't tell where the sound was coming from. Was it behind her? Ahead? She didn't know.

She scanned the forest, sick with fear. In the dim light, she spotted a small woven basket just up ahead, alongside the stream.

She rushed forward to examine it. Inside was a large red apple, some berries, and a garland of the wild pink roses that were abundant in the forest. A feeling of peace flooded her.

"*It is safe*," the forest seemed to say. "*Eat*."

Issylte sniffed the apple and red berries. The fruity scent made her mouth water. She took a small bite and waited a moment to see if it had an odd taste. It tasted delicious.

She devoured half of the apple and a few of the berries, reserving the rest as a precaution in case she couldn't find the cottage. She quenched her thirst from the stream, picked up the basket, and continued her perilous trek through the Hazelwood Forest.

Once again, she had the sensation of being followed. She heard the patter of feet, the rustling of leaves. This time, when she glanced to her right, she glimpsed some sort of small creature which scampered into the woods.

Hushed whispers—of children? —seemed to come from the forest.

Despairing that it would soon be too dark to see, Issylte spotted a trail of light pink wild roses leading from the stream into a thicket of trees.

"*Follow the trail,*" the forest whispered. Her veins thrummed in response.

The wild roses led to a dense wooded hamlet where several trees with low-lying branches covered in vines concealed a small cottage with a thatched roof. The smell of smoke from the chimney wafted through the air. Golden light glowed from the two shuttered windows on either side of the entrance door. Thick trails of ivy embedded with pink flowers clung to the stone walls. The floral vines covered the entire front of the cottage, concealing it from view. Wild roses led right up to the carved wooden door.

Issylte had found the witch of the Hazelwood Forest.

Chapter 6

The Knighting Ceremony

As a reward for the Tournament of Champions, King Marke presented a *destrier*—a warhorse—to each of ten winners from the kingdom of Cornwall. The generous king also gifted each of the champions a new suit of armor, with a surcoat bearing the knight's coat of arms, for the journey to Camelot. The knighting ceremony had officially begun with a sumptuous feast of fresh fish, roast boar, spring vegetables and assorted fruits, followed by the ritual bathing and dressing in white for the Night Vigil in the castle chapel. This morning, Tristan and his fellow knights, traditionally attired in red cloaks and black breeches, followed Lord Gorvenal to the entrance of the Great Hall of Tintagel where the dubbing ceremony—the *adoubement*—would take place.

The long rectangular Great Hall of Tintagel was made of stone, with columned arches along the eastern wall, where morning sun shone through the stained glass ogival windows. Four enormous chandeliers hung from the intricately carved wooden embellishments which graced the high, curved ceiling. A large oval window stood high above the raised dais of pine-scented gleaming fruitwood where King Marke, in a splendid red velvet cape with ermine at the collar and front, a golden crown adorned with glittering gemstones atop his regal head, sat the tufted red velvet throne, flanked by four royal guards in finest livery.

The animated voices of lords and ladies, resplendent in bright satins, jewel toned velvets and rich brocades filled the vast room. Joyous music of fiddles and pear-shaped rebecs soared through the air. Lovely daughters of marriageable age, clad in softest silk, tittered with excitement at the prospect of finding a handsome husband. Wealthy nobles displayed their affluence in fur lined capes fastened with golden brooches which glinted in the morning light. The heady scents of rosewater, jasmine, and lavender perfumed the air.

The herald's trumpet resounded through the Great Hall, announcing the arrival of Gorvenal—the First Knight of Tintagel—and the ten accolades. The jubilant throng of spectators parted to allow the procession to form a queue upon the carpeted area before the king. At once, all heads bowed before King Marke as he stood to welcome the ten champions who would journey to Camelot and become Knights of the Round Table of King Arthur Pendragon.

One by one, the accolades knelt before the dais to pledge their oath of fealty. King Marke dubbed each knight, bestowing the title of "Sir" with the official *adoubement*.

As Tristan approached the dais to kneel before the king, his stomach clenched; his mouth went dry. Wavy brown locks fell forward as he bowed his head humbly before his uncle, lowering himself to his knees. In a deep voice which rang out through the Great Hall, Tristan pledged his vows as a knight of Tintagel, his right fist chested in fealty.

"I swear my allegiance to you, King Marke of Cornwall. I swear to always protect and defend a lady. To show loyalty, honesty, and integrity. To defend the weak and the poor. This I solemnly swear, my sacred oath of chivalry."

King Marke stood before Tristan. He unsheathed his royal sword Plantamort and dubbed his nephew's right shoulder, then the left. "I dub thee Sir Tristan, the Blue Knight of Cornwall. My nephew, my champion, and my heir."

The king sheathed his sword and raised Tristan to his feet. As he searched his uncle's bearded face, crinkled in a rugged smile, Tristan saw pride shining in the king's deep blue eyes, filling him with joy. He grinned from ear to ear as his uncle wrapped him in a hearty embrace.

Celebratory music began anew as the lively chords of fiddles rippled through the Great Hall. Jubilant spectators rushed forward to greet and congratulate the ten newly dubbed knights, who followed their squires to the area designated for donning the new armor, gift of the generous King of Cornwall.

Tristan saw Gorvenal approach, carrying a white surcoat displaying King Marke's royal coat of arms. Clad in fine chain mail armor of his own, his mentor's brutal, scarred face was stretched tightly in a broad, fraternal smile. He unfurled the magnificent surcoat before Tristan's admiring eyes.

Upon its white background, the side profile of the head of a Cornish *chough*—a black sea raven—was centered amidst an ocean of blue waves, outlined in a perimeter of the fifteen gold *bezants* of his uncle's royal heraldry. Like the cherished ring, whose brilliant blue topaz eye glinted in the morning sunlight upon the largest finger of his left hand.

"The Blue Knight of Cornwall," Gorvenal chortled. "The king's champion…and heir." He slapped Tristan on the shoulder, his teeth gleaming white. "Congratulations, Sir Tristan of Lyonesse!"

Tristan laughed from his belly as Gorvenal helped him don the new chain mail armor and the magnificent surcoat bearing his uncle's royal heraldry.

King Marke stood in regal splendor upon the dais before his velvet throne. With a grand sweep of his mighty arm, he gestured towards the banquet hall and bellowed to the exuberant crowd. "And now, in honor of the ten newly dubbed knights of Cornwall, let us feast. Come one, come all. ENJOY!"

The inviting aroma of roasted meats and spices wafted through the air as servants scurried to serve the elegant, seated nobles chattering at the tables in the bright banquet hall. Silver goblets glistened in the candlelight of the four chandeliers, suspended over the rows of rectangular tables. Colorful gowns and rich brocade tunics of the royal guests embellished the gaily decorated room, where garlands of ivy woven with fragrant yarrow adorned the wooden walls. At the royal table where King Marke awaited, ten places had been reserved for the newly dubbed knights, with Gorvenal placed at the end opposite the king.

Now seated to the right of his uncle at the royal table, Tristan caught the eye of his companions, his fellow knights who would train with him under the legendary Sir Lancelot of the Lake. Tomorrow, they would begin the two-week trek across southeastern Britain to the wondrous Castle of Camelot. Their faces beamed with pride, a hearty grin spread from ear to ear, as they feasted on stuffed pheasant, roast venison, and imbibed in King Marke's delicious ale.

His voice exuberant, his heart filled to the brim, Tristan raised his goblet to toast their success. With the same cheer that Vaughan had shouted at the celebration feast after the tournament of champions, Tristan roared with joy.

"To Camelot!"

Chapter 7

Églantine

Issylte peered through the thick oak branches which
concealed the ivy-covered cottage. A glow of fire or
candlelight illuminated the two windows on either side
of the carved wooden entrance door. Smoke trailed from
the chimney of the thatched roof, the enticing aroma of
food making her mouth water. Her scratched face stung
as the temperature of the spring evening plummeted with
nightfall. Crisp woodsmoke promised the welcome of
warmth as the trail of wild roses beckoned her to the
door.

She sheathed the dagger Lord Cian had given her to
the strap at her ankle and removed the gold ring from the
bodice of her gown. The pulse of the forest pushed her
forward. Issylte knocked hesitantly upon the front door.

A white-haired woman with skin like crinkled
parchment paper appeared, a wary regard in her seasoned
eye. "Yes, my lady? Have you lost your way in these
woods?"

Issylte stood trembling on the witch's doorstep—
filthy, exhausted, injured and alone. Radiant firelight
emanated from the warm cottage behind the open door.
A delicious scent wafted from the simmering pot over
the blazing hearth.

"I am sorry to disturb you," Issylte stammered,

glancing down at her feet. "I was told to come here. That you might help me. To offer you this ring as payment for shelter." Issylte outstretched her palm, where the jewel glinted in the golden light. "Please help me. I have nowhere else to go," she implored the wizened witch.

****

On the other side of the entrance door, Maiwenn's keen eye took in the fine quality of the girl's gown, the elegance of her embroidered cape, the courtly manner of her speech. The fairy witch searched the forest behind the intruder but saw no one. She opened the door wider, allowing the girl to enter.

She closed and bolted the door and helped the visitor remove her cloak, which she hung on a hook in the corner of the tiny entrance foyer. Taking the basket from the girl's hand, Maiwenn glimpsed a glittering gold coronet, adorned with emeralds; a half-eaten apple; some *groseille* berries; and a garland wreath of wild pink roses.

She set the parcel down on the table in the small kitchen and led the frightened girl toward the welcoming hearth. She wrapped a warm woolen blanket around her visitor's shoulders and seated her in a well-worn chair before the crackling fire. The poor girl was trembling.

"Sit down, my dear. You are tired and cold. Warm yourself before the fire. My name is Maiwenn, and you are welcome here in my humble cottage."

The fairy witch went into her tidy kitchen and lowered two ceramic mugs from her wooden cupboard. She measured some herbs from a small jar on the shelf, placing the mixture into the two cups. Wrapping a thick towel around her gnarled hand, Maiwenn lifted a kettle from the fireplace and poured steaming water over the herbs.

She retrieved the basked by the front door and placed it on the table in front of her guest seated before the hearth. Maiwenn then returned to the kitchen and fetched the two mugs. Offering one to the girl, and keeping one for herself, she sat down beside her guest in front of the welcoming fire.

"Drink this, my child. It's chamomile tea. In my native *Bretagne*, a cup of herbal tea like this is called a *tisane*. Its warmth will soothe you, and the herbs will calm your nerves, as you explain to me why the Emerald Princess has appeared this evening at my doorstep."

The girl looked at her in astonishment. "You know who I am?"

"Of course I know who you are, my dear. You are the Princess Issylte, the only child of King Donnchadh. Everyone knows and loves the Emerald Princess. And, it would seem, you are beloved by the Little Folk as well."

"The Little Folk?" inquired Issylte, sipping her *tisane*.

The girl seemed to luxuriate in the warmth of the blanket and the fire. Maiwenn smiled inwardly and nodded.

"Yes, the Little Folk. Some call them the forest fairies; to others, they are the *Old Ones*—the small woodland creatures who protect those with a pure heart, such as yourself."

Maiwenn set her cup down on the small table and assessed the lovely blonde girl. Her pitiful face was badly scratched, caked with dried blood. She would need to clean it and apply some of her comfrey salve. That would be soothing and ease the sting. She had some on her bedroom table.

"You might have spotted them in the forest." The fairy witch picked up the basket and peered inside at the rustic garland of wild roses. She chuckled at the half-eaten apple and red *groseilles* still in the panier. "It does appear that you enjoyed their gifts."

The girl's dark green eyes glowed in the firelight. She nodded emphatically, her blond hair falling over her shoulder, down her arm. "Yes, I did see something in the forest. I felt as if I were being watched—and followed. I even imagined hearing the voices of children whispering in the woods. It must have been the *Little Folk* that you described."

Maiwenn chuckled warmly. "Indeed it was, child. I am certain they followed you, covering your tracks, and guiding you here to me. They will protect you in this enchanted Hazelwood Forest, as they have me, for many years."

She removed the garland of wildflowers from the basket, running her bony, gentle fingers over the small pink blossoms.

"In *Bretagne*, these wild roses are called *églantines.* Here in Ireland, they're called "sweetbriar" or "briar rose".

She peered at the distraught girl, who seemed a bit more relaxed, snuggled in the warm blanket, comforted by the chamomile *tisane*. The fairy witch rose to her feet and placed the garland upon Issylte's head as if it were a crown.

Maiwenn kissed the top of the girl's head. "The Wild Rose of the Hazelwood Forest," she mused, a wide grin crinkling her soft, wrinkled cheeks.

She sat down beside Issylte, whose golden hair glistened in the firelight.

"Let me tend to your wounds, dear. I have a healing ointment that will ease the pain. I'll be right back."

Maiwenn tenderly washed Issylte's torn skin with homemade soap made from wild roses and yarrow, sponging it with a soft, clean cloth and warm water from a basin. She meticulously applied the healing salve—a soothing blend of rosemary, comfrey, and cedar— murmuring words of comfort with her gentle, knowing touch.

"Thank you very much, Maiwenn. My face hardly hurts anymore." The princess smiled gratefully and took a sip of her *tisane* as the fairy witch cleared away her herbal soap and medicine, pleased that the girl seemed less frightened.

Maiwenn headed to the fireplace, wrapped her hand once again in the thick cloth, and removed a lid from the pot which was simmering over the hearth. A tantalizing aroma wafted into the room.

"Rabbit stew, with fresh herbs and vegetables from my garden—which I will show you tomorrow." She grinned at Issylte, cocooned in the blanket before the warm embers of the fire.

The old woman heaped a ladle full of the thick stew into two earthenware bowls and placed them upon a small table against the far wall of the cottage, nestled behind the seating area of the hearth.

She then set two spoons, the two cups of *tisane* and two goblets, into which she poured some fresh water from a pitcher. She fetched the remainder of a loaf of fresh bread and brought two small jars from the small kitchen, placing them upon the table as well. Satisfied with the simple yet appetizing display, she flashed a welcoming smile at Issylte.

"Come, dear princess, sit here with me. Let's eat, for you must be famished."

Maiwenn seated the girl at the table across from her and watched in delight as she dug into the savory rabbit stew.

"Mmmm," she hummed contentedly. "This is delicious!"

"I am very glad you enjoy it. While you eat, I will tell you a bit about myself so that we can get better acquainted."

She offered the girl the nutty bread, the pot of fresh butter churned from goat's milk, and a bit of honey from the small jar. Issylte joyously accepted them all. Maiwenn smiled as the princess buttered the bread, poured honey over the top, and bit into the delicious confection, licking the sweet golden ooze from her lips with obvious glee.

"I have lived in this cottage for nearly forty years," Maiwenn began, her voice filled with nostalgic love.

"My late husband Pierrick built it for us when we first came to Ireland all those years ago. At the time, King Tuathal—your grandfather—was expanding the castle and had commissioned the construction of the north tower. Since my Pierrick was an experienced stone mason, we came to Ireland for the stability of the work."

Maiwenn ate some of her rabbit stew and sipped her chamomile *tisane.* Her tone became sorrowful.

"We lost our beautiful daughter Solenn and her husband Donall—may the Goddess bless their souls— twenty years ago, when our grandson Branoc was just three years old. We raised him in this cottage with us, and he now lives in the village with his young wife. He comes to visit when he can, chopping wood for my fireplace, helping me tend to the animals. Tomorrow, I will introduce you to my hens and goat, and show you my workshop where I make my herbal tinctures and ointments. I'll teach you how to make them. And the sweet-smelling soap with wild roses and yarrow."

She smiled at the princess, who had devoured every bite of the stew and was soaking up the broth with the crust of her bread. Maiwenn sat back in her chair and gazed into the expressive emerald eyes that now beheld her with apparent satisfaction and gratitude.

"Now, my dear, it's your turn to tell me why King Donnchadh's beloved daughter was wandering alone—in the dark—in the midst of the enchanted Hazelwood Forest."

The princess, fidgeting with her gown, told her about the queen's huntsmen. The orders to kill her and bring back her heart. Maiwenn saw the stark terror on the girl's face as she described in a quavering voice the malevolent stepmother with black eyes and icy hands.

Maiwenn sipped her tea, staring at the fire. She'd heard rumors in the village that the beautiful young queen was barren. Of course. With the queen unable to produce an heir, the Emerald Princess seated at her meager table had the rightful claim to the Irish throne. And therefore, posed the greatest threat to her stepmother's feeble grasp of power.

The fairy witch rubbed her forehead, searching for a plausible way to keep the girl's identity hidden. She perked up suddenly as the idea came to her. "The Goddess has sent you to me, my princess. I will shelter you here and keep you safe. And I will call you *Églantine*, after these wild roses that the forest fairies have chosen for you." She smiled at the rustic garland of elder wood twigs and interwoven pink blossoms crowning the girl's blond head. Maiwenn removed the wedding ring from her left hand and gave it to Issylte. "You must wear my wedding ring. We'll say that you are Églantine, my sister's granddaughter, a young widow who has come all the way from *Bretagne* to live with me as your only surviving relative." She took a sip of *tisane* and met Issylte's wondrous eyes over the rim of the ceramic mug. "It will be easier to hide your identity if we pass you off as a married woman. I'll lend you a frock, an apron, and some ordinary shoes. We'll store your fine clothing—and golden crown with those lovely emeralds—in a hidden compartment behind the armoire in the bedroom."

Taking a couple bites of the stew, and another sip of her herbal tea, she smiled affectionately at the young princess. *Églantine.*

Issylte nodded, fingering the silky velvet of her elegant robe. A hesitant smile spread across her torn face as she lifted her eyes, widened with hope.

"We'll braid your hair high upon your head, as the married women in the village do. You must always keep it covered with a scarf or bonnet to hide its distinctive blond color. We'll go into the village, where I'll present you to Branoc—that's my grandson—and his wife Dierdre. I usually go once a week to barter my ointments, salves, and tinctures for the supplies I need. We'll fetch some fabric to make you two or three simple dresses, and have the cobbler make you some leather shoes. Your lovely boots are much too fine for a peasant woman. I'll lend you a pair of mine—we'll say that yours were ruined by the salt water on the boat coming over from *Bretagne*. And you must call me *Tatie*—Auntie—as the

French girls do in *Bretagne*."

The dark green eyes of the young princess shimmered, her lips quavering with emotion. "You are most kind, dear Maiwenn. I mean, *Tatie*. I cannot thank you enough. I only hope that someday, somehow, I'll be able to repay you for the kindness you have shown me. I am so very, very grateful."

Issylte covered her face in her hands, the tears leaking through her long fingers.

Patting the princess' arm to comfort her, Maiwenn rose from the table. "Let me show you the room that used to be Branoc's. It will be yours now. Come, Églantine. Follow me."

Maiwenn led her into her into the small room which held a bed, a night table, and a wooden armoire. A stone fireplace flanked one wall, and a table and chair were centered under a window where moonlight filtered through the gauzy curtains into the peaceful room.

The fairy witch lit the candle on the night table beside the bed, and the soothing scent of rosemary and sage filtered into the air. Maiwenn indicated the chamber pot in the corner of the room, the pitcher and basin on the table beneath the window. "You may wash in this basin. Here's some of the soap that I make with my herbs and oils. I'll teach you how to make it, as well as my ointments and salves. There is so much knowledge I will share with you. It will be wonderful, having you here." She took hold of the girl's trembling hand and gave it a tight squeeze. "It will almost be as if my Solenn were with me again."

Maiwenn swallowed the painful lump in her throat, smoothing the sides of her brown homespun gown.

She opened the doors to the armoire, gesturing to the

shelves inside. "We won't need a fire in the bedrooms until late fall, but I keep extra blankets here on the top shelf if you should feel chilled. I'll bring you one of my nightgowns, and when you have changed, we'll store your things in the hidden compartment behind this armoire. We must hide your fine gown, your crown with emeralds, your father's ring upon your hand—and the cloak which bears his coat of arms. All would identify you instantly, should the queen's guards ever come searching for you here."

Maiwenn left to fetch a white nightgown from her own bedroom and returned to lay it on the narrow bed. "Wash up now, then change into this. My room is right next door. I'll be back in a few minutes so we can hide your things."

A few moments later, she knocked at the door, bringing the carefully folded cloak and boots that the princess had been wearing. Maiwenn wrapped the emerald-adorned coronet, royal ring, and emerald gown inside the deep green velvet cloak, placing the boots on the floor at the foot of the bed.

With Issylte's help, she moved the armoire away from the wall to reveal a hidden compartment in the wooden paneling. She pushed against one of the panels, causing a small door to open. Inside a hidden vault for storage lay a small pouch with a drawstring closure.

"This is where I keep my silver. Although it's not much, we might need it one day."

Storing the cloak-wrapped items and the fine quality boots inside the hidden compartment, Maiwenn closed the wooden paneled door. Issylte helped her push the armoire back into place against the bedroom wall.

The fairy witch walked to the bed and turned down

the blankets invitingly. Patting the bed with a gnarled hand, she spoke in a soothing, gentle voice.

"Sleep now, Églantine. We'll have boiled oats with goat's milk, honey, and wild berries for breakfast. I'll show you my workshop and introduce you to the animals. We'll load up baskets to carry my wares into the village so we can barter and get supplies. We'll pick up some fabric for your gowns and visit the cobbler for your shoes. Sleep well, my dear," she said, tucking the blankets around Issylte, who had crawled into comfortable, inviting bed.

"May the Goddess watch over you and bring you pleasant dreams." She kissed the girl's cheek goodnight, extinguished the candle, and slipped from the room.

Maiwenn returned to her small kitchen, gazing out the window to the shadowy forest, illuminated by the waning crescent moon. She prepared another *tisane*, the tangy herbal fragrance soothing as she sat down in her wooden chair before the dying fire. The sweet taste of chamomile lingering on her tongue, Maiwenn stared into the glowing embers. Reflective. Contemplative. Pensive.

Twenty years ago, she'd forsaken her magic. Cursed it. Damned it.

Because her magic had failed her. When she'd needed it most.

Maiwenn, one of the trio of fairies who'd studied with Merlin himself in the enchanted Forest of Brocéliande. *La Fée Verte de la Forêt*—the Green Fairy of the Forest—with seemingly limitless knowledge of its sacred trees, plants, and herbs. The skilled enchantress whose healing powers seemed boundless and infinite.

Until she'd failed to save her beloved daughter.

Maiwenn, who knew all the secrets of the

Hazelwood Forest, had been unable to squelch the raging fever that had claimed both Solenn and Donnall.

Her powerful magic had failed.

So, she'd abandoned it. Cursed it. Forsaken it.

Tamped it down into the bubbling cauldron of rage, despair, and guilt that smoldered in her shattered soul.

Yet tonight. . . the Goddess had sent the Emerald Princess to her doorstep.

And Maiwenn had sensed the thrum of the forest pulsing in the girl's veins.

A latent, potent force yet to be discovered.

A fecund, virid power yearning to be released.

The verdant, dormant magic of a forest fairy.

Reawakening her own.

Chapter 8

Lust for Power

Morag stood between the mauve velvet draperies of the ceiling-high windows in her lush royal chambers, watching the handsome young Master of Horse ride the dappled gray mare.

At her husband's request, Lord Liam rode the palfrey daily across the grassy plains of the courtyard. She knew the king would now be seated in his comfortable chair, a warm blanket wrapped around his bony shoulders and another across his weakened legs, staring out from his forlorn bedroom window, clutching desperately to the memory of his beloved daughter.

In the eight months since Issylte's death, King Donnchadh had become more and more withdrawn, preferring the solitude of his isolated royal chambers—tucked away in the farthest corner of the first floor of the castle, far from her own rosy bedroom on the second floor, where she now observed the last living link between King Donnchadh and his dearly departed daughter.

She experienced a rare pang of jealousy. Not because she no longer attracted her husband's interest. Quite the contrary. His reclusive, nearly catatonic state had given her the freedom to enjoy more frequent trysts with her lusty lover. No, she did not regret the loss of her husband's desire.

She was jealous that a father could love his daughter so very, very much.

For Morag had never known paternal love. She'd been the greatest disappointment of her father's life since the day she'd been born female. Her father, who had so desperately wanted a son, had rejected not only the worthless infant, but the useless wife incapable of bearing him a male heir. Her mother, in turn, had blamed the child for the loss of her husband's affection, seeking solace in newfound piety amidst the company of scornful priests in her private, inaccessible, royal chapel.

Neglected by her regal parents, the little princess grew up craving affection that was never given, learning instead to fill the hollow ache in her young heart with a different sort of attention. The sort that she'd seen burning in the eyes of every lord she met once her feminine curves had blossomed into the voluptuous petals of an irresistible flower they longed to pick.

Every noble lord, striving to please the beautiful, disdainful princess. Every lovestruck suitor, spoiling her with exquisite jewels, elegant silks, and the finest furs. Every loyal knight, eager to defend her honor—or warm her bed—with their mighty swords.

Lust. The source of her power over men.

And the means to satisfy the lust for power in her cold, withered heart.

A knock at the door interrupted Morag's reverie. Her attendants cinched the corset of her shimmering lilac gown a bit tighter, adjusting the strand of flawless pale amethysts at the base of her throat. A pair of silver combs held the sides of the long, black locks cascading down her back. Scented with lavender, his favorite smell on her. Like the silken sheets in her tantalizing, lavender-scented bed.

Just the thought of him in those sheets created a painful throb deep inside. She shivered with delight.

Her servants opened the door and scurried out like squirrels as the Morholt strode into her royal chambers and feasted his hungry eyes upon the lavender queen. He dropped to one knee, his head lowered in homage. "My queen."

The deep rumble of his voice sent a thrill rippling through her body.

She slid across the floor, the silk of her lavender gown rustling as she approached, placing a slender white hand upon his massive shoulder. The salty tang of sweat and a hint of smoke emanated from his dark green woolen tunic as she raised him to his feet to stand before her. Although Morag was quite tall, her eyes only came to the level of his throat, which she kissed seductively, humming her contentment at his presence.

He touched the glittering amethysts at her neck. "My gift pleases you."

"Truly. I am most pleased."

She rested her hand upon his. Her Viking had brought back many gifts, but this was by far her favorite. The color of lavender. Another ripple of pleasure flooded through her.

Her Black Knight's brutal raiding expeditions had indeed been most profitable—the sleek bottomed *drakaar* longships could not only traverse the seas, but venture inland for miles, sailing up rivers to raid foreign monasteries and churches, brimming with gold and valuable jewels. Such as the brilliant lavender amethysts sparkling at her throat in the early morning light.

He lowered his lips to the side of her neck, sending a wave of longing down her spine. Her breasts tingled at his touch.

"The color of lavender," he whispered, burying his nose into her hair and inhaling deeply. "The scent of passion." His eager lips returned to her swanlike neck.

Then, just as Morag expected to feel his hands caress her soft, silken bottom...he turned abruptly away and walked over to the window.

Something was wrong. He *never* resisted her. Morag's pulse quickened as he turned to face her, his eyes filled with longing. And regret.

"What is it? Something is troubling you. Tell me." She squelched the urge to fling her arms around his neck and pull him towards the bed.

"My queen, with the taxes you have raised, I now have every sea wright in the kingdom of Ireland constructing *drakaar* warships. Hundreds of knights training here at Castle Connaught, with thousands more preparing for battle with my men-at-arms."

Where was he leading with this? What was he saying? Morag's heart hammered in her chest.

"My raiding expeditions have been most profitable. I have made you a very wealthy queen."

His deep green eyes blazed with fire. Her mouth went dry as she lost herself in their verdant depths.

"But I wish to offer you more than jewels and gold. A gift to please you immeasurably. A treasure you will value beyond all others."

He strode forcefully across the room and halted abruptly right in front of her. The indomitable Viking warrior who cowered even the most courageous kings. She locked eyes with him, the hum of power filling her veins.

"The Cornish crown."

He took her hand and lowered his lips to caress it. Her knight raised his eyes to meet hers, his full lips upon her hand, cradled in his own.

Intrigued, Morag withdrew her hand and placed it at her side, stroking the soft silk of her lavender gown. To calm the tremors of thrill rippling up her long, lean legs.

"I have been raiding Cornwall for months. Pummeling them with incessant, brutal attacks. Weakening their forces. Capturing slaves."

He began to pace. A lion ready to roar.

"The men, I force to row our Viking longships. To plow the fields and harvest the crops to feed my expanding army. The women, I give to my soldiers. To produce more slaves and make us all the richer. The beautiful ones, I sell to wealthy nobles who tire of their boring wives and long for the heat of passion to warm their frigid beds."

He strode across the room and seized her, bending her over one arm as he lowered his lips to her throat, covering the swell of her breasts with his warm, wet lips. Lips that every inch of her body ached for.

He stood her back up, his eyes fierce as they bore into hers.

"But, to give you the Cornish crown, I must first beg your leave."

Her mind raced. He wished to leave? Why?

"I do not understand. Morholt, explain."

He began pacing again, a fury simmering beneath his rugged muscles. A power yearning to be released.

"I wish to transform the seaport of Dubh Linn into a Viking fortress, where I can launch slave expeditions in full force. Where my *drakaar* longships can have direct access to the Celtic Sea, while still being protected by the harbor and stone defense walls surrounding the city. I can store *hundreds* of vessels there. Fortify the naval forces of Ireland. And conquer Cornwall for you, my queen."

Morag saw the potent desire that blazed in his eyes. That's why he thrilled her. His lust for power matched her own.

He would bring her the Cornish crown. Thank the Goddess she'd eliminated her simpering stepdaughter. To think that she'd considered marrying the girl to King Marke, when her Black Knight could accomplish so much more!

He'd bring her gold and silver, flawless gemstones, slaves to empower the kingdom of Ireland. And her Morholt would bring her the Cornish crown. She nearly swooned with desire.

His feral gaze never left hers. He was waiting, her virile red lion. Her Viking warrior, the scourge of the Celtic Sea. Her indomitable knight, ready to crush the Cornish king. And bring her his glittering crown.

Morag could no longer hold back. She flung her arms around his neck and pulled his face down to hers. Her chest was heaving, her body quivering against his. She could feel his desire, straining against her hips.

"You have my leave, Morholt." She exhaled into his face, tugging his lip with her teeth.

"Transform Dubh Linn into the most powerful seaport in all of Europe. A Viking stronghold for your merciless slave raids."

She teased his lips, sucking them into her warm, inviting mouth. He pressed firmly against her hips, his desire enflaming her own.

"Weaken the Cornish king. And bring me his crown."

Her beloved Black Knight growled into her neck, unlaced her corset, and slid the lavender silk gown to the floor.

He scooped her up into his arms, carried her nude body across the room, and threw her down upon the lavender scented bed. He grinned ferally as he unstrapped his sword, letting it clatter to the tiled floor.

He removed his boots and his tunic, which he flung across the room, his savage eyes locked upon hers. Her breath hitched as he offered her the magnificent view of his expansive chest, covered in dark russet hair, brutal scars, and tensely coiled muscles, poised to strike.

He removed his breeches and crawled onto the bed, her red lion ready to pounce. He hovered over her, his eyes blazing, as he pushed her legs apart roughly with his powerful thighs.

And drove Morag wild with his ardent, amorous assault.

Chapter 9

The Hazelwood Forest

In the morning, Issylte awakened to sunlight streaming in through her window and a delicious aroma emanating from the small kitchen of the cottage. She rose from the warm covers, made the snug little bed, washed her face and hands in the basin, inhaling the lovely scents of yarrow and dogwood in the handmade soap. She donned the homespun brown peasant dress that Maiwenn had left for her on the table and headed towards the kitchen, where she spotted the fairy witch stirring a pot over the hearth.

"Good morning, Églantine! You seem very well rested, my dear. Did you sleep well?" Maiwenn flashed her a bright, welcoming smile.

"Yes, *Tatie*. The bed was very comfortable, thank you." Issylte peered into the pot to see what Maiwenn was cooking.

"Boiled oats and fresh fruit. This morning, we have gooseberries and wild strawberries, with fresh honey, too! But first, let's go meet the animals. I'll teach you how to milk the goat, Florette. We can have fresh goatmilk with our oats and fruit."

Maiwenn put the lid back on the pot and set the large spoon down on the nearby shelf. She took Issylte's hand to lead her outside, behind the cottage, to a small wooden building with a grilled door, centered within a metal gate enclosure that encompassed a large grassy area. The stream she had followed to discover the hidden cottage flowed into the fenced area behind the building and back out into the forest again. Maiwenn opened the door of the small wooden stable and greeted the animals inside.

"Good morning, ladies! Who's hungry?" At this, four plump brown hens and a small white goat rushed outside to greet the woman and the girl. "Églantine, meet Jojo, Lulu, Belle and Sophie," Maiwenn said, indicating the chickens, who pecked at the grass, searching for delectable insects.

"And this is Florette! Isn't she lovely?" Maiwenn stroked the goat's white fur and went inside the small stable to fetch a metal pail. Pulling up a wooden stool, she sat down beside Florette and began milking the goat, motioning for Issylte to watch. As she demonstrated, a stream of milk entered the clean pail, and when she deemed it a sufficient amount, the fairy witch stood up, replaced the stool, and allowed Florette to graze in the grassy area behind the cottage. Issylte noticed that the goat and hens drank from the stream and understood the ideal positioning of the fence.

"After breakfast, I will show you my two gardens. I have one for vegetables and another for herbs," Maiwenn explained, indicating two rectangular areas that were also enclosed within the grilled iron fence. This is my workshop," she said, gesturing to a small adjacent stone building that abutted the cottage. "In the winter, I open these doors which connect the workshop to the cottage. I keep the animals in there when it's too cold outside. That way, they have the warmth from the fireplace, and I can still tend to my herbs."

The Wild Rose and the Sea Raven

Issylte followed Maiwenn past the two gardens. Plants and vegetables were in one garden area, with small green tomatoes forming on the vines, and what appeared to be herbs growing in another.

"I'll teach you how to harvest the herbs and vegetables, and how I preserve them to last through the winter. I'll take you into the forest and show you where I find the most delicious berries, like the ones we have for our breakfast this morning." Collecting four eggs from the henhouse, Maiwenn said cheerfully, "We'll have an *omelette* with goat's milk and fresh mushrooms for supper. I'll show you where I find the edible ones and teach you which are poisonous. Come now, let's go back inside and have this fresh milk with our boiled oats and fruit."

Issylte followed her *tatie* into the cottage, and the two enjoyed the delicious porridge topped with fresh milk, fruit, and honey. Washing up the dishes in a basin on the shelf, Maiwenn handed Issylte a towel so that she could dry them, indicating where they were to be stored in the small wooden cupboard.

"Come now, let's go tend to the vegetables and herbs. I'll show you how." Returning to the back yard, Maiwenn rinsed out the bucket which had held the goat's milk and filled it with water from the stream. She carried the bucket over to the garden area, watered the vegetables, and returned several times to fetch more water until both gardens had been sufficiently irrigated.

"I do this every morning unless it has rained. Next, I prune them if necessary and remove the weeds. If there are any caterpillars or beetles on any of the plants, I feed them to the chickens. They *love* them!" She chuckled.

Maiwenn showed Issylte how to harvest the

vegetables that were ready to be picked, explaining that the scraps from peeling or pruning would be tossed into the nearby pile which she maintained to form a rich compost that she added to the garden. "The insects lay their eggs in this dark soil, and the fat grubs feed the chickens. The Goddess provides for us all."

After storing the herbs and vegetables in the kitchen, Maiwenn led Issylte through the Hazelwood Forest, indicating the gooseberry bushes and wild strawberry plants which were full of fruit. Issylte learned where the edible mushrooms were found, and that the poisonous ones often had white gill caps, or cup-like structures at their base, a red color or perhaps a ring in the stem. She discovered where herbs could be found in the wild, and Maiwenn promised to teach her of the medicinal properties of the forest.

As they continued their trek through the woods, Maiwenn explained to Issylte, "In Bretagne, a woman blessed by the Goddess with the *gift* of the forest may study herbal medicine to become a *guérisseuse,* or advanced healer. She learns which plants prevent a wound from festering, which form salves to soothe tired muscles or ease aching joints, and which herbs promote fertility or prevent a babe from being conceived." Lowering her head to fit under a thick branch, she motioned for Issylte to follow, and continued walking at a brisk pace, as if pursuing a predetermined destination.

Following closely behind, Issylte listened as Maiwenn continued. "I learned herbal medicine in the Forest of Brocéliande, in my native *Bretagne.* In that sacred realm, there are Druids who follow the teachings of the famed Merlin, and women priestesses who have mastered all three of the sacred healing elements of the

Goddess—forest, water, and stone—to earn the prestigious title of *guérisseuse*." Turning to face Issylte as they reached a clearing at last, the old woman smiled enigmatically. "Who knows? Perhaps it is your destiny to embark on this journey. Indeed, perhaps that is why the Goddess has brought you to my doorstep." Upon finishing these words, Maiwenn revealed the purpose for this trek through the forest.

They had arrived at the edge of an enormous lake, gleaming in the morning sunlight, surrounded by dense woods and ledges of high rocks. The water was an intense blue, calm and serene; birds soared overhead amongst the scattered white clouds. The loamy, earthy scent of the rich black soil mingled with the fresh tang of the lake and the pine scent of the forest, inundating Issylte with its striking natural beauty.

"Where is this place? It is magical!" She sighed, taking in the vast expanse of the lake, the enormity of the rocks on the distant shoreline, and the density of the Hazelwood Forest from which they had just emerged.

"This is *Lough Gill*, which means shining lake. See how the water glistens? The Lough Gill drains into the river to the west. From there, it flows into an estuary, a tidal bay which leads to the ocean. I often go there to harvest shellfish, such as oysters, cockles, clams, and mussels. The village of *Sligeach* is a seaport there, with lots of local fishermen selling their wares. My grandson Branoc has a blacksmith shop there in the village, where I go to the market every Saturday. I'll bring you with me this week and introduce you to him, and to some of the townspeople as well. We'll get some fresh seafood, a few supplies, including the fabric for your dresses—and your new pair of leather shoes. It will be such a lovely day."

Maiwenn beamed.

Issylte was speechless, still marveling at the beauty of the lake before her and the forest around her. She thought of her father, whom she missed so much her stomach ached, and of Gigi, who had mothered and comforted her throughout her entire childhood. She missed the castle of Connaught, and even the attendants who always yanked her hair into tight braids with the emerald silk ribbons Gigi adored. She longed to ride Luna, her beautiful gray mare, and to see the handsome face of Liam who had taught her not only to ride and care for her horse, but also the thrill of a wild gallop, the wind whipping her hair as it stung her cheeks. But above all, she missed her father. His warm hugs, his twinkling hazel eyes, his generous heart.

Emotions flooded Issylte, and tears welled up into her eyes. A wave of terror flooded through her as she sensed her stepmother's icy hands draining her strength. Her legs trembled at the memory of the ordeal in the forest when Lords Cian and Bolduc had been ordered to kill her. Shaking, crying, and overwhelmed, Issylte fell to her knees and sobbed into her hands.

The gentle touch of Maiwenn's hands soothed her. Issylte raised her tear-soaked, crumpled face to search the kind eyes of this loving old woman who had welcomed her into her own home.

"Thank you so much, *Tatie*. For everything. For bringing me here to this enchanted place, for offering me shelter. For feeding me, protecting me, teaching me…I will always be grateful to you for the kindness you have shown me." Her lower lip quivered as tears flowed into the scratches on her still-torn face.

Maiwenn pulled the girl into her arms. She stroked

her hair, kissed her cheek, and cooed, "Ah, there now, dear heart. Don't cry. I know you miss your father the king and the life you had at the castle. Poor thing, you've had such a fright, and you've been through so much. But, please, look at me, dear."

Issylte lifted her tear-strewn face to meet her *tatie's* affectionate gaze.

"I am very, very glad that you are here with me now. I thank the Goddess for bringing you into my life. It is wonderful to feel needed again. I have been so lonely for such a long time. For far too long."

Issylte offered a soft smile, drying her eyes with the hem of her plain woolen dress.

Maiwenn reached into the basket and retrieved a metal hook. She flashed Issylte an impish grin. "And now, I will teach you how to fish!"

Chapter 10

The Road to Camelot

Tristan, Vaughan, Connor and the other seven recently sworn knights from Cornwall proudly displayed their new armor and fine surcoats as they traveled northeast across the southern countryside of Britain atop their gifted warhorses. Each knight brought a page and a squire, with tents, bedrolls, and provisions to last for the long trek to Camelot.

Tonight, as the group neared the legendary castle and its surrounding villages, the men decided to stay at the inn just up ahead along the well-traveled road. Exhausted after days in the saddle, Tristan envisioned a warm bed, a hot meal, and a much better night's sleep than what he had been experiencing on the hard ground inside his small tent.

Securing the horses in the stables with the grooms, Tristan and his fellow knights entered the wooden building, where they were greeted in a large hall by a friendly innkeeper and several serving women, who were bustling around with trays of food and tankards of ale for the guests who were already seated. After procuring rooms for each of the knights, with adjacent ones for the squires and pages, the travelers settled down at several tables to order food and drinks.

Tristan, Connor, and Vaughan were seated with

three knights who hailed from different regions of Cornwall. At a table across the room, Tristan observed Indulf sitting with the remaining knights, with the pages and squires settled at two other tables nearby. The atmosphere in the inn was lively, with merchants and wealthy lords conversing loudly, obviously enjoying the hospitality and vibrant ambiance of the establishment.

A serving girl set goblets of ale and platters of roast boar before them, a warm smile on her face. The delicious aroma made Tristan's stomach growl.

"Will any of you fine lords be wantin' some female company this evenin'?"

Kaden, one of the knights at Tristan's table, put his arm around the young woman and grinned.

"Only if it's you, darlin'!"

She laughed, promising to take care of Kaden's every need after the knights had finished eating.

A short while later, she cleared off the table, brought the dishes into the kitchen, then returned, smiling provocatively at Kaden, who rose to his feet to greet her. With a nod of her head, she indicated that there were several other lovely ladies available for the remaining gentlemen, should they be interested. Catching the attention of a dark-haired co-worker, she motioned to the young woman, inviting her to approach the table.

"This is Mirren. Isn't she lovely, m'lord?" the barmaid said to Tristan as she seated the young brunette upon his lap. "She may seem a bit shy, but she's really very friendly, aren't you, Mirren?" Taking Kaden by the hand, she led him away as he grinned to his fellow knights and hollered, "Good night, lads! Tomorrow, it's Camelot—if I survive tonight!" The men at the table roared with laughter, adding a few bawdy comments.

Tristan squirmed uncomfortably and shot a pleading look at Vaughan.

Tristan helped the serving girl rise to her feet from his lap. "You are quite lovely, my lady, but…" to which Vaughan interjected, "but he has a sweetheart back home, and he's promised to be true to her, isn't that so, Tristan?"

The young Mirren smiled demurely, excused herself politely, and walked back behind the wooden bar to join the other servers, who were pouring more goblets of ale.

Vaughan teased, "She was pretty, Tristan. Just not interested?"

Tristan stared into his tankard. "You know me, Vaughan. I'm a bloody bastard. My only interest is fighting." He took a long pull of ale and met Vaughan's mirthful eyes. "And killing bloody Vikings!" He grinned, downed another big gulp of his brew, and wiped his mouth on his sleeve.

Vaughan seemed pensive as he drank from his own goblet. After a few moments, he leaned towards Tristan and confided, "Elowenn is hoping you'll come back to her, you know. My father would be most pleased. And I would be thrilled to have you as my sister's husband. We would be brothers by marriage, as well as in arms."

Tristan didn't know how to respond. He knew what Vaughan wanted to hear. But he couldn't lie to his best friend. Vaughan waited a few moments, as if hoping his words would have the intended effect.

"Do you plan to marry her, Tristan? She has loved you ever since the first summer you spent with us at Kennall Vale. You stole her heart, you know. She won't even consider anyone else."

Tristan reflected upon the summer when he'd first

kissed Elowenn. Three years ago. He thought of her light brown hair and soft blue eyes, her gentle nature. He cared for Vaughan's sister, but he also knew that she would never be the right wife for him. The kisses they'd shared had been chaste. Like kissing his own sister.

Elowenn was pretty enough, but she rarely spoke. She was timid, vapid, sedate. She had few interests, other than needlepoint, and Tristan simply could not envision a life with her, sitting by a fire in silence while she embroidered his tunics. Perhaps many a man would appreciate such qualities in a wife, but Tristan wanted a woman who was more his equal in temperament, intelligence, and fire.

And it was all intricately more complicated than just Tristan's preferences, for he understood that, as his uncle's presumptive heir to the throne of Cornwall, he would be expected to marry a princess, not the daughter of a lesser lord such as Vaughan's father. Tristan realized that Lord Treave and Lady Melora hoped that a royal marriage of their daughter to King Marke's heir would elevate the position of their entire family, and that Elowenn, as Tristan's wife, would live in the castle of Tintagel and one day rule Cornwall as its queen.

But none of that mattered anyway, for Tristan knew in his heart that no woman would ever want a foul-tempered, angry brute of a man such as himself. No, it was better if he avoided women altogether. It was safer—and easier—that way.

There was a sudden commotion at Connor's table, and Tristan, shaking himself out of his reverie, noticed that Indulf had pulled the serving girl, Mirren, to his lap, where he held her pinned with an arm wrapped around her waist. Muttering something incoherent that made the other knights at the table burst out laughing, Indulf ravaged Mirren's neck, holding her tightly against his chest as she pleaded with him to stop. Her face crumpled in fear as Indulf roughly groped her breasts, grinding himself into her backside. She yelped and struggled to break free, desperately trying to escape. But Indulf had her locked in place, thrusting against her as she wriggled, thoroughly enjoying her pain and fear.

Tristan's chair toppled to the floor as he shot to his feet. His voice was feral, gruff. "She asked you to stop. Let her go. Have you so quickly forgotten our oath of chivalry? To *honor a lady*?"

Undeterred, Indulf continued pawing Mirren, whose tearful eyes implored Tristan. With a cruel grin, Indulf sneered, "She's no lady, now is she?" He burrowed his snout into Mirren's neck, snuffling like a pig.

Tristan was revolted. His heart hammered in his chest. His sister, Talwyn…she'd been only ten years old. And the fucking Vikings had dragged her behind the wall… He could still hear her blood curdling screams, tearing out his heart.

He'd been too young to fight. To protect her. To stop the bastards. But Tristan would stop Indulf. Even if he had to kill him.

Like a raging bull, Tristan charged across the room, tore Indulf's arm away from Mirren, and helped the girl to her feet. He spoke into her ear, his lethal eyes never leaving the repulsive swine. Mirren dashed into the kitchen as Tristan, his breath heaving, turned to face a snickering Indulf, pompously relaxed at the table, one side of his face drawn up in a sneer.

The flames of rage engulfed him. Tristan unleashed his fury, swinging his fist in a powerful arc that connected with Indulf's jaw, knocked him backwards over his chair, crashing down upon the hard wooden floor.

Vaughan launched himself at Tristan, wrapped an arm around his shoulder and across his neck. Tristan, straining against Vaughan's choke hold, was shaken back to his senses by his brother's strength as he was pulled away from Indulf, who lay ignominiously on the floor, spitting blood from his ruined lip.

"Tristan," Vaughan shouted, his voice straining with exertion. "We can't have the Blue Knight of Cornwall thrown out on his arse for brawling before we even get to Camelot! C'mon, man—save it for Sir Lancelot's training field! Let's go have another ale, shall we?"

Tristan, still roaring with adrenaline, glowered at Indulf, whose legs were splayed awkwardly across his overturned chair. Vaughan, his arm still around Tristan's neck, was patting his back, soothing the savage beast, reminding him of the paramount trek to Camelot.

It was all he could do to restrain himself from pummeling Indulf's porcine face.

The blond knight spat out another mouthful of blood and glared daggers at Tristan. Indulf put his hand to his jaw, wincing as he moved it side to side. Tristan filled his lungs with calming air, exhaling forcefully as Vaughan released his grip and stepped back. Tristan rolled his shoulders and stretched his neck, then glanced around the room as his simmering fury abated.

The inn keeper and several other patrons were watching, as if waiting for the two combatants to draw swords. Indulf was still laying on the floor, sizing him up, taking in Tristan's superior height and weight. Apparently deciding it would be in his best interest to feign humor, Indulf rose to his feet and brushed himself off. He set his chair to right and reached for his mug of ale.

Raising his goblet, he guffawed, "Aw hell, Tristan, I was just havin' a bit o' fun. No harm done, eh?" The swine gulped his frothy brew, wincing as the mug thumped against his swollen lip.

Tristan allowed Vaughan to drag him back to the table and buy him another tankard of ale. With the brawl narrowly averted, the raucous revelry of his companions resumed in full force. Indulf glowered at him across the room.

Just as Tristan and Vaughan were preparing to leave the large hall to retire to their room, one of the well-dressed patrons and his cadre of armed personal guards stood up from a table and headed for the exit.

The obviously wealthy lord, surprisingly short in stature, had a dark and withered face, misshapen and contorted. The baron, followed by his armed guards, stopped at Indulf's table to speak with the blond knight.

The lord's personal guards bore gleaming swords at their hips, a surcoat with the image of a wild boar over their chain mail armor. The diminutive baron and Indulf conferred, glancing repeatedly in his direction. Tristan realized that he was obviously the topic of their conversation; he could feel their watchful, predatory eyes assessing him. Plotting. Conspiring. His warrior instincts told him to beware.

A barmaid was wiping off a nearby table, and Tristan motioned for her to approach. He asked the woman if she recognized the baron who was speaking to Indulf. She cast a quick glance over her shoulder and turned abruptly back to Tristan, her eyes widened in fear.

"The dwarf? Aye, m'lord. That's Frocin, a shipping merchant. He owns a fortress just east of here, in the Forest of Morois. He's very wealthy, 'cause he's the one they hire when there's money owed, or property to be seized, or vengeance to be had. Some say he's an assassin; others, that he delves in the dark arts. Best to stay clear of him, m'lord. Frocin's dangerous and deadly, that he is."

The mercenary, having finished his intense discussion with Indulf, headed towards the exit with his entourage of heavily armed knights. The dwarf's malevolent stare made the hairs on the back of Tristan's neck rise. A chill rippled through him as Frocin grinned wickedly, sauntering past Tristan's table.

He watched the dwarf slither from the inn, a dozen guards in his wake. He wondered what the hell Indulf had said to put that bloody smirk on Frocin's gnarled face. Something sinister. About him. He finished his ale and went upstairs with Vaughan to their room.

"Thanks for saving me, brother. I wanted to kill the bastard." Tristan unbuckled his sword and placed it beside his bed. He glanced over at Vaughan, sitting on his own bed, removing his boots.

"I know, Tristan. I know." Vaughan's eyes reflected empathy. And stern reprimand.

Tristan's temper often got the best of him. And tonight, he'd nearly lost everything.

He would have killed Indulf. To stop him from hurting her.

Because he had not been able to stop the Vikings from ravaging his beautiful sister.

The guilt and rage consumed him. Thank the Goddess Vaughan had saved his ass tonight. Because he would have killed Indulf.

And been hanged for murder.

It was a long time before sleep finally found him.

****

The next morning, the ten knights broke their fast and loaded up the warhorses to complete the last leg of the journey to Camelot. As they headed northeast, the incline of the forested terrain became increasingly steeper as they crossed the foothills through the dense woodlands of southern Britain. Finally, as the sun approached its zenith, the travelers glimpsed the magnificent white stone castle and the treacherous bridge across a precipice which provided the only access.

Built atop a mountain, Camelot was an impenetrable fortress, surrounded at its base by an immense stone outer curtain wall with a drawbridge protected by a metal gated portcullis. On either side of the gated entrance stood enormous defense towers, with battlements and ramparts extending around the outer perimeter of the castle. Multiple levels of its glistening stone towers and turrets rose high above the mountain, reaching up into the heavens, proudly displaying the red pendragon of King Arthur's heraldry on the many golden banners that rippled in the crisp spring winds.

The walled stone bridge which traversed the ravine and led to the castle permitted only three riders at a time, so each knight crossed with a page and squire riding at his sides. When all ten winners of the Tournament of Champions had crossed, the knights of Cornwall entered the bailey of the castle, where they handed their horses and gear to the awaiting stable hands. Servants ushered them to their quarters, informing the knights that a formal reception awaited them in the massive Great Hall.

Tristan washed up with the pitcher of water and basin in his chamber, then donned a clean tunic and breeches, after which his squire Lionel helped him with his new armor—including the surcoat bearing the Cornish *chough*—and his sword, *Tahlfir*. He joined Vaughan, Connor, and the others in the corridor, following servants to the Great Hall where an elaborate feast welcomed them.

As the new knights stood at the entrance to the Great Hall, Tristan beheld the opulence of the Castle of Camelot.

The intricate ceiling consisted of three pointed wooden arches, painted in gold and adorned with red dragons, overlooking a vast room of glittering, gilded walls. An elevated seating area, suspended high above the main floor, gave a splendid view of the sumptuous feast to a dozen of the highest-ranking nobles, the preferred guests of King Arthur Pendragon. On the main floor, long tables—perpendicular to the royal dais— were covered with white damask tablecloths where centerpieces of ornately gilded pheasant, stuffed boar's head and aromatic arrays of spiced meat pastries beckoned the royal guests. Silver goblets of wine and ale glinted in the candlelight from the chandeliers overhead. The enticing aroma of exotic foods wafted through the air, carried upon melodic currents from harmonious harps and violins.

King Arthur was seated in a golden throne upon a dais at the royal table, where Sir Lancelot stood to his right. The First Knight of Camelot was tall and lean, with shoulder length wavy brown hair and a friendly countenance upon his handsome, youthful face. Several other nobles sat at the royal table, with a blond queen dressed in white seated beside the king. *Queen Guinevere,* Tristan realized.

Lords and ladies, all dressed in fine silks and brocades, were seated amongst knights in shining armor at the elegantly decorated tables throughout the vast room. Ten empty seats awaited the honored guests—the new knights representing the kingdom of Cornwall—at the table of distinction closest to the royal dais.

The herald trumpeted at the entrance to the Great Hall. Sir Lancelot of the Lake—the First Knight of Camelot—announced their arrival as he bowed and gestured to his king.

"Knights of Cornwall, Welcome! I present to you his Royal Majesty, King Arthur Pendragon, the High King of all Britain!"

The ten knights knelt before their royal sovereign, their heads bowed in fealty. They were then ushered to the table of honor, seated ceremoniously, and offered gleaming goblets of rich red wine.

King Arthur, splendidly attired in a red velvet cape and golden crown, adorned with magnificent gemstones, boomed joyously to greet them.

"Knights of Cornwall. Winners of the acclaimed Tournament of Champions. I congratulate you on your victory!"

Applause rippled through the jubilant crowd.

"My First Knight, Sir Lancelot of the Lake, will train you most vigorously for the next two years. Upon completion of your training, you will join my prestigious Knights of the Round Table. And defend all of Britain!"

Enthusiastic cheering ensued as the king raised his chalice of wine above his gilded head.

"To the winners of the Tournament of Champions.

Welcome to Camelot!"

Tristan, Vaughan, Connor, and the others lifted their goblets as the joyous crowd roared. Sir Lancelot raised his silver goblet high.

"To the ten newest Knights of the Round Table. May you always prove worthy of this greatest honor!"

Beaming with pride, humbled with gratitude, Tristan and his fellow Cornish knights raised their goblets and drank.

Tristan grinned ferociously at Vaughan and Connor, his brothers in arms.

Their two-year adventure had begun.

Chapter 11

A Verdant Power

Maiwenn did indeed teach Issylte to fish. She showed her how to unearth the fat, wriggling worms that the sea trout, pike, and perch in the lake of Lough Gill loved best. The first day at the lake, the very first time she had ever fished in her entire life, Issylte caught two sea trout, giggling in delight as the fish squirmed at the end of the stick which she held tightly underneath the oak canopy at the side of the shining lake.

Maiwenn, who had caught four perch, put two of the fish in a small basket, to which she added some berries, nuts, and a few jars of her herbal tinctures. The fairy witch placed the basket under a tree at the edge of the Hazelwood Forest, explaining to Issylte, "I always leave a gift for the *Little Folk*. I consider it an offering to the Goddess, since they are Her people."

Taking her small dagger, she showed Issylte the technique of filleting the fish that they had caught. Tossing the entrails and bones of the cut fish back into the water, Maiwenn washed her knife in the lake, wrapped the fresh fillets in a clean cloth, and placed it all in a large basket.

"Come, dear, let's return to the cottage. I'll show you how to bake the fish with rosemary, thyme, and sage. We'll harvest a few early carrots and turnips, and an onion. It will be a feast!"

Later that afternoon, seated at the wooden table in the cozy cottage, the old woman and the peasant princess savored the delicate flavor of the herbed trout and steaming vegetables. Once they finished their dinner, Maiwenn served a delicious dessert, which she called *tarte aux mirabelles,* a fruit pie made from the wild sweet plums that were abundant in the forest during spring and summer.

Each day, Maiwenn taught Issylte about herbs—those she cultivated in the garden, for seasoning the savory meals they prepared, but also the wild herbs which they collected in the forest, which were needed for the tinctures, potions, ointments, and salves that they bartered in the village. Issylte learned which herbs would soothe the cramps she suffered each month when her courses came; she learned which would help promote fertility or prevent a babe from being conceived. Maiwenn taught her how to harvest fresh flowers and prepare essential oils, to which they would add herbs for healing wounds, or to soothe aching joints and muscles.

One day, Maiwenn led Issylte along the stream to a sheltered grove where an abundance of beautiful purple and white wildflowers grew amidst ivy-entwined evergreen shrubs and yew trees. The fairy witch motioned for Issylte to kneel at her side among the flowers. Her luminous brown eyes twinkled in the filtered sunlight.

"Every tree, plant, flower and herb has an essence. A spirit. A life force." She gestured to the verdant forest all around.

Issylte raised her eyes to the lush canopy of trees overhead, the blue sky peeking through the fluffy clouds.

She inhaled deeply, the green notes of pine mingling with the rich scent of earth and the tangy fragrance of blossoms in the early summer breeze.

"The essence of the forest can be beneficial. Benevolent. Essential for healing." She picked up a sprig of red clover and handed it to Issylte with a knowing smile. "Yet others are harmful and deadly." Maiwenn gestured to the alluring deep purple flowers before them.

Issylte's breath caught in wonder. She sensed an aura. A tingle in her veins.

Maiwenn's chestnut eyes bore deeply into hers. "Have you ever felt the thrum of the forest in your veins?"

Issylte nodded, her eyes wide with discovery and delight. She held Maiwenn's gaze, nearly breathless with anticipation.

"That, Églantine, is *power*." Maiwenn's eyes were brown, like the nourishing earth of the Hazelwood Forest.

"You, my dear princess, are a *forest fairy*. Like me."

With a quick intake of breath, Issylte placed her hands over her mouth in wonder.

"The Goddess has blessed us both with a divine gift. The ability to sense the essence of a plant. To wield its power. The warm, soothing aura of a beneficial herb. The icy sting of a poison." Maiwenn gestured to the field of flowers. "Use your gift. Tell me which flowers are harmful."

Issylte stood, straightening her brown homespun frock. She stepped cautiously among the flowers. A pervasive sense of dread and doom engulfed her as she neared the deep purple blossoms. She turned to Maiwenn. "These flowers are poisonous. I can sense death."

Maiwenn nodded proudly, her eyes glowing in the dappled sunlight. "Wolfsbane. Deadly poison." She wobbled to her feet, rubbing her hip with a gnarled hand, and crept towards Issylte. "Wolfsbane slows—then stops—a beating heart." She took hold of Issylte's hand and led her to the deep pink flowers growing nearby. "And these?"

Issylte sensed the sting of danger, tempered with a wave of hope. "These…can be fatal in large doses. But beneficial in small amounts." She reached out with her gift, probing the nuances of the aura surrounding the flowers. "This plant affects the heart also. Is it used to prevent death from wolfsbane?"

Maiwenn's wrinkled cheeks puckered in a grin of delight. "Yes. This deep pink flower is foxglove. It can accelerate and strengthen the heart. If someone has been poisoned with wolfsbane, it can prevent death."

The fairy witch pointed to the white flowers. "What about those?"

There were two very similar types of blossoms. Both very pretty, like delicate lace, but one flower had a repulsive odor and purple splotches on the stems. An icy cold permeated her veins, warning of danger.

"This one is deadly. What is it?"

"Irish hemlock. Very deadly indeed. And the other?"

Issylte sensed a wave of peace and calm. "It is harmless. Am I right?"

"Yes. Cow parsley. Well done, Églantine. Come, I will teach you so much more."

As the weeks passed, Maiwenn taught Issylte which herbs—such as basil, nettle, red clover, and burdock root—cleansed toxins from the blood. The young forest fairy learned to distinguish between the lethal cherry laurel and the beneficial bay laurel, between toxic lily of the valley and edible violets. That rhubarb stalks yielded a delicious fruit, yet consumption of the leaves was often fatal.

Issylte developed her newfound power, learning to draw upon the curative essence of the Hazelwood Forest with the verdant magic which flowed in her veins. Little by little, under Maiwenn's loving tutelage, the young forest fairy discovered her divine gift.

And Maiwenn rediscovered her own.

****

Every Saturday, they ventured into the village of Sligeach, uniquely placed on a tidal bay in the estuary of the river which flowed from the lake, Lough Gill, to the sea. Maiwenn taught Issylte how to dig clams when the tide was low, for the recessed water revealed an enormous mud flat, abundant in shellfish. The fairy witch pointed to the small holes which indicated where the clams were hidden, and Issylte dug into the thick, sandy mud with her long fingers, being careful not to slice them open on the sharp shells of the mollusks.

They harvested oysters, mussels, clams, and cockles. They caught crabs and crayfish whose tender, sweet meat Issylte found delicious, especially when flavored with butter that Maiwenn churned with Florette's milk. On each trip into the village, the two women coordinated their shellfish harvest with the tides, sometimes collecting their seafood on the way in, and sometimes stopping to dig clams on the return home. Maiwenn taught Issylte that, by placing the bucket of seafood in the cool water of the fast-flowing steam near the cottage, the shellfish stayed fresh for two or three days. They feasted frequently on the delectable *fruits de mer.*

Each week, Maiwenn brought baskets of herbal remedies into town, bartering her wares for flour and honey, grain for the hens, fabric for Issylte's frocks, a pair of boots or gloves—whatever supplies were needed. She introduced Issylte as her sister's granddaughter Églantine, the young widow from *Bretagne*, presenting the princess to the local shopkeepers and villagers, who soon welcomed her with a friendly smile.

Maiwenn helped the young forest fairy learn to wield her magic, bringing her protégée to various homes in the village, where Issylte created elixirs to heal the sick, assisted with the difficult delivery of a baby, and helped young mothers produce more milk with fenugreek tea. She learned about the healing power of raw honey, how to prepare poultices which could withdraw toxins from a festered wound, and how sometimes it was necessary to administer a sleeping draught in order to cut out decayed flesh or remove a gangrenous limb.

As the months passed, Issylte learned to wield the power of the forest and heal with the magic of her touch. Her kind smile, gentle demeanor, and ever-increasing skill with the herbal remedies she administered gained Issylte respect among the local villagers, her *Tatie* always at her side.

One evening, an urgent knock interrupted their light supper. Maiwenn opened the cottage door to find a frantic young man in dire need of a healer.

"It's my daughter," he wailed, wringing his hands in distress. "She's very sick. Please help us."

As Maiwenn donned her cloak, Issylte grabbed the basket of herbal medicines. The two healers hurried to keep up with the young man as he raced through the forest, arriving at a small wooden house with a thatched roof. At a nearby pond, several goats were grazing peacefully under the golden setting sun.

The villager flung open the front door and burst into the room. As she and Maiwenn entered, Issylte spotted a young girl, five or six years old, curled up on a cot. She was clutching her stomach, moaning, writhing in pain.

Issylte quickly shed her cloak and rushed to the girl's side. The child was trembling, with sweat beading on her brow. She, the young healer, knelt beside the bed and took hold of the little girl's hand.

A wave of frost shivered up Issylte's spine. The icy chill of her stepmother's grip—the numbness and tingling, draining her energy and sapping her strength—blasted through her like a biting winter wind. Issylte jumped to her feet, recoiling in horror. She stumbled back, her chest heaving, unable to speak.

Maiwenn rushed forward and took Issylte's place beside the girl. The child's frantic mother, her eyes fixed upon Issylte with terror, was rocking back and forth at the foot of the small bed. Maiwenn asked her to fetch a cup of water. Issylte, who had found shelter behind a chair near the front door, watched helplessly as her *tatie* withdrew a vial from the basket of supplies, placed a drop of liquid into the cup, and helped the child sit up enough to drink a few swallows.

Maiwenn fetched an ointment from the basket, massaging it briskly into the girl's arms and legs, rubbing the frail limbs as if to improve the flow of blood. She covered the little patient with a woolen blanket and stroked the child's damp hair. After a few minutes, the moaning and writhing stopped. The young girl smiled weakly at Maiwenn, a gap from a missing tooth in her innocent grin.

"My tummy feels better now," she whispered. "And my arms and legs don't feel all prickly anymore."

Maiwenn wiped the child's brow and leaned down to plant a soft kiss upon her forehead. "Sleep now, sweetheart. And stay away from those purple flowers. That's what made you sick."

The child nodded, snuggling into the warm blankets, relief spreading across her sweet face.

Maiwenn motioned for the girl's parents to approach. Issylte listened by the door.

"She might have diarrhea for the next day or two. Give her plenty of water and rest. She will be fine. But you must keep her away from the dark purple flowers near the stream. They are poisonous."

The young parents, their eyes filled with grateful tears, nodded earnestly, thanking Maiwenn with eager handshakes. The girl's mother paid the healer with a basket of fresh vegetables from her garden, and the young father escorted Maiwenn and Issylte back to their stone cottage. He bowed in gratitude before Maiwenn and returned gratefully to his humble home.

Maiwenn lit a candle, for it had grown dark, adding another log to the fire in the hearth. She seated Issylte at the little table, set the yarrow scented candle before the shaken princess, then went into the kitchen to prepare two cups of *tisane*. Returning with the steaming chamomile tea, Maiwenn sat down across from Issylte, her large brown eyes tinged with worry.

"What happened when you touched the girl's

hand?"

Issylte shuddered at the memory. She sipped her *tisane* to bolster her courage. "I sensed my stepmother's icy hand, draining my strength. The same numbness and tingling creeping up my arm. Like *death*." Issylte's lips quivered. She groaned in despair. "I couldn't save her, *Tatie*. That little girl would have died. I was too frightened to save her."

Maiwenn took Issylte's hand. She gazed at the flickering flame of the fragrant candle. Inhaled the soothing, sweet scent of yarrow. "Sometimes we falter. Lose faith in our gift." Maiwenn's large brown eyes glowed in the soft light. "I did, twenty years ago. When I failed to save my daughter Solenn and her husband."

Issylte glanced up in shock. Maiwenn squeezed her hand, her eyes blazing like the flame before them.

"I tried everything, Églantine. Herbs, tinctures, potions, ointments. Whispers, enchantments, prayers. Nothing worked. My gift failed me. And when my beautiful daughter died, my heart shriveled up like a neglected flower. I scorned my magic. Abandoned it. In my rage, grief, and guilt, I blamed it for their deaths. I, *la Fée Verte de la Forêt*, abandoned the divine gift of the Goddess. Until She sent you to my door."

Maiwenn kissed Issylte's hand, her expressive eyes glimmering. "I, my dear princess, have learned from you, as you have from me. Through you, the Goddess has reawakened my power. And tonight, because of that, I was able to save a life." Maiwenn took hold of Issylte's other hand and shook both at once, as if to impart the urgency of her message. "Never abandon your gift, Églantine. Never wallow in the darkness as I have so foolishly done all these long, lonely years. Face your fears, dear heart. If you fail, don't give up. Learn from your mistakes and become even stronger. And always cherish your gift. Shine the divine light of the Goddess as you wield your power. To *heal*."

Maiwenn kissed Issylte's hands. "I thank Her for returning my gift through you. Tonight, I was able to save that child. Thanks to you." Maiwenn's beautiful, wrinkled face shone with divine light.

Pensive, the fairy witch took a sip of her *tisane*, gazing at the crackling hearth. "Your gift is even stronger than my own, Églantine." Maiwenn turned to face her. Issylte's heart caught in her throat.

"Some fairies have the gift of *sight*. A power that reveals itself when images appear on water, foretelling the future. Sometimes, the gift of *sight* occurs through touch. When a fairy can envision forthcoming events, such as what you experienced when you sensed the icy hand of your stepmother the queen."

Maiwenn sipped her tea, meeting Issylte's enrapt gaze. "That little girl had ingested wolfsbane. The purple flowers we saw near the stream. When you touched her hand, you sensed the poison with your gift of *sight*. Just as you did when your stepmother took your hand. Your *sight* has shown that the queen will somehow use wolfsbane, perhaps as a means to acquire power. Your gift was warning you of the danger."

That evening, Issylte found sleep elusive.

Fear had prevented her from saving the little girl. She felt ashamed, guilty, and weak. But Maiwenn's message inspired her. She did need to face her fear of the wicked queen. Overcome it somehow. Develop her strength and skill. She was thrilled to be a *forest fairy*, like Maiwenn, with the power to wield the healing essence of the forest. Yet the queen terrified her.

Tendrils of tingling numbness crept up her arm as her stepmother's icy fingers gripped her hand. She shivered, rubbing her arms to ward off the frost.

Her stepmother had already tried to kill her once. If she discovered Issylte was still alive, she would try again. Perhaps with the poison wolfsbane. Issylte shuddered, pulling the blankets around her tightly.

She needed to discover more about her gift, to defend herself from the wicked queen.

She would develop her power. Overcome her fear. And find a way to save her father.

Chapter 12

Lancelot of the Lake

Tristan and his fellow knights from Cornwall, along
with approximately thirty other newly knighted warriors
who represented different regions of Britain, trained
under the supervision of the First Knight of Camelot, Sir
Lancelot of the Lake. Every day, the men awoke early,
ate a hearty breakfast, and began a routine of rigorous
training in such weapons as mace, battle axe, crossbow,
and longbow, in addition to Tristan's preference, the
sword. They scaled walls for siege attacks, engaged in
mock battles and jousts, and with Lancelot's
unparalleled horsemanship, developed even more
impressive equestrian skills atop the destriers that King
Marke had gifted them in the knighting ceremony at
Tintagel.

In addition to the new armor and surcoats displaying
their coat of arms, the knights in training now also
enjoyed donning elegant tunics of silk and brocade, with
breeches of velvet and wool for the many occasions at
Camelot where they were expected to be chivalrous and
dashing. As part of their upbringing as squires—where
they'd studied French, Latin, music, and poetry, learning
to dance with courtly grace—the new knights now
reveled in the feasts, balls, and holiday celebrations
which enabled them to display their charm and wit.

Distinguished lords, ladies and visiting royalty frequented Camelot, and the young, brightly attired knights often danced with lovely maidens whose fathers were seeking husbands for their daughters, offering substantial dowries and inheritances.

Along with the intensive warfare training with Sir Lancelot and the royal festivities of King Arthur's court, Tristan, Vaughan, and Connor enjoyed another favorite pastime—falconry.

In the forests of Kennall Vale during their youth, Vaughan had hosted Tristan every summer and had taught him to hunt stag and boar. Under Vaughan's guidance, Tristan had learned to use trained peregrine falcons to bring down ducks and cranes who flew beyond the reach of the bow and arrow. Now, at Camelot, he and Vaughan enjoyed the hunt once again, for the woodlands surrounding the castle were abundant in wild fowl.

Sometimes, they enjoyed gaming with dice, or playing chess with ladies of the court, often listening to troubadours and musicians who sang ballads accompanied by harps and flutes. In King Arthur's royal court, there was always sumptuous food, fine wine, lively music, and beautiful ladies, to the delight of most of his companions. Although his friends reveled in the gaiety, Tristan often preferred to remain seated alone at a table, lost in his chalice of wine, as he was this evening in the glorious palace of Camelot.

Lancelot of the Lake observed Tristan from the perspective of his table across the room. Taking in the somber mood and distant solitude of the renowned Blue Knight of Cornwall, Lancelot wondered why Tristan drove himself harder than anyone on the training field, pushing himself beyond the point of endurance. Despite his enormous strength, Tristan was never satisfied; indeed, it seemed as if he were punishing himself physically for some perceived failure. Sensing in him the same emptiness that plagued his own troubled spirit, Lancelot felt an affinity for the dark, lonely knight who preferred King Arthur's fine *bordeaux* than the company of the beautiful brunette nearby who was trying in vain to attract Tristan's attention.

He, too, suffers a deep wound. Perhaps, like me, he longs for a woman he cannot have, an impossible love that torments his dreams and sickens his soul. We are the same, you and I, Tristan of Cornwall.

Lancelot strode over to Tristan's table and held up his goblet of wine. He raised his eyebrows and asked cheerfully, "Mind if I join you, Tristan?"

Tristan glanced up from his chalice. He quickly stood and pulled up a chair. Bowing his head, he offered it respectfully and replied, "I'd be honored, Sir Lancelot."

With a friendly grin, Lancelot settled down into the proffered chair as Tristan sat back down in his. He took in the knight's dark wavy hair, the stubble on his sullen face, the deep blue eyes glowering at the jubilant dancers, twirling upon the joyous music of the lively fiddles. He leaned forward with a conspiratorial grin, a challenging gleam in his twinkling blue eyes.

"Why is it that all of your companions are enjoying the pleasure of female company this evening, while you remain here alone, drowning yourself in King Arthur's delicious wine?" At this, he raised his chalice, inhaling the bouquet of the exquisite *bordeaux,* savoring the earthy, fruity fragrance. With chivalrous *panache,* he swallowed a mouthful and leaned back comfortably in his chair, crossing an arm behind his head. He grinned at Tristan again, awaiting his response.

"I'm not much for dancing, my lord. I'm too awkward," Tristan replied, pointedly ignoring the pretty brunette who was still trying to catch his eye.

"You are anything but awkward on the training field, Tristan. Quite the opposite. Could it be perhaps that you have a lady waiting for you back home in Cornwall?"

Tristan hesitated a moment before spluttering, "No, it's not that, my lord. I just prefer to keep to myself. That's all."

Lancelot leaned forward intently, his face expectant.

"The men have earned a summer's respite from training. Many are going home to see their families or their sweethearts." He eyed Tristan with interest. "Do you plan to go back to Tintagel?"

****

Tristan stared into his goblet. He considered Sir Lancelot's question. He had no plans to return home. No, he wanted to remain in Camelot and train all the harder. It was why he was here, his whole purpose for living— to atone for his failure. To punish himself for surviving when his family had not. To forge the rage and guilt into his lethal sword. No, he did not want to return to Tintagel for a celebration. He wanted to fight.

He realized with a start that Lancelot was waiting for him to respond. "No, Sir Lancelot. I plan to remain here and train hard all summer long. I have no desire to return to Cornwall."

Tristan took a long pull from his wine. He knew that Vaughan was expecting him to come to Kennall Vale, as he'd done every summer. But he also knew that accepting the invitation would be interpreted as an agreement to the betrothal of Elowenn, for she was expecting him, too. Tristan was damned either way, for a refusal would be seen as a rejection of not only the marriage, but of Vaughan's friendship, which was already strained by Tristan's reluctance to wed his best friend's sister. And he would insult Lord Treave and Lady Melora, who had always treated him like a son. Tristan's stomach clenched in a knot.

Lancelot seemed to read his thoughts. "Tristan, each summer, I travel to northwestern France, to the region called *la Bretagne*. There, I oversee my château—*la Joyeuse Garde*—and the surrounding territories that I own." He edged forward on his chair, his eager face convincing.

"This year, you'll accompany me. I have several loyal knights that I want you to meet. It will it be a tremendous learning opportunity for you to see a new land, and to train with these truly exceptional men." Lancelot took another long pull of wine from his goblet. A boyish grin illuminated his handsome, clean-shaven face.

"We depart the day after tomorrow, from a port on the southern coast of Britain. The sea voyage takes a week to ten days, depending on the winds and tides. We'll return at the autumnal equinox—in time to rejoin the knights for the final year of training here at Camelot."

Tristan gazed incredulously at his mentor. He couldn't believe what he was hearing. He'd be traveling with Lancelot to France? To his personal *château*? To train with extraordinary knights? His heart pounded with adrenaline. He took a large gulp of wine to quench his parched throat.

"For now, enjoy our king's fine wine, and perhaps dance with her," Lancelot chortled, indicating the brunette who was still observing Tristan from the corner of her eye.

Lancelot rose from the table, as did Tristan, bowing his head in deference to the First Knight of Camelot. His mentor finished his wine, slapped Tristan on the shoulder and grinned. "Good night, Tristan. I'll see you in the morning." With a friendly nod, Lancelot left the table and headed towards the exit of the grand ballroom.

Tristan sat back down at his solitary table, shaking his head in disbelief. He took another swallow of wine, envisioning the sea voyage to Bretagne, the chance to visit Lancelot's *château,* and the opportunity to train with exceptional knights.

He would need to tell Vaughan in the morning of his decision not to go to Kennall Vale. He stared into his goblet, wincing at the effects of that rejection. At least now he would have a good reason to decline. Maybe Vaughan would understand. An invitation from Sir Lancelot of the Lake simply couldn't be refused.

But eventually, he'd have to tell Vaughan the truth. That he couldn't marry Elowenn. His heart wrenched with guilt.

Tristan watched Lancelot cross the lively ballroom where the joyous music still filled the air and breathless dancers continued their fervent revelry. His lord's gaze lingered on the beautiful blond queen seated beside their king as he passed the royal table. Lancelot's eyes were filled with longing and regret as he lowered his head to bow before King Arthur and his queen.

As the First Knight of Camelot walked solemnly toward the exit door, Tristan observed Queen Guinevere.

Her eyes followed Sir Lancelot's retreat, the same intense longing on her empty, pearlescent face.

At the door, Lancelot turned for one last glimpse of her before he left. As Tristan saw the passionate, desperate glance that Lancelot and Guinevere shared, the stark reality dawned upon him as if he'd been slapped in the face.

Sir Lancelot of the Lake loves the queen!

Chapter 13

The Village of Sligeach

Maiwenn introduced Issylte to her grandson Branoc
and his wife Dierdre, who lived in the village of Sligeach
on the tidal bay. The couple lived in a wooden house with
a gabled roof in the center of the bustling village, with
Branoc's blacksmith shop attached to the side of their
residence. There, he shod horses, crafted tools and plows
for the local farmers, and made wheels for the wagons
needed in town. He forged hammers, nails, and hardware
for builders to use in construction. He created
arrowheads, daggers, and swords, and because he was
also a skilled armorer, he configured chain mail, metal
plates, helmets and shields for the knights who often
stopped into the port during their various voyages at sea.

A man of average height and stocky build, Branoc
had kind eyes that reflected in his warm smile. He was
dark-haired, with enormous arms and brute strength,
thanks to the heavy hammer, anvil and bellows he used
every day in his forge. His wife Dierdre was in her early
twenties, like her husband, but unlike him, she had red
curly hair, green eyes, and freckles dusted across her
face.

Issylte found Branoc friendly and outgoing, yet his
spouse seemed reserved and scornful. As the months
passed, no matter how many times she and her *Tatie*

stopped into the shop for a friendly hello, nor how many Sunday afternoons they spent sharing the delightful meals in Maiwenn's cottage, Dierdre never seemed to warm up to Issylte at all.

This afternoon, they were all seated together enjoying baked trout from the lake and vegetables from the garden. Branoc was informing his grandmother about the recent increase in activity in his blacksmith shop.

"I've taken on two more journeymen and four new apprentices, *Mamie!* It seems that King Donnchadh is building new lodges at the castle for hundreds of knights. They'll all be needin' armor, and weapons, and of course, their horses will need to be shod. The farmers'll be needin' more plows, and tools, to feed all those hungry soldiers, and I'll be busy craftin' all the locks and doorknobs that they'll be needin' for the new structures. The Goddess be praised, I'll be busy for the next two or three years, at least!"

At the mention of her father, Issylte nearly choked, but with great difficulty, managed to hide her distress. Maiwenn smiled warmly at her grandson.

"That's wonderful news, dear. The Goddess be praised indeed!" Sipping her *tisane,* Maiwenn met Issylte's gaze as if to remind her to keep her composure and remain calm.

Deirdre continued, picking up the thread of conversation.

"There's talk in the village that it's really the Queen who's orderin' the lodges to be built and wantin' all the knights to come live at the castle. They say that Black Knight of hers, the one they call the Morholt, is reinforcin' the castle and buildin' an army. Well, whatever it is that they're doin', we're surely grateful for the extra work, and that's a fact."

Maiwenn stood, clearing the dishes from the table, and said to Issylte, "Églantine, would you please fetch the *tarte aux mirabelles?*" Turning to Branoc, she grinned from ear to ear. "I know it's your favorite, dear. And there's fresh cream to top it off!"

Everyone loved the delicious pie—the perfect ending to the wonderful meal—and, after Branoc and Dierdre had returned home to the village, Issylte was finally able to relax and unburden her troubles to Maiwenn.

"Oh, *Tatie,* when they mentioned my father, I nearly choked. I miss him so much!" She turned her face away to hide her tears as she dried the ceramic plate and stacked it in the cupboard. "I wonder why the queen is building new lodges for so many knights. She must be planning something. What do you think?"

Maiwenn frowned as she washed a cup and handed it to Issylte to dry. "Perhaps they want to reinforce the defense of the castle. It's a show of strength that we have a fine army. The Goddess be praised, Branoc will have lots of new orders and will make a fine profit. When we go into town this week, we'll ask around. See if anyone has heard any more news. But for now, there's no use worrying. Come, let's give these scraps to Florette and the hens."

That Saturday, when they went into town for their weekly excursion, no one in the village had heard any new developments from the castle. So, for the time being, Maiwenn and Issylte continued cultivating herbs, harvesting bark to prepare potions, picking fresh mushrooms and berries, and stocking up for the approaching winter. The fairy witch taught her how to smoke fish and salt meats, how to preserve fruits by making jellies and jams, how to store nuts and grains which they would need when the weather was too cold or the snow too deep for trips to the village.

When winter finally did arrive, they kept the animals in the adjacent stone workshop. The stable door allowed the bottom half to remain closed, preventing Florette and the hens from coming into the cottage, but Maiwenn kept the top half open so that the heat from the fireplace could keep the stable warm.

Branoc visited the cottage every week throughout the winter when the weather was too cold or the snow too deep for Maiwenn and Issylte to venture into town. Arriving on horseback, he brought supplies from the village, often bringing the fresh catch that the local fishermen had been selling, chopping firewood, and bringing feed for the goat and hens.

When Issylte had first come to live at the cottage, Maiwenn told Branoc that Issylte had come from an abusive family and needed shelter. Although he knew that Issylte was not truly his cousin, everyone—including Dierdre—believed that Églantine was a member of the family who had come from *Bretagne* to live with Maiwenn, her sole surviving relative. Maiwenn had explained that she needed Branoc to keep up the pretense for the safety of the young woman she was protecting. He had promised his grandmother that he would.

Two years passed as Issylte developed her powers of healing, learning to wield the herbal essence of the forest under the loving tutelage of her *Tatie*.

During the summer, they harvested fresh herbs, fruits, and vegetables, going frequently to Lough Gill, where Issylte learned to swim. Maiwenn taught her to row the small canoe which she kept near the water's edge so that they could fish toward the center of the lake. They feasted on fresh shellfish, wild berries, mushrooms, and nuts, with an occasional *tarte aux mirabelles*—Issylte's favorite dessert.

During the winter, on clear days, when the sun reflected off the snow and the weather seemed warmer, the two women often ventured into town. They were able to continue harvesting shellfish throughout the colder months, since the estuary and bay did not freeze, thanks to the salt content in the water and the continuous movement of the tides.

Now in her third year of living with Maiwenn, Issylte saw another winter pass, and with the return of spring, the salmon were once again abundant in Lough Gill. With the lake finally thawed after winter's deep freeze, the fairy witch and her *protégée* were once again able to catch and rediscover the pleasure of eating the delicious pink fish, along with the ever-present trout, perch, and pike which they ate year-round.

One Saturday, as they were preparing for their usual weekly excursion into the village for supplies, Maiwenn remarked, "We'll need to purchase some fabric, Églantine., to make you two or three new dresses. The bodices of these are now much too tight."

Maiwenn's large brown eyes twinkled, her cheeks crinkling in a grin. "You, my dear princess, have blossomed into a woman."

Issylte's cheeks heated as she smiled back at the loving, knowing gaze.

In the village, the fabric merchant, knowing how much Issylte loved the color green, showed them a beautiful deep emerald fabric, which Maiwenn purchased with a few jars of salves. Upon their return home, the two women began sewing, and soon finished two simple gowns. Clad in darkest green, so dear to her heart, the forest fairy was once again the Emerald Princess.

As spring gave way to another summer, Issylte often ventured into the forest, collecting herbs, berries, and mushrooms. Sometimes, she would find a garland of lovely wild roses, the *églantines* for which she'd been named, a gift of nature from the *Little Folk* of the Hazelwood Forest.

Today, as she meandered in the woods, she noticed a trail of the pink flowers, beckoning her to follow the stream. *Just like the églantines I followed to find the cottage!*

She sensed the pulse of the forest, the need to heed the call of the woodland creatures. Keeping to the edge of the stream, she soon came to a beautiful waterfall, cascading over a ledge of smooth rocks, the roar of water splashing furiously into a deep pool in the midst of the stream. The forest air was thick and humid, fragrant with the crisp scent of dense oaks and rich, fertile earth. The midsummer sun was beating down through the canopy of leaves onto her scarf-covered head. She'd been walking for hours and sweat trickled down the back of her bare legs. The cool ebullient water was so inviting, Issylte just couldn't resist.

She took off her scarf and unbraided her long hair, shaking it out vigorously in wild, joyous freedom. She disrobed, laying her dress and chemise on a nearby rock. Stepping cautiously into the water, she waded out deeper and slid down into the refreshingly chilly pool.

Every pore in her body shivered in delight, a ripple of pleasure caressing her scorched skin. Diving under the water, she swam from one side of the pool to the other, flipping like the salmon in Lough Gill. She swam over to the waterfall, letting it shower over her body in wicked delight. When she finally emerged from the pool, Issylte shook out her hair and laid down upon a rock, basking in the sun as it warmed her cool skin. When she'd dried off, she got dressed, picked up her basket, and skipped back to the cottage, eager to share her discovered treasure with Maiwenn.

She burst in through the front door, her damp hair cascading down to her waist.

"*Tatie*, I found a *waterfall*! And a pool! Just up ahead in the stream."

She dropped her basket and ran into the kitchen, where Maiwenn was stuffing a chicken with rosemary and garlic to roast over the hearth. Issylte was breathless with excitement.

"I went swimming and diving—the water was cold, but I loved it! I stood under the waterfall, letting it shower all over me. Oh, *Tatie*—it was wonderful." She spun in a circle, a dance of delight. Spotting the vegetables Maiwenn had been peeling, she picked up a carrot and chomped it with relish. "Do you know where it is?"

Maiwenn's laughter rippled like cascading water. "Indeed I do! Pierrick and I used to bring Branoc there when he was a boy. He loved to slide down the rocks and splash into the pool! It's so beautiful there, isn't it now?"

Issylte's heart nearly burst with joy as her *tatie* wrapped loving arms around her, showering her with kisses and giggles. From that day forward, the secret waterfall became her favorite spot to bathe each morning throughout the long, hot, humid summer.

The months passed by, and winter followed autumn. Branoc and Dierdre often visited, bringing supplies, and sometimes staying for dinner. Even though it had been four years since Issylte had come to live with Maiwenn, Dierdre still remained as aloof and suspicious as ever. Indeed, Issylte often sensed the unsettling gaze of Branoc's wife following her every move.

She blushed at the apparent increase in Branoc's attention as well. He gazed at her quite differently from his scornful wife, with an intensity that made her feel self-conscious and uncomfortable. She frequently caught him staring at her breasts, as if he, too had noticed that she was no longer a child. He perked up whenever she spoke or entered the room. His eyes lingered wherever she walked, and Dierdre scowled at the appreciative glances he stole at Issylte when he thought no one was watching. Issylte tried to ignore his obvious infatuation, but Branoc's presence made her palms sweat and her entire body feel jumpy.

****

Maiwenn taught Issylte to harvest white willow bark to make fertility potions, jewelweed leaves for skin ointments, muellin flowers for earaches, and valerian root for sleeping tonics. Each week, they delivered herbal remedies to shopkeepers who sought relief for various ailments, sometimes stopping by the house of a villager too ill to travel into town. In her four years of study at Maiwenn's side, developing her divine power, Issylte had become a gifted *guérisseuse,* a verdant fairy of the Hazelwood Forest.

One morning, while they were at Lough Gill,

preparing to fish, Issylte was near the water's edge, searching for worms to use as bait. Something caught her eye—a reflection on the lake's surface. She knelt on the muddy bank and leaned over to get a closer look.

The air around her suddenly darkened, as if a storm were rapidly approaching. She was woozy and disoriented as she gazed deep into the lake. Her muddy fingers dropped to her sides as the thrum of power surged through her.

A kaleidoscope of images appeared on the dark surface of the lake—indistinct at first, but increasingly clear—until one emerged like a mirror before her. She glimpsed her father, pale and sickly, laid out on his bed in his royal chamber. His eyes were closed, and his body was covered in leeches for bloodletting. Issylte shivered with cold.

Beside the bed stood her stepmother the queen, dressed entirely in black, her head bowed as if in prayer. A tall, wiry man, also dressed entirely in black, stood beside the queen, murmuring what seemed to be an incantation. As Issylte stared at the image, the man in black lifted his gaze, his yellow reptilian eyes meeting her own, as if he could sense that she was watching. A biting cold rippled through her, freezing her in his baleful, powerful stare. The icy sensation of tingling and numbness crept up her hand—the same as her stepmother's frigid touch—draining her strength and freezing her in place. Issylte was shivering, shaking, trembling—when, from afar, she became aware of Maiwenn's distant voice, calling her name.

"Églantine, Églantine, come back to me… Come back to me!"

Tatie was tapping her cheek, shaking her shoulders

gently.

Slowly, her senses returned. She inhaled the fresh tang of the lake, the fecund richness of the black earth beneath her knees. The warm sun caressed her frosty cheeks, Maiwenn's presence a comfort at her side. Issylte threw her arms around her *Tatie,* shaking with cold and fear. Her mouth was dry, her hands like ice. She swam in the depths of Maiwenn's worried eyes.

"*Tatie*, I had a vision. I saw my father, lying in bed, covered in leeches. My stepmother was at his side, and a man dressed in a black robe was standing beside her. He was frightening, *Tatie!*" Issylte rocked back and forth on her knees, shuddering. Maiwenn rubbed her back soothingly. "He had eyes like a serpent. Evil, yellow slits. He stared right at me, *Tatie,* as if he could see me watching!" Issylte shivered with dread. "I had the same sensation of numbness and tingling, creeping up my arm. Just like when my stepmother touched my fingers. Like when I held the little girl's hand. The one who had eaten the wolfsbane." Issylte grasped Maiwenn's arms. "He stared right at me, as if he knew I could see what was happening. As if he could sense me watching. And the tingling and numbness—the poison of wolfsbane. What does it mean? I think my father is in danger, *Tatie!* What can I do?"

Maiwenn wrapped her arms around Issylte, pulling her close. "I don't know, sweetheart. But when we go into town this weekend, we'll see if there's any news from the castle. Maybe we can discover who this man in black is." She fixed her eyes on Issylte, her voice serious and earnest. "But we have discovered a new facet of your power, Églantine. Your gift of the *sight* is not just through physical touch, but also through water. The second of the three sacred elements of the Goddess." She kissed Issylte's cheek, a twinkle in her eye. "Your divine gift is powerful indeed."

Maiwenn rose to her feet and brushed off her frock. "Come, let's go back to the cottage. We'll have a *tisane* and try to relax. You've had quite a shock. We'll fish another time."

Issylte nodded and rinsed her muddy hands in the lake water, drying them on a cloth from the basket, which she fetched to carry home.

Back in the haven of her cozy cottage, Maiwenn settled Issylte into the well-worn chair before the hearth and prepared the *tisane*. As they sat together before the fire, sipping chamomile tea, she gazed at the blond head she loved so fiercely, envisioning the evil black wizard with yellow, reptilian eyes who now threatened her sweet Églantine. Whoever he was, the fairy witch of the Hazelwood Forest vowed to do everything in her power to protect and defend her beloved Emerald Princess.

Chapter 14

The Queen's Royal Advisor

Morag stood beneath her mauve velvet draperies, staring out the window of her royal chambers at the lush green grass, the distant dense forest, the morning sun peeking through the scattered clouds across the summer sky.

She missed the Morholt. He'd been gone for three years now, amassing his powerful army. Building an unstoppable fleet of *drakaar* warships. Transforming Dubh Linn into a formidable Viking stronghold. Launching lucrative slave expeditions to batter and weaken King Marke of Cornwall. Preparing for the invasion which would bring her the Cornish crown.

She touched the amethysts at the base of her throat. Imagined his full lips and skilled tongue ravishing her neck. Her breasts. Her entire body. A deep ache throbbed in her loins.

As tantalizing thoughts of the Morholt washed over her, Lord Liam rode the dappled gray mare out onto the courtyard greens. Morag scoffed, jolted out of her sensual reverie.

She eyed the Master of Horse, her lip raised disdainfully. In the four years since Issylte's death, King Donnchadh's only interest was that damned horse. He cared for nothing else. He refused to leave his bedroom, neglected his royal duties, and rejected nearly all visitors. As if the palfrey alone kept his daughter alive in his withered, empty heart. Morag stormed away in disgust. A trail of simpering servants followed her to the throne room to await her invited guest.

The disgruntled queen took her seat upon the gilded throne, tufted in rich deep green velvet, flanked by royal banners displaying the great white hawk of Castle Connaught. Six royal guards in finest livery stood attentively at her sides, their swords gleaming in the sunlight which shone from the massive ogival windows behind her along the eastern wall. When the herald's trumpet announced his arrival, Morag straightened her regal spine, smoothed the voluminous folds of her sapphire gown, and assessed the appearance of the expected visitor who waited at the entrance door.

He was as tall as the Morholt, and though he lacked the massive warrior bulk of her beloved Black Knight, his shoulders were broad and his step nimble as he entered the room and knelt before her. A luxurious mane of thick black hair covered his bowed head, his elegant hands revealing long, slender fingers that exuded skill and strength. At her command, he rose to his feet, rippling the room with an aura of power. His lean, narrow face was balanced by an aquiline nose and full lips, filled with promise. Morag inhaled sharply at the sight of his startling eyes, golden and glowing like a luminous dragon of legend. A wicked thrill shivered deliciously up her spine.

"Lord Voldurk. I welcome you to Castle Connaught." She lifted her chin to expose her swanlike neck, straightening her back so the velvet gathered bodice of her sapphire gown could fully accentuate her feminine curves.

"I am at your service, Your Majesty." Golden eyes gleamed in the gilded light.

"I am told that you are an Archdruid who studied with Lord Merlin, the Royal Advisor to King Arthur Pendragon."

"Yes, my queen. In *Bretagne*, in northwestern France. Deep in the enchanted Forest of Brocéliande."

Morag dazzled him with the brilliance of her most regal smile. "You have the reputation of being a great healer. A wizard of tremendous power." She glanced up at him from lowered lashes, raising her eyes seductively. "I am in need of a Royal Advisor to treat my husband, King Donnchadh, whose health has declined dramatically since the death of his daughter four years ago. The king is withdrawn, melancholy, unresponsive. I need a medical advisor to undertake his care, to expel the evil humors which plague and sicken him." She smoothed the soft velvet folds of her deep blue gown, then gazed at the darkly handsome wizard with golden, mesmerizing eyes. "Lord Voldurk, I should like to offer you that position. What say you?"

The wizard's white teeth sparkled against his bronzed skin. "I am deeply honored, Your Majesty. I gratefully accept the position as Royal Advisor to the Queen."

Morag grinned with wicked glee. "Excellent. You shall have your own chambers, my lord. Anything you need is at your disposal. Herbs, elixirs, ointments. Potions, *poisons*." As her eyes locked with his, Morag saw the glow of comprehension gleam in his serpentine eyes.

"Thank you, my queen. You are most generous." He

bowed majestically, his black robes rustling upon the polished, wooden floor.

Morag motioned for two servants to approach. "These attendants will usher you to your quarters. They will see to your needs, help you to settle in and make yourself comfortable. Inform them of any request. I shall send for you in an hour. You'll accompany me to my husband's royal chambers. There, I shall introduce you to the king, and you will have the opportunity to examine him and advise me of your plan of treatment. You are dismissed, Lord Voldurk." She nodded to the servants, who led the dark wizard from the throne room. Ripples of power shimmered in the air.

Morag shivered with delight. Perhaps she had found an enchanting bedwarmer until the Morholt returned. A golden dragon to breathe fire into her icy veins. A wizard whose magic touch would fill her hollow ache.

And enable her to wear the sole crown of Ireland.

Chapter 15

Deirdre

Maiwenn promised Issylte they would inquire in the village of any recent news of the castle after the disturbing vision of her father covered with leeches, the ominous man in black, and the wicked queen standing beside the bed-ridden king. The yellow eyes of a snake haunted Issylte's dreams as much as the chilling numbness of her stepmother's icy hands. She was desperate to hear news of her father as they headed into town.

They chatted with several merchants as they bartered for provisions. They heard rumors that the king had been quite ill since his daughter's death. That the worried queen had sent for a powerful healer, who had administered potent remedies and numerous bloodlettings, all to no avail. Some even said—although never too loudly, for one dared not speak against the queen—that the healer, Lord Voldurk, was more of a dark wizard than a physician and was likely the queen's lover as well as her spiritual advisor.

As they entered the blacksmith shop, Issylte noticed that Branoc was occupied, showing a new plow to a farmer, but that Deirdre was greeting customers from behind the counter. Maiwenn kissed her grandson's wife on each cheek in greeting—*la bise* of her native

Bretagne.

"Good morning, Dee! How are you today, dear?" Maiwenn said cheerfully.

"I'm fine, thank you, *Mamie*. Branoc's busy at the moment, but he'll be over shortly to say hello. We've had quite a few customers this morning, and with the warmer weather, lots of new orders, especially for weapons and armor. It seems like every week, there's dozens of knights comin' in, needin' their horses shod, or some chain mail for their squires, or a fancy shield. Branoc is even takin' on an engraver, to do the gold and silver inlays on the shields for the wealthier knights. Business is good, and we are indeed grateful. At least we'll be able to pay the new taxes that the queen is imposin'. Most folks are havin' a real hard time of it, I hear."

Branoc, wiping his hands on his apron, came over to greet Maiwenn and Issylte, kissing them both on each cheek with a friendly grin. "It's good to see you, Mamie and Églantine! I'm sorry I don't have much time for a visit now, but I'll come by the cottage soon and have a look at your fence. I noticed there's a section that's rusted and will need replacin'."

When another customer needed his attention, Branoc excused himself, kissed the two women once again, and returned to work. Maiwenn and Issylte kissed Deirdre goodbye, promising to stop in again next Saturday, and left the blacksmith shop to return home to their stone cottage in the woods.

That evening, Issylte was in the kitchen preparing a mushroom omelette with fresh spinach for their supper, when she saw Maiwenn quietly and surreptitiously leave the cottage. Intrigued, Issylte glanced out the front window to see her *tatie* speaking urgently with four small men. Taking in their dark, weathered skin, their *otherworldly* faces, the homespun clothing in the dark green and brown colors of the forest, Issylte realized that these were the *Little Folk,* who had left the trail of *églantines* to help her find the way to Maiwenn's cottage.

The woodland creatures were listening intently, nodding in comprehension, as if Maiwenn were conveying a message of utmost importance. They quickly disappeared, and Issylte watched as Maiwenn brushed off her apron and straightened her dress, as if to regain her composure before entering the cottage.

Issylte rushed back to the kitchen to resume chopping the mushrooms. After Maiwenn had come in, closed and latched the front door, Issylte asked, "Where did you go, *Tatie*?"

Seeming flustered and ill at ease, the old woman responded, a bit too quickly. "Ah, one of the villagers needed a remedy for a stomach ailment. I gave him some ginger and fennel, so all should be fine in a day or two."

As they enjoyed the delicious *omelette*, Issylte wondered why her *tatie* was lying. The only plausible reason why Maiwenn had not disclosed the truth was that the message to the woodland creatures must have been about Issylte. But why would her *tatie* keep something from her? A tight fist clenched her heavy heart.

The weeks passed, and summer returned. Issylte spent the days exploring the Hazelwood Forest, collecting *mirabelle* plums, fresh strawberries, plants, and herbs. She often helped Maiwenn hang herbs to dry from the ceiling of their workshop, using mortar and pestle to grind and prepare the tinctures and elixirs they brought to the village. Sometimes, Issylte would find a little basket with a garland of *églantines*—the lovely pink roses called "sweetbriar" here in Ireland—and some of the *groseilles,* or red currants, that Maiwenn especially loved.

One morning, while Issylte was out gathering fruit and herbs in the forest, Maiwenn heard the pounding hooves of horses approaching the front entrance of the cottage. She opened the door, delightfully surprised to see Branoc and Deirdre dismounting, bringing tools for her garden. She kissed them both in greeting and exclaimed, "Bran! Dee! What a pleasant surprise! I wasn't expecting you today. Come in, both of you! Welcome!"

The two visitors entered the cozy cottage. Maiwenn closed the door after them and said to her grandson, "What brings you here today, dear?"

Branoc glanced around the kitchen as he laid the basket on the shelf. "I've brought these tools for your garden, *Mamie*. And I've come to see about that rusted section of your fence. I can craft the chain links in my shop and replace it easy enough. Shouldn't take me but a week or two." As Deirdre sat down at the little table, he asked, "Where is Églantine?"

Maiwenn dried her hands on her apron. "She's out gathering some berries and herbs, as she does most mornings. She'll be back in an hour or two. Won't you stay for dinner? Églantine and I went to the lake yesterday, and we've plenty of trout. If she brings back some of the sweet plums, I can even make a *tarte aux mirabelles* for dessert! How does that sound?"

Branoc grinned. "Sounds perfect, Mamie!" Kissing Deirdre's cheek, he suggested, "Why don't you two have a *tisane,* and I'll go check out the fence?"

After Branoc had left, Maiwenn could sense that

something was troubling Deirdre, but knew enough to wait patiently until her grandson's wife could muster the courage to find her words. Finally, the younger woman, seeming a bit embarrassed, asked Maiwenn, "*Mamie*, do you have any herbs that could help me to conceive a babe? Each month, my courses come, and it just breaks my heart. We've been tryin' for so long... Can you give me anything that might help?"

Patting Deirdre's hand in a gesture of comfort, Maiwenn replied, "I do indeed, Dee. I have just the herbal remedy for that." She went to her cupboard and took out some white willow bark, yarrow, and wild raspberry leaves. She measured each herb, placed the mixture in a small pouch and handed it to Deirdre. "Add a teaspoon of this into a cup and pour boiling water over it to make a *tisane*. Let it steep for three or four minutes, strain out the leaves and drink the tea each morning and night. It's helped a few women in the village, so I hope it will help you as well."

Deirdre was exuberant, nearly jumping from her chair with joy as she accepted the precious pouch and kissed Maiwenn's cheek. "Oh, *Mamie!* Thank you so much! It means the world to me. I want a baby so much, it's just killin' me, you know. Thank you, *Mamie*. Truly."

Heading to the door, Dierdre turned and said, "I'll go say hello to Florette and the hens and see how Bran's doin' with the fence. Then I'll come back in and help you peel the vegetables for dinner. Thank you again, dear *Mamie!*"

Maiwenn busied herself in the kitchen, assembling the pots and utensils she would need to prepare a lovely meal for her unexpected guests. Églantine should be home soon and, hopefully, she'd have some *mirabelles* with her. Otherwise, there were still plenty of wild strawberries that would be delicious with some fresh cream.

As Maiwenn prepared the herbed trout and fresh vegetables, Deirdre wandered into the back yard where the animals were enclosed within the metal fence. The hens were picking at the pile of vegetable scraps, searching for the grubs they loved so much, and Florette was grazing in the grass. Deirdre stroked the goat's soft white fur, searching for Branoc.

She saw the rusted area of the fence that he wanted to replace for *Mamie* and his tools on the ground, but he was nowhere to be found. Wondering where he'd wandered off to, Deirdre let herself out through the door of the gate, closing it behind her so the animals would not stray, and ventured into the forest to find her husband.

Following the stream, she walked for a few minutes until she heard splashing and what sounded like a woman's voice humming. Perplexed at the singing and the rushing of water, Deirdre scanned the forest and noticed Branoc up ahead, in the strangest position. He was crouched behind a cluster of trees, as if he were hiding from view. He was staring intently at something in front of him, just beyond the trees. *He's hunting. He must have spotted a hare, or maybe even a stag!* Yet, as she observed more closely, she realized that he had no bow and arrow, nor did he have a dagger. Still, he had the look of a predator on his face, and Deirdre was determined to discover what held her husband's rapt attention.

Taking a few steps to her left, Deirdre saw how the

stream near the cottage flowed into a large pool just up ahead from where she stood. A splendid waterfall cascaded down over a high wall of smooth rocks into a deep, natural basin. As she watched in disbelief, she saw a totally nude Églantine bathing in the pool, rinsing soap from her hair as she stood beneath the waterfall.

Deirdre had never seen Églantine's hair, for it had always been pinned up and covered by a scarf. But now, as she stood with her mouth agape, Deirdre saw the pale blond tresses which fell to Églantine's curved hips. Mesmerized, Deirdre stared in horror as the blond woman turned, revealing full, round breasts and hips, a small, delicate waist, and a tuft of blond hair between her long legs.

Numb with shock, Deirdre returned her gaze to her husband and was mortified to see that he had the front of his breeches open, his erect manhood in his hand, pleasuring himself while he stared at Églantine! As she watched in horror, Branoc convulsed with pleasure, his sacred seed spewing forth in an arc which puddled in a pool of waste on the forest floor.

I want him to spill his seed in me, not waste it on her! Here I am trying to conceive a child, and he throws it away! He can't bed her, so he does this instead. By the Goddess, I hate her! Why did she have to come into our lives?

Trembling, shaking, sickened with jealousy, Deirdre backed slowly away in silence, not wanting her husband to see that she had witnessed his lust, his longing, his sexual act for another woman. She felt betrayed, as if he had committed adultery. She hated Églantine for enticing him, for seducing him. Dierdre had seen the way her husband's eyes followed Églantine everywhere, how his gaze lingered on her breasts, how he watched her hips sway as she walked. *She has bewitched him. I hate her!*

Deirdre staggered into the cottage, and *Mamie* rushed to her side, helping her into a chair at the little table. *Mamie* pulled up a chair, taking Dierdre's trembling hands into her own. "Dee! What happened, dear? You're so pale. You've had a terrible shock. What is it, dear?"

Horrified, ashamed and humiliated, Deirdre recovered enough to reply. "I feel quite ill, *Mamie*. I'm afraid we can't stay for dinner. I want to go home. I feel sick to my stomach. I'm sorry, *Mamie*." Tears welled up in her eyes, and it was all she could do to hold them back until she got home, where she would allow herself to weep until her eyes were dry.

Branoc strolled in a few minutes later, aglow with pleasure, a contented smile plastered upon his traitorous face. He saw Dierdre and his face dropped. He glanced at his grandmother, as if sensing the tension in the air. At the obvious distress on his wife's face, he rushed to her side and dropped to his knee. "What is it, Dee? What's wrong?"

He tried to comfort her by touching her cheek. Deirdre thought of what he had just done with that filthy hand, and she recoiled from his touch. She replied coldly, "I feel quite ill. I want to go home. I told *Mamie* we can't stay for dinner. Please, Bran, let's go home. I feel sick to my stomach."

She couldn't hide her pallor, her obvious distress. She couldn't breathe. And her legs were shaking uncontrollably.

Branoc replied, his voice filled with concern, "Of course, Dee. I'll go see to the horses and be right back.

I'll just be a few moments." He gathered his tools and saddled the horses. Returning, he said sadly to his grandmother, "I'm sorry, Mamie. We'll see you Saturday when you come into town. Give our regards to Églantine."

At the mention of her name, Dierdre once again envisioned the nude body in the pool, her husband's lust, the opened breeches, and the wasted seed that could perhaps have given her the child she so desperately wanted. Overcome with jealous rage, she rushed outside and heaved the contents of her stomach onto the ground, just as her husband had heaved his precious seed in the forest.

They rode in silence back to the village, the image of Églantine's voluptuous body taunting Deirdre as her jealous mind kept chanting, *I hate her! I hate her! I hate her!*

The summer evolved, and her husband stopped touching her altogether. He blamed fatigue or the increased workload in the shop. Still, he found plenty of reasons to visit the cottage frequently, bringing a new plow he had fashioned to till *Mamie's* garden, repairing the thatch on her roof, or replacing yet another section of the fence.

And, as the Hazelwood Forest bloomed, verdant and fertile, Deirdre's heart withered, as barren and empty as her womb.

Chapter 16

A Tale of Two Knights

The new knights at Camelot were returning home to their respective families for the summer reprieve. The more experienced Knights of the Round Table were remaining to oversee the training and continued chivalrous education of the pages and squires who would stay at the castle for the summer. Vaughan was among the many who were loading up their horses for the journey home.

As Tristan sauntered over to bid his friend farewell, he swallowed a lump of tremendous regret that this would be the first summer since he had come to live with his uncle at Tintagel that he would not be accompanying Vaughan to Kennall Vale.

"All set?" Tristan handed Vaughan one of the bags that the squire had placed beside the horse, to be loaded with the rest. With an apologetic smile, Tristan said gently, "Give my best to your parents and Elowenn. I'll miss hunting with you this summer. Shoot a stag for me, huh?"

Vaughan accepted the bag and strapped it onto his horse's back. He said stiffly, "Sure thing, Tristan. Enjoy your trip to Bretagne. *Bon voyage.*" With a nod to Connor, who was already astride his horse, Vaughan mounted his own. As Tristan waved farewell to see them off, his brother at arms reined his horse, exited the castle grounds, and rode across the stone bridge into the dense forest beyond.

He watched Vaughan retreat into the woods surrounding Camelot, flooded with grief and guilt. By declining the invitation to Kennall Vale, he had not only lost his best friend, but had been replaced as such by Connor. Pain sliced like a knife.

Lancelot joined him as they watched the knights file across the bridge to gallop off into the forest, his quiet presence supportive.

When the last of the knights had disappeared into the woods, the First Knight of Camelot turned to Tristan. "Our horses are ready. We'll ride to the coast and board the ship to *Bretagne*. A dozen of my best knights—they travel with me every year—will accompany us and stay at the *château* for the summer. Come, let's bid farewell to Arthur and take our leave." Clasping Tristan on the shoulder, Lancelot led the way back into the castle.

They road south to the eastern coast of Britain, where Lancelot and his knights arranged lodging for the horses in the local stables, to be groomed and cared for until their return in mid-September. The vessel for the voyage to *Bretagne* was a square sailed round ship with a crew of twenty, who had stored the supplies they would need below deck in the cargo hold. As they sailed away across the Narrow Sea towards the coast of France, the knights settled into their berths to rest awhile after the long journey from Camelot.

There was a galley kitchen where meals were served, and cots and benches where the crew slept, but most of the ten-day voyage was spent on the main deck, observing the wind whipping the enormous sail of their ship, the white capped waves rolling and breaking onto their craft, the sea gulls squawking and flying overhead amidst the clouds.

This morning, the sun shone bright and clear, the briny tang of the ocean sprayed by the waves crashing against the hull. Tristan was leaning over the taffrail on deck, gazing out over the vast expanse of ocean, lost in thought, when Lancelot joined him.

The First Knight gazed at the ripples in the sea. "I was raised in Bretagne," he said pensively, "in the sacred forest of *Brocéliande*—the heart of the mystical land of druids, fairies, and magic." Lancelot grinned as Tristan raised his eyebrows, his curiosity piqued.

"The woman who raised me, whom I call *mère,* or mother, is the fairy Viviane—once the beloved pupil of the wizard Merlin." Tristan listened aptly, honored to hear the mysterious tale of Lancelot of the Lake.

"Merlin was so enamored of my beautiful mother that he shared all his magical knowledge with her. He taught her all sorts of spells and enchantments. He even created for her a gleaming castle—*le Château de Comper*—in the midst of the sacred forest of Brocéliande."

Lancelot tossed his brown hair back from his face with a boyish grin. "*Comper—kemper,* in my native Breton language—means "confluence." And my mother's splendid castle, where I was raised, lies at the junction of four sparkling lakes in the very heart of the sacred forest. Indeed, that's why she is called the Lady of the Lake, and I am *Lancelot du Lac.*"

He glanced again at Tristan and shot him a promising grin. "I'll bring you to her *château* this summer. Its pure white stone is so brilliant, it is said to be a castle made of crystal."

One of the members of the crew came up, offering Lancelot and Tristan a chalice of wine, which they gladly accepted. Tristan drank deeply from his, savoring the dry, fruity blend of the same fine French *bordeaux* that King Arthur served in Camelot, granting Lancelot the time he needed to continue his tale.

"As I grew older," the First Knight continued, after a hearty gulp, "my mother wanted me to be trained as a knight. She brought me to the realm of the Elves—the fiercest warriors in the Celtic kingdoms. On one of the seven islands where they reside, she founded Avalon, a renowned center for healing, where she and eight other priestesses now devote themselves to the practice of natural medicine and the worship of the Goddess."

They each drank more wine, gazing across the Narrow Sea which would lead them south to *Bretagne*. Although he was filled with questions, Tristan listened patiently, knowing more was yet to come. The ship's steward returned and filled their goblets of wine. Lancelot nodded his thanks as he picked up the thread of his tale.

"The Avalonian Elves—the warriors who trained me—are exceptional with the bow and arrow, but unparalleled with the sword. Descended from the gods and endowed with magic, they live throughout the islands of an archipelago off the coast of *Bretagne*. The realm of Avalon." He took a long pull of wine. Tristan was enthralled.

"Their master blacksmith Gofannon was the Avalonian Elf who, along with his son Ronan, forged the sword Excalibur for King Arthur. And it was my mother, Viviane, who had Arthur's sword forged in *dragonfire*, by the blacksmith of the gods himself, on the mystical island of Avalon." Tristan stared at the rhythmic waves, entranced in Lancelot's past.

"When the sword was completed, my mother sent for Merlin to bring Arthur to Avalon. She vowed that the king would never be wounded in battle, nor lose a drop of blood, so long as he wore the sacred scabbard she'd had crafted, and that his sword Excalibur would never fail him." Lancelot's cerulean eyes gleamed in the sunlight, as brilliant a blue as the Celtic Sea flowing beneath their ship.

"But before my mother gave him the sword and scabbard, she made Arthur swear that he would grant her one request." Lancelot grinned at Tristan. "Of course he consented." He drank again from his chalice, as did Tristan, the two men gazing at the expanse of ocean from the deck of their ship.

"Her request was that Arthur would accept an unknown soldier—"the White Knight"—to his Round Table. The king promised to accept the knight, but only if he proved himself worthy by accomplishing a nearly impossible quest. To free Arthur's illegitimate son, held captive by a brutal Saxon king, in the castle called *La Douleureuse Garde*—the Sorrowful Keep."

Lancelot paused for a moment to take another long pull from his goblet. "The White Knight would have to siege the castle, kill the Saxon king, and banish the evil enchantment cast upon the dwelling. To free the imprisoned boy and return him safely to his father in Camelot."

Tristan took another gulp of wine. He grinned at Lancelot, nodding in comprehension. "And you, Sir Lancelot, were the mysterious White Knight."

Lancelot slapped Tristan on the shoulder and boomed with laughter. "Bravo, Tristan! Yes, I was in fact the White Knight of Avalon. And, as a reward for the safe deliverance of his son, King Arthur appointed me First Knight of Camelot and gave me the infamous *Douleureuse Garde*—the enormous castle and surrounding territories of the Saxon king I had killed."

His boyish grin stretched from ear to ear. "I have since renamed it *la Joyeuse Garde*—the Joyous Keep. It's now my personal residence, dedicated to what we French call," he said, raising his goblet to toast Tristan, "*la joie de vivre.*"

Tristan clinked his chalice against Lancelot's. "Here, here. I'll drink to that!"

Their goblets were refilled, and as the wine flowed freely, so did the words between the two knights, weaving together the strong bonds of friendship with the fabric of their tales. Lancelot, having completed the story of his past, now turned to Tristan, and inquired with his intense blue eyes. "And what of you, Sir Tristan? What darkness lurks within and prevents you from seeking the company of beautiful women and the very *joie de vivre* that we toast right now?"

Tristan huffed, turning to face the choppy sea. He'd never released all the guilt and anguish that tormented him, not even to Vaughan, who knew only that Tristan's family had been slaughtered in a brutal Viking raid. Tristan had always chosen to immerse himself in relentless training, becoming a hardened warrior as he hardened his grieving heart.

Yet, Tristan sensed in Lancelot the same emptiness that hollowed his own soul and felt the need for the first time to unburden his grief.

Taking a large gulp of wine to muster his courage, Tristan began. "My mother Blanchefleur—the sister of my uncle Marke—was beautiful, with soft, silky hair and a gentle, soothing voice. I remember finding comfort in her loving arms and courage in her proud eyes. I loved her so very much," Tristan choked, swallowing down his pain with another gulp of wine.

"My father was King Rivalen of Lyonesse. He fell in love with my mother when he visited her brother, my uncle Marke, in Cornwall. They were married in Tintagel and settled in Lyonesse, the islands off the southern tip of England, where my sister Talwyn and I were born. All of us lived in the castle *le Château d' Or*, amidst the villages, farmlands, and fishing ports along the craggy coast."

They sipped their wine, the ship sailing across the Narrow Sea seemingly transporting the two knights into the past. "I was a squire at my father's castle, training under the supervision of a knight named Sir Goron. One day, when I was eight years old, returning from the hunt, my lord and his fellow knights stopped suddenly at the edge of the forest and dismounted, forcing me to do the same. Sir Goron restrained me, his hand clamped over my mouth, while Sir Konan, another knight, prevented me from running to the castle, which was under attack."

Tristan's body shook with anger and guilt, his stomach clenched in a knot. "I stood there, powerless, protected by the knights who were defending me—the heir to the throne of Lyonesse—and watched helplessly as the Vikings tore through the village like a herd of animals. They set fire to the thatched roofs with their torches. They slaughtered the people trying to defend their homes. And they took the young, strong men and pretty women as slaves, dragging them off screaming to their ships."

Tristan groaned, his body shuddering. "The castle had been breached. Two Vikings dragged my father in chains and forced him to kneel before a fucking giant of a Viking. The bloody bastard made a great spectacle of beheading my father right there, at the entrance to his magnificent castle." Tristan sobbed, shaking his head as if he could dispel the agony. "I watched him raise his fucking sword high above his head. He dropped it down like an axe and sliced off my father's head."

Tristan choked, spewing out the hatred which sickened him. "I was physically restrained from helping Talwyn, my ten-year-old sister. They dragged her behind a section of the stone wall. They took turns." Tristan gulped big breaths of air as he struggled to breathe. "I still hear her blood curdling screams. Even now."

Lancelot placed his hand quietly upon Tristan's back.

"Two other Vikings held my mother, the beautiful queen of Lyonesse, as she struggled, trying desperately to save Talwyn. She was kicking, shrieking, and biting so much that the bastard who had just killed my father turned around and impaled her with the same goddamned bloody sword." Tristan bent against the rail of the ship, struggling to catch his breath.

"They dragged Talwyn—my beautiful sister Talwyn—from behind the wall. She was beaten, bloody. Mutilated." He gasped for air. "They slit her throat. They threw her on top of our mother's lifeless body, right beside my father's corpse." Tristan leaned over the taffrail and heaved the anguish from his stomach.

When he finished retching, he wiped his mouth with

his sleeve and spat on the deck of the ship. "And me? Did I fight to defend them? Did I die with them? Hell, no—I survived! I was too weak to save them. And here I am now. *Alive*. By the Goddess, I should have died that day, too!" Tristan leaned against the taffrail and buried his face into his bent arms.

Lancelot placed his hand on Tristan's back. "You couldn't have saved them, Tristan. There is nothing you could have done, nothing which would have altered the outcome. Your death would have been both tragic—and futile." Lancelot paused for a moment, as if to let his words reach Tristan's ears.

"Although you punish yourself for what you perceive as a failure, I ask you to consider this instead. Perhaps the Goddess herself chose to save you... for a fate which has yet to be revealed."

Tristan raised his anguished face and gazed into the eyes of this knight whom he respected and served in a sacred oath of fealty. Lancelot's wise eyes bore into his very core.

"You are destined to rule, Tristan. I will impart to you the very skills I acquired from the Avalonian Elves. I will forge you into the lethal weapon you must become as you inherit the throne of Cornwall. And restore your father's kingdom of Lyonesse."

Tristan was infused with strength at the intensity of Lancelot's gaze and the conviction of his words. The White Knight of Avalon locked eyes with the Blue Knight of Cornwall.

"You were powerless before—yes. You were a child, Tristan. A mere boy." He placed both hands on Tristan's shoulders as if to impart the weight of his words. "Rather than despair at the impotence of youth, embrace your fate and empower your sword. Become the king you were destined to be."

Tristan raised his head as their round ship sailed across the Narrow Sea towards the distant land of *Bretagne*. He raised his goblet of wine and the two knights toasted the future, the friendship, and the fate which entwined them both.

During the remainder of the ten-day sea voyage, Tristan and Lancelot sometimes fished, played chess, or diced with the other knights on board the ship. Yet, each day, they continued weaving together the ties of friendship that had begun to bind them.

The first time they had shared tales, it had been Lancelot who told of the past, and now, it was Tristan who revealed the present as the two men sipped ale and leaned on the taffrail over the Celtic Sea.

"After the attack on *Château d' Or* and the slaughter of my family," Tristan began, "my uncle Marke had me brought to Tintagel so I could continue my training as a squire under his master-at-arms, Lord Gorvenal. It was there that I met Vaughn, a fellow squire a couple years older than me. An expert with the bow and arrow. He'd spent every summer throughout his childhood hunting in the forests of Kennall Vale. In the east of Cornwall, with his father, Lord Treave." Tristan glanced at Lancelot, took a gulp of his brew, and continued.

"At Tintagel, we squires had mock battles, siege attacks and even jousts. We trained hard, and I fueled the rage burning inside me into my sword. I'd picture that Viking bastard who killed my parents, and my hatred drove me to become strong as an ox. I loved the thrill of competition—it helped me keep the guilt at bay."

A pod of dolphins swam by the ship. Tristan smiled

wistfully, watching them arc playfully into the waves. He smiled at Lancelot and took a long pull of his ale. "Vaughan invited me to go hunting stag with him to Kennall Vale the summer I was thirteen. His parents, Lord Treave and Lady Melora, approved of our friendship. Over the years, as I spent each summer at their estate, they became like second parents to me." He took another sip of ale, glanced at Lancelot, returning his gaze to the endless sea.

"Vaughan was with me when I brought down my first stag that summer. He taught me to use falcons so we could hunt geese and ducks. We trained as squires together, spent our summers hunting together, and I am a skilled archer today because of him."

Lancelot nodded, took a draught from his goblet, and wiped his mouth on his sleeve. "Why didn't you go along with him this summer? What made you decide to stay at Camelot?"

A corner of Tristan's mouth curved upward. "Vaughan has a younger sister, Elowenn. She took a fancy to me a few summers ago. I kissed her a couple of times. She's pretty, but when I kissed her…it was just *wrong*." Tristan leaned away from the taffrail, stretching his broad back and shoulders.

"Elowenn is quiet and timid—it's hard to have any kind of a conversation with her. I know her parents are hoping I'll ask for her hand, because it would elevate her whole family to royal status if she became my wife…the future queen of Cornwall."

Tristan leaned forward, positioning his elbows against the taffrail. "But, it's more complicated than just my personal preference." He took another long pull of ale, watching the stern of their ship plow forth across the

Narrow Sea. "As the heir to the kingdom of Cornwall, I know my uncle expects me to marry a princess. Not the daughter of a lesser lord." Tristan stared off at the horizon.

"I knew that if I accepted the invitation to Kennall Vale this summer, it would be as if I were agreeing to the betrothal. Yet, by declining their hospitality, I have affronted Lord Treave, offended Elowenn, insulted Vaughan, and lost the friend whom I loved like a brother."

Taking another gulp of ale, Tristan turned to Lancelot and searched his knowing eyes. "I don't know if she even exists, Lancelot, but I want a woman who makes me feel *alive*! I want her kisses to arouse my passion, her heart to sing to mine. I want a muse to inspire my song, a lady to whom I would pledge my sword—and my life." Tristan shook his head and sighed. "Is such a love even possible?"

The First Knight of Camelot responded with a sad smile. "It is indeed possible, Tristan." Lancelot turned his pensive gaze to the vast expanse of sea. "In French, we call such a love *l'amour fou*—a passion so intense… it can drive you mad."

Lancelot glanced back at Tristan, a forlorn smile reaching his intense blue eyes. "When you find such a woman, Tristan, the love she gives you fills every empty hollow in your soul. She completes you; she invigorates you; she thrills you. And, when you consummate such a love, the exquisite blend of the spiritual and physical realm will satisfy you more than the finest wine or the greatest victory in battle. The love she gives you with her body will transport you to the stars, and you will never experience a greater joy."

And, though he smiled, Tristan saw that the First Knight emanated loneliness, suffering, and sorrow. As Lancelot returned his gaze across the faraway sea, Tristan knew that the White Knight of Avalon longed for the beautiful blond queen of Camelot.

Chapter 17

The Master of Horse

Dierdre had been drinking the herbal tea that Maiwenn had given her, following *Mamie*'s instructions religiously, but it made no difference, since Branoc had not touched her for weeks. *Not since he saw that witch Églantine in the waterfall. He never wants me anymore—he lusts for her! How can I possibly conceive a child when he wastes his seed on her? I hate her!*

As Deirdre stood behind the counter of the blacksmith shop, despairing over the loss of her husband's affection, a handsome lord entered and greeted her cheerfully.

"Good day, my lady! I need to have my horse reshod. The nails have come loose on her right rear hoof. Is it possible to have her shoe replaced while I wait?"

Branoc, who had been working in the back of the shop, came forward to greet the gentleman. "Good day, sir. Yes, I can repair or replace your horse's shoe. Bring her on in, and I will take good care of her, rest assured," he said with a grin, wiping his blackened hands on his apron.

As the customer brought in his horse to be shod, Deirdre could not help but notice the fine quality of his clothing, the cleanliness of his shiny blond hair, and the confident air in which he carried himself. *He is a wealthy lord,* she mused. *He is someone of importance, to be sure.*

With a courteous smile, Deirdre attempted to make small talk while the gentleman waited for Branoc to reshoe his horse. "It is such a fine day today, a lovely day for a ride. Are you headed to the castle, my lord?"

The customer replied courteously, a friendly smile spread across his handsome, youthful face. "As a matter of fact, I am coming *from* the castle, my lady, delivering a dozen horses, including this lovely gray mare." He gestured to the horse in Branoc's care.

"I am Liam, the Master of Horse at the castle of King Donnchadh. I am bringing these fine animals from the royal stables to their new owner, just outside this village of Sligeach." He smiled warmly at Deirdre, who blushed under his gaze.

She preened at his attention, smoothing the folds of her dark blue homespun frock. "We are most fortunate that you have brought your business here to us today, my lord." Glancing out the window, Deirdre noticed half a dozen royal guards, as finely dressed as the one before her, tending to several horses just outside the shop.

The Master of Horse responded kindly, "And I am fortunate to have found a blacksmith on my way to deliver these magnificent animals."

Liam gestured to the horse that Branoc was busily reshoeing. "That lovely dappled gray mare is named Luna. She was the Princess Issylte's horse, the king's daughter who died in a tragic accident four years ago. Do you remember?"

Dierdre had a vague recollection of the events surrounding the death of the princess, but she wanted to hear more. "I do remember hearing something about that.

Wasn't it an accident with her horse?" She observed the palfrey in her husband's care. "Is that the mare she was riding when the accident happened?"

The lord replied sadly. "Indeed, it is. Princess Issylte was riding with her guards along the coast, where the cliffs overlook the sea." The Master of Horse stared off into the distance as if remembering the past.

"The edge of the cliff was unstable, and her horse reared when it started to crumble." He glanced down at his feet and whispered, "The princess was thrown into the sea. The king's guards searched for days, but her body was never found." When he raised his eyes to meet hers, Dierdre saw in his forlorn expression how much he had cared for the king's daughter.

"The princess loved this horse so much that the king refused to sell her. He insisted that I ride her every day below the window of his royal chambers, where he sat watching, as if it kept the memory of his daughter alive." He gazed up at Dierdre and smiled sadly. "But now, with King Donnchadh bedridden and ailing, the queen has decided to sell Luna after all. Along with these other fine horses from the royal stables." He paused for a moment to admire the pretty gray mare, his eyes filled with regret. "The Morholt—the one they call the Black Knight— needs war horses for his army, not gentle palfreys like Luna."

Liam gazed at the dappled gray mare, as if lost in reverie. "She was such a lovely girl, the princess. I used to ride with her every day—giving her equestrian lessons, teaching her to care for the horse herself."

He glanced back at Deirdre. She saw a mask of pain across his handsome face. "We'd gallop across the plains near the castle, and through the forest that she loved so well. They called her the Emerald Princess, you know."

The Master of Horse was clearly fond of the princess, his eyes sorrowful as he held Dierdre's gaze. "I can see her now, her long blond hair whipping through the wind, her cheeks pink from the thrill of the ride…She was so beautiful…. such a tragic loss. She was only fourteen years old." The Master of Horse glanced down at the floor, scuffling his feet as if he could wipe away the pain.

At that moment, Branoc brought Luna over to the handsome blond lord, handing the reins to the Master of Horse with a hearty grin.

"There now, she's as good as new. The nails had come loose, so I removed the shoe, filed her hoof properly, and replaced it. It's even better than before." Dierdre shot Branoc an eager look, indicating she had something important to tell him. Branoc said to the Lord Liam, "That'll be twelve shillings, please, my lord."

The Master of Horse paid his bill, led Luna out of the blacksmith shop and, with a cheerful goodbye to Branoc and Deirdre, rode off with royal guards to deliver the horses to their new owner just outside the village.

Dierdre turned quickly to her husband, breathless with excitement. "Did you hear the man, Bran? He said he's the Master of Horse at the castle! Imagine that! And the horse you shod—she belonged to the Princess Issylte, the king's only child!" Branoc seemed to be barely listening as he took stock of the orders he had yet to fill, planning his afternoon and prioritizing his work.

Deirdre was insistent. "Bran! Are you listenin'? That gentleman, Lord Liam, he said that the princess had long blond hair and that she loved to ride. He said she was fourteen years old when she died four summers ago."

At the mention of the princess' long blond hair, Branoc turned to face her. Finally, she had his attention.

"That would make her eighteen now, wouldn't it? The same age as *Églantine*." Deirdre sneered, fixing Branoc with a stark, determined gaze. "Isn't that a *coincidence*, Bran? That Églantine shows up out of the blue at the very same time that the princess has a tragic *accident*? They never found her body, you know? I do remember that. I remember how they were searching everywhere, but she had been thrown into the sea, and they never found a single trace of her."

The pieces of a puzzle were falling in place. Deirdre scoffed, "I don't remember you ever mentionin' that you had a cousin in *Bretagne*. I never heard *Mamie* talk about a sister, either. And now, suddenly, at the very same time that the princess dies in a tragic accident, with no trace of her body ever found... Églantine arrives at *Mamie's* cottage."

She paused for her words to sink in, her face contorted with disdain. "She's the same age, Bran. She loves horses, she's a skilled rider, and she loves the forest. Just like the Emerald Princess did."

Dierdre leaned forward to lock his eyes as she fit the final puzzle piece in place. With a sly grin, she smirked, "And—she has *long blond hair,* just like the princess, doesn't she, Bran?"

****

Branoc dried his hands on his apron, trying not to reveal how fast his heart was pounding. How his wife's words had rattled him. The sinister appearance on Dee's face made his mouth run dry. She'd been acting peculiar lately—watching him constantly, pestering him about

wanting a baby to the point of obsession. Although she'd
wanted a child ever since their marriage five years ago,
it seemed that now Dee was all the more desperate for
him to make love to her, frantically craving his affection.
Yet, the more she tried to entice him, the more she
repulsed him. He could barely stand to be near her and
recoiled from her touch. He thought of the beautiful
blond nymph he watched nearly every day in the
waterfall. She'd captured his heart. He longed for her
with an ache so intense it suffocated him. He had to
protect Églantine from his crazed, jealous wife. With the
intense hatred that he saw blazing in her eyes just now,
Branoc knew he had to think fast to deflect Dee's
suspicions.

His mind flashed through the events surrounding
Églantine's arrival. *Mamie* had never told him the truth
about the girl's background, saying simply that she had
needed protection and shelter. Now, Dee threatened
Églantine's safety. If she talked about her suspicions to
customers and the other shopkeepers in the village…
Bran needed to reaffirm the story his grandmother had
told everyone. Églantine was his distant cousin, who had
come to Ireland to stay with her grandmother's sister, her
last surviving relative.

A knot clenched in his stomach as he realized that
Dee had uncovered the truth. Églantine was indeed the
Princess Issylte. It made perfect sense now. He had to
protect her, the innocent victim of jealousy and hatred.
He feigned indifference to his wife's intense glare.

"That's ridiculous, Dee!" he scoffed with a laugh.
"Of course I remember Mamie talking about her sister! I
never met Églantine before, because I was born here in
Ireland, and she was born in *Bretagne*. But, by the

Goddess, she's my cousin and that's all there is to it. Now stop with your crazy accusations! I have work to do!"

He stormed off, pretending to be exasperated with her, watching out of the corner of his eye. She was not at all dissuaded by his words. She puttered about, shelving items in the shop and tidying up as she prepared to go to the house and fix dinner. But he caught her scornful stare. "Say what you will, Bran. But I know, as sure as I'm standin' here right now, lookin' at you, that our *sweet little Églantine*," she spat with disgust, "is the king's daughter Issylte, the Emerald Princess herself!"

In a desperate effort to distract Dierdre from her fixation with Églantine, Branoc tried to shower his wife with the attention she craved. He smiled at her frequently and kissed her cheek from time to time as he worked in his shop and crossed her path. He even forced himself to make love to her, hoping that his feigned interest would keep her occupied, deflect her attention, and protect Églantine.

Deirdre did seem to thrive on the newfound affection and did not mention again the visitor from the castle, the horse named Luna, or the tragic death of the Emerald Princess—until Maiwenn and Issylte came into the blacksmith shop on their usual Saturday excursion.

****

When Issylte entered the shop with Maiwenn, she saw Dierdre bustling about, wiping off the countertop, tidying up. She and *Tatie* greeted Dierdre with kisses on the cheek and bright smiles. Dee seemed barely able to contain herself, as if she had exciting news to share.

"Mamie! Églantine! You'll never guess who came into our shop just a few days ago! A fine gentleman by the name of Lord Liam, the Master of Horse in King Donnchadh's castle! Can you imagine?"

At the mention of Liam's name, Issylte's knees buckled underneath her. She grabbed the countertop to steady herself as Maiwenn responded brightly. "The Master of Horse! My goodness, fancy that! Did he come here to purchase a weapon?"

Issylte sensed Dierdre's scrutinizing gaze. Branoc's wife smirked, seeming to watch Issylte's reaction. "No, *Mamie*, he was here to have his horse reshod. A pretty *dappled gray mare* whose name was *Luna*."

Issylte nearly choked—her beloved horse was *here*! In this very shop. With Liam!

The blacksmith's wife continued, as if meting out the cruelty of her words and savoring their sweet effect. "Lord Liam, the Master of Horse, explained that the palfrey—Luna—had belonged to the king's only child, his daughter the Princess Issylte." Dierdre busied herself, wiping off the countertop, yet Issylte could feel her watchful stare as she struggled to keep her emotions in check. She cast her eyes to the ground, flustered, while Maiwenn did all the talking.

"How fortunate for you to have earned his business. I'm sure he paid handsomely for Bran's fine work."

Issylte adjusted the lacing on her boot, trying desperately to hide her dismay.

Dierdre continued, seemingly delighted at the effect the poison of her words was having on Issylte. "Yes, we are most grateful for his business. It seems that Lord Liam was on his way to deliver the horse Luna and some other palfreys from the royal stables to a buyer near the village when her horseshoe came loose. While Bran did the repairs, Lord Liam and I had a *very nice chat*."

Issylte shot Maiwenn a pleading look, hoping to extricate her from Deirdre's attack. Branoc was still occupied near his forge and could not rescue them.

"Lord Liam told me how the king had been terribly distraught after his daughter's death. How he just could not part with the horse, for the princess had loved the mare so much. But now, with the king bed-ridden and ailing, the queen decided to sell Luna and the other palfreys. It seems the Morholt—her Black Knight—was needin' only *warhorses* for his army."

Bile rose in her throat. She had to escape *now*.

Just as Issylte could bear no more, Branoc finally came over to greet them, wiping his hands and grinning at the sight of the visitors. "*Mamie*! Églantine!" he beamed, "how are you today?" As her husband kissed the two women, Dierdre gloated, "Bran, I was just tellin' *Mamie* and Églantine about Lord Liam, the Master of Horse at the castle who came in this week with the gray mare to be reshod."

Branoc shot a worried glance at his grandmother and turned to stare at Issylte. The blood drained from her face. Her legs shook under her gown.

"It's most peculiar, *Mamie*. Lord Liam said that the Princess Issylte," Dierdre crooned, malice burning in her bleak stare, "had long, blond hair—and was quite beautiful. That she was just fourteen when the *accident* occurred four years ago." Maiwenn was assembling her baskets, preparing to leave. Dierdre's steely voice was a razor-sharp blade. "Four years ago… the same time that *you* came to Mamie's cottage. From *Bretagne.*" Dierdre shot daggers at Issylte, who dared not meet the malevolent stare.

"Isn't that just an incredible *coincidence*? And, to

think that here you are—eighteen years old now, the exact same age that the princess would have been if she'd survived." A devilish grin contorted Dierdre's taunting face.

Maiwenn seemed to be trying her best to remain unruffled. "Yes, Dee, it is indeed a tragedy. I've heard it said throughout the kingdom that she was a lovely child. Such a terrible loss for His Majesty, the king."

Turning to Branoc and adjusting the basket on her arm, she announced, "We'll be headin' home now, dear. It was good to see you both. Come now, Églantine. Let's go make that seafood stew with the clams and mussels we found this morning."

Maiwenn took Issylte's arm and firmly steered her towards the door. Issylte could barely stand as she leaned on her *tatie* for support. "Bye now, Dee. We'll see you soon." Maiwenn flashed a bright smile as she led Issylte out the door.

Maiwenn's voice was quiet but stern. "Hold your head high and keep your composure. I am sure that Dee is watching from the window. Do not react at all until we are out of view. Come with me, dear. Calmly."

Once they were no longer in sight of the blacksmith shop and well into the forest, Issylte collapsed onto her knees. "Oh, *Tatie*… Luna was there! And Liam! And my poor father… He's bedridden, just like I saw in that vision on the lake!" She shuddered, her breath heaving.

"The queen sold Luna. She belongs to someone else now." Issylte was inconsolable, her body wracked with grief. "I'll never see her, or Liam—or my father—ever again. Oh, *Tatie*, I just can't bear it!"

Maiwenn stroked Issylte's back, her touch soothing. "There now, dear. I know it hurts. It's all right, sweetheart." Maiwenn wrapped her arms around Issylte in a grandmotherly hug, as if to absorb her pain.

After a few minutes, Issylte raised a crumpled, miserable face to her *tatie*. Maiwenn helped Issylte to her feet. "Come, let's go home to the cottage. I have something important to tell you."

Seated at the cozy table behind the hearth, Issylte sipped the chamomile tea as her *tatie* stored the provisions they had procured in the village earlier that day. Returning with her own *tisane*, the fairy witch who had so lovingly cared for her for the past four years sat down at the table. Large, luminous brown eyes twinkled in the firelight.

"My dearest Églantine," she said, her eyes glistening. "I love you as if you were my very own granddaughter." Maiwenn reached across the table and squeezed Issylte's hand. Issylte's heart was in her throat. Where was this leading? A wave of panic washed over her.

"You have given me so much *joy*, sweetheart. I thank the Goddess every day for bringing you to my doorstep." Wiping her tears and straightening her back, her *tatie* seemed to be gathering her resolve. She met Issylte's gaze, her wise eyes resolute and firm.

"You cannot remain here any longer, my princess. It has become much too dangerous. Dozens of knights are arriving each week, headed to the castle. The Black Knight has got every sea wright along the coast building warships for his army, preparing for an invasion of Britain." Issylte's lip quivered and her legs shook under the table. "Soon, there will be lumberjacks felling the trees here in the Hazelwood Forest. More royal guards coming into the village. And now, I fear Dee suspects the truth, after what she said in the shop today."

Issylte, her heart fluttering, watched Maiwenn sip her tea.

"Do you remember several weeks ago, you saw me talking to someone in front of the cottage, near the woods?"

Issylte nodded, taking a sip of *tisane*. Her hands trembled, and her stomach clenched. She was downright ill with tension and dread. What was *Tatie* saying?

Maiwenn continued, her voice at once soothing yet discomforting. "I told you that a villager was asking for a remedy for a stomach ailment," she said, seeming embarrassed at the lie. "But those were my *messengers*—the *Little Folk*—the woodland creatures of the forest."

Issylte gazed at Maiwenn in confusion. Where was this leading? What was *Tatie* trying to say? Her stomach was twitching. She wiped damp palms on her dress.

"I sent an urgent message to my trusted friend Viviane, asking if she could take you in. I explained who you were, the queen's attempt on your life, and that I could no longer keep you here with me." Maiwenn's eyes blazed with conviction.

"I received a response not long after, saying yes, you could stay with her, and that she would be sending her guards to escort you there."

Issylte panicked. "Escort me where, *Tatie*? I don't want to leave. I want to stay here with you. I love you, *Tatie*. Please don't send me away!" She clutched Maiwenn's hands.

The fairy witch rose to her feet and threw her arms around Issylte's shoulders. Maiwenn rested her cheek against Issylte's head. Issylte's heart was a tight fist. She loved her *tatie* so very much. She couldn't leave!

"I know, sweetheart. It breaks my heart to send you away, but that is exactly what I must do. It is too dangerous for you to remain here. You know that is true. If the queen learns that you are still alive, she will hunt you down and *kill* you."

And you, Tatie, for sheltering me, Issylte realized with horror. *By the Goddess, I must leave before it's too late. For Tatie's sake!*

Maiwenn returned to her seat at the table, composing her face with her posture. Her wide, brown eyes—so full of love and light, yet stark and resolute—locked on Issylte's.

"You, my dearest princess, are the heir to the throne of Ireland." Maiwenn took Issylte's trembling hand. "I believe with all my heart that the Goddess sent you to me. So you could discover your divine gift, learning to wield the magic essence of the forest. So that you could become a powerful healer. So that you can one day reclaim your birthright." She met Issylte's eyes with wonder and awe. "So that you, the Emerald Princess, can become the *Emerald Queen.*"

Maiwenn turned to gaze at the fire in the hearth as if the flames held the answers she sought.

"I have taught you all the secrets of the forest. You can wield your power to determine which herbs can heal, which can kill. You can create medicines, elixirs, poultices, and salves. Verdant magic is within you, my forest fairy. It protects and guides you, just as it has me, all my life." Maiwenn cast a loving glance at Issylte, her luminous eyes glowing in the firelight.

"You have mastered the first of the three sacred elements of the Goddess—the forest. And now, you have also shown evidence of the gift of *sight*—a magic to be wielded through water. It is time for you to develop that divine gift as well. To master the second of the three sacred elements—*water.*"

Issylte, bewildered, repeated her urgent question. "Where, *Tatie*? Where are you sending me?"

Her face alight with wisdom and love, Maiwenn responded with a soft, knowing smile.

"To Avalon."

Chapter 18

The Fountain of Barenton

After nearly two weeks at sea, Tristan, Lancelot, and the accompanying knights finally reached the craggy coast of *Bretagne*, where they docked and procured horses for the three-day trek to Lancelot's domain. Leaving the rocky coves and rugged cliffs behind, they rode southwest through dense forest, stopping to rest the horses and grab a quick meal, sleeping on bedrolls at night, until at last the salty tang of the estuary and the roar of the river announced their arrival at *la Joyeuse Garde*.

Built upon a hill, the *château* faced south, over the Élorn river which flowed into the Atlantic Sea. To the north and west, fertile plains and dense woodlands led to the ocean, but to the east lay the sacred forest of *Brocéliande* where Lancelot had been raised. As the riders approached, the white limestone castle gleamed as the setting sun sparkled in the rippling waters of the wide river.

Lancelot had sent messengers ahead to inform the servants of their impending arrival. The travelers were greeted warmly by the stable hands who accepted their horses as they rode through the opened gate. The *châtelain*, or lord of the castle, as Lancelot was known here, invited the traveling knights inside, where smiling servants were waiting, ready to usher the guests to their chambers.

"I am hosting a welcoming reception and feast this evening, gentlemen. There are pages available to assist you in preparing a bath. I, myself, cannot *wait* to wash the brine of the sea from my hair," he said, extending a matted and gnarled sample of his normally shining brown locks, "and don a finely embroidered tunic and soft breeches. My clothing is *stiff* from the salt air of our voyage." He laughed, touching the inflexible fabric of his tunic with a frown.

With his dazzling boyish grin, he added enthusiastically, "There will be delicious seafood—oysters, mussels, fresh fish from the river. With stuffed duck, roast venison, fresh fruits and vegetables. And, of course—exquisite French wine!" At this, the knights roared their approval, and Lancelot concluded with the *pièce de résistance*.

"And, since you have suffered the company of such filthy brutes as myself and Tristan here—" he joked, gesturing to his companion, who was grinning as broadly as his host—"for nearly a *fortnight*," he drawled, a mischievous smirk on his face, "I have invited some of the loveliest ladies in all of *Bretagne* to regale you with their beauty…and delight you with their *charms*." Then, with a dramatic bow, Lancelot departed, withdrawing to his own private chambers and a much longed for bath.

The remaining knights laughed heartily as they, too, headed for their chambers, commenting about what a magnanimous host Lancelot was, how they could not wait to sample the fine food, the exquisite wine, and the *delicious* women.

A page approached. "Sir Tristan, please follow me.

I will lead you to your rooms and draw your bath, my lord." Tristan followed him from the entry foyer, down a long hall, up a set of stairs to the second level, to a large chamber at the end of another hall.

The bedchamber was expansive, with large, windowed doors extending from floor to ceiling and taking up nearly the entire wall opposite the entrance. The glass doors were opened wide, letting in the salty summer breeze and the mellow sunlight flickering through the dense trees behind the *château*. Gossamer white curtains fluttered in the gentle wind, the crisp air of the brackish river embalming the room with the scent of the sea. A large bed with fine linens faced the windows from the opposite wall.

Beside the bed was a table with a pitcher, basin, cup and candle. A chair was neatly tucked underneath, with a chamber pot on the stone floor in the corner of the room. Perpendicular to the windows was a fireplace, where a squire was heating water for Tristan's bath over the flaming hearth.

A magnificently carved fruitwood armoire with double doors, gleaming with the fresh scent of pine oil, towered between the two enormous windows. Peering inside, Tristan glimpsed an array of richly colored tunics, breeches, hats, cloaks, gloves, and boots. *Our host thinks of everything,* Tristan mused with a smile.

The squire filled the porcelain tub in the adjacent bathing room, then entered Tristan's bedroom. "I've prepared your bath, Sir Tristan. It is good and hot, my lord. Shall I help you, or do you prefer privacy, Sir Tristan?"

Replying that he preferred to bathe unassisted, Tristan disrobed and eased into the hot water, sighing with relief as his tense muscles relaxed. After two weeks at sea and three days in the saddle, his back was tight from sleeping on the hard ground and his thighs protested their abuse. *Lancelot is right*, he thought, lathering up with the chamomile soap provided by his host, *it does feel good to wash the brine from my hair.* He slipped under the water with a moan of delight.

Once he finished bathing, Tristan dressed in a tunic of dark green with gold embroidery, breeches of the finest brown wool, and dark brown boots of the softest leather he'd ever worn. As he exited his room, a page came in and quietly removed his dirty clothing to be laundered. The squire who had prepared his bath said, "This way, my lord. Sir Lancelot's guests are arriving, and the feast will be in the banquet hall. Follow me, Sir Tristan."

The banquet hall was sumptuously decorated, with tables set with white linens, silver chalices and utensils, adorned with large bouquets of fragrant white lily flowers. Along the side walls, attendants were carving roasted meats whose tantalizing aroma wafted through the air while servants delivered goblets of wine to the elegantly dressed lords and ladies being seated all around.

An enormous ballroom extended from the banquet hall, where glittering chandeliers of crystals sparkling with candlelight hung from the high vaulted ceilings. Enormous, windowed doors graced the entire length of both rooms, opening onto a large courtyard enclosed by a high stone wall.

Flowering vines and trees in bloom beckoned, embalming the air with the fragrance of jasmine. A pair of swans floated upon a large pond; water lilies dotted its surface with fragrant white flowers. Under a canopy of oaks enlaced with ivy and wisteria, stone benches welcomed guests to watch the moonlight dance on the shimmering waters of the lake. *La joie de vivre,* reflected Tristan, remembering Lancelot's description of this *château,* which offered all the elegance of King Arthur's palace, yet with more intimacy than the much larger and more formal Camelot.

As he was ushered to Lancelot's table, which seated twelve, Tristan noticed that his host was chatting amicably with a dark haired, enormous knight on his left. At Tristan's approach, the *châtelain* rose to his feet, welcomed him with a hearty grin and a friendly slap on the shoulder as he introduced the Blue Knight of Cornwall to his fellow guests.

"Tristan, allow me to present Sir Esclados, the Red Knight, and his beautiful wife, the Lady Laudine," Lancelot exclaimed as the dark knight stood and extended his rugged hand. With a firm shake and a respectful nod of his head, Tristan accepted the greeting, turning to place a chivalrous kiss upon the lady's delicate fingers.

"Sir Esclados and his gracious wife are the lord and lady of the castle of Landuc, in the forest of Brocéliande, not far my mother's castle of Comper." Lancelot grinned broadly at the tall, dark knight, who took his seat beside his auburn-haired wife.

"Lord Esclados and Lady Laudine are the Knight and Lady of the Spring—the holy Fountain of Barenton—in the heart of the sacred forest." Lancelot sat down with the Red Knight on his left, gesturing for Tristan to take the reserved, empty chair on his right.

Tristan seated himself beside his host with a

respectful nod to Lord Esclados and Lady Laudine. He first met the dark, intelligent eyes of the Red Knight, then the expressive green ones of the exquisite redhead. Tristan sensed an aura of power emanating from the defenders of the sacred spring.

"Tristan is the nephew of King Marke of Cornwall," Lancelot continued, "one of the ten winners of the Tournament of Champions held last summer at the castle of Tintagel. He is training to become one of King Arthur's Knights of the Round Table in Camelot." At this, Sir Esclados nodded his approval, while Lady Laudine smiled, her elegant white hand gracefully tossing back a long tendril of her luxurious red hair.

Lancelot gestured to the knight seated on the far side of Lady of the Spring. "This is Sir Agrane, First Knight to Lord Esclados and Lady Laudine, at their castle of Landuc." Upon his introduction, a tall knight with long blond hair and a deep scar across his right cheek rose to shake hands with Tristan.

"Sir Agrane leads a regiment of sixty knights who reside at the castle. All have sworn an oath to protect the sacred fountain—and the sacred Forest of Brocéliande." The intense blue eyes of Sir Agrane held his gaze as Tristan nodded in homage and finally returned to his seat beside the First Knight of Camelot.

The conversation among Lancelot and his fellow knights resumed, and Tristan observed the remaining guests seated at the host's table. There were four other ladies, adorned in brightly colored silk gowns, bedecked with sparkling jewels at their throats and ears. They chatted gaily with the knights seated beside them, who were all as bulky and enormous as Tristan himself. Curiously, they all displayed the same tattoo on their inner right wrist that he had noticed on the inside of Lancelot's sword arm.

The tattoos were triangular, with each of the three corners extending down, like an outstretched arm, curving inward into a protective spiral. *An emblem of brotherhood,* Tristan reflected, *a Celtic symbol of some kind. Perhaps Lancelot will grace me with another of his fine tales when he explains its significance.* Hiding his grin, Tristan lifted his chalice and drank deeply of the rich burgundy wine.

When the final course of the meal was finished and the dishes cleared away by discreet and diligent servants, fiddlers and flutists began performing in the ballroom. The four distinguished couples seated at their table rose to join the many other lords and ladies who had flocked to the dance floor, leaving Tristan, Lancelot, Esclados, Laudine and Agrane to chat more freely.

Taking advantage of the lull in conversation, Tristan decided to satisfy his curiosity and inquire about the mysterious tattoos. "I've noticed that you all bear the same mark on your inner wrist," he began with a quiet smile. "What is the meaning of the tattoo you share?"

Lancelot stared proudly at the green design on his wrist, glancing up at Tristan with a grin. "It's the emblem of the Tribe of Dana—the Goddess of Nature. We're the defenders of Her realm—the sacred *forest*, such as Brocéliande; the sacred *waters*, such as the Fountain of Barenton, and the sacred *stones*, such as *les Menhirs de Monteneuf,* which are portals to the *Otherworld.*"

Tristan glanced at Sir Esclados and Lady Laudine. Their faces glowed with the same reverence that shone in Lancelot's bright blue eyes.

Tristan noticed that Laudine also bore a similar

tattoo, with the same curves ending in spirals but with thinner, more delicate scrolls. Laudine, observing his inquisitive expression, explained the meaning of her tattoo. "My tattoo is given to priestesses of the Tribe of Dana who have defended the sacred waters of the Goddess. I am the guardian of the sacred spring of Barenton. I wield its holy power to heal and protect." Her face glowed, a warm smile reflected in her kind eyes.

Lancelot flashed his boyish grin at the lovely Lady of the Fountain. "Laudine studied with my mother Viviane—the Lady of the Lake—who bestowed upon her the curative powers of the sacred fountain. Many a wounded warrior has been healed by the lovely Lady of the Spring, in our sacred Forest of Brocéliande." Lancelot raised his goblet of wine in a toast. "To the Tribe of Dana! Defenders of Her sacred realm!"

Tristan joined his fellow knights in the tribute to the Goddess as he clinked his goblet to theirs, drinking in the spirit of brotherhood with generous swallows of his host's fine wine.

The merriment and revelry continued for three days, with Tristan strolling along the lilied pond and under the floral trellises with Lady Laudine, galloping into the forest for hunting and falconry with Esclados, Lancelot, and Agrane. Nightly feasts offered jubilant revelry, with troubadours, harpists, and fiddlers entertaining the joyous dancers in the expansive ballroom. Each evening at their dinner table, Lancelot planned maneuvers with Esclados and Agrane as they included Tristan in the knights' training at *la Joyeuse Garde*.

Most of the royal guests then departed, returning to their *châteaux* and stately manors. Some of the knights escorted the ladies home—including Laudine—

returning to *la Joyeuse Garde* for vigorous training with Lancelot, Esclados and Agrane. As the weeks flew by, Tristan saw a marked increase in his strength, accuracy with a bow and arrow, and dexterity with the sword.

One afternoon, when Lancelot and his knights were in the midst of their midday meal, a horseman arrived at the *château* with an urgent message. A servant ushered him into the *La Joyeuse Garde* while a stable hand tended the slathered horse.

Breathless, the rider gasped as Lancelot and his knights gathered to listen. "Sir Lancelot, Lord Esclados—I have come from the *château* of Landuc. The castle is under attack!"

The horseman wheezed, winded from hard ride. Esclados rushed forward, his eyes blazing. "My wife. Has she been harmed?"

The messenger shook his head, panting. "No, my lord. The Lady Laudine is inside the castle. She is well protected by two dozen knights. With two dozen more manning the defense towers."

Lancelot helped the horseman to a seat and knelt beside him, his expression grave. "Who is behind the attack? How many soldiers?"

The rider fixed his desperate eyes on Esclados. "It is the dwarf Bédalis, my lord. He has an army of knights surrounding the castle. He knows that you and most of your men are here training with Sir Lancelot. So, he has attacked now—while you are away." He gulped some water that a servant offered. "The dwarf has demanded that Laudine surrender the castle."

Lancelot rose to his feet, his brows lowered. "Bédalis delves in the dark arts. He wants control of the spring. If he abducts Laudine—"

The Red Knight interrupted Lancelot and began barking orders. To Agrane, he commanded, "Summon the Tribe. Leave immediately. Meet at *Comper*." He glanced at Lancelot, who nodded in confirmation. Agrane and six knights rushed into armor and strapped on their swords while the grooms raced to ready the horses. Lancelot dispatched a messenger for Comper, with orders to prepare the *château* for his imminent arrival.

Esclados turned back to the rider from Landuc and fired more questions. "Has the castle been breached? Are there armed men inside the gate?"

"No, my lord. When I left—three hours ago—they had not yet breached the outer wall." The Red Knight paced back and forth in front of Lancelot and Tristan. "Agrane and his men can summon two—perhaps three— dozen members of the Tribe. We can bring sixty knights with us, and still leave a minimum of guards here for defense. If we surround the dwarf's men and block any escape—the element of surprise is in our favor."

Lancelot shouted to his knights. "At arms! We ride to Comper. We attack tonight. Now go—make haste. To Comper!"

Esclados approached again, pensive and grave. "As Lord of the Spring, I also wield its power. For its *defense*."

Tristan watched the Red Knight pace, forming his battle strategy. Esclados turned abruptly to Lancelot.

"If I can reach the fountain, in the heart of the forest, I can summon a storm. Lightning, thunder, winds, hail. By drawing forth the divine power of the sacred spring."

Adrenaline flooded Tristan's veins as the dark eyes of the Red Knight blazed in the setting sun.

"There's a sacred pine tree beside the well. Where the spring forms the Fountain of Barenton. A golden basin hangs from one of its branches. I can summon a tempest by pouring three drops of the sacred water from the fountain onto *le Perron de Merlin*—the wizard's ancient stone."

The thrill of battle surged through Tristan as he listened, enthralled.

"With lightning, tremendous winds and hail appearing out of nowhere, Bédalis' men will be terrified. They'll suspect an evil enchantment."

Lancelot's eyes were aflame, caught up in Esclados' plan. "We attack from behind. Overpower them. With the element of surprise, the terror of the storm, the cover of darkness—all in our favor."

The three men nodded, quickly donning their armor and swords. They dashed outside to the awaiting horses as Lancelot gave instructions to his servants.

"Most of the knights will return tomorrow. I'll keep a half dozen with me at my mother's *château.* I'll return in three or four days." With a quick nod to Tristan and Esclados, they mounted their destriers and rode off to join the warriors of the Tribe of Dana.

At the Castle of Comper, Lancelot, Esclados, and Agrane were outlining plans in the Great Hall. Knights were sharpening their weapons, checking their armor and horses, preparing for battle. Lancelot, his chain mail gleaming in the candlelight, addressed the tribe.

"Esclados, you and Tristan disguise yourselves as beggars, with a large cloak to cover your armor. Approach the spring slowly, with stooped backs, as if you're elderly. If you're stopped and questioned—say that you're pilgrims, on your way to the chapel of the

179

Goddess Dana. That you stopped to rest and quench your thirst at the fountain."

Both knights nodded solemnly. "Tristan, sit down on Merlin's perch—the sacred ancient stone—while Esclados fetches the golden basin. To summon the storm." Tristan's muscles were tightly coiled, screaming for release.

Lancelot turned to address one of the tattooed warriors of the Tribe who had been summoned by Agrane. "Kirus," he said, garnering the instant attention of a tall, burly soldier with dark brown hair and a brutally scarred face. "You and the Tribe will wait in the trees west of the spring. When the storm begins, bring Esclados and Tristan two horses and proceed to the front of the château. If the castle has been breached, engage in battle." Kirus nodded, his regard savage and fierce. Tristan's heart thumped through his armor, the wings of a sea raven ready to take flight.

"Agrane, you and your knights approach from the rear of the castle. Engage the enemy from the east and prevent any escape." Lancelot locked eyes with the First Knight of Landuc. "Take *no* hostages." Agrane nodded gravely.

Lancelot turned to face another senior knight from his own command. "Judoc, you and your men approach from the south." Another nod of comprehension. "And I will lead from the north. All right, men. Get into position and wait for the storm. May the Goddess Dana assure our victory! We ride!"

The moonlight shone through the thick canopy of trees. Tristan and Esclados waited in the darkness of the dense forest until the warriors of the Tribe of Dana were in position, surrounding the dwarf Bédalis' unsuspecting men. The two knights donned their long, dark cloaks and assumed the hunched backs of elderly pilgrims, slowly approaching the sacred Fountain of Barenton.

A clearing stood in the heart of the dense forest, illuminated by the moon and starlight above. An owl hooted in the distance. Twigs snapped and leaves rustled as the horses waited impatiently in the thick woods.

Tristan spotted a low wall, composed of dozens of smooth stones, encasing a hole in the forested ground. Water from an underground spring gurgled and bubbled, forming a fountain which pooled into the stone-enclosed well. He observed the sacred pine tree behind the well, with the golden basin hanging from a low-lying branch. His heart pounding with adrenaline, Tristan slowly lowered himself onto the smooth, sacred stone named for the famed archdruid. Staring into the blue eye of the sea raven, he kissed the ring upon his left hand.

Tristan's muscles quivered with anticipation. He watched Esclados retrieve the golden basin from the sacred pine tree and fill it with water from the spring. No one questioned them, and soon Tristan slowly stood and tottered towards the fountain, as if to quench his thirst.

Esclados cautiously poured three drops of the sacred water onto Merlin's stone. Instantly, a whirlwind arose, as if a cyclone encompassed the entire clearing. Though it was already dark, what little moonlight had been visible was now totally obscured by ominous clouds that rumbled with thunder. A current sizzled through the night air.

Lightning flashed as a furious wind whipped the trees. Hailstones the size of walnuts began falling from the sky, clattering onto the branches of trees and the stones near the well. Amid sudden shrieks and shouts, the sound of metal clashing announced the beginning of the onslaught. Tristan and Esclados cast aside their cloaks, uncovering their armor, as Kirus and his men rode into the clearing with the two horses. The two knights quickly mounted and raced through the forest to the *château*.

Esclados led the Tribe to the front entrance, where the lowered drawbridge indicated the castle had been breached. Two dozen knights were valiantly defending the front entrance, but were being pushed back, outnumbered by Bédalis' men. Swords clashed; the shrieks of dying men tore through the dark forest, illuminated by flashes of lightning as hail pummeled metal helmets and shields. Gale force winds battered the heavy branches of oaks as torrents of rain fell in buckets from the black sky.

The Red Knight and Tristan engaged the dwarf's army from the front, while Kirus and the Tribe surrounded the enemy from behind. Tristan blocked a thrust, dodged another strike, landing a fatal blow just as he saw the dwarf Bédalis run into the castle on foot. Quickly dismounting, Tristan raced to follow, his sword drawn, his shield up.

Inside the castle, he heard Laudine scream just as he caught sight of the dwarf's lunge. He barely managed to deflect the sword, which gouged his cheek with the tip of the blade. Recovering quickly, Tristan launched a barrage of strikes in quick succession, overwhelming the frantic dwarf. With one final massive blow, Tristan cleaved his sword into the side of Bédalis' neck at the shoulder, nearly decapitating him. He quickly removed his bloodied blade, ran up the stairs, and found a trembling Laudine huddled with her frightened attendants, desperately clutching each other behind an overturned chair. Her face was streaked with grime, but she nodded to Tristan, who raced down the hall.

He ran into the remaining chambers, finding more terrified servants but no attacking knights. He flew down the stairs and tore through the castle but found only his fellow members of the Tribe defending the front entrance, their massive swords drawn, their gruesome faces bloodied.

Outside, the storm had stopped. Amid puddles of mud and blood, dozens of slain enemy bodies were scattered across the castle grounds. Tristan stood at the entrance of Landuc as Lancelot rode up from the north. Judoc—Lancelot's First Knight of *la Joyeuse Garde*— and his men approached from the south. Agrane— Esclados' First Knight of Landuc—returned from the rear of the *château*. On every face, Tristan saw savage grins of victory, tempered by the pain of loss. They had liberated the castle, freed Laudine, yet several of their brothers had fallen in battle. Tristan's blood pounded in his ears as battle frenzy surged in his veins. The copper tang of blood assailed his nostrils as he wiped the flow oozing down his face from the bite of the dwarf's treacherous sword.

Lancelot dismounted and beckoned for the leaders to follow him into the castle. Esclados tore up the stairs, threw his arms around his wife, showering her with kisses as she sobbed onto his chest. He helped her to her feet, and she leaned against him as they came downstairs to join Lancelot and Tristan in the Great Hall.

"Report?" Lancelot inquired of each of his commanders. Judoc replied first. "None escaped. We lost four, with two wounded." He nodded to an area across the room where Laudine and her priestesses were tending to the injured, washing off blood and grime, herbal remedies in hand.

Agrane responded next. "We lost two men. Several wounded." He turned to Esclados. "We recovered about three dozen horses from the dwarf's men." A grin spread across his bloodied face. "A good addition to the stables of Landuc."

Lancelot questioned Kirus. "And the Tribe?"

The lead warrior of the Tribe of Dana said proudly, "We lost none. And none injured." His brilliant eyes blazed with triumph.

Lancelot reported the loss of one man, with three wounded. He then ordered quietly, "Bring the bodies of our seven fallen knights into the Great Hall. Cover them with sacred cloth. Tomorrow, we'll bury them near the sacred stones. And honor their sacrifice." Several knights rose at once, exiting in solemn silence.

Laudine and four priestesses of the Tribe of Dana had set up a makeshift hospital in the Great Hall where the wounded were being carefully laid onto cots quickly set up by servants. With the sacred, curative waters of the fountain and the medicinal herbs of the Forest of Brocéliande, the *guérisseuses* tended the battered knights who had been injured defending the castle.

Laudine came over to Tristan to treat the gouge on his cheek and clean the dried blood from his filthy face. With a soft cloth and a basin of water from the sacred spring, she gently washed his face with herbal soap and applied a soothing ointment over his wound. She whispered in his ear, "It is not deep. This salve will aid healing and prevent it from festering." She quietly rejoined her priestesses to care for the rest of the wounded.

Tristan sat down upon the floor of the Great Hall beside many of his fellow knights. Faces were streaked with blood and grime; everyone was drenched from the storm. Despite the injuries, he saw the savage thrill of victory on the battered, brutal faces all around him. Lancelot's commanding voice carried across the heads of the knights and warriors of the Tribe of Dana leaning against the sturdy walls of the Castle of Landuc.

"Tomorrow, our fallen knights receive the sacred burial. We burn the bodies of the enemy." Heads bowed in remembrance of those who had fallen.

Tristan observed the men around him. Some cleaned their bloodied weapons, others nursed painful wounds. All were listening intently, their eyes fixed on Lancelot. Their revered leader.

"Each one of you displayed courage and valor tonight in defending Landuc." Lancelot walked through the men, his eyes glowing with respect, pride, and honor. "Victory is ours. May the Goddess be praised!" Cheers rippled through the ragged voices of the bloodied men. Swords frapped against shields, the savage applause of warriors. A thrill rushed up Tristan's spine.

"We liberated Laudine. Defended Landuc. Protected the sacred Fountain of Barenton."

Lancelot met the shining eyes of his valiant men. "Victory is ours because of your prowess. Your courage. Your skill. Men, I salute you." White teeth shone in the dim firelight, faces alight with honor and respect.

Lancelot turned to the First Knight of Landuc. "Agrane, take my men to join yours in the knights' lodge." To his own men, he directed, "Sir Agrane will lead you to the knights' lodge, which can accommodate one hundred. There are cots and bedding for everyone. In the morning, we honor our fallen. For now, go and rest. May the Goddess bless you all. Good night, men. Well done!"

The knights gathered their weapons and followed Agrane across the courtyard to the lodge near the stables. Tristan saw Lancelot and Esclados conferring quietly with the Tribe of Dana in a far corner of the Great Hall.

Once the knights had left, and the wounded soldiers were resting peacefully, Laudine and her four priestesses joined Lancelot and the Tribe. Esclados motioned for Tristan to approach. He rose to his feet, a new thrill surging through him.

"Tristan, tonight you valiantly defended the castle of Landuc. You slew the infamous dwarf Bédalis. And protected the sacred Fountain of Barenton." The Red Knight nodded to the other members of the Tribe of Dana, including Lancelot.

"Because of the valor you showed in defending the sacred realm of the Goddess, we invite you to join us. To become a member of the Tribe of Dana. What say you, Blue Knight of Cornwall?"

Tristan was speechless. Lancelot flashed him the familiar boyish grin, encouragement shining in his proud eyes.

"It would be my greatest honor to join the Tribe of Dana," Tristan stammered. "I humbly thank you, Lord Esclados!"

The Red Knight responded with a hearty grin. "Excellent! Tomorrow we honor our fallen with a tribute and sacred burial. We burn the bodies of the enemy. Once night has fallen, we will conduct your initiation ceremony in the clearing. Where we summoned the storm."

A gleam twinkled in Esclados' expressive dark eyes. "And Tristan, as a reward for rescuing my wife, the Lady of the Fountain. For your valor in defending the sacred element of *water*—I will present you an additional, most precious gift. Which you will receive in a special ceremony tomorrow night."

Tristan beamed as Lord Esclados slapped him heartily upon the shoulders. The Red Knight then turned to the members of the Tribe of Dana. "Fellow warriors, allow my servants to escort you to our guest chambers. You all fought heroically tonight. We defended the sacred fountain…and the sacred Forest of Brocéliande. The Goddess Dana is most pleased with Her tribe."

With a nod to Tristan, he announced to the men, "Tomorrow, we induct a new member, with the traditional ceremony in the sacred forest."

The dark, burly Lord Esclados turned to his wife and placed an arm around her shoulder, pulling her into a warm hug. As the servants ushered the Tribe members to their chambers, the Red Knight said in parting, "Good night, everyone. Sleep well."

Tristan bid good night to Esclados, Laudine, and Lancelot, following a servant to his guest room. He disrobed, washed the grime from his body, and curled into the comfortable bed, his mind racing, reliving the thrilling events of the tumultuous day.

He'd defended the castle and had single-handedly defeated that damned dwarf Bédalis. He'd saved Laudine and her priestesses and had helped Esclados invoke the storm. The divine power of the Goddess.

And now, I will become a member of the Tribe of Dana.

As he drifted off to sleep, Tristan of Lyonesse felt a true sense of belonging. A camaraderie here in the Forest of Brocéliande. A sacred brotherhood to fill the bitter emptiness inside his savage soul.

Chapter 19

The Escort from Avalon

Maiwenn knew she had to act quickly. From the sound of the horses' hooves, there were several riders at least, so it wasn't just Bran and Dee. She raced into the woods behind the cottage, her heart pounding furiously, praying that the Goddess would protect her beloved Églantine. Drawing from the deep well of her newly reawakened magic, the Green Fairy of the Hazelwood Forest—*la Fée Verte de la Forêt*—summoned her loyal woodland creatures.

****

Issylte was returning to the cottage, a basket of wild plums on her arm—savoring the sweet taste of the *tarte aux mirabelles* that *Tatie* would make for dessert—when she noticed a trail of pink flowers leading away from her normal route home. Intrigued, knowing that the *Little Folk* had left them for her, she followed the *églantines* to the same area of hazelwood branches covered with vines where she had first glimpsed the hidden cottage four years ago.

She knew immediately that something was wrong. Her heart hammered in her chest. Her legs were wobbly and weak.

The hens were squawking, their wings flapping wildly. Florette was bleating madly, running around in circles at the side of the cottage. Issylte's stomach dropped, along with the basket of *mirabelle* plums from her arm.

She couldn't see any horses, yet the grassy area in front of the cottage was churned up by the imprint of many hooves. Huge clumps of dark mud were scattered everywhere near the entrance door. *Dear Goddess, where is Tatie?* A shiver of dread crept up her spine. *I must help her!*

Just as she was about to race to the cottage, a strong hand clamped over her mouth from behind. A heavily muscled arm pulled her back against a chest as hard as the trunk of oak. Panicked, Issylte struggled to break free, but his grip was like iron. A stern, deep voice spoke quietly into her left ear. "Do not cry out. I will not harm you. We are the escort from Avalon."

Issylte nodded in bewilderment. Her weakened legs could barely support her weight. Her mouth was bone dry. *I have to help Tatie!*

"The queen's men are in the cottage right now. Waiting for you to return. They have slain Maiwenn, her grandson, and his foolish wife who betrayed you."

Issylte's legs gave out. The strong arm supported her; the hand clamped over her mouth muffled her guttural moan.

He spoke sternly into her good ear. "You must be silent. The queen's guards will hear you."

Issylte nodded grimly. He relaxed the grip over her mouth ever so slightly. She was sick to her stomach. Could she vomit through his hand?

"Maiwenn summoned the *Little Folk* to leave the trail of flowers. To draw you here, so that I could intercept you before you reached the cottage. It was her last act—*to save you.*"

Issylte collapsed in his arms, grief blinding her vision. *Tatie! No....*

The escort lowered his voice in sorrow. "We saw the three bodies behind the cottage. There is nothing you can do. We must leave *immediately.* The queen knows that you live. Her knights are hunting for you as we speak." Issylte's heart thumped in her throat.

He withdrew his arms from the hold which had pinned her to his chest. Issylte turned numbly to face the rider from Avalon who towered over her. She raised her face up to him with a blank stare.

A dark felt hat covered most of his face. Like a huntsman himself. Frantically, Issylte raked her eyes over the wooded area behind him. Were the queen's guards in the forest? Where could she run?

"If we are questioned, you are my wife Petra and I am your husband Odrec. We are booking passage to Cornwall from the port of Sligeach."

Before she could respond—or even blink—he lifted her effortlessly onto a horse and leapt up behind her. He motioned to six other riders hidden among the nearby trees. The escort reined his horse and dashed off into the forest, away from the beloved cottage.

Issylte was shivering in the saddle. The rider held her tight, his arms wrapped around her to grip the reins. They thundered through the thick forest towards the setting sun in the west.

Maiwenn is dead? Bran, too? And Dee betrayed us? Too stunned to even cry, her body trembling in shock, Issylte sat numbly before the horseman as they galloped towards the coast.

Suddenly, Odrec raised a fist in warning. The riders

abruptly halted their horses and hid in a thicket as a dozen armed knights went barreling past. The queen's huntsmen. Just like Lords Cian and Bolduc, who'd been ordered to kill her. She remembered the terrifying ordeal in the forest. Cutting out the heart of a stag. And now, a dozen more were hunting her. Like prey. A mouse hunted by swarms of hawks. She shivered uncontrollably as Odrec held her tight.

After a few moments, her escorts continued through the dense forest, towards the village of Sligeach and the sea. Yet, instead of riding directly into the village, Odrec and his men halted near the lake where Issylte had always fished with Maiwenn. At the sight of the beloved Lough Gill where she and *Tatie* had caught so many fish, Issylte sobbed into her hands and moaned from the pit of her stomach.

He spoke gently into her ear. "Princess, we stop here for a moment. I'll be right back."

Odrec dismounted, handing the reins of his horse to one of his men with a nod that said, *"guard the princess."* He whistled—a bird call—and after a moment, received a similar signal in response. Issylte wiped her eyes with a fold of her dress and glanced up to see a man and a woman emerge from the forest on horseback. They approached the escorts and dismounted. Odrec walked over to them, and the three conferred in hushed voices. He returned to Issylte. "My lady, come with me."

He gently pulled her from the horse, his strong hands under her arms, and placed her on the ground. Odrec gestured to one of his men, who dismounted his own horse, and came to Issylte's side. To stand guard. *As if I could run away!* she thought bitterly.

Odrec returned to the couple, and as Issylte watched, the woman removed her cloak, revealing pale blond hair, similar to her own. Issylte examined Odrec, able to see him more clearly now in the setting sun.

He is enormous! Issylte noticed that her escort stood a whole head taller than the lord who was traveling with the blond lady. Odrec's entire body was as huge as an oak—a massive chest, expansive shoulders, and thick, muscular legs. His jawline was square, his neck corded with muscle, his light skin burnished gold from the summer sun.

Under his hat, Odrec's hair was a pale, silvery blond, tied back at the nape of his neck with a leather cord. His features were sharp and angular, like those of a warrior. A bow and a quiver of arrows were on his back, like the other riders in her escort; all were armed with intricately carved swords sheathed in elaborate scabbards as well. Issylte glanced at the six men who accompanied Odrec. All were of the same enormous height and bulk as their leader, but he was the only blond among them.

Her escort returned, carrying the woman's cape over his arm. "Please give me your cloak, Princess. Don this one instead."

As she complied, Odrec gestured to the woman and her companion. "This couple will book passage on a ship to Cornwall, departing with the tide. When the queen's knights discover that a young blond woman wearing your cloak set sail to Britain, her guards will pursue a false path, enabling us to take a different route to Avalon."

Issylte fastened the borrowed cloak. "If we are interrogated, you must say that my name is Odrec, and that you are my wife, Petra, as I instructed. But I want you to know that my true name is Ronan."

He returned to the couple, handing Issylte's dark green cloak to the blond passenger, who spread it across her shoulders. The woman fastened the hood under her chin and covered her light hair. Ronan gave further instructions to the gentleman, who nodded affirmatively as the couple mounted their horses. Ronan waved goodbye and walked back to Issylte as the couple rode off towards the village of Sligeach.

With a quick nod to his men, who mounted their horses in response, Ronan informed Issylte of their plan. "We shall head south, deep into the forest. From there, we ride west to the coast where a small boat will transport us to my ship." He lifted Issylte back into the saddle, then mounted behind her. "The trip to Avalon will take three weeks. Have you ever sailed before?"

Issylte had never left Ireland and had never been on a ship. She shook her head. She was numb and empty inside. Like her heart had left her chest.

"The voyage at sea can be rough. If you are ill, come up from your quarters to the top level of the ship—the deck—and stare out towards the horizon. The fresh air will help." Ronan nudged his horse, and they headed south, with two riders ahead of them, two behind, and one on either side.

Issylte was drowning in grief. She couldn't swallow, her throat was so tight. A suffocating weight squeezed her heart; she couldn't breathe. The pain was too heavy to bear. *Tatie is dead because of me. And Bran and Dee. If I had never come to the cottage, they would all still be alive. It is my fault. Tatie, how can I live without you, too? I've lost my father, Gigi, Luna…and now you? Oh,*

Tatie...

She wept the whole way to the coast—her face blotchy, her eyes nearly swollen shut. Her nose was so congested she had to breathe through her mouth. Her temples were pounding, her muscles twitching. *The queen's men could be anywhere. This time, they'll bring her my head.*

After what seemed like hours riding through the darkening forest, the travelers arrived at a port where several ships were harbored along two docks, near a few wooden buildings and an inn. Ronan and his men stopped their horses at the edge of the forest and dismounted. He helped Issylte to the ground as well. She collapsed in a heap among the leaves.

Ronan emitted another bird call whistle and waited for the return signal. A group of eight woodland creatures short in stature, with dark wizened skin, long black hair, and homespun clothing—*the Little Folk*—emerged from the woods. Conferring quietly with Ronan, the leader of the forest creatures turned to his brethren and motioned for them to approach the riders from Avalon. All six members of Issylte's escort joined Ronan in handing their horses to the woodland creatures, who led the animals quietly away into the forest.

Ronan helped Issylte to her feet. She brushed the leaves off her dress and stood unsteadily. She could barely see, her eyes were so swollen.

"Those men will sell the horses in the neighboring village. The animals are payment for the services they rendered to Maiwenn, to the Lady of the Lake Viviane, and to us, her escort from Avalon."

He took her hand and said gently, "This way, Princess." Ronan led her to the water's edge where a boatman awaited. Issylte's enormous escort seated her on the small vessel, then climbed aboard with his six men, taking up oars. They rowed the boat through a series of tributaries toward the sea-worthy ship that awaited them just offshore.

Issylte and her escorts climbed up the rope ladder from their small boat into the larger vessel which would sail west into the Atlantic Ocean and south to Avalon. As the crew hoisted the small boat onto the deck of the larger one, Ronan gave her a tour of the ship, indicating her quarters below deck. He showed her where the ship's crew would prepare and serve their meals, and where he and the escort from Avalon would be sleeping.

Alone in her cabin, Issylte watched her beloved Ireland disappear in the distance. Wracking sobs choked her; grief blurred her vision. The ship was taking her away from all that she loved.

Oh, Tatie! If it were not for me, you would still be in your beautiful cottage, collecting herbs and tending the animals... The four plump hens and sweet little Florette. A heaviness smothered her.

If I had not come to your cottage—you, Bran and Dee would all still be alive! It is all my fault.

She fell onto her bed, smothering her face in the pillow. How could she help her father now that she was no longer in Ireland? How could she ever see Gigi again? And she would never see *Tatie* again. Ever. She struggled to catch her breath.

The queen now knew she was still alive. She would hunt her down and kill her. Like she'd already tried to do. *Twice.* Issylte shivered, the blood freezing in her veins.

The icy cold hands of her stepmother tingled up her

arms, leeching her strength. The queen would find her. Even in Avalon. Issylte shook with numbing cold.

And, as the strong ocean winds carried the ship across the endless blue sea, Issylte—wracked with sobs, drowning in grief and guilt—wept and retched all the way to Avalon.

Chapter 20

A Powerful Ally

Her long, slender fingers clutched the arms of the velvet tufted throne, extracting every precious drop of regal power from the carved, gilded wood. An elaborate golden crown, encrusted with enormous emeralds, sat atop an equally elegant crown of intricately woven braids of lustrous black tresses coiled upon her royal head. Morag straightened her spine, smoothed the voluminous folds of her deep green silk gown, and raised her imperial chin to reveal her swanlike neck. She glowered at the six royal guards cowering at her feet, dutifully awaiting the fatal judgement of the livid, scowling queen.

"You have failed in your duty. Because of your incompetence, the prisoner has escaped. You scoured every inch of the Hazelwood Forest. *Where is she?*"

The captain of the guards, his head bowed, replied solemnly. "A young blond woman in a deep green cloak was seen with a male escort in village of Sligeach. They booked passage to Cornwall from the inn at the seaport. The vessel departed three days ago, my queen."

She flashed a furious glance at Lord Voldurk, silent in his black silken robes at her side. His dragon eyes glowed in the golden light.

"And Lords Cian and Bolduc?" Her eyes sliced like a blade across the lowered heads humbled before the wooden dais.

"There is no trace yet, my queen. But our soldiers are hunting them. The traitors will be found."

"And you will bring me their heads. Or I shall have yours." Morag hissed, her lethal stare fixed upon the captain of her royal guards.

"Yes, my queen. As you command."

The guards quickly rose to their full impressive height, bowing graciously before the glacial queen. Turning as one, they exited the throne room with military precision, the clatter of metal swords against the gleaming chain mail armor, glinting in the morning sun.

Morag's frosty voice gusted through the vacant throne room. "Bring wine, with a platter of cheese and fresh fruit to my royal chambers. At once."

Four meek attendants scurried from the room like frightened squirrels. Morag addressed her Royal Advisor, her voice iced with anger. "Lord Voldurk, come with me. I am in need of your sage counsel."

****

Morag stared out the window beneath her mauve velvet draperies, gazing at the courtyard where Lord Liam had so often ridden the dappled gray mare. *A sight I no longer have to endure,* she sighed inwardly. Now that her husband was weakened by violent purgings and frequent bloodlettings, his strength sapped by merciless, insatiable leeches—he could no longer watch the Master of Horse ride the palfrey from his bedroom window. The king could no longer stand, let alone rule. Thanks to her husband's royal physician, who now stood at her bedroom table, pouring two silver goblets of rich ruby wine.

Yes, she'd gotten rid of the damned horse, Morag

199

thought bitterly, as she turned to face the dark wizard and drained the proffered chalice. But her stepdaughter still posed an intolerable threat to her tenuous hold on the Irish crown. A hold Morag intended to solidify with the powerful ally in silken black robes whose golden eyes glowed deeply into hers.

"My stepdaughter is still *alive.* I cannot fathom it. For years, I believed her dead. Those guards—who happened to pass through that village blacksmith shop one day—received the report that the princess had been hiding in the Hazelwood Forest all these years. Living with that damned witch!"

Morag hurled her empty goblet across the room to clatter against the white limestone wall. The grating sound of metal scraped on the tile as it rolled over the cold, hard floor.

Voldurk removed his black robe and draped it across one of the two chairs tucked under the lace covered table. His long dark hair touched the wide shoulders of the black velvet tunic she longed to touch. She raked appreciative eyes over his lithe, powerful form, the dark breeches clinging to the tight muscles of his long, lean legs. Sensing her attention, he gazed at her with sultry, golden eyes. The blazing eyes of a dragon, enflaming her frozen veins.

He placed his goblet upon the table and sauntered toward her, his towering presence comforting as he wrapped her into a strong embrace. He lowered his full, warm lips to her bare shoulder, his tantalizing tongue teasing her pale, frosty skin. A ripple of pleasure shivered through her as she leaned back into his hold and exposed her swanlike neck.

He kissed her pale throat softly, the trail of his lips

weakening her quivering legs. Yet, instead of the bed, as she had hoped, he led her to the table, where he sat her down upon the lush velvet chair, refilling his own goblet and handing it to her.

"Drink, my queen. It will abate your anger, and warm you to the idea I wish to propose."

He walked across the room and retrieved the chalice from the floor, wiping it with a napkin from the platter of fruit. As he filled the goblet and drank deeply, his eyes locked with hers. Morag swooned in the golden, glowing pools.

"I wish to sail to Cornwall, my queen," he said cautiously, pulling his chair up beside hers as he lowered himself to her side. "For there is someone I wish to meet. A powerful ally to aid in our quest."

Morag raised an eyebrow, sipping her delicious wine. Intrigued, she tingled with anticipation.

"The dwarf Frocin, my queen. A wealthy baron who lives in the dark Forest of Morois, on the outskirts of Cornwall. An *otherworldly* creature with a most unique power of clairvoyance."

He grinned slyly at Morag, sending a thrill up her spine. "Frocin can not only read the stars and see the future. He also has the extraordinary ability to track the gift of *sight.*"

Voldurk knelt at her feet and took her hand, warming her icy fingers with his wicked lips. Her breath hitched at his touch.

"Like you, my queen, I believed the princess dead." His golden eyes bore into hers. "Once, as I covered the king with leeches to suction his blood, I sensed someone watching. A presence, an aura of power. The deep green eyes of a young blond woman observing me, transfixed with terror. I had no idea who she was. Until we received the report that the princess still lived." He rose, peered down at her, the golden gleam of challenge in his serpentine eyes.

"Princess Issylte has the gift of *sight*—a form of magic that leaves a telltale trace whenever it is used. A trail that Frocin, with his clairvoyance, can track for us." He pulled Morag to her feet, his eyes glowing like embers. "Frocin will follow the verdant trail of her magic. He'll find her for us. And his merciless mercenary knights will eliminate the sole threat to your throne." He raised her chilled fingers to his fiery lips. She shivered with sensual delight.

"May I have your leave, my queen, that I may sail to Cornwall? To garner the alliance of the dwarf Frocin?"

Morag raised her eyes to his, a sultry smile spreading across her face. "Yes, my loyal Royal Advisor. Obtain this powerful ally. And return quickly to your most grateful queen." She pursed her luscious lips into a provocative pout, tantalizing him with the tip of her dainty tongue as she tasted the rich, ruby red wine.

His snakelike eyes devoured her as he roughly pushed the lacy sleeves from her shoulders to expose her bare breasts. Morag moaned as his molten lips assaulted them, his tongue a flickering flame melting her like a wax candle. He led her at last to the bed, unlaced her corset, and grinned wickedly as her dress fell in a puddle of silk at her feet. He laid her back upon the bed, deftly removed his tunic and breeches, hovering over her, his serpentine eyes blazing with golden desire. Morag wrapped her slender legs around his hips and pulled her dragon deep inside, engulfing them both in flames.

Chapter 21

The Tribe of Dana

The acrid smoke stung Tristan's eyes. The corpses
of the dwarf's men crackled as the flames consumed
them in the courtyard of Castle Landuc. They'd already
buried their fallen, in a ceremony of tribute amidst the
sacred stones in the heart of the forest of Brocéliande.
And now, as the flames of the pyres diminished into
embers, and the remaining knights were departing for *la
Joyeuse Garde*, Tristan followed Lancelot and Esclados
back into the castle. Tonight, he would be inducted into
the Tribe of Dana. His blood pulsed with adrenaline.

In the banquet room, the deep undertone of male
voices and the clatter of metal goblets filled the air,
perfumed by the delicious scent of sizzling ham and
freshly baked bread. The warriors of the Tribe of Dana,
seated at several rectangular wooden trestle tables, were
finishing up their meal as Tristan and Esclados sat at a
table to join them. Servants soon brought them a platter
of meat, porridge, bread and ale, which the two men
devoured with relish. As Tristan wiped the grease from
his mouth, a contented grin across his healing face,
Lancelot approached the table, accompanied by a young
priestess with astonishing amethyst-colored eyes.
Lancelot flashed Tristan a mischievous look, delight
dancing in his brilliant blue eyes.

Tristan smiled at the priestess. She was tall and lithe, with sleek black hair that cascaded to her hips. The long, flowing sleeves of her deep blue robe nearly touched the floor and rustled with her movements like gentle wings. Her alabaster skin glowed softly, the green notes of fragrant herbs emanating from her like the scent of the sacred forest. She smiled discreetly at Tristan and pushed a lock of hair from her lovely face with long graceful fingers. He noticed that she bore the emblem of the Tribe of Dana inside her right wrist.

"This is Nolwenn," Lancelot positively purred, presenting the beauty to Tristan. He rose to his feet and bent his head to kiss her proffered hand.

"She is the priestesses who tattoos the sacred emblem inside the wrist of each member of our Tribe. The first step in initiation." The White Knight of Avalon smiled at Nolwenn, who observed Lancelot with her striking violet eyes.

"When she has finished your tattoo, she'll escort you to the Fountain of Barenton, where the Red Knight summoned the storm. That's where we'll conclude the initiation ceremony." Lancelot grinned at Tristan, his enthusiasm contagious. "Esclados—the Lord of the Fountain—will bestow upon you an extraordinary gift. To show his gratitude for saving Laudine."

Lancelot nodded to the skilled artist beside him, then said with a sly grin, "Go with her now. So that she can mark you as one of our own."

Nolwenn took Tristan by the hand, leading him away from the banquet room, down a long hall, into a chamber where two enormous windows bathed the room in summer sunlight. Diaphanous white curtains rustled in the gentle breeze, wafting the crisp, clean scent of tangy herbs throughout the immaculate room.

Between the windows lay a flat stone table, draped with a long, white cloth. Two smaller tables flanked the center one, each topped with a white cloth and displaying an assortment of tools, a small bowl with green liquid, and several small vials. Tristan observed a pitcher of water, a basin, and a chalice on a table against the wall, where a lit candle emitted a soothing fragrance of sage.

Nolwenn closed the door to the chamber behind her. She approached Tristan and said in a melodic voice, "Please remove your tunic and lay on your back upon the long table. Relax your arms at your sides, and place your right wrist so that it faces up." She turned to prepare her tools as Tristan complied.

Once he was inclined on the table, Nolwenn removed her blue robe, revealing a thin white chemise. Tristan saw the outline of her small breasts and narrow hips. Her arms were long and lean, yet sculpted and muscular, and she moved with the grace and agility of a warrior. She deftly plaited her long hair in one thick braid down her back, tying it with a strand of leather cord. She placed her folded robe on the side table near the pitcher and poured some water into the basin. She washed her hands with a fragrant soap that delighted Tristan's senses, drying them with the white cloth. She returned to Tristan. He quivered in her aromatic presence.

Nolwenn opened one of the vials and poured a couple drops of scented oil onto his inner wrist. With her long slender hands, she massaged it gently. "The herbs in this oil will cleanse your skin and ease the sting of the needles." Spotting the gouge on his face from the dwarf's blade, she gently rubbed some of the oil onto his cheek with delicate fingertips. "The herbs will help this wound heal and prevent it from festering," she said softly. He inhaled the clean herbal fragrance of her glistening skin.

She gestured to the bowl on the table beside her. "The green liquid you see is a mixture I have prepared from the sacred herbs and plants of the forest. This water is from the sacred fountain that you fought to defend."

Nolwenn fixed Tristan with her amethyst eyes, her soft voice filled with reverence. "This emblem will mark you as a member of our Tribe. Sworn to defend the sacred elements of the Goddess Dana."

As she massaged more oil onto his wrist, she gazed at his broad chest, lingering on the dark hair, following the trail down his taut abdomen, past his navel. His body stirred at her attention, her touch, her closeness, her scent. Pulling a stool up to the table, she sat down beside him, and for the next three hours, marked Tristan with her artistry and skill.

"The trilogy of this symbol," she explained as she began her work, "represents the three sacred elements of the Goddess, which the warriors of our Tribe defend." She gently dabbed at the green liquid on his wrist. "The three branches of this emblem—which I carve upon your sword hand—curve downward into a swirl, signifying the arm and protective hand of the warrior."

Nolwenn's voice was soothing and melodic, captivating him with the secrets of her art. "This first arm represents the sacred *forest*, such as our beloved *Brocéliande*, but many others as well. Even as far north as the enchanted Hazelwood Forest of Ireland." Tristan watched her meticulously puncture his skin with the needle and green dye, admiring the sheen of her black hair in the warm afternoon sun.

When she completed the first arm of the emblem, Nolwenn continued her story as she began the next. "This second branch represents the sacred element of *water*, such as the Fountain of Barenton that you defended with prowess and valor. It also symbolizes all the waters of the Goddess Dana, such as *le Miroir aux Fées*—the Mirror of the Fairies. A sacred, mirrored lake in the heart of *Brocéliande*."

Nolwenn gently wiped his wrist and examined her work. "Le *Miroir aux Fées* lies in the enchanted woods, near the Château of Comper, the crystal castle of the fairy Viviane. She is the Lady of the Lake, the enchantress who raised Sir Lancelot, one of the leaders of our Tribe."

The priestess dabbed his skin again with the white cloth, applied a few drops of the herbal tincture, and regaled Tristan with more of her enchanting tale. "The waters of the sacred fountain protect our Tribe. The sacred spring of Édern promotes fertility among our women. And *la Fontaine de Jouvence*—the Fountain of Youth—bestows an extraordinarily long life to Druids such as Merlin and Odin." She gazed deeply into his eyes, the wisdom of ages glowing in their amethyst depths.

Tristan lay expectantly on the table, watching this dark-haired beauty with intoxicating eyes grace his arm with precision and skill. Marking him as one of the Tribe. His body was taught as a bow, an arrow nocked in its string. Nolwenn advanced to the third branch of his tattoo. "The final arm shelters the third sacred element— *stone*."

Her deep purple eyes held Tristan's rapt gaze. "The *menhirs* and *dolmens* where the Druids perform their sacred ceremonies are found throughout our realm. Some are holy burial sites, such as *le Tombeau des Géants*, where today we honored the knights who had fallen, defending our sacred fountain."

She blotted the green ink from Tristan's arm and added more drops of the soothing tincture. Her melodic voice lulled him as she massaged his burning wrist. Her touch sent tingles up his arm which rippled through his body, her touch as intoxicating as her enchanting tales.

"Some of the sacred stones are portals to the *Otherworld*, such as those in the *Hôtié de Viviane,* where the Lady of the Lake seeks celestial wisdom. And the *Menhirs de Monteneuf,* the universal portal of the Druids."

Her artwork complete, Nolwenn concluded Tristan's lesson on the significance of the emblem which now marked him as a member of the Tribe of Dana. "The sacred element of stone includes not only the megaliths that serve as sacred burial grounds or portals to the *otherworld*." She massaged his wrist and forearm with an aromatic oil that was both soothing and stimulating. His skin tingled under her skilled fingers. She smiled up at him with her astonishing amethyst eyes.

"The sacred element of stone also includes the treasures of the mineral world. The crystals and gemstones—amethyst, emerald and moonstone—which channel the energy of the earth. The divine power of the Goddess herself. Into our hearts, minds, spirits. And bodies." Her touch was igniting Tristan's skin.

Nolwenn, seemingly satisfied with the emblem she'd engraved upon his wrist, placed her needle on the table and retrieved a different vial. She poured a few drops onto Tristan's wrist, massaged the essential oil into his arm with her gentle touch. The clean scent of sage filled his nostrils as she wiped her hands on the white cloth from the nearby table.

Tristan sat up and examined the amazing artwork on his skin. It was truly magnificent. Nolwenn turned to face him, withdrawing from under her chemise a silver necklace with an intricately scrolled bezel cradling a large, brilliant amethyst stone. The same deep purple hue as her exquisite eyes.

She walked close enough to Tristan so that her shoulder touched his as she showed him the extraordinary jewel. "Many gemstones are protective talismans, like this one. Amethyst is my sacred stone. It helps me to convey relaxation and to cleanse negativity as I create my art." She took Tristan's hand and laid the brilliant purple gemstone in his palm. Her breasts touched the side of his arm, sending a shiver of pleasure washing through him.

"Amethyst helps me imbue the protection of the Goddess as I mark the new members of Her Tribe." Tristan admired the incredible gem and gently placed the talisman back against her chemise. His fingers longed to stroke her skin underneath.

Nolwenn massaged a bit more oil into his skin. He inhaled the herbal essence of her fragrant skin and hair. She added a few more drops into her hand and rubbed her palms together. She massaged his wrist, moving up his arm to his bicep, which she gave extra attention with firm, skilled hands. His shoulders relaxed under her touch, working magic up his neck and down his back, across his other arm, concentrating on his knotted bicep. Nolwenn finished with a delicate massage of his hands, leaving every part of his body tingling and alive. Her

209

sacred amethyst stone had indeed channeled relaxation and contentment into his spirit, but his awakened body longed for more.

Nolwenn gestured to Tristan's ring. The gift from his uncle Marke when he was dubbed the Blue Knight of Cornwall. The eye of the sea raven glinted in the sun. "Blue topaz is also a sacred stone, like the amethyst I wear."

She lifted Tristan's hand and stroked the glittering gemstone with her thumb. "It stimulates self-confidence and courage. It connects us to the divine spirit of the Goddess." Her skilled fingers touched the blue gem, stroking the *chough,* admiring the intricate details of the royal bird of Cornwall.

"Blue topaz connects us to the sacred element of water. Like this sea raven." She dazzled Tristan with a glorious smile. "And you, the Blue Knight of Cornwall, defended the divine fountain of the Goddess Dana. Blue topaz is indeed your sacred stone. And water is your sacred element."

He lost himself in the depths of her amethyst eyes.

"I am certain that is why Esclados, Lord of the Fountain of Barenton, intends to bestow a precious gift upon you at the ceremony tonight." She lowered her eyes and smiled softly. His heart sank as she released his very warm hand.

"You must be hungry after spending several hours in here. We'll eat a light meal that the servants have prepared for us in the alcove by the kitchen. After that, I'll lead you to the clearing at the sacred spring, where the others await. To induct you into our Tribe." Nolwenn handed him his tunic with a soft smile. Her violet eyes sparkled with anticipation. "Please put this on and come with me."

As Tristan dressed, Nolwenn unbraided her long hair and shook out the rich, dark tresses. She adjusted her blue robe with the long, fairy-like sleeves, placing her talisman underneath, close to her heart. The alluring artist cleansed her tools and replaced the stoppers in the vials, verifying that everything was in order. She turned back to face Tristan and flashed him a bright smile. His breath caught in his throat.

Taking him by the hand, she led him to the kitchen alcove, where they ate a light meal of an *omelette aux fines herbes* and fresh summer fruit. The pungent burst of basil and tarragon and the juicy sweetness of strawberries delighted his palate. He and Nolwenn washed everything down with rich, earthy wine, then exited the *château* into the front courtyard, where two awaiting grooms brought forth their saddled horses. He watched her effortlessly glide into the saddle, the warrior priestess of Dana whose touch still lingered upon his alert body. He mounted his own horse and followed Nolwenn as she rode off into the forest to join the members of the Tribe of Dana.

When they arrived at the clearing, the muffled roar of the fountain bubbled in the underground well where Esclados had summoned the storm. The dark, enchanted forest of *Brocéliande*, embalmed with the crisp scent of pine and the earthy richness of decaying leaves, sheltered the sacred spring in the verdant, protective embrace of the Goddess.

Encircled by smooth stones, the flickering flames of a small campfire danced and crackled in the darkening twilight. Stars were just beginning to twinkle in the sky, and the crescent moon smiled down upon the sacred ceremony which would welcome Tristan into the Goddess Tribe.

Tristan recognized many familiar faces seated around the circle of stones, where acrid smoke from the campfire emitted the heady scent of burning herbs. Kirus, leader of the Tribe, with his brutally scarred face. Dagur, his black beard and bushy hair reminiscent of a cave bear. Solzic, whose blond hair gleamed golden in the firelight. Lancelot raised his head, his twinkling eyes shining with brotherhood and pride as he flashed him a hearty, boyish grin. Tristan's body thrummed, his heart thumping in his throat.

Nolwenn and Tristan dismounted, and two members of the Tribe came forth to take the horses. They led the animals to an area where others grazed, tied to nearby trees.

Esclados greeted Tristan, and Nolwenn went to sit among the warriors and priestesses gathered around the fire. The Lord of the Fountain motioned for Tristan to come forward and face the Tribe as he addressed the group.

"Members of the Tribe of Dana, we meet tonight to induct a new member." Esclados grinned at Tristan, nodding his head in approval. "Sir Tristan of Lyonesse. The Blue Knight of Cornwall, heir to King Marke of Tintagel."

The warriors and priestesses smiled among themselves, the murmurs of their hushed voices carrying words of praise and acknowledgement to Tristan's heightened ears. He took in the eager faces of the heads nodding in approval as the Tribe smiled upon him, welcoming him as one of their own.

"Sir Tristan, you have been invited to join our Tribe.

In recognition for your courage in defending the sacred Fountain of Barenton." Esclados gestured to the well behind him, the sacred spring where he had summoned the storm.

The Red Knight turned to face him, his commanding voice reverberating across the campfire. "Kneel before the sacred Fountain of Barenton. At the base of the sacred stone of Merlin. In the heart of the sacred forest of *Brocéliande*."

Tristan knelt, bowing his head in reverence. Every muscle in his body was tightly coiled, ready to leap. Sweat dampened his trembling palms.

"Place your right fist upon your heart. Raise your left hand and swear your oath of fealty to the Goddess Dana."

The baritone voice of the Red Knight bellowed through the sacred forest. "Do you, Sir Tristan of Lyonesse, the Blue Knight of Cornwall, solemnly swear to defend the sacred elements of the earth, the magic of the Celtic Druids, and the divine power of the Goddess Dana?"

Tristan's mouth was parched, his muscles quivering. From the depths of his pounding heart, his deep voice rang out clear and strong. "I do so solemnly swear."

Esclados turned to the sacred pine tree and removed the golden basin, which he filled with water from the sacred spring. He carried a silver chalice to Tristan, still kneeling before the Fountain of Barenton. The Red Knight poured the water into the goblet and handed it to Tristan.

"Drink, Sir Tristan. May the water of the holy fountain you defended nourish your body. And grant you the sacred protection of the Goddess."

Tristan drank deeply from the goblet. Esclados, Lord of the Sacred Spring, pronounced, "Welcome to the Tribe of Dana, Sir Tristan of Lyonesse. The Blue Knight of Cornwall."

Esclados took the chalice from Tristan and placed it—and the golden basin—on top of the sacred stone. The members of the Tribe seated around the fire cheered heartily amid cries of "Welcome to the Tribe of Dana!"

Tristan, beaming with pride, thrumming with adrenaline, noticed a Druid—with long white hair and an equally long white beard—emerge barefoot from the forest. He wore the white robes of a priest, and carried in his arms a parcel, carefully wrapped in white cloth, which he reverently placed atop the flat surface of the sacred stone where Esclados had summoned the storm.

The Druid took the golden basin to the fountain, withdrew water from the sacred spring, and washed his hands, which he dried with a white cloth. Next, he refilled the basin, carried it to the flat stone, and placed it beside the silver goblet.

He cautiously unwrapped the white cloth of the parcel he had carried, revealing an unusual plant. From his robe he withdrew a small vial, which he placed beside the basin, followed by a golden sickle, with which he meticulously carved a small section of the plant, placing it in the silver goblet. Tristan saw the Druid's lips move, as if murmuring an incantation. He placed three drops from the vial and a small amount of the sacred water from the spring, pouring it into the chalice from the golden basin. The Druid lifted the goblet from the stone, cradling it in his hands, while he made three revolutions around the sacred fountain and stone, his head bent as if in prayer, wguspering incantations as he walked. When he completed his ritual, the Druid walked to Tristan, who still knelt before the spring, and spoke in a voice wizened by age and knowledge.

"Tristan of Lyonesse, Blue Knight of Cornwall, I have been requested by Sir Esclados, the Lord of the Fountain of Barenton, to bestow upon you a most prestigious gift of Druidic magic." The solemnity of the Druid's words rang like a heavy *bourdon* bell across the sacred forest.

"Lord Esclados has chosen the gift of *l'herbe d'or* —the golden herb—to express his gratitude for the safe deliverance of his beloved wife Laudine, the Lady of the Fountain." Tristan, still kneeling before the sacred spring, searched the crinkled eyes of the ancient Druid. A thrum of power and mystery radiated from the bent, wizened frame.

The Druid handed Tristan the goblet. He accepted the silver chalice with damp palms and shaking hands.

"The golden herb will grant you the means of communication with certain creatures of the Goddess." The archdruid fixed Tristan with sage eyes, his face withered by wisdom of the ages.

"You will be able to communicate wordlessly with birds, dogs, and wolves. Command them with your thoughts. Understand messages which they convey to you." The Druid motioned for Tristan to drink.

Tristan raised the goblet to his lips. "Drink this sacred brew, the gift of Druidic magic from the Lord of the Spring. May this divine blessing of the Goddess Dana protect you, valiant warrior of Her Tribe, as you defend the sacred elements of the Celtic realm."

Tristan consumed the bitter draft, which burned his throat like liquid fire as he gulped it down. He returned the chalice to the Druid, who replaced it on the flat stone. The priest returned the golden basin to the branch of the tall pine tree next to the well. He carefully rewrapped the plant in white cloth, which he carried in his arms like a great treasure as he nodded to the Red Knight and departed into the forest as mysteriously as he had arrived.

Esclados helped Tristan to his feet, turning him to face the Tribe as he shouted, "Welcome to the Tribe of Dana!" As cheers erupted from the Tribe, Nolwenn rose from the group and approached Tristan, a sparkle of delight in her brilliant amethyst eyes.

"Go with Nolwenn," the Red Knight instructed, "to conclude the initiation ceremony."

Tristan's breath caught as the dark-haired beauty took him by the hand. She led him away from the campfire, deeper into the sacred forest. They arrived at a clearing where a rapid stream flowed across large smooth stones into a gurgling, effervescent pool. Moonlight sparkled in the bubbling water as it cascaded over the rocks, the brilliant gems of a glorious, natural necklace of the Earth Goddess Dana.

Surrounded by dense woods, the clearing was carpeted with thick, soft moss, lulled by the music of the bubbling stream splashing into the deep pool. Stars winked in the night sky; the distant hoot of an owl rang out in the dark. Wings of a sea raven fluttered in Tristan's chest.

To the right of the mossy clearing lay several large stones which formed a protective border. Nolwenn reached under her long blue robe and removed a white cloth, which she spread over the soft forest floor. Retrieving a vial and cup from the pocket of her robe, she placed them on a nearby flat stone.

Tristan stood still, breathless with anticipation, watching Nolwenn take the cup to the bubbling pool. Beckoning him to join her, she said, "Come, see the waters of this sacred spring." He walked over to her as she knelt by the stream, pointing to the effervescence. "The bubbles flow from the center of the earth and nourish us with precious minerals." She filled the cup, rose to her feet, and handed it to him, moonlight reflecting in her luminous eyes. "Let us drink this gift from the Goddess as we conclude your initiation into Her Tribe."

As he drank, the bubbles bursting in his mouth, Tristan delighted in the rich, earthy taste of the pure spring water. He returned the cup to Nolwenn, who drank from the spring and smiled up at him. "I am the physical embodiment of the Goddess, who welcomes you tonight into Her Tribe."

She raised up on her tiptoes to reach him, placing a soft kiss upon his eager lips. Liquid fire flowed in his veins. Nolwenn removed his tunic slowly and, leading him to a flat stone, unbuckled his sword and placed it carefully on the ground.

Next, she gently sat him down on the flat surface of the rock and removed his boots, massaging his feet with capable hands. Reaching for the small vial, she poured a few drops of oil onto her fingertips, knelt beside him, and gently cleansed the wound on his cheek. The clean scent of sage floated in the night air.

"The herbs in this oil will soothe your skin and promote healing," she murmured into the shell of his ear as she stroked his face. Tristan breathed in the scent of her—green and earthy, like the forest itself—as she touched his cheek softly. He stared at the silkiness of her black hair, watching as she gently massaged his inner wrist with fragrant oil. She rose to her feet and placed the vial on top of the flat stone. Taking his hand, she led him to the white cloth which she had spread upon the moss. Kneeling beside the cloth, she patted the ground and smiled up at him softly, beckoning him to lie down upon it.

Once he was reclined on the moss, Nolwenn rose to her feet and walked over to fetch the silver cup, which she refilled in the bubbling spring. Placing her fingers inside the chalice, she cast droplets of the sacred water as she walked in a wide circle around the clearing. She seemed to murmur an incantation, casting a spell of enchantment around the entire area, including the freshwater spring. Tristan watched in amazement as a shroud of mist arose from the droplets, encircling them with protective magic. She took a handful of small gemstones from the pockets of her robe and, murmuring softly, placed them on the ground inside the mist which encircled the clearing.

When she finished, Nolwenn explained to Tristan, "I have cast a triple layer of enchantment for us, with the sacred water of the spring and the sacred stones, here in the heart of the sacred forest. The Goddess will protect us as I welcome you into Her Tribe."

Nolwenn turned to face Tristan, locking his eyes with her own, as she removed her blue robe, folding it gently and placing it on the stone next to the vial. She lifted her chemise above her head, removed the amethyst talisman from her neck, and placed both beside her gown upon the stone.

She stood magnificently nude before him. Tristan drank in the beauty of her lithe body—her small breasts, long limbs, toned muscles and narrow hips. Her dark hair cascaded down past her waist, framing her face with black silk. He trembled as his eyes rove over the length of her, taking in every detail, finally resting on the dark hair between her legs. His body strained painfully against his breeches.

Seeming to sense his discomfort, Nolwenn knelt beside him and released him from the confines of his clothing, leaving him naked on the white cloth. Her hair brushed his arm as she leaned over him, her appreciative eyes raking over every inch of his warrior's body. He wanted to jump out of his skin.

"You, Sir Tristan of Lyonesse, the Blue Knight of Cornwall, have fought courageously to defend the sacred elements of the Goddess." Nolwenn kissed his face, his neck and chest, her warm lips igniting a fire beneath his skin. When she finally tasted his lips, he groaned softly.

"And I, priestess of the Goddess Dana, wish to express Her gratitude. And welcome you into Her Tribe."

Her soft mouth caressed his lips, parting them with the tip of her tongue. She sucked his lips and kissed his neck, straddling him with her lean thighs. Tristan moaned, his body straining to reach hers as she kept her hips elevated above him. She placed a nipple playfully in front of his lips, which he swallowed into his mouth, delighting in her soft moan.

He reached for her hips, lowering her onto him, aching to find the entrance he sought. Instead, she guided his hand between her thighs, driving him wild with the wetness he found as he stroked the delicate skin.

Finally, when he could no longer bear it, Nolwenn welcomed him into her body, plunging down onto him, enveloping him with her plush, silky warmth. She rose rhythmically up and down, stroking his body with her own, her lips seeking his with passion and fire. He gripped her hips tightly, pulling her down roughly onto him and thrusting deep. Her moans of pleasure intensified his own.

Nolwenn slumped forward, convulsing, the rhythmic contractions of her release clamping him tightly within her. Tristan grasped her hips and thrust hard, erupting with pleasure as he filled her depths with his abundant seed.

He lay quivering, panting, sweaty and breathless. Nolwenn kissed him and murmured against his lips. "Welcome to the Tribe of Dana, Sir Tristan." Disengaging her thighs, she lay down beside him, placing her head against his chest as he wrapped his arms around her in a protective embrace. His body sated, his spirit content, Tristan fell asleep cradled in the arms of the Goddess, the roar of the bubbling stream Her soothing lullaby.

When he awoke, several hours later, the light of dawn and the fresh green scent of pine greeted him. Nolwenn was gone, along with her blue robe, vials of oil, and silver cup. Tristan sat up, noticing that the enchanted mist still enshrouded the clearing. After seeing to his needs, he washed away the lingering traces of Nolwenn's welcome, smiling and feeling his body respond to the memory. *If only she were still here. I would love another welcome*, he mused greedily.

He donned his clothes and strapped on his sword, shaking out the white cloth which belonged to the dark-haired beauty who had embodied the Goddess Dana last night. He folded it carefully and retrieved the crystals she had placed on the ground around them. He tucked them into his pocket, grinning at the chance to see her again when he returned them. Strolling over to the bubbling spring, he cupped his hand and quenched his thirst. The rich taste of minerals rolled over his tongue; the effervescence tickled his nose. As Tristan strode away from the clearing, the mist dissipated, revealing the mossy bed that he had shared with the goddess Nolwenn in the sacred forest of *Brocéliande.*

When he arrived at the campsite, the fire had been extinguished and several members of the Tribe were sleeping on bedrolls nearby. Lancelot emerged from the woods, grinning from ear to ear. "The welcome is without a doubt the best part of the initiation ceremony, wouldn't you agree?"

Tristan raised his face to the sky, closed his eyes, and moaned with pleasure. "Without a doubt."

Lancelot slapped him on the shoulder and laughed deeply. "Water the horses in the stream while I wake the Tribe. We'll head back to Landuc, break our fast, and return to *la Joyeuse Garde.* We'll arrive late this afternoon." He paused to face Tristan, his eyes sparkling in the early morning light. "She's indeed a beauty, isn't she?" Tristan answered with a bright, expansive smile, his entire being alight with pleasure. The glittering eye of the sea raven winked on his left hand.

They rode through the verdant forest back to the imposing castle of Landuc. The members of the Tribe of Dana were loading up their horses, preparing to depart, bidding goodbye to the Lord and Lady of the Fountain. Kirus, Dagur, and Solzic welcomed Tristan once again, turning to say fond farewells to the brotherhood of the Tribe. Esclados and Laudine thanked Tristan for defending the sacred spring and slaying the wretched dwarf who had attacked the *château*.

"It was a great honor to fight by your side, Tristan," Esclados said as he shook the knight's hand. "May the gift of *l'herbe d'or* grant you the protection of the sacred spring. May the Goddess Dana bless your return to *La Joyeuse Garde*. And your voyage across the sea, all the way back to Britain."

After he and Lancelot bid *adieu* to Esclados and Laudine, Tristan spotted Nolwenn standing near the door, as if waiting to say goodbye. He fetched the white cloth from the tabletop where he'd placed it and removed the stones from his pockets. His heart thumping wildly, Tristan strolled briskly across the room toward the lovely priestess. She smiled at him, her alluring amethyst eyes glowing like the magnificent amulet gleaming upon her breast. He swallowed a huge lump in his throat.

"I brought these back for you," Tristan whispered, handing her the cloth and the gemstones.

"Thank you," she hummed. She raised her beautiful eyes to his, dazzling him with violet light. "May the Goddess grant you a safe return home."

She rose to kiss him softly on the lips. Tristan inhaled her fresh herbal scent, his body responding at once. Nolwenn smiled gently and walked away. Tristan watched the sway of her slender hips, the train of her deep blue robe softly brushing the cold tiled floor. Lancelot approached, with a smirk on his face. He joked, barely able to restrain from laughing. "Will you be able to ride, Tristan?"

Tristan grinned, adjusting his breeches. "Give me a few moments, and I'll be fine." Unable to contain his mirth, the First Knight of Camelot burst out laughing and slapped Tristan on the back. Nolwenn smiled as the two knights went into the courtyard and mounted their horses. As they rode away, Nolwenn blew him a kiss farewell. Tristan flashed her his most dazzling smile.

Accompanied by Lancelot and his loyal knights, Tristan rode southwest through the forest of *Brocéliande,* back to the castle of *La Joyeuse Garde*. The rich scent of the forest reminded him of Nolwenn's exquisite embrace, welcoming him to the Tribe of Dana. *Lancelot was right,* he mused. *A woman's body does indeed transport you to the stars!*

Chapter 22

The Island of Healing

Ronan's crew anchored their sea-worthy ship at a wooden dock along a curved outcrop of craggy coast which jutted into the choppy sea. Issylte now sat in a small boat, headed towards an island enshrouded in mists. Her Avalonian escorts rowed toward the shore, where the princess glimpsed a sandy beach sheltered by the rocky coastline, with dense forests visible in the distance through the hazy sky. Sea gulls squawked amongst the clouds, the salty air was crisp and fresh, and the summer sun was warm upon her grief-ravaged face.

The flat bottom of their boat slid easily onto the sand, and as Ronan jumped out of the vessel to help Issylte onto land, they were met by a woman with long black hair streaked with silver, adorned in a white, gracefully flowing robe with gossamer sleeves. She wore an intricately scrolled silver necklace where three large white stones glimmered in the sunlight at the base of her throat. Beside her stood two other women, dressed in similar robes, but of a deep blue; they were flanked by four enormous men, armed with swords at their waists and bows and arrows strapped to their broad backs. The woman in white was smiling, as if to welcome Issylte to Avalon.

Ronan stood on the sandy beach before the woman

in white. He removed his hat, inclined his silvery blond head, and placed his right arm across his stomach as he bowed in homage. "My lady, I have returned safely with the princess, at your request."

Now that his head was bare, Issylte could see that Ronan's ears were long and pointed, like the other members of her escort, who had also removed their hats in deference to the woman in white. All of the Elves who had escorted her from Ireland were broad as oaks and tall as pines. They exuded an aura of power that thrummed in Issylte's veins. *They are otherworldly, like the Little Folk. But, while the woodland creatures are small, the Elves of Avalon are enormous!*

The Elven oarsmen carried the small boat up a path from the beach to a forested ledge where they stored it in a wooden cabin. Ronan turned to introduce Issylte to the woman in white. "Princess, may I present Viviane, the Lady of the Lake, High Priestess of Avalon."

Viviane approached Issylte and said warmly, "Welcome, dear Princess." She took Issylte's two hands in her own and smiled sadly. "Our beloved Maiwenn would be most pleased to learn that you'd arrived safely to Avalon."

At the mention of *Tatie's* name, Issylte lowered her face in grief. Viviane murmured, "You will be safe here. Far from the reach of the wicked queen."

She glanced up. Affection and concern shone in Viviane's sparkling eyes, the same deep blue as the Narrow Sea which had brought Issylte to Avalon. *She, too, is sheltering me from my cruel stepmother. Just as Tatie did in the Hazelwood Forest so many years ago.* Issylte swallowed the enormous lump in her throat.

The Lady of the Lake gestured to the women in blue

225

who were standing just behind her on the shoreline. "May I present two of my priestesses. This is Nyda," she said, as a small woman with long, light brown hair and twinkling hazel eyes came forward to take Issylte's hand. "And this is Cléo," Viviane continued, as the taller brunette priestess with expressive brown eyes greeted her with a kind smile.

Viviane's expression became solemn. "Maiwenn sent you to Avalon for your protection. We must adopt a new name to keep your identity secret. So that the queen will never learn you are here." Viviane stared pensively at the wild, savage ocean. White froth sprayed high into the air as choppy waves crashed upon the rocky shore. The Lady of the Lake cast her wise gaze back to Issylte. The trio of moonstones sparkled in the sun, the flow of magic swirling at her pale throat.

"Maiwenn named you Églantine, the wild rose. A flower of the sacred forest. Here in Avalon, you shall be Lilée, the waterlily. A flower of our curative waters. You'll learn to wield its divine power. The healing essence of water—the sacred element of the Goddess we serve."

The Lady of the Lake turned back to address Ronan and his men. "I am most pleased with the exemplary performance of your duty in safely escorting Lilée to me. You are my most trustworthy warriors, and I am sincerely grateful for your faithful service."

The Avalonian Elves bowed their heads to the Lady of the Lake as she dismissed them with honor. "Return to your homes now, and rest after your long journey. Thank you, and may the Goddess bless you all."

As the Elven warriors strode towards the forest where stable hands awaited with horses saddled for their departure, Vivian called out to Ronan, beckoning him to approach. The blond Elf came up to the High Priestess, who stood beside Issylte. "Ronan, we must keep Lilée safe. I would like you to be her escort while she remains in our care." Viviane turned back to Issylte.

"Ronan is not only our master blacksmith," she said, grinning proudly at him, "but he is also our Master of Horse. His stables house many magnificent animals, some of which you see today."

Her eyes twinkling, Viviane added, "Maiwenn informed me of your love for horses." The Lady of the Lake locked eyes with the massive Elf. "I am sure Ronan will be delighted to accompany you whenever you wish to ride." A glimmer of hope fluttered in Issylte's fragile heart. *Horses! I can ride again!*

Viviane seemed to notice the spark of light in Issylte's eyes. She spoke again to Ronan. "Please take Lilée to ride frequently. Show her our island. Where we harvest shellfish, where the farmers raise our fruits and vegetables, where the sacred springs are located. Where she may ride through the forest that is so dear to her heart."

Ronan nodded, accepting orders as a dutiful knight. The Lady of the Lake graced them both with a kind smile. "Nature is at the heart of *all* healing. And that is precisely what our dear Lilée needs right now."

Ronan replied, "It will be my honor, Lady Viviane." To Issylte, he offered, "I will come tomorrow afternoon so that we may ride together through the forest. I'll take you on a tour of the island and introduce you to some of the villagers." With a hint of a smile, his deep green eyes beheld hers briefly. "And to my horses." With a nod of his head, Ronan bid the two women good day and returned to his awaiting men.

As the Elves rode off through the forest, Viviane and Issylte watched the blond warrior disappear into the trees. "Your outings will be as good for Ronan as they are for you, Lilée," Viviane murmured sagely. "He, too, has a great need for healing." Turning away from the retreating escort, Viviane led Issylte toward the two priestesses and four guards who were waiting for them at the edge of the forest, horses in hand.

An additional mount had been brought for Issylte, and as she stroked the dark brown muzzle of the beautiful animal, the memory of Luna washed over her in a sudden wave of grief. "Good girl," she murmured to the horse, as she had done countless times into the ears of her beloved mare. Swallowing the lump in her throat, she hoisted herself into the saddle, reined her horse, and followed the priestesses, flanked by the protective knights, into the forest and away from the rocky beach.

Viviane rode up beside her and indicated a path leading off to the left, deeper into the forest. "That road leads west, to the village, mainly populated by the Avalonian Elves. However, many humans live there as well, having decided to remain among us, often after seeking treatment for an illness or injury. We all live together in harmony with nature, blessed by the bounty of the Goddess." She flashed Issylte a cheerful smile.

As their horses trotted at a gentle pace, the Lady of the Lake pointed to a second path, leading off to the right. "To the east lies another village, where fishermen live with their families in stone cottages all along the coast. There are dozens of boats, and the sailors frequently travel to the many islands in our realm." With a conspiratorial grin, she chortled, "Perhaps Ronan can take you to an island or two. Not only is he our master blacksmith, but an excellent boatsman as well."

Vivian's bright smile lit up her beautiful face. In many ways, the Lady of the Lake reminded Issylte of *Tatie* and the warmth with which she'd welcomed her— the frightened princess—at the door of the ivy-covered cottage. Now in Avalon, as in the Hazelwood Forest, Issylte shuddered at the thought of her stepmother's icy fingers, leeching her strength with a chilling numbness. The queen's royal guards hunting her. Killing *Tatie*, Bran and Dee. She took a deep breath, shook her head, and furiously rubbed the dreadful tingle from her arms as they rode through the dense trees along the forested path.

"Beyond this forest," Viviane continued, "lie fertile plains where farmers raise animals and produce the fruits and vegetables for our island. The fishermen share their harvest, the farmers share their crop, the villagers produce many of our necessities, and we trade with other islands to import the goods we cannot produce here."

She gestured to the forest around them with a slender white hand. "The *Little Folk*—the forest denizens—live in the woods throughout our entire realm." Viviane pointed to a nearby wooden hut with a thatched roof. "That is one of their cottages. The woodland creatures collect berries, mushrooms, and nuts for all of us to enjoy; many of them are skilled in woodworking, construction, and cabinet making as well."

Viviane leaned forward to stroke her white horse's mane. "Many of the women among the *Little Folk* are skilled at spinning wool from the sheep they tend, knitting warm blankets for the villagers. They also weave the fabrics we need for our clothing. When we care for their sick loved ones, they often pay with the products they create. The Goddess provides for us all."

They continued on, riding through the thick, verdant forest. In the distance to the north, Issylte perceived a clearing beyond the edge of the forest, where a flat-topped hill emerged from the grassy plain. Upon its summit, a white stone building glimmered in the afternoon sun. A wide, smooth, cobbled stone path led from the base of the plateau to the entrance of the structure at the top of the hill.

Abundant trees were blooming everywhere, a profusion of white flowers lining each side of the stone path. The *château* itself was surrounded by smaller trees, with delicate white blossoms. A vine-covered trellis, resplendent with fragrant white flowers, graced each side of the entrance door. The sweet scent of jasmine wafted through the fresh air as a flock of white gannets cawed to each other in the brilliant blue sky.

"These trees will produce delicious red apples in autumn," Viviane explained, referring to the lovely white blossoms lining the path as they rode up the hill. "The smaller trees produce my sacred flower—*les aubépines*—which in Britain are called white hawthorn." Viviane indicated the delicate white blossoms surrounding the gleaming white stone building. "We use the leaves, berries and flowers of *les aubépines to* treat ailments of the heart."

The Lady of the Lake pointed to the fragrant white blossoms on the vine-covered trellises. "These jasmine flowers perfume the air that we breathe and provide natural medicine for diseases of digestion. We extract essential oil from the blossoms, which we use to produce

sweet-smelling soaps and treatment for skin ailments."
With a knowing smile, Viviane crooned, "The Goddess
has indeed blessed us with Her bounty."

To the west of the clearing, Issylte glimpsed a large
lake, extending behind and beyond the hill which
supported the white building. Its deep blue surface was
covered with water lilies; a pair of white swans swam
gracefully amid the pearly white blooms. Taking in the
apple blossoms, the hawthorn flowers, the water lilies,
and the jasmine-covered trellises, Issylte marveled,
*everything is white—pristine and sparkling in the
sunlight.* She took a deep breath, filling her lungs with
fabulous floral fragrance.

Viviane seemed to notice Issylte's wonder at the
white stone *château*, the hill resplendent in white
flowers, and the lake covered with white blossoms. "I
chose the name Lilée for you because of these water
lilies. You are beautiful and pure, like they are." With an
impish grin, Viviane chuckled, "White is my favorite
color…as you may have noticed." Her white moonstone
necklace sparkled in the sun.

They rode up the cobbled stone path to the top of the
hill, finally arriving at the gleaming white limestone
building. The High Priestess dismissed the four
Avalonian Elves who had accompanied them, and they
rode off into the forest, back to their village. Nyda, Cléo
and Viviane dismounted, followed by Issylte, handing
their horses to grooms who led the animals into nearby
stables. The two priestesses in deep blue gowns entered
the *château*, with Viviane walking beside Issylte as she
familiarized the princess with her new surroundings.

"This white building is our center for healing, which
we call *Le Centre*. It is here that we cure the sick and

tend to the wounded, where we store our herbs and remedies, as well as the sacred stones we use for healing." As the four women walked down the hall of the enormous white stone building, Issylte noticed the spacious, open rooms with large windows overlooking the apple blossoms and white hawthorn flowers. "This is where the priestesses care for the ill and injured who seek treatment," Viviane explained, indicating the six rooms on either side of the wide central hall.

Issylte was amazed at the expansive rooms, the glistening white stone walls, and the sunlit windows which revealed the trees in bloom. Serenity and calm washed over her.

"This next building is the library," Viviane continued, indicating a gray stone building just beyond the windowed exit doors of *Le Centre,* "where we store the sacred books of herbal lore."

Viviane paused as Issylte gazed out the window to examine the library. "Many of our most valued treasures are kept there—the ancient scrolls and manuscripts which contain spells for protection and healing." A gleam sparkled in her wise blue eyes. "Many of which belonged to the famed wizard Merlin, who taught a trio of fairies in the enchanted Forest of *Brocéliande.*"

Issylte's breath caught in her throat as her eyes locked with Viviane's. The trio of fairies!

Viviane's eyes were the deep blue waters of the lake, flooding Issylte with fluid magic.

"*La Fée Verte de la Forêt* —the Green Fairy of the Forest, our beloved Maiwenn. *La Fée Blanche des Rochers*—the White Fairy of the Sacred Stones, the powerful Morgane. And *La Fée Bleue des Eaux Sacrées*—the Blue Fairy of the Sacred Waters—I, the

Lady of the Lake."

Issylte's hands were damp. Her stomach quivered. The wings of her magic fluttered in her chest, a white dove soaring in her heart.

"Maiwenn followed the love of her life to the Hazelwood Forest of Ireland." Viviane pushed a long blond lock from Issylte's face. "But Morgane and I came here to Avalon, to establish this Center for Healing. We brought with us the sacred knowledge of our venerable mentor. A priceless treasure for you to discover as you learn to wield the healing power of our sacred waters."

Issylte swam in the limpid eyes of the mysterious Lady of the Lake.

They exited the rear of the white limestone building through the windowed doors, emerging onto a cobbled stone courtyard where a bubbling underground spring sprayed froth high into the air. The central fountain was enclosed by smooth stones and encircled by welcoming stone benches. The roar of the cascade, the fragrance of white flowers of apple trees, *aubépines,* and jasmine vines, the glimmer of the deep blue lake, the lull of the distant, crashing ocean waves—all flooded Issylte with an aura of peace on this beautiful island of Avalon.

The High Priestess gestured to the ebullient water. "This is the sacred *Fontaine de Jouvence,* the Fountain of Youth. It flows from the same underground source as the one in the Forest of *Brocéliande*, where I was born. Where I studied, as part of the trio of fairies under Merlin. Where I developed my sacred powers of healing. And where I raised my son, Lancelot." Viviane gazed pensively into the waters, her expression as dreamy as the cottony clouds scattered over the lily-strewn lake.

"When I first came to Avalon and discovered this

sacred spring, I knew that it would be at the heart of the healing center I wished to establish on this island."

The Lady of the Lake locked her Blue Fairy eyes on Issylte. "In *Brocéliande*, the *Fontaine de Jouvence* bestows a long life to Druids such as Merlin." Her graceful white hand flowed to the water before them. "This sacred fountain is not only a source of healing the sick and injured. It also grants the Avalonian Elves—the *otherworldly* inhabitants of this enchanted realm—the same extended lifespan." Viviane's smile gleamed like the trio of gems glimmering at her throat.

From her perspective atop the plateau, Issylte examined the surrounding buildings and panoramic view behind *Le Centre*. To the west and north lay the enormous lake, covered in white water lilies, extending far into the distance, where the forest began anew. To the east and south were more dense woods, surrounding the grassy plains at the base of the gently sloping hill where they now stood. And, beyond the forest, to the east, the princess could perceive the jagged rocks and cliffs of the far-off coastline and the white-capped waves of the turbulent turquoise ocean.

Mists rose from the lake, shielding the healing center of Avalon with the divine essence of water. Encircled by thick forests, high stone cliffs, and the waters of the lake, the thrum of magic called to her. The three sacred elements of the Goddess that *Tatie* had told her so much about. *You are safe here, Emerald Princess*, the voices of Nature whispered. A latent power was awakening, pulsing in her verdant heart.

Viviane interrupted her reverie as she held her palm towards the blue expanse in front of them. "This is *le Lac Diane*, named after the body of water in the Forest of

Brocéliande where Merlin built my *château*." A sorrowful smile clouded the Lady of the Lake's face as she observed the gleaming white building of *Le Centre*. "The white stone of the palace he built for me—the Crystal Castle—glistens in the sun, just like this beautiful center of healing." As if collecting herself once again, the High Priestess of Avalon said to Issylte, "Come, I will show you to your quarters."

As they passed the fountain and followed the cobbled stone path from the center courtyard, Issylte noticed three gray stone buildings extending in a long row to the left. Each building stood two stories high, with windows opening onto the fountain in the central courtyard. Viviane gestured to them and explained, "These are the residences for acolytes, such as yourself, who have come to study the healing arts here in Avalon. We have the capacity to house four women in each of these three residences. Although we can accommodate twelve, we currently have only eight—now that you have joined us."

Nyda and Cléo entered the farthest of the three buildings, with Viviane and Issylte close behind. A central stairway led to the two quarters on the upper floor. On the ground floor to the left, an entrance door led to an acolyte's chamber. Issylte followed Viviane and the two priestesses down the long corridor to the entrance on the far right. Viviane led Issylte into her new quarters. "This will be your room," she said, indicating a spacious chamber with two large windows on opposite ends. One faced the fountain to the east; the other looked upon the lake to the west. The setting sun basked the room in a golden glow which shimmered on the ripples of the lily strewn water.

A small night table stood beside a comfortable bed on the wall opposite the entry door. A large wooden armoire stood beside the window near the lake; a large table and chair were centered under the eastern window, offering a spectacular view of the fountain.

"The morning sun will shine in this eastern window, making the fountain sparkle with light," Viviane said cheerfully. She turned to the west. "And the setting sun reflects off *le Lac Diane* from this window." The Lady of the Lake beamed. "You will be enlightened by the Goddess every day."

Retuning Viviane's bright smile, Issylte brought her attention back to the details of the room. A small table sat in the corner, holding a candle, a pitcher, and a basin, with a chamber pot on the floor underneath. Nyda and Cléo stood near the window by the lake, waiting patiently for Viviane to finish showing Issylte the features of her new residence.

The Lady of the Lake opened the door to the armoire, which held several light blue garments, extra linens for the bed, a bar of soap, and several small jars of ointments. The High Priestess gestured to the clothing on the shelf. "As an acolyte, you will wear one of these light blue robes, and a soft white chemise as an undergarment." Indicating the soap and jars on the shelf, she explained, "Nyda and Cléo will show you where the baths are located. Each morning, the priestesses wash in the sacred spring, and use soaps, such as this one," she said, holding up the bar and inhaling its fragrance, "which is made from our jasmine flowers. Mmmm," she murmured contentedly, smiling at Issylte.

"The priestesses make our soap, as well as ointments, such as these," Viviane continued, holding up one of the jars. "We extract delicate oils from the flowers and make salves which are wonderful for our skin. And essential for healing many of the wounds which we treat here at *Le Centre*."

Viviane turned to Nyda and Cléo. "I am certain Lilée would like to wash after her long sea voyage and rest before our evening meal. Please take her to the spring where she may bathe, and show her the dining area, where we'll meet when the bells chime."

The Lady of the Lake faced Issylte once again, giving her hands an affectionate squeeze. "I am most pleased to welcome you to Avalon, Lilée. You'll enhance your impressive knowledge of herbal medicine that you acquired with Maiwenn in the Hazelwood Forest. And learn the healing properties of water—and sacred gemstones—here in Avalon."

With a kiss on each of Issylte's cheeks—the familiar French *la bise* that Maiwenn had always used —and a nod to her two priestesses, Viviane left the room with a smile. She crossed the courtyard, passed the spraying fountain, and headed back to the pristine white limestone walls of *Le Centre*.

Nyda, the smaller priestess with light brown hair, took a few items from the armoire and said to Issylte, "Come with us. We'll show you where to bathe. After that, we'll return here to deposit your things, and you can let us know if you prefer to rest until supper or walk around *Le Centre* a bit more." She gestured with her head, inviting Issylte to follow. "This way."

The bathing area was to the north, adjacent to Issylte's acolyte residence. A freshwater spring, fed from the same underground source as the central fountain, bubbled into a large pool, encircled by smooth, flat stones. A high stone wall, covered with jasmine vines in bloom, surrounded the bathing area and ensured privacy. Cléo said cheerfully, "Here's a clean white chemise and light blue acolyte's robe to put on when you've finished bathing."

She set down a bar of soap and a towel on one of the flat stones. "This jasmine soap will wash the salt from your hair after the long sea voyage." With a soft smile, the dark-haired priestess crooned, "The water of the spring is rich in minerals from the earth, which your body and hair will absorb. When you emerge from the water, your skin will tingle, and you will feel rejuvenated. That's why it's called *la Fontaine de Jouvence.*"

Nyda said, indicating with her head, "We'll wait for you just over there, on one of the benches by the fountain. Take your time and enjoy the sacred waters of the Goddess." The two women left Issylte to bathe in the cool, bubbling spring.

As she slipped into the gurgling water, Issylte remembered the delightful pool where she'd bathed near Maiwenn's cottage. The waterfall, the clear stream which flowed into the grassy back yard. Where *Tatie* had her two gardens. Where Florette and the hens loved to drink. The enormity of loss smothered her, and Issylte sobbed, letting the tears flow freely, a catharsis which cleansed her soul as the water of the spring washed away the brine of the sea.

When the well of her emotions finally ran dry, she dipped her head underwater and washed her long blond hair with the jasmine soap. The floral fragrance was as sensual a delight as the cool kiss of water on her skin. Emerging from the bath at last, she did indeed feel rejuvenated, her skin enriched by the nourishing minerals of the underground spring. Issylte dried off with the towel Cléo had placed on the rock and dressed in the light blue acolyte's robe. She gathered her soiled clothing, the soap, and the damp towel, walking toward the fountain where the two priestesses waited for her with a welcoming smile.

"Doesn't your skin feel *alive*?" Nyda exuded, her eyes alight with pleasure.

"It does feel wonderful, just as you said," Issylte agreed with a faint smile as she followed the cheerful priestesses back to her residence.

Nyda pointed to the table in the corner of her room. "You may place your soiled clothing here, to be laundered by the village women that we employ at *Le Centre*. They will change the linens on your bed each week and restock the supplies in your armoire." With a warm smile, she added, "They take very good care of us, and we provide healing services and protection to all inhabitants of the island in return. We live in harmony, among ourselves, and with the earth."

Cléo flashed her a bright grin. "Would you prefer some time to rest, or would you rather see more of your new surroundings?" Issylte would cry miserably if left alone. "I'd prefer to walk around, please." With the hint of a smile, she added softly, "Thank you both very much for your kindness."

Nyda and Cléo took Issylte around *Le Centre,* showing her the residence where Viviane and the priestesses lived, the conservatory where patients convalesced with music. They paused for a few moments at the doorway to the vast open room, listening to a priestess play the flute. As she gazed out the window at the bubbling waters of the fountain, the melodic music made Issylte's heart soar, lifting her spirits with its pure, crystalline notes. *Music is a powerful source of healing, too.* She spotted a magnificent golden harp in the corner of the room near the window. *Perhaps I can learn to play one day.*

They took her to the dining area, explaining how meals were served three times a day, announced by a chiming of bells. They visited the library, where priestesses and acolytes hovered studiously over manuscripts on smooth tables in front of rows and rows of precious books.

When Issylte arrived at the area where herbs were stored and processed, women were preparing ointments and salves, in much the same was *Tatie* had shown her in Ireland. The crisp, clean scents of sage, chamomile and rosemary filled her nostrils with nostalgia. Her throat constricted; her heart gripped in a vise. Swallowing the lump of sadness, she followed the two priestesses to the room which housed the sacred stones.

Wooden shelves lined the walls of the enormous white room, where hundreds of brightly colored gemstones and sparkling crystals were laid upon pieces of cloth or stored in clear glass containers. Brilliant rubies, emeralds, sapphires, and moonstones glistened in the afternoon light from windows at each end of the long rectangular room. An aura of power emanated from the gems, calling to the verdant magic simmering in her soul.

Cléo seemed to notice Issylte's fascination with the brightly colored gems. "I am one of the priestesses here who will teach you the many healing properties of our sacred stones." She picked up a luminous white gem, glowing from within. "Moonstone is the Lady Viviane's sacred stone—you may have noticed the necklace she wears." She turned the gem so that it glowed softly in the light. "It is a stone of great power…and protection. You will learn to channel the divine energy of the Goddess as you enhance your skills as a gifted healer."

The bells chimed, indicating the evening meal was being served, so Nyda and Cléo escorted Issylte to the dining area. As they walked past the ebullient fountain, acolytes and priestesses hurried past them, chattering gaily. Their faces were merry, carefree, their hearts young and full of life. Issylte felt isolated, sorrowful, and withdrawn—in stark contrast to their exuberance and joy.

Guilt flooded her again, choking her with grief. She thought of *Tatie* and the little stone cottage that she loved so much. *If not for me, Tatie, Bran, and Dee would all still be alive. It's my fault they are dead. How can I ever be happy again, like these women? I do not belong here. I bring nothing but death to the ones I love.*

Viviane caught up to Issylte and her two escorts, rushing to join them. Her voice was as bright as her brilliant blue eyes. "Ah, Lilée! I am glad I found you. I'll present you to the acolytes and priestesses, then join you for supper. That is, if you do not mind my company?" she asked with a cheerful grin. Issylte replied softly, "That would be lovely, Lady Viviane."

The banquet room sat across from *Le Centre* on the opposite end of the courtyard, with a wall of windows facing the spraying fountain. As they entered the building, the Lady of the Lake introduced Issylte to the other acolytes and priestesses, who were seated at four long rectangular tables, eagerly chatting as they enjoyed their meal. They glanced up from their conversations to

241

greet her with a friendly smile, then returned to their light banter and giggling, oblivious to Issylte's pain.

The kitchen staff had set up a generous banquet table, where two large urns of steaming vegetable soup emitted the enticing blend of onions, carrots, green beans and potatoes. The delicious smell of fresh, crusty bread and the sweet scent of succulent strawberries, ripe cantaloupe and fat, juicy grapes perfumed the air. The familiar herbal scents of rosemary, garlic and sage evoked painful images of *Tatie's* cozy kitchen, where they'd chopped vegetables and herbs from the gardens together, cooking savory meals over the glowing hearth. Issylte's stomach clenched. She doubted she could eat, despite the appetizing array of food. Pitchers of water from the sacred underground spring sat beside ceramic goblets atop crisp white linen tablecloths throughout the cheerful, sunlit room.

"We serve ourselves," the High Priestess demonstrated, ladling the hearty soup into a ceramic bowl, "and sit together to discuss the lessons we have learned. Or request further practice sessions, or plan treatment for our patients." Issylte heaped some of the steaming soup into her bowl, took a slice of bread and a few pieces of fruit, as Viviane did. She followed the Lady of the Lake across the room to where Nyda and Cléo were sitting with two priestesses and two acolytes, with two seats reserved at the table for Viviane and Issylte.

They joined the group, who were deep in a discussion of herbal treatment for one of the injured patients. While the conversation continued in the background, Viviane spoke softly to Issylte.

"Most of the acolytes rise early and wash before the

morning meal, which is served at seven." She took a spoonful of soup and hummed in contentment. "Mornings are devoted to lessons taught by the priestesses, who will demonstrate herbal preparations, the curative properties of the different waters on our islands, and how to channel the healing energy of crystals and gemstones." She spooned more of the savory soup into her mouth, wiping it delicately with the corner of her linen napkin. "The three sacred elements of the Goddess—forest, water, and stone." Her brilliant blue eyes glinted in the setting sun.

Viviane offered Issylte some of the nutty whole grain bread and freshly churned butter. "After classes have finished, the bells chime to announce the midday meal. Afternoons are free to study in the library, travel to one of the villages, practice new treatments or spells, bathe in the spring, or simply enjoy music in the conservatory." With a sad smile, she mused dreamily, "Although we do have a magnificent harp, no one here is skilled enough to play. Perhaps one day, someone will grace us with its musical magic."

The Lady of the Lake seemed to perceive the somber mood and lack of appetite of her newest acolyte. She placed an arm around Issylte's shoulder in a comforting embrace and whispered, "I know you're overwhelmed with your new surroundings, especially given the circumstances of your arrival." Her luminous eyes shone with compassion.

Viviane's voice was soothing. "You're still in shock from Maiwenn's tragic death, and I know you were very close to her grandson Branoc and his wife as well." She paused, as if to allow her gentle voice to calm Issylte. "I know you're frightened of the wicked queen, but you are safe here with us. I have cast powerful spells of enchantment which protect all of Avalon. No evil can harm us here. We will take good care of you, Lilée, and I truly hope you will learn to be happy among us." After another pause, she added, with a smile, "Perhaps Ronan can help, with his horses."

Issylte tried—and failed—to hide her sadness as she nodded in silence. Perhaps, as she'd done when her father had remarried, she could find solace in the saddle. Horseback riding might prove once again to be her salvation.

The next day, Issylte followed the acolytes to wash in the spring, take the morning meal, and report to *Le Centre* for lessons. She was placed with two other novices who were working with a priestess in preparing salves for the treatment of skin conditions. Soon, the bells chimed for the midday meal, and Viviane joined Issylte once again. "How are you today, Lilée? Are you becoming acquainted with *Le Centre*?" she asked brightly.

Issylte nodded and replied softly, "Yes, my lady. Thank you."

After they finished eating in the dining area, Viviane indicated, with a tilt of her head, the familiar blond warrior who had brought Issylte to Avalon. "It seems Ronan is here to escort you around the island." Motioning for him to approach, the High Priestess said gaily, "Good day, Ronan! Lilée is ready for today's excursion. I hope you will show her the village of Briac and your blacksmith shop. Perhaps introduce her to some of the horses in your stables."

"It will be my pleasure, Lady Viviane," Ronan replied. He turned to Issylte. "I have a horse ready for you to ride. The same chestnut mare that you rode yesterday. Her name is Maëva, and she is eager to run. Shall we?" he asked, politely offering his hand to help her up from the table.

Issylte accepted it timidly, said goodbye to Viviane, and headed off to explore Avalon with Ronan.

The afternoon sun was shining off the waters of the glistening lake where the pair of white swans swam peacefully amid the pearlescent water lilies. Jasmine vines, apple blossoms and fragrant *aubépines* perfumed the air as they rode from *Le Centre* down the cobbled stone path towards the densely wooded forest. Her chestnut mare galloped across the plain, and Issylte let her hair flow freely, grateful that she did not need to keep it covered, as she'd done in Ireland. The wind whipped her hair, the sun kissed her cheeks, and the thrill of being back in the saddle lifted her heavy heart.

When they reached the edge of the thick woods, they slowed to a trot, and Ronan said, "Today I'll take you to the village of Briac, on the western side of the island. I'll show you my shop and introduce you to my horses. Follow me, my lady."

Issylte spoke up. "My name is Issylte, but while I am her in Avalon, Lady Viviane wants me to be called Lilée." She leaned forward to stroke Maëva's mane. "You may call me either, but please, there's no need to address me as *my lady.*"

To which Ronan replied, "Very well. But you must call me Ronan, Issylte."

How wonderful it is to hear my own name again. She'd been *Églantine* for the past four years in Ireland and was now Lilée to everyone in Avalon. It was liberating to just be herself and not an imposter—at least with Ronan.

As they rode through the forest, he stopped suddenly and pointed to a garland of *églantine* flowers, placed near the path they were following. He dismounted, picked it up, and brought it to her. With a deep chuckle, he grinned, his eyes as verdant as the dense woods. "It appears the forest fairies wish to welcome *Églantine* to Avalon."

He handed her the floral wreath, and, at the sight of the flowers for which *Tatie* had chosen her name, Issylte was flooded with emotion as tears welled up in her eyes.

She was grief-stricken with loving memories of *Tatie* and the horror of her death. The loss of Bran, Dee, and the life she'd known in the Hazelwood Forest. Yet, she was also delighted by the generosity and kindness of the *Little Folk* who had made such a lovely gift to welcome her. Deciding that the woodland creatures might well be observing her reaction from some hidden spot among the trees, Issylte placed the wildflower headpiece atop her golden hair, wiped her eyes, and smiled gratefully.

As if pleased to see her bedecked in flowers like a forest nymph, Ronan grinned and climbed back onto his horse as they continued their journey.

The village of Briac reminded Issylte of Sligeach, where she and Maiwenn had gone each week for provisions. Many of the buildings here, like there, were residences built atop or beside open shops which displayed everything from leather saddles, boots, and shoes, to pastries, clothing, pottery, fruits and vegetables…even live animals. A glass blower was entertaining some of the local children with his wondrous creation. The music of their joyful laughter rang through the salty air. The quaint village was both vibrant and welcoming.

Ronan seemed to be well-known and well-liked, for he greeted many of the shopkeepers by name as they rode through the town. Most of the buildings were made of gray stone, with thatched roofs, very much like Maiwenn's cottage in the Hazelwood Forest. Once again, Issylte swallowed a lump of sadness, forcing herself to try to enjoy the outing and the chance to be on horseback, the sun on her face and the wind in her hair.

Ronan's blacksmith shop and stables were a short distance from the village, with a stone cottage where he lived alone, abutted by a large forge under a covered, sloped roof. Several Elves were working over the fire, hammering metal into various shapes as they shod horses and made tools for the villagers. As he rode by, Ronan waved to his workers, who greeted him in return, and Issylte followed his lead to the nearby stables.

He dismounted and gave his horse to a stable hand, then helped her down from Maëva's back, handing the chestnut mare to another groom. Turning to face her, the Avalonian Elf said kindly, "Come this way, Issylte. Come meet my horses."

Behind the stables, a huge grassy plain extended to the forest, and approximately thirty magnificent horses grazed freely. The outer perimeter of the grassland was encircled by a wooden fence, allowing the animals room to roam while keeping them contained and protected. A few scattered trees offered some shade, but the wide, open field offered lots of fresh grass for nibbling.

They entered the fenced area, and at Ronan's whistle, a pretty chestnut mare, similar to the one Issylte had been riding, came trotting over to munch on the

247

carrot he held out to her. "This is Marron, and she just loves carrots," he explained with a grin. "She carries a foal and is due to give birth in the spring. I bring her carrots now, and in autumn, I will spoil her with the delicious fruit of our abundant apple trees."

As Marron crunched the carrot happily, Issylte stroked her soft muzzle. She thought of caring for Luna, the exhilaration of riding through the forest with the handsome Master of Horse Liam. A life she had lost because of the evil queen.

She turned away to hide her distress, pretending to adjust her dress as she composed herself. When she at last straightened and returned to stroke Marron's dark mane, Ronan seemed to notice the streaks on her cheeks but wisely said nothing. He watched her stroke Maëva's muzzle, feed Marron another carrot, and said, his deep voice gentle and soothing, "I must return you to *Le Centre*. Soon it will be time for the evening meal."

She gazed into his deep green eyes, trying to hide her disappointment. She loved caring for the horses. It was almost like home. Before the wicked queen.

"If you like, I can show you the fishing village of Rochefort next week," Ronan offered gallantly. "Do you like seafood?"

She perked up immediately. "I *love* sea food! My *Tatie*—Maiwenn—taught me how to dig clams, harvest shellfish...even how to catch salmon and perch in the lake of Lough Gill."

Ronan grinned. "Excellent! I know a shop where they serve delicious *potage*—a soup made with seafood and fresh vegetables. Seasoned with herbs from their garden. I'll bring you there next Tuesday. For now, let's head back to *Le Centre*."

They returned to the stables so that the grooms could bring their horses. "I hope you enjoyed today's ride." Ronan smiled at her, stroking her mare's mane. "Maëva certainly did."

Issylte beamed at him, her love of horses filling her heart. "I thoroughly enjoyed it, Ronan. I loved riding Maëva, exploring the village of Briac. Seeing your blacksmith shop. And especially meeting Marron, the carrot lover." She chuckled softly. "Thank you very much."

When they arrived back at *Le Centre,* Ronan helped Issylte to dismount as Viviane came to greet them. She flashed Ronan a warm smile. "Thank you for taking Lilée for an excursion today."

The Lady of the Lake grinned at the flower garland in Issylte's hair. "A gift?"

Nodding, Issylte replied, "From the *Little Folk.*" She met the Elf's deep green gaze. "Ronan said they were welcoming me—*Églantine*—to Avalon." She smiled with delight.

Viviane's astute eyes darted between Ronan and Issylte. The Lady of the Lake asked Issylte cheerfully, "How did it feel to go riding again?"

"Incredible! I let my hair flow in the wind…. It was so nice to not have to keep it covered, like I did in Ireland." Glancing up at the enormous blond male at her side, Issylte added, "Ronan is going to show me the fishing village of Rochefort next week. It will be lovely to see a tidal bay, like the one in Sligeach, where my *Tatie*—Maiwenn–taught me to collect shellfish."

Ronan said goodbye, wished them a pleasant evening, and rode off through the forest, back to the village of Briac. Viviane and Issylte joined the other priestesses and acolytes for the evening meal. As she savored the herbal flavor of her *omelette aux fines herbes,* drinking the mineral rich water of the sacred spring, Issylte looked forward to the future for the first time since she'd left the Hazelwood Forest.

The day Ronan arrived to escort her, he brought Maëva, much to Issylte's delight. Once again, she reveled in the thrill of galloping across the plain to the forest, her long hair blowing in the wind. This time, they headed east, to the opposite side of the island, where brightly colored boats and lovely stone cottages—many decorated with blooming floral vines—dotted the rocky coast.

The sandy beach was scattered with large rocks, sheltered by cliffs jutting out over the turquoise sea, which glimmered in the afternoon sun. A large, sinuous path led down to the shore, where Issylte could see fishermen returning with baskets and nets brimming with their fresh catch. Ravenous sea gulls squawked loudly, diving for the scraps tossed their way, as powerful waves crashed against the rocky cliffs, splattering salt spray and the tang of brine into the summer breeze.

In the village, people were bustling about, bartering for goods, selling their wares. Shops offered brightly colored pottery, woven baskets, fishing supplies, clothing, leather goods, fruits, and vegetables, and plenty of freshly caught fish.

As Ronan had promised, he took her to a small inn where patrons were enjoying delicious seafood beneath bright blue awnings draped over outdoor tables, bedecked with white tablecloths and deep blue ceramic dishes. Issylte's mouth watered as the tantalizing aroma of fresh seafood wafted through the air. When the serving girl placed heaping bowls of the *potage* before them, Issylte inhaled deeply, savoring the familiar aroma of scallops, oysters, and mussels that she had grown to love in Maiwenn's cottage.

Ronan filled her mug from the pitcher on their table and offered it to her with a gleam in his forest green eyes. "This water comes from an underground spring that is filled with bubbles." Issylte accepted the cup and tasted the sweet, fresh water, wrinkling her nose at the effervescent tickle. The hint of mint tingled her tongue.

"This fresh mint adds a wonderful flavor. Perfect for a warm, sunny afternoon." She smiled at Ronan, delighted with familiar flavors and new sensations.

The *potage* was delicious—full of succulent clams and mussels, the creamy broth flavored with garlic, butter, and herbs. The fresh bread was filled with nutty grains, and the mint-flavored spring water delighted her tastebuds. Ronan talked of his horses, of Marron's expected foal, of the Elves who worked for him, the contentment of the island villagers. Issylte spoke of her lessons with the priestesses, of Viviane's warm welcome, of Maiwenn's herbal tutelage in the Hazelwood Forest, the similarities between the villages of Rochefort and Sligeach. He laughed when she described fishing for trout with wriggling worms, digging for clams in the tidal bay, churning butter from Florette's sweet milk.

The friendly conversation, savory seafood, refreshing mint water, warm sunlight, and spectacular view of the ocean made for a most delightful afternoon. Soon, it was time to return, and they headed back through the forest to *Le Centre*. This time, when they dismounted, Ronan offered to return the following week to take her to the south side of the island, where there were lovely shells to collect and beaches to explore.

Issylte agreed eagerly, stroking Maëva's soft brown muzzle as the Avalonian Elf mounted his black stallion Noz, promising to return the following Tuesday. As he rode off, Viviane came up to greet her with a warm smile, and the two women headed towards the fountain to sit and chat while they waited for the bells to chime for the evening meal.

When Issylte rode to the south side of the island the following week with Ronan, she gasped in delight at the white, sandy beach at the base of the hill from where they now sat atop the forested ledge. "Let's water the horses here, in the stream," he said, heading into the edge of the forest, where he dismounted, helping her do the same.

After the animals had quenched their thirst, Ronan tied them to nearby trees, where there was a grassy area for the horses to graze.

As she stood near him, Issylte breathed in his scent—the clean smell of sweat, a hint of leather, a touch of smoke from the fire of his forge—which stirred something deep inside her. She gazed up into Ronan's intense green eyes, sensing immense power radiating from him. *He is of the forest, like I am. I sense an otherworldly force in him. A verdant magic, like my own.*

She tore her attention away from his magnetic eyes and watched as he took a sack out of his saddle bag, slung it over his shoulder, and turned to her with an exuberant smile. When he took her hand in his, Issylte thrilled at his touch as she followed him down a long, winding path from the top of the cliff to the white shore below.

The beach was wide and flat, and from this perspective, at the base of the ledge, she could see the steep, rocky cliffs which protected the coast, with the forest high above them. Still holding her hand, Ronan led her to a large rock, beckoning her to sit beside him as he removed first his boots, then her shoes.

"The sand feels delightful," she exclaimed, reveling in the sensation, as she walked with him along the shoreline.

The ocean was gentle here, as if the force of the turbulent sea crashed upon the distant rocks, sending soft cascades to caress this white sandy shore. Overhead, dozens of seabirds squawked in the sky, their white outstretched wings soaring through the clouds. Her face was flushed from the warm afternoon sun, the sky a brilliant blue above the turquoise sea.

Pungent seaweed tickled her nose as the gentle waves lapped at their feet. Issylte raised the hem of her robe to keep it dry.

"Here, allow me," Ronan offered, bending forward before her to tie the lower half of her dress in a knot. With his head so close to her, Issylte took in his silvery blond hair and pointed ears, his enormous shoulders and back, the strength exuding from him like a shield to protect her. He raised his head, an exuberant grin on his face, and said triumphantly, "Now your hands will be free to collect the many shells I want to show you."

Indeed, the shoreline offered many treasures—rose-colored scallop shells nearly as large as her hand; snail shells that curved in a soft, gray spiral; and a large white shell that resembled a horn, with extraordinary shades of purple inside. Ronan seemed delighted at her enchantment, placing the shells she collected in the sack on his shoulder as they strolled along the shore, the afternoon sun glimmering on the ripples of the sea.

"Next week, I will show you another of the many wonders of this island," he said, barely containing his enthusiasm. "There's an underground spring on the north shore which is breathtaking. You will love it, I am sure."

Issylte, her heart content, beamed at Ronan. "I can't wait!"

She approached him timidly, gazed up into his dark green eyes, and murmured softly, "Ronan, thank you so much for bringing me here. For taking me to Rochefort. For showing me the island. You have been a wonderful guide, and I am truly grateful." She wanted to kiss his cheek, but didn't dare, so she graced him with a genuine smile that she saw reflected in his twinkling eyes.

****

Ronan absorbed the marvel of her—the long blond hair, tossed by the salt air, the expressive emerald green eyes, so often filled with sadness but now glinting with joy. The fragile heart, nearly broken by grief. He wanted to wrap his arms around her, to protect her from the cruelty of life. Instead, he took her hand, lifted it to his lips, and placed a tender kiss on the curve of her fingers.

He gazed at the setting sun and said softly, "We must return now. Next Tuesday, I will show you the sacred spring." Taking her hand and carefully placing the sack over his shoulder, Ronan led Issylte back up the steep path to the horses and returned her to the white stone building of *Le Centre*.

****

Ronan worked most afternoons in his blacksmith shop, crafting tools to barter in the villages of Briac and Rochefort, forging Elven weapons and armor to sell in nearby kingdoms. Issylte kept busy with her lessons, learning to diagnose various ailments among the local inhabitants, studying with her mentors, trying to learn as much as possible. Yet, despite her dedication to her craft, she often found herself thinking of Ronan and the tender care he showed his horses, the quiet strength he exuded which calmed her troubled spirit. She found herself longing for Tuesdays, when he would take her exploring—revealing the secret delights of Avalon, so appropriately named the Island of Healing.

When her class finished and she'd shared the midday meal with the other priestesses and acolytes, Issylte was thrilled to see the familiar rugged face and pale blond hair when Ronan arrived with Maëva for this week's excursion to the north shore of the island. With a quick goodbye to Viviane, Cléo and Nyda, she rode off with her handsome Elf to discover another of the sacred springs of Avalon.

Once again, they tied the horses to trees at the edge of the forest, where Issylte observed more of the same rocky cliffs she'd seen on the south side of the island. She followed Ronan's lead down an equally steep path to reach the shore of the sandy beach, partially enclosed by a curve in the high rocky cliff behind them.

Beckoning her to sit on a stone, Ronan said with a grin, "I will start a fire now, and while it burns, I will take you to the spring." He gathered driftwood for kindling and started a small fire, which he encircled with smooth, round stones that he collected at the base of the cliff. He took a large sack off his shoulder, placed it on the sand and approached her with an extended hand. "Come, the spring is this way."

She placed her hand in his, a tingle shivering up her arm and through her body at his touch. She saw the dark blond hair that peeked out of his green tunic at the base of his throat. His strong jaw was covered in stubble, and his scent wafted to her, drawing her in, as she followed him away from the campfire, around the curve of the stone wall.

To her amazement, they came to a hidden sea cave at the base of the cliff, and Ronan's eager grin thrilled her as he led her inside. Her body awakened, and her senses heightened, as the roar of an underground spring reverberated off the limestone walls of the cave into her very bones. A turquoise green pool bubbled from the center of the floor of the cave, with a wide stone path on either side of the gushing spring. The sides and back of the grotto were walls of pearlized gray stone which glimmered in the light from the entrance behind them. Issylte's magic came alive. *There is otherworldly power in this cave*, her instincts whispered.

Ronan's eyes were lit with excitement as he shared his delightful secret with her. He went farther into the cave, knelt down and said, his deep voice sonorous, "The water bubbles from an underground spring. Taste how sweet it is." He cupped his calloused hand and drank deeply, the cool water spilling down his square chin.

Issylte knelt beside him and placed her hand into the chilly turquoise water which glowed from within. The water from the underground spring tasted fresh and clean, the hint of minerals lingering on her tongue. The roar of the jet spray thundered in her ear.

"This is *la Grotte de l' Étoile*—the Cave of the Fallen Star," Ronan explained in a reverent hush. He motioned to the light glimmering in the water. "See how the bubbles burst forth? They form a pattern which resembles a star."

As she examined more closely, Issylte noticed how

the water from the base of the spring separated into five jet sprays under the surface, forming a star. Sunlight from the entrance to the cave reflected off a bed of crystals beneath the bubbling waters, as if starlight were radiating from the bottom of the spring. "It is magical!" she exclaimed with a sigh, "as if the Goddess herself illuminates the water." She cupped her hand and drank again from the sacred spring. Magic hummed with the song of the spring.

The walls of the cave were dewy with moisture, echoing and amplifying the music of the gurgling water into a thrilling roar. She shivered with delight.

"Some say this is a portal to the *Otherworld*," Ronan whispered into her left ear. "One of the most sacred sites among the islands in this realm." His breath caressed her cheek.

Issylte absorbed every detail of the treasure he had offered. The musty scent of the limestone walls, the turquoise brilliance of the icy water, the radiant starlight beneath the turbulent bubbles. Her magic sang within her, like the music of the sacred spring.

Finally, Ronan said, "Come—the fire should be ready now." Again, he took Issylte's hand in his and again, his touch sent a ripple of pleasure through her as they exited the cave and walked back to the firepit on the sandy beach.

"Perfect," Ronan said, bending over the fire. "In a few minutes, it will be reduced to embers." To her surprise, he took a bag from his sack and opened it to reveal a large cluster of fresh mussels. "I harvested, cleaned and prepared these for us today."

A gleam of excitement lit up his handsome face. "Look what I made in my shop with pieces of scrap metal." Reaching back into his bag, he produced a strange tool with tongs that clamped a finely woven metal grill. Extending from either side of the grilled enclosure were two long metal handles.

As she watched in wonder, Ronan put the large clump of mussels inside the tongs and suspended the small grilled area over the embers by placing the long arms of the tool on top of the rocks which outlined the firepit. "We'll roast the mussels until their shells crack open, which only takes a few minutes." He reached into his sack and produced two silver cups and a flask. Pouring some deep red liquid into each cup, he offered one to her and placed one on the rock beside him. She sat down on a flat rock near the fire as he closed the flask, then sat down at her side.

"Elderberry wine." Ronan grinned as Issylte tasted the delightful fruity beverage. "A shopkeeper in the village makes it from the berries of the elder tree. It is delicious," he promised, reaching for his cup. His eyes locked onto hers, Ronan raised the chalice and whispered, "To new discoveries, and shared treasures."

Issylte smiled brightly, her heart full. "And to friendship." They clinked glasses, drank the earthy, rich wine. The warmth slid down her throat and spread deliciously though her body.

Ronan stood and walked over to the firepit. He wrapped his hand with a cloth, removed the tongs from the embers and placed the grill on a nearby rock to cool.

As they sipped the elderberry wine, waiting for the mussels to reach the right temperature for eating, Issylte told Ronan, "I put the shells we collected the other day on the table in my room that faces the fountain." She took another large swallow of the heady wine, savoring the richness and the mellow glow in her body. "Every day when I see them, I remember the day on the beach when we found them." She met his deep green gaze, luminous in the afternoon sun. A thrill raced down her spine. "And now, the fountain that I see from my bedroom window will remind me of the sacred spring we saw today in *la Grotte de l' Étoile*." The satisfaction on his face and in his smile warmed Issylte as much as the elderberry wine.

Ronan stood, retrieving two stoneware plates from his bag. He took the cooked mussels out of the metal grill and placed some upon each of the two plates. The aroma of fresh seafood and the salty tang of the sea delighted her nose as much as the fruity fragrance of the delicious wine.

Ronan turned towards her, a plate of steaming mussels in each hand, a delighted grin plastered across his handsome, blond stubbled face. He served her first, then himself. As Issylte placed the plate of steaming mussels upon her lap, Ronan sat down close beside her to demonstrate how to eat them.

"Be careful not to slice your fingers on the shells," he said gently, unsheathing his dagger. He wiped it clean and cut some of the tender meat for her with the sharp blade. He offered the delectable treat to Issylte, who cautiously took it from his knife, popping the warm delicacy into her salivating mouth. "Delicious," she hummed contentedly.

He ate directly from his blade, expertly cutting more for her. This time, she carefully placed her mouth on the blade and ate the mussels as she'd seen him do, thinking of how his lips and tongue had just been where hers were right now. Ronan watched her, delight shining in his deep green eyes.

When she had eaten her fill, he finished the rest of the mussels and refilled their glasses. The fire was warm, the setting sun glowed on the ocean, and Issylte, a bit heady from the wine and the sultry taste of the fresh seafood, was blissfully content and very aware of how close Ronan was beside her.

As she gazed up at him, he reached over to push a strand of hair from her face. "You are very beautiful, Issylte," he said, meeting her eyes with a look of longing. As he leaned his face close to hers, she could feel his breath on her cheek. Her body tingled with anticipation.

He moved closer to her on the rock and placed one arm behind her. With his other hand, he gently lifted her chin and lowered his mouth to graze hers. The silky touch of his lips sent a wave of pleasure through her, making her thighs tremble. Wanting more, Issylte was disappointed when he stood, brushed himself off, and glanced out at the ocean, cast in shadows. "I need to take you back to *Le Centre*. The sun is setting. Soon it will be dark."

He gathered the cups and plates they'd used and brought them, along with the grill, to the water's edge. He rinsed them out, tossing the empty mussel shells for the crabs to pick over and nibble. Ronan returned to Issylte and gently wiped the sand from her feet with his bare hands, sending waves of delight up her long legs. He put the shoes on her clean feet, then donned his own boots. As if sensing her disappointment in having to leave, he offered, "Would you like to visit Marron and my horses at the stables next week? She'll be glad to see you." His grin told Issylte that Marron was not the only one who'd be glad to see her.

Issylte's spirits brightened. "That would be lovely. I

can't wait to see her again!" They packed up the supplies, extinguished the fire, and climbed back up the steep slope to the tethered horses. As they rode home through the forest, she sensed Ronan's eyes lingering on her through the dimming light dappling through the trees. Her face flushed as she remembered the feel of his lips on her own. She flashed him a brilliant smile, grateful for another glorious day with her handsome blond Elf.

****

The following week, when Ronan brought her through the village of Briac, they stopped at the vegetable stand to purchase carrots for the horses. As they remounted to head towards his stables, Issylte asked, "I noticed you paid the merchant with coin, rather than bartering, as my *Tatie* always did. Do you sell items from your shop?"

Ronan replied as they rode through the forest. "Avalon is inaccessible to anyone other than the inhabitants of this realm. But many of our merchants do travel elsewhere to sell their goods." He cast her a glance as he urged his horse into a trot.

"I do the same, traveling every few months to sell the tools that I craft, as well as the swords and armor that we forge in my blacksmith shop." With a proud grin, he beamed. "The weapons forged by Avalonian Elves fetch a *very* good price. Our swords are the finest in the Celtic realm."

Marron was indeed glad to see Issylte, especially after Ronan handed the princess a carrot, which the mare happily crunched from her hand. The other horses came trotting over to greet her as well, and Ronan continued providing Issylte with carrots to feed their inquisitive muzzles. Atop Maëva who loved to run as much as her rider, Issylte galloped beside Ronan across the wide, open field. Her wind-kissed cheeks were warm in the late spring sun.

When they returned to the stables, Issylte watched Ronan do much of the stable hands' work himself. He cleaned out stalls, replaced fresh hay, and brushed the horses, allowing—even seeming to enjoy—her help. Together, they fed the animals fresh oats and provided clean water from the nearby well. Issylte, remembering the years that Liam had taught her to care for Luna, was delighted to be able to groom horses once again.

In many ways, Ronan reminds me of Liam—gentle, patient, strong, hard-working. And though both males were handsome, Ronan had the rugged, forged body of a warrior, which Issylte found herself thinking about more and more frequently lately. In fact, right now, as he brushed Noz's glossy black mane, she found her eyes wandering over Ronan's bent back, the muscled arms covered with hair—exposed from the rolled-up sleeves of his tunic— blond hair tied back at the nape of his neck. Remembering the kiss on the beach, Issylte's lips longed for his touch once again.

When they finished with the horses, they washed their hands and drank from the underground spring which fed the well. "The water is so sweet." She sighed with pleasure.

Smiling, Ronan nodded his agreement. He replaced the bucket at the well, walked up to her, and gazed down into her eyes. "Your love for horses shows in the gentle way you care for them." He lifted her chin to meet his gaze and said softly, "Thank you," as he planted his lips gently on hers.

Tears welled up in her eyes. Immense joy at being with Ronan, yet longing for Luna, Liam, her father, the castle, Gigi—as if caring for the horses today had revived the wounds in her heart. She missed T*atie* so much her stomach twisted. A wave of shame washed over her. Her face reddened at the pleasure she'd shared with Ronan, as if she'd forgotten her grief and guilt. She hid her face from him, ashamed, as painful memories of the past compounded her grief with tremendous guilt.

Ronan brought her gently into his arms, and she buried her face into his chest, breathing in his distinctly male scent, comforted by his strong embrace. He seemed to understand without words, and simply held her, until she whispered, "I miss my father, my nurse Gigi, and my horse Luna." He stroked her hair gently, encouraging her to continue. She raised her gaze to his dark green eyes, feeling her tear-streaked face crumple with pain. "I miss *Tatie,* and Bran, and Dee. If it weren't for me, they would all still be alive."

Issylte buried her face in the broad Elven chest once again. "It is my fault they are dead, Ronan. If I had not gone to *Tatie's* cottage, none of them would have been killed. It is all my fault."

He held her in his strong arms, rocking her gently, allowing her grief to spill. When her shudders finally subsided, he lifted her chin and said firmly, "Issylte, it is *not your fault* they were killed. It is Queen Morag's fault, and hers alone."

Issylte tried to reject his words, drowning in guilt. Ronan gently but firmly pulled her chin so that she would face him. "Issylte, look at me. *Look at me.*"

She met his steady gaze with imploring eyes. Ronan's deep voice was filled with conviction. "You, my princess, are the *victim*, not the guilty. Do not hold yourself responsible for the evil of another."

Taking her face between both of his hands, he planted a luscious kiss upon her quivering lips.

Issylte's knees gave way as she leaned into his embrace. Ronan wrapped both arms around her, cradling her against his chest. He kissed her more deeply and passionately, parting her lips with his own, teasing her with a gentle probe of his tongue. His hands roamed down her back, to her hips, pulling her tightly against him, the hardness of his body creating deep within her a hollow ache that yearned to be filled.

"I will keep you safe, Issylte. I will protect you. Always." At these words, he crushed her into his arms, kissing her lips, face, and hair—washing away the sorrow and guilt.

Ronan then pulled away, as if striving to regain his composure. Once again, Issylte was disappointed that he had stopped, for she wanted *more* of him. He touched her face gently, smiling to see her grief assuaged. Adjusting his clothing, Ronan shook his head—*like a horse*, Issylte thought. Then, with a look of regret, he said gently, "Come, we must head back now."

Issylte followed him reluctantly to the horses. He helped her onto Maëva's back, climbed into the saddle atop Noz, and led the way back through the thick, verdant forest.

Arriving at *Le Centre*, they dismounted to say goodbye. Ronan hovered near her, seeming to struggle for the right words. He finally managed, "I will be leaving tomorrow, to sail to Armorique. On the mainland of *Bretagne*, in northwestern France. I'll sell the weapons and armor that I have been forging in my shop."

Seeing the disappointment on her face, he added reluctantly, "I'll be gone for eight weeks, possibly ten." Issylte's heart sank. He would be gone for two or three months!

Ronan lifted her chin to lock her eyes with his own, which were filled with light and hope. "When I return…the apple trees will be full of autumn fruit." Placing a soft kiss of promise on her lips, he whispered, "The horses love apples…"

Swallowing her disappointment, Issylte smiled into his deep green eyes. "Hurry back to me, Ronan. I will miss you every day that you are away." To which he replied, drawing her into his arms and kissing her deeply, "I will, my princess. I will."

As the weeks passed, Issylte tried to keep busy, missing Ronan desperately. Focusing on her lessons, she learned to steep sweet woodruff in wine to cleanse toxins from the body. She made poultices from comfrey to knit broken bones and heal wounds. She discovered even more of the healing properties of sacred trees, such as beech, willow, hawthorn, and elder.

She explored the beloved forest, learning where to find the plants and herbs she needed to prepare remedies, tinctures, and salves in the workshop of *Le Centre.* Immersing herself in the love of the forest, just as she had done in Ireland with her beloved *Tatie,* Issylte found that nature soothed her suffering. The verdant magic of the forest flourished in her virid soul.

She accompanied the priestesses to the villages, treating sick children with ear drops she created from the bark of elder trees; she soothed skin disorders with ointments made from beech bark; she eased aching muscles and joints with salves made from the sacred willow.

The priestesses taught Issylte which waters were used to enhance fertility, which streams were best for purification of wounds, and which springs, such as *la Fontaine de Jouvence,* could prolong life.

Cléo taught Issylte to channel the energy of sacred stones, such as amber, to alleviate pain; black coral, to promote male fertility, and ocean jasper, to calm and soothe nerves. Viviane taught her spells of enchantment to imbue gemstones with protective energy. Issylte learned to create crystal grids, to harness the power of the earth and dispel disease. She crafted talismans to bestow the blessings of the Goddess into sacred crystals to protect from harm. And discovered the power of her own sacred stone—the emerald—to heal a broken heart.

As Issylte learned to channel the healing properties of the sacred element of stone, one of the most amazing crystals she discovered was a tree-shaped agate called *merlinite*, named after the famed wizard himself. With this sacred gem, Issylte perfected her magic, learning to absorb the healing essence of minerals, accessing the *otherworldly* knowledge of the master enchanter, and channeling the divine power of the Goddess through sacred stones.

Summer faded into autumn, and Ronan had not yet returned. Issylte spent many afternoons in the library, studying spells and incantations, learning the properties of minerals, crystals, and gemstones, practicing and refining her skills. She quickly surpassed her fellow acolytes.

And finally, as Maiwenn had suggested so long ago in the enchanted Hazelwood Forest, Issylte mastered the three sacred elements of the Goddess, attaining the highest ranking among priestesses of Avalon. *Guérisseuse*—Sacred Healer. *Tatie* would be so proud.

Viviane was most impressed with her progress as well. Today, as they walked together near the lake, the High Priestess said, "You have become a gifted healer, Lilée. A *guérisseuese.* A most prestigious distinction."

Issylte gazed at the white lily flowers which had inspired her name. "Thank you, Lady Viviane. I am very grateful for the knowledge I have acquired here in Avalon."

They strolled along the water's edge, the hint of autumn in the crisp, cool air. "Maiwenn told me that you were a forest fairy. Wielding its verdant, healing magic. Indeed, you've demonstrated your extraordinary skill with the many herbal remedies you've prepared here at *Le Centre*. The patients you've cured in the village." Issylte's pulse quickened. Where was Viviane leading with this?

"You've mastered the curative properties of our healing waters and sacred gemstones. You have earned the prestigious title of *guérisseuse*. A truly exceptional honor."

Viviane rewarded Issylte with a proud smile, continuing to walk along the water's edge. "Your *Tatie*," she said affectionately, "mentioned that you once experienced a *sighting* in the waters of Lough Gill." Viviane stopped to lock eyes with her. "Perhaps you could tell me more about that encounter."

Issylte shuddered at the memory. The leeches covering her father's body, the wicked queen at his bedside. The frightening man with the yellow eyes of a snake. Watching her. A ripple of dread slithered down her spine.

"Yes, I had a vision. I saw my father King Donnchadh—bedridden, covered with leeches, with my stepmother beside the bed. There was also a man in black at her side. Muttering a sort of incantation." She rubbed her arm as if to wash away his memory.

Her hands trembled. "He was horrible. With yellow eyes like a snake. During the vision, he stared at me from the bed—as if he *knew* that I was watching."

The Lady of the Lake cast her gaze upon the expanse of blue before them, her expression reflective and contemplative.

"Some are gifted with the *sight*—the ability to see beyond the realm of ordinary vision." She took Issylte's hands in her own. "You have been blessed by the Goddess with this divine talent, and I would like to help you further develop your skill. Your magic. The essence of water."

They stopped before the waves which lapped upon the shore. "Your first vision was at Lough Gill. A lake. Perhaps *le Lac Diane* might offer you another *sighting.*"

Viviane indicated a smooth area of white sand just up ahead of them. "Kneel here, and gaze into the lake. Clear your mind, concentrate. Let the magic in your veins flow into the sacred essence of water. Become one with the Goddess."

The sand was warm beneath her knees, the sun gentle upon her back, the breeze wafting the fragrance of the lilies. She shut off the awareness of her surroundings, focusing on the depths before her. The waves lulled her, rocked her, flowed into her. She floated in the dark blue pool, the cool kiss of water caressing her skin, entering her pores, filling her soul. Leaving her physical body behind, Issylte cast her spirit into the profound blue depths of the lake.

Darkness enveloped her in an unearthly stillness, and jumbled visions began to appear. As she focused, one emerged clearly —Gigi, her bags in hand, being escorted from the castle as four royal guards waited on horseback for her to join them. Issylte's heart pounded wildly. She remembered how Lords Cian and Bolduc had led her into the woods. To kill her.

In the vision, Issylte saw the queen's guards ride hard with Gigi deep into the forest, where they stopped abruptly and pulled her roughly from her horse. Two guards in gleaming armor pinned her thin arms behind her back as an inconsolable Gigi pleaded with them, struggling against their unyielding hold, tears streaming down her desperate face. While two armored guards held her pinned tightly against them, a third horseman grabbed a handful of Gigi's hair and yanked her nurse's head back to expose her vulnerable neck.

Issylte, her heart thumping out of her chest, watched in horror as a fourth guard unsheathed his sharp dagger and tore open Gigi's throat before her very eyes. Blood spurted from the beautiful neck, Gigi's frail life force flowing freely into the dead, rotting leaves. The huntsmen threw the fragile body to the ground, covering it hastily with thick branches. The four royal guards, resplendent in their finest livery, mounted their magnificent horses and galloped away, abandoning Gigi's crumpled body in the darkest shadows of the Hazelwood Forest.

Gasping, unable to breathe, Issylte became aware of a voice calling from far away. Viviane gently tapped her on the cheeks, crying out, "Lilée... Lilée... Come back to me!"

The darkness cleared, the water lilies welcomed her, and the sunlight reflected off the lake once again. Slowly, her breathing calmed, and she was able to speak to the distraught High Priestess beside her.

"Viviane, I saw what *really* happened to my nurse!" Issylte panted, sobbing, struggling to get the words out.

"I had been told that she was dismissed. That the queen decided I no longer needed a nursemaid. The entire castle had been told that Gigi was being returned to her sister." Her heart pounded frantically. "But I saw what really happened. The wicked queen had her *killed*!" Issylte jumped to her feet, flailing her arms, pacing along the sandy shore of the lake. "My evil stepmother tried to kill me—*twice*. She forced me to flee my father's castle. Later, I had to flee the Hazelwood Forest. She killed *Tatie,* Bran and Dee. And now, I find that she killed Gigi, too!"

Issylte fell to her knees and buried her face in her hands, tearing at her hair in frustration and anger. "That wretched queen even sold Luna. She has taken everything and everyone that I love!" Issylte grasped Viviane's hands. "My father is in *danger*. The queen is going to kill him, too. I know it. I must do something, before it is too late." Issylte implored the Lady of the Lake. "I must help him, Viviane. He *needs* me. The leeches, the bloodletting…they are not healing him. They're *killing* him. I must go to him. I must help him."

The Holy Priestess of Avalon held Issylte in her arms, consoling her with soothing words and a comforting embrace. When Issylte was finally able to listen, Viviane said gently, "I know you are desperate to help your father. You fear for his safety—and rightly so. You're the victim of the queen's evil wrath. I am so terribly sorry she has caused you such pain. Killed so many you love." She hugged Issylte, rocking her in cradled arms.

A few minutes later, when Issylte's whimpers had abated, Viviane whispered, "We did discover something today. You do indeed have a tremendous gift for the *sight*. I am sorry the vision was so horrific."

Viviane lifted Issylte's face, the depths of her blue eyes as profound as *le Lac Diane.* "One thing is for certain, Lilée. You cannot return to the castle. The queen would *kill* you before you could even reach your father. She'd have you arrested the moment you set foot into the castle. And execute you at once."

Imparting words of wisdom to Issylte's unwilling ears, the Lady of the Lake said solemnly, "You are the sole heir to the kingdom of Ireland, and the greatest threat to her power."

And, with nearly the same counsel that *Tatie* had given her years ago in Ireland, the High Priestess of Avalon said sagely, "It is difficult to be patient when we feel compelled to act. Yet often, we must wait, knowing that the Goddess has determined our fate—which has yet to be revealed."

The Lady of the Lake kissed Issylte on the head and rose to her feet, beckoning her to stand as well. "Come," she said gently, "let us go to *la Fontaine de Jouvence,* and be rejuvenated by the sacred spring. You've had an arduous ordeal, and it will help to restore you. There is nothing you can do to help your father right now. You *must* be patient—no matter how difficult it is—and trust that the Goddess will reveal your fate, when the time is right. For now, let us heal your troubled heart with the sacred waters of Avalon."

They walked slowly back up the hill, where the sight of the apple trees abundant with ripe, red fruit made Issylte think of Ronan, who had promised to return to her soon. At the memory of the handsome Elf, a wave of longing washed over her. She was simultaneously suffocated with tremendous guilt and overwhelmed with yearning for him. *I am safe here, amid this natural beauty, awakened by the passion of Ronan's kisses, while my father lies ill in his bed, threatened by the wicked queen and her horrid wizard. I must find a way to help him. Before it is too late.*

At *la Fontaine de Jouvence*, Issylte drank the rejuvenating water of the sacred spring under the watchful gaze of the Lady of the Lake. Deep within her grieving heart, the Emerald Princess vowed to help her father. Somehow, she would find a way to save him and stop the wretched, wicked queen. Before it was too late.

Chapter 23

A Call for Aid

After his induction into the Tribe of Dana, Tristan returned to *la Joyeuse Garde* and spent the rest of the summer learning the *otherworldly* sword-fighting techniques that Lancelot had mastered while training with the Elves of Avalon. Every day, Lancelot and his knights Judoc, Darius and Gaël drilled Tristan mercilessly. He loved every minute of it. But now that summer was ending, Lancelot and Tristan were sailing back to Britain in the morning, in time for the autumnal equinox in Camelot and the final year of training to become a Knight of the Round Table of King Arthur Pendragon.

This evening, the Blue Knight of Cornwall sat with his host Lancelot in the vibrant banquet room on the final night before their sea voyage. Servants were clearing away platters of roast boar, refilling goblets of rich burgundy wine. Lively music of fiddles filled the jasmine scented air as knights and their ladies began to dance in the adjacent ballroom under the soft candlelight of the sparkling crystal chandeliers. Couples strolled in the moonlight along the glistening lake, where the pair of swans swam among the water lilies. Lovers kissed under the wisteria vines as Tristan and Lancelot sat contentedly at their table amidst the music, gaiety, and romance.

Tristan saw Judoc kiss a lovely brunette in a deep blue gown. He thought of Nolwenn's long dark hair, lithe limbs and intoxicating amethyst eyes. His body stirred at the memory of the delicious welcome into the Tribe of Dana. His tongue loosened by several cups of wine, Tristan leaned towards his companion, his mouth curved upward in a smug grin. "You never told me how *you* became a member of the Tribe. How did the legendary Lancelot of the Lake get inducted?"

Lancelot leaned back in his chair and extended his long legs. The White Knight of Avalon took a long pull from his goblet of wine, swirling it in his mouth to savor the dry fruity flavor. With his boyish grin, he fixed Tristan with blue eyes filled with mirth.

"The Priestesses of Dana are the guardians of the sacred waters, wielding the divine curative powers of the Goddess. Laudine is the Lady of the Spring—the sacred fountain where you and Esclados summoned the storm." He took another mouthful of the fine burgundy, smacking his lips as his eyes twinkled in delight.

"When I was sixteen, living in the Forest of Brocéliande in my mother's *Château de Comper,* a young priestess named Lysara had just been appointed *La Dame du Serein*—the Lady of the Fairy Waterfall." He took another large swallow of wine and grinned at Tristan. "She wasn't at Landuc this summer, but you might meet her next year. She's petite, brunette... *beautiful."* Lancelot's deep blue eyes swam in the soft light.

"My mother Viviane created a beautiful moonstone necklace—imbued with magic—as a protective talisman for Lysara. A gift to celebrate her becoming a Priestess of Dana." Lancelot retracted his legs, reached his arms over his head, and stretched his broad back. He glanced out at the dark lake, glimmering in the moonlight, his thoughts lost in the past.

The music played in the ballroom, the fragrance of wisteria blossoms wafting in from the open doors overlooking the courtyard and lake. As he gazed at the moonlight reflecting on the gentle waves of the deep water, Tristan envisioned the young priestess with her enchanted moonstone necklace.

"Dwarves inhabit the forests of *Bretagne*. Like Bédalis, whom you slew to save Laudine," Lancelot continued. "Many of them practice dark magic. They try to obtain our sacred objects—like Lysara's magic talisman. A dwarf named Gorin learned of the necklace. He knew its value was immeasurable, because of the magic my mother had imbued into the moonstone gems."

A servant refilled their goblets of wine. Tristan leaned back to enjoy the rich, earthy taste, enthralled by another of Lancelot's captivating tales.

"One day, when Lysara was bathing in her fairy waterfall, she laid the necklace on a nearby stone. Gorin, spying in the woods, grabbed it and dashed off into the forest. Lysara came running back to my mother's castle, hysterical with grief, desperate to retrieve her precious talisman."

Lancelot gulped from his goblet and smirked. "I flew into the saddle, raced through the forest, and tracked him down. I slew him as he crouched over it, laughing greedily, muttering to himself." Pride gleamed in his warrior eyes. "I was invited to join the Tribe for saving the precious talisman." He took another gulp of wine, a big grin illuminating his bemused face. "Lysara showed her appreciation by welcoming me into the Tribe."

Tristan, remembering the luscious night with Nolwenn, returned Lancelot's wicked grin. He raised his chalice, spilling wine on his tunic as he swayed slightly in his chair. "To the warm welcome of the Tribe of Dana!" The two knights clinked goblets, emitted a guttural laugh, and drained the rest of their wine.

The revelry was winding down as the musicians stopped playing. Guests were heading off to their respective chambers; the servants were tidying up. Stretching his arms in a luxurious yawn, Lancelot bid goodnight to Tristan as they parted ways until morning, when they would sail for England with the tide.

Tristan lay in bed on this last night in *la Joyeuse Garde*, the cool chill of autumn air blowing through the open windows. He observed the full moon in the night sky, the salty breeze from the brackish river reminding him of the impending sea voyage home, reflecting on the events of the summer which was ending.

He'd traveled to *Bretagne*—the craggy coast of northwestern France, where he'd honed his skills as a swordsman, training with Lancelot's knights, learning the techniques of the Avalonian Elves—the fiercest warriors in the Celtic realm. He'd defended the sacred *Fontaine de Barenton* and rescued the Lady Laudine. He'd become a member of the Tribe of Dana and been *welcomed* by the goddess Nolwenn. All were chivalrous pursuits worthy of the most gallant knight.

As he finally drifted off to sleep, Tristan enjoyed a sense of pride of accomplishment—and, for the first time in many years, a true sense of belonging.

The return sea voyage was uneventful, and soon Tristan and Lancelot—with the guards that had accompanied them to *La Joyeuse Garde*—reached the coast of Britain, where the horses had been stabled for the summer. As they rode northwest to Camelot, the red and gold-colored leaves of the trees, the bite of the chilly winds nipping their faces, and the crisp woodland smells of fall reflected the subtle changes of the season. It would soon be the autumnal equinox—the final nine months of training. When Tristan would at last become one of King Arthur's prestigious Knights of the Round Table.

Everyone who had gone home for the summer was now returning to Camelot to complete the final months of training with Lancelot of the Lake. Tristan spotted Vaughan unloading his saddlebags, alongside Indulf and Connor. He strode over to greet his friends with a hearty welcome.

"How was the summer in Kennall Vale? Hunting good?" Tristan asked, clasping Vaughan on the shoulder as he grinned from ear to ear.

"Not bad, not bad," Vaughan replied as he unloaded supplies. "Connor shot an eight-point buck, and I got a twelve pointer." One side of his mouth extending in a half smile, he joked, "Two more sets of antlers to adorn the study in Lord Treave's stately manor." Connor grinned and shook Tristan's extended hand. He searched around to greet Indulf, but the blond knight had already left. *Didn't even say hello. The bastard.*

Lancelot strolled over to greet to the new arrivals, whose squires were handing the horses over to grooms and hauling bags to take to their lords' quarters. "Welcome back, everyone. Tonight, there is a reception in the banquet hall. King Arthur wishes to extend his greetings. Today, we rest after our long voyage. Tonight, we feast. And tomorrow, we train. Good day, men. Until this evening!"

As the First Knight strolled away, Vaughan smirked, "Enjoy your *séjour* in Bretagne, Tristan? Fuck any French girls?" His eyes, deep brown like bitter coffee, held Tristan's gaze with undisguised contempt. "Elowenn sends her regards." Then, with a grunt of disgust, he spat, "Not that you care." Vaughan hoisted his bag over his shoulder and sauntered away, the ghosts of summers past haunting the deepening void between the estranged friends.

The feast was splendid, as the receptions in Camelot always were, and soon, autumn unfolded. The knights adapted to the rhythm of training—engaging in mock battles, siege attacks, defense tactics and military strategy. Occasionally, Lancelot would plan an outing, such as today's hunting competition, to break the monotony and entertain the men.

Some of the more experienced knights, such as Bedivere, were joining them this afternoon. Four teams of six were hunting wild boar and deer in different sections of the forests surrounding Camelot, with two teams pitted against each other in both divisions. Every member of the two winning teams would receive a highly prized hunting falcon as a reward.

Lancelot's team, which included Tristan, was competing against Bedivere's group, which counted Indulf, Vaughan and Connor. In another section of the forest, King Arthur led a group, as did the veteran knight Lamorak. The weather was crisp and cold, the afternoon sky overcast and gray. A dense carpet of red and gold leaves blanketed the forest floor. Anticipation and the thrill of the hunt was in the air.

The men in his group were readying their horses and

donning their bows and arrows. Tristan heard a sudden loud rustling in the trees. He examined the copse of woods, darkened by shadows and haze in the dense forest. As he searched the source of the disturbance, he spotted the enormous head of a large gray wolf emerge through the dense foliage. Intense amber eyes fixed his own, as if to convey an urgent warning. With the Druidic magic of the golden herb flowing in his veins, Tristan understood the lupine message wordlessly.

You are in grave danger. The man with hair the color of wheat does not hunt the wild boar—he hunts you. His companion, the small evil creature with wrinkled skin, lurks behind the trees near the stream. Four others await with him. All have weapons. To kill you. Stay clear, Warrior of Dana. We—the Wolves of Morois—will defend you.

Shaken, Tristan quietly told Lancelot of the encounter with the wolf. Lancelot led the team in the opposite direction—away from the stream —to begin the hunt. A few minutes later, horrific screams pierced the silent woods. Vicious snarling and growling, savage snapping of jaws and bloodcurdling shrieks shattered the stillness of the forest. Tristan's team quickly drew their bows and nocked their arrows. Lancelot led the way as they rode cautiously forward, towards the stream.

The mutilated, bloody corpse of a knight lay at the scene. His throat had been ripped open, his body covered in vicious bite marks. Blood was splattered everywhere—over broken branches of trees, across scattered leaves—puddling in deep, dark pools near the multiple gashes on the victim's ravaged body.

Bedivere was on foot, bent over the victim, examining the evidence. He held up the knight's shield to those who had just arrived at the scene. "This boar's head is the coat of arms of the dwarf Frocin." He pointed to the blood, patches of gray fur, and broken branches surrounding the body. "He was obviously killed by wolves. But why," he frowned, gesturing to the riderless animal who stood faithfully beside the fallen knight, "would a pack of wolves kill a human, yet leave his horse untouched? If hungry enough to attack a man, would they not *consume the body*? It makes no sense. If the wolves were famished enough to attack a man, they certainly would have eaten the horse as well."

Bedivere rubbed his beard, eyebrows lowered in puzzlement. He scanned the forest, hand on his sword. "It speaks of enchantment. Those wolves were *bewitched!*"

At that moment, a group of hunters emerged from the forest, with Indulf, Vaughan and Connor among them. All were pale and haggard—as if in shock—as they rode up to the mutilated body.

Lancelot stepped forward to address them. "This knight was one of the dwarf Frocin's men. His coat of arms is on the shield. Did any of you see anything?"

Vaughan replied, a tremor in his voice. "We saw four men on horseback, fleeing a pack of huge gray wolves. The wolves were growling, snapping at the horses' legs, their teeth bared—in hot pursuit. I fired an arrow but missed as a wolf leapt over a fallen log. The pack veered off together into the forest, as one. Moving in unison. An enormous wave of wolves." He raked his fingers through his hair, looked down at his boots, and shivered. "It was chilling, uncanny… *unearthly*."

Bedivere motioned for two squires to lift the corpse onto the riderless horse just as Arthur and the remaining knights joined the shaken men. Barking orders, the king commanded that the body be brought to Camelot to be burned, indicating that the fallen knight's weapons and shield be retained for proof of Frocin's treachery. "I do not know what his purpose was here today, but he has no right to hunt in my forest, nor may he trespass onto my territory. Bring the weapons so that they may be safeguarded. I will decide what action to take upon our return."

Two days later, the dwarf Frocin appeared in the throne room of Camelot, where the wizened creature now knelt before the High King upon the dais. Surrounded by the Knights of the Round Table, the lords and ladies of the royal court, the king bellowed to the humbled dwarf before him.

"Frocin, the body of one of your knights was found near my castle of Camelot. Witnesses saw you and several of your armed men riding through my forest. You are forbidden from hunting in these woods. You now stand accused of trespassing upon my royal territory. What say you?"

Frocin, his voice trembling, stammered, "I do most humbly beg your forgiveness, Your Majesty. We were in pursuit of a wild boar, which had been injured in our hunt. My men and I and did not realize that we had traveled so far east as to encroach upon your royal domain. I do apologize most sincerely, Your Highness, and respectfully request your clemency."

Arthur, in his red velvet cloak lined with ermine, his gilded crown heavy upon his golden head, glowered at the quivering dwarf. The king's deep voice thundered through the throne room.

"You shall be fined one hundred silver coins. I shall

send men in ten days to collect the debt." The king bellowed, his craggy face crinkled in rage. "Be forewarned, Frocin—if you or any of your men trespass again upon my lands, your lives will be forfeit. Now go. Return to your domain in the Forest of Morois. You shall pay the hefty fine in ten days' time."

Tristan watched Frocin and his guards slither from the castle, dismissed by the High King of Britain. The barmaid's warning came to mind as the dwarf cast him a grim, baleful glare. *Some say he's an assassin. Others say he delves in the dark arts. Stay clear of him, my lord. He's a dangerous man.*

The Blue Knight of Cornwall vowed to heed the woman's advice and avoid the malicious dwarf, grateful for the Druidic magic of *l' herbe d'or*—and the Wolves of Morois—which had spared his life in the thick forest of Camelot.

****

Autumn passed into winter, the knights' regimen of training continuing unabated, until finally, the Yuletide season arrived. Evergreen garlands and holly with bright red berries bedecked the glorious castle with the fragrant splendor of pine. Boughs of mistletoe, sacred plant of the Celtic people, hung above doorways, bestowing the inhabitants of Camelot with the blessing of the Goddess for a prosperous new year.

For today's holiday feast, the enormous banquet room was resplendent with candlelight glistening in crystal chandeliers, fragrant pine branches on the mantelpiece of the enormous fireplace, and garlands of dark green holly and sweet-smelling hellebore blossoms draped across the gleaming wooden walls. The savory aromas of stuffed pheasant, roast venison and rich meat sauces wafted through the air, and the sparkling array of silver and glass on the tabletops twinkled like stars in the dark night sky.

Guests arrived, bedecked in furs, jewels, and embroidered brocades, ushered to tables by attentive servants who served goblets of exquisite French wine, followed by courses of aromatic soup, fresh seafood, roasted meats, vegetables, cheeses, and pastries. When the last course was finished and the platters cleared away, musicians began playing, luring jubilant guests onto the magnificent dance floor with lively, lyrical melodies.

Elegant ladies in silken gowns and glittering jewels enticed the knights at Tristan and Lancelot's table with dazzling display. Soon, all were dancing, and Tristan found himself once again brooding over his wine with the First Knight of Camelot at his side. At a nearby table, a lovely lady in a sapphire blue gown was desperately trying to get Lancelot's attention, to no avail. The White Knight of Avalon only had eyes for the beautiful blond queen seated upon the elevated dais next to King Arthur, where the red dragon of her husband's royal heraldry blazed upon golden banners in the light of the Yuletide fire.

A servant refilled their wine goblets. With a nod of his head, Tristan smirked, "That pretty brunette would love to dance with you," indicating the young woman in the deep blue gown.

With a sad smile, Lancelot replied, "I, like you, am a bloody brute whose only interest is fighting." He downed a large gulp of wine and leaned back in his chair to observe the brightly attired nobles swirling on the dance floor, dazzling in colorful brilliance.

Tristan saw his friend's forlorn gaze return to the blond queen at the royal table. Her luminous face reflected every bit of longing as that of the lonesome knight at Tristan's side who could but love her with his eyes.

Before he could stop them, the words tumbled out of Tristan's mouth. "Your love for her. Is it *l'amour fou*?"

Lancelot's astonishment soon turned to shame. He stared gloomily into his goblet. "*Oui, c'est l'amour fou.*" A desperate yearning blazed in Lancelot's gaze as he beheld the pale, fragile queen.

The eyes are the window to the soul, Tristan thought, witnessing his friend's suffering for an impossible love and the loneliness which smothered him. Lancelot, unburdening his grief, confided at last to Tristan.

"My mother Viviane brought me to Avalon when I was eighteen, to train with the Elves," he began, smiling sadly as he drank deeply of the rich red wine. "The Elves of Avalon are unparalleled warriors. Incredibly strong, tall, agile. With weapons of inimitable quality and exceptional performance. Forged with *otherworldly* skill. Imbued with magic." Tristan gulped more wine, his pulse quickening as he listened.

"My mother, the Blue Fairy, was Merlin's best pupil. She enchanted my armor and my sword, imbuing me with superior strength, speed, and agility. To equal that of the Avalonian Elves who would train me."

Lancelot gazed unseeingly at the dazzling dance floor, lost in the past. Tristan took another long pull of wine from his silver chalice, grateful and proud that the White Knight considered him a close enough friend to share his grief.

"The training was intense, as I expected, but there was one most unanticipated delight." Lancelot shot Tristan an impish grin. "The priestesses."

The White Knight leaned forward, his white teeth gleaming in the candlelight. "They take lovers whenever they wish. And many took me." He took another big gulp of wine, wiped his chin with his sleeve and grinned ear to ear. "My preparation for the battlefield was matched only by my education in the arms...and between the legs...of the priestesses of Avalon."

Lancelot chuckled huskily, drank more wine, and continued his tale. "Seven years ago, when I was twenty, a new acolyte arrived. Sent by her father, King Leodegrance, to become a healer on the island of Avalon. Exquisitely beautiful. Light blond hair, icy blue eyes. Lithe, elegant. Irresistible." He gazed at the regal beauty across the room. Caressed her with his desperate, loving eyes.

"She had a kind, gentle manner. A magic touch. I was attracted to her in ways I'd never experienced. Ever. I found her not just physically beautiful. I was magnetically drawn to her. Like never before." He downed the rest of his wine and motioned for more. A servant hurried to comply.

Tristan glanced at the ethereal queen seated beside King Arthur. Regal, proper, elegant—all the attributes expected of a monarch—yet emanating the same sadness that choked the chivalrous knight who loved her madly.

"Guinevere and I became friends, then lovers." Lancelot gazed into his goblet of wine, his hair hanging forward on either side of his distraught face. "In her body, I found ecstasy. In my heart, ... sublime joy. Our souls touched. Our spirits merged. Our bodies joined together…we truly became *one*."

He desperately searched Tristan's eyes, seeking recognition and comprehension. Lancelot gazed back at the royal dais where his heart sat beside the king. He exhaled sorrowfully, his longing and suffering whispering her name.

"I envisioned her becoming my wife. Having children together…raising a family. The Elves would accept us as their own. We'd live peacefully on Avalon for the rest of our lives." He drank deeply from his goblet, drowning his grief in the rich French wine. The brilliance of his eyes dimmed in bitter defeat.

"But the Goddess had a different fate for Guinevere and me." The White Knight leaned back in his chair and turned to face Tristan. Lancelot clenched his jaw.

"My mother had her lover, the Avalonian Elf Gofannon—*the blacksmith of the gods*—craft a sword for Arthur. With the help of his son Ronan, one of the fierce Elven warriors who trained me, Gofannon forged Excalibur. When the sword was finished, my mother sent for Merlin, who brought Arthur to Avalon."

Tristan remembered that Viviane had the Avalonian Elves forge Excalibur. But there was much more to Lancelot's story. He took another gulp of wine, his jittery foot bouncing under the table. Tristan wiped his damp palms on his lap.

"My mother gave Arthur the sword in return for his promise to grant her one request. That he would accept me, the White Knight of Avalon, to the Round Table. This you already know, Tristan. But what I didn't tell you on the deck of the ship was that Arthur, upon meeting Guinevere—my love, my muse, my heart—decided that he wanted her for his *queen*." Lancelot impatiently motioned for more wine, waiting until the servant filled his goblet before continuing.

"I was off in Bretagne, on the quest to free the king's imprisoned son. While I was gone, Arthur sent word to King Leodegrance, requesting Guinevere's hand in marriage. Of course, her father accepted. Arthur was the High King of Britain. How could he possibly refuse?" Lancelot's bark of bitter laughter was a wretched sob.

"Why would he even want to? Guinevere would become the High Queen of Britain. The greatest honor he could ever hope for his lovely daughter." His face distorted with pain, Lancelot shook his head and gazed into his goblet, as if it held the answers he sought.

"And now, my friend, you understand my suffering." Lancelot's eyes glistened with bleak, bitter acceptance. "The love I have for the queen is indeed *un amour fou*—a love so intense it drives me mad. I love her with every depth and breadth of my soul, yet she is the wife of the king to whom I have sworn the chivalrous oath of fealty. A king whom I also love and would *never* betray. Yet…whose wife I love to the point of madness."

His noble face crumpled with grief, Lancelot downed the rest of his wine and motioned for more. At a loss for words, Tristan swallowed his rich satisfying wine with the empty bitterness of Lancelot's sorrow.

****

Spring returned, and with it, the much-anticipated dubbing ceremony. As King Marke had done in the castle of Tintagel, Arthur—the High King of Britain, his magnificent sword Excalibur gleaming in the sunlight of the Great Hall of Camelot—officially dubbed the ten winners of the Tournament of Champions. Sir Tristan of Lyonesse, the Blue Knight of Cornwall, was at long last a valiant Knight of the Round Table of King Arthur Pendragon.

A celebratory feast and tournament followed the dubbing ceremony, allowing the new Knights of the Round Table to display their chivalrous skills in two events—jousting and sword fighting—before dozens of lords and ladies assembled on either side of the castle grounds. The ten winners of the Tournament of Champions proudly donned the surcoats bearing their coat of arms gifted by King Marke of Cornwall. Excitement filled the air as the new knights competed to garner prestige, recognition, and, for the winners—generous prizes. New and experienced knights alike hoped to gain the favors of the ladies whose colors they wore in the joust.

Tristan and his fellow knights sat atop their *destriers*—the war horses that King Marke had gifted them for winning the Tournament of Champions in Cornwall. The magnificent animals were adorned with *caparisons,* the ornamental drapery which featured the rider's heraldry, as the ten new Knights of the Round Table competed against the more experienced knights who had trained them. Each rider charged with a wooden lance, hoping to unhorse his opponent, as frenzied cheers from the crowd of brightly attired nobles rippled through the crisp spring air. Lancelot, bearing the flowing white scarf of Queen Guinevere, emerged as the victor of the celebratory joust. The jubilant crowd went wild.

Panting, grinning, his face streaked with grime and sweat, Tristan stood triumphant as the champion of the individual sword fighting event, having earned the distinct honor of being the first to ever defeat the infallible First Knight of Camelot. His teeth clenched in a wicked grin, Tristan muttered under his breath, "You let me win. So that I would share in your joy of triumph today."

Lancelot, his dark brown locks plastered to the sides of his handsome face, grinned savagely in return. "No, Tristan. Truly, I did not. You are the first—and *only*—knight to ever disarm me. The Goddess help any warrior who challenges you in battle. You, Sir Tristan of Lyonesse, are a champion of kings." He wrapped an arm around Tristan's shoulder, leading him off the tournament field to claim their prizes, revel in victory, and enjoy another sumptuous feast.

Two weeks after the official dubbing ceremony and unforgettable celebratory tournament, the Knights of the Round Table were assembled in the throne room of Camelot as King Arthur explained the purpose of his royal summons.

"Knights of the Round Table. I have received an urgent request from my ally, King Marke of Cornwall." Tristan, his heart pounding at the mention of his uncle's name, flashed an anxious glance at Vaughan, whose desperate eyes reflected the same panic that was now racing through his icy veins.

"The Morholt—the Black Knight of Ireland—has been pummeling the coast of Cornwall. Taking slaves. Burning villages and crops. Weakening King Marke's defenses." Heated voices rippled among the knights. Arthur's deep voice bellowed across the room.

"The Morholt has demanded the Cornish crown. If Marke refuses to surrender, the Black Knight will invade with his ruthless Viking army. And dozens of *drakaar* warships." Shouts broke out among the knights from Cornwall. Pressure throbbed in Tristan's temples. *My uncle needs me. I'm his champion. His sword. His heir.*

"Marke has refused to surrender. He has called for the aid of Camelot to defend against the Irish attack." Lancelot had come to stand beside Tristan, whose entire body was shaking with adrenaline. And rage.

Another fucking Viking threatens to destroy the only family I have left. He glanced down at the glistening blue eye of the sea raven on his trembling hand. *I will defend my uncle. Or die in battle!*

Once again, the massive arm of the bearded Viking raised the lethal sword. Tristan's stomach dropped like the weapon which fell like an axe to slice off his father's humiliated head. Liquid rage flowed like fire through Tristan's veins as the Viking brute impaled his struggling, defenseless mother with the odious, bloody blade. His sister's horrific shrieks scraped across his soul.

I am no longer the simpering boy too weak to fight. Too young to defend his family. I am the Blue Knight of Cornwall. The heir to the throne. And I will defend my family—and my kingdom—to the death.

Arthur's deep baritone tore Tristan from the past.

"I will send twenty of my Knights of the Round Table, each with a command of a hundred men, to defend the kingdom of Cornwall. Bedivere, as my Marshal, will select who among you will depart for Tintagel, and who will remain here to defend my lands. If you are among the twenty selected for battle, prepare to ride on the morrow."

As expected, the ten knights from Cornwall were returning to defend their homeland, along with ten more experienced Knights of the Round Table. Lancelot, as Arthur's First Knight, and Bedivere, as the king's

Marshal, were leading the army, departing at first light.

Tristan sharpened his sword *Tahlfir* as he prepared to return to Cornwall for the first time in two years. Immeasurably grateful for the exhaustive training here in Camelot. In *Bretagne*, where Lancelot had taught him the inimitable maneuvers of the fearsome Avalonian Elves. In the sacred Forest of *Brocéliande*, where he'd mastered extraordinary skills among his brethren, the fierce Celtic warriors of the legendary Tribe of Dana.

He stared at his chain mail armor, gleaming in the setting sun streaming in through his open window. The sharp cry of a falcon tore through the air. Tristan gazed at the distant forest he would cross in the morning, riding hard with an army of two thousand men to defend Tintagel.

To defend his uncle, the only remaining member of his brutally slaughtered family. To defend the kingdom he had sworn to protect.

He, the king's champion, the Blue Knight of Cornwall, would face the same Vikings he'd been too young to battle as a squire in Lyonesse.

But this time, by the Goddess, he was ready.

Chapter 24

Ronan

The autumn air of Avalon was crisp and cool, the apple trees bursting with ripe, red fruit. Issylte was returning to *Le Centre*, a basket on her arm, when she saw the silvery blond head of the enormous warrior at the top of the hill.

Her heart skipped a beat, the frantic wings of a white dove fluttering in her chest. She dropped her collection of herbs, raced up the hill and shouted, "Ronan!" as he dismounted from his black horse. With a squeal of glee, she threw herself into his arms, clasping him behind his thick, muscular neck. Tears sprang into her eyes, relieved at his return.

"I'm so glad you're back," she whispered into his pointed ear, burying her face into his broad chest, inhaling the familiar scents of pine, leather, and horses. With a deep chuckle, he wrapped his corded arms around her, lifted her off the ground and swirled her around in a circle of joy. He gently placed her back down on the thick grass and planted a kiss upon her lips that conveyed how much he had missed her, too.

"Let's go find Viviane, so I can deliver these supplies she requested," he suggested, his rugged face lit up in a handsome grin. "After, we can pick some of these beautiful apples to bring to the horses. Sound good?"

She nodded brightly, and they headed into *le Centre* to find Viviane.

Once he'd greeted the Lady of the Lake and some of the priestesses who had come to say hello, Ronan and Issylte harvested two baskets of the ripe, red fruit to bring to his stables. The white dove in Issylte's heart soared with joy.

Marron was delighted to see her, especially when Issylte offered the pregnant mare two delicious apples, which she crunched with relish. Maëva and Noz devoured their fruit, as did the other horses who came to greet Ronan and his familiar guest, delighted with their special treat.

Once all the horses had welcomed him back and had eaten at least one apple, Ronan led Issylte into his gray stone cottage to warm her from the chilly autumn wind.

A long rectangular living area extended from the front entry, with a simple kitchen to the left and a fireplace in front of a wooden settee. At the far end of the cottage, Issylte glimpsed a bedroom and a hall leading to a second bedroom behind the living area. Ronan sat her upon the fruitwood settee as he lit a fire against the chill. Soon, flames were crackling and the scent of woodsmoke from a thick oak log welcomed her with cheerful warmth.

The enormous Elf went into his small kitchen to pour two goblets of hard cider. He returned to the living area where Issylte sat before the fireplace. He offered her a chalice as he sat down beside her before the comforting hearth. The spicy scent of cinnamon, the fruity aroma of apples and the effervescent bubbles of the cider delighted her nose.

Ronan stirred his goblet with the cinnamon stick,

took a hearty gulp, and smacked his lips with a grin. Placing a long arm behind her on the back of the settee, he turned to face her, his deep green eyes glowing in the firelight.

"I traveled to the seven islands here in the Avalonian realm," he began, "then sailed to the mainland of Bretagne, to the region called Armorique. It has a coastline of pink granite that is especially beautiful." He sipped his cider and flashed her a dazzling smile which took her breath away. She buried her face in the goblet, delighting in the rich apple flavor sweetened with spice. And the distinctly male scent of leather, horses and pine that beckoned her forest fairy soul.

"I brought these back for you." He grinned, withdrawing from the bag at his feet several exquisite pink and white seashells.

Issylte gasped in delight. "Oh, Ronan, they are beautiful! Thank you so much. I *love* them!" She cradled the treasure in her palms, the pearlescent shells and pink swirls glistening in the firelight. She hummed with delight. He grinned, content that his gift had pleased her.

"I'll place them on my table near the fountain. Next to my giant scallop shell," she murmured, her voice hushed with exuberance. "The one we found the day you took me to the fishing village at Rochefort." She gazed at him, feeling a flush heat her face. "I always think of you... every time I see it." She took another swallow of cider and averted her eager eyes.

Ronan smiled again, took her hand, and kissed it. After a moment, he told Issylte more of his voyage to the mainland of *Bretagne*.

"I sold all of the weapons and armor I had forged in my shop to King Hoël of Armorique. They were so impressed with the quality," Ronan added, placing his cup of cider on the table before them, "that King Hoël and his son Kaherdin have placed an additional order. Which I will deliver in the spring, after Marron has birthed her foal."

Issylte's heart dropped. Ronan would be leaving again. But at least he would be here in Avalon for several months. As if reading her thoughts, he promised with a grin, "We'll have plenty of time together before I leave again." He rose, stretched his long arms above his head, taking their two goblets into the kitchen to refill their cups. He sat back down beside her, placed his arm back along the settee, and asked with a smile, "And you, my princess? What news do you have to share with me?"

The horrific vision in the waters of *le Lac Diane* shuddered through her. Issylte took a large swallow of cider, the fruity spice and warmth of alcohol giving her courage to speak.

"One afternoon, when I was with Viviane, I had a *sighting* on the lake." She shivered, the yellow reptilian eyes of the dark lord slithering up her spine. Ronan cradled her hand in his, his deep green eyes protective and fierce.

"When I was fourteen, living in my father's castle, my stepmother abruptly dismissed my nurse Gigi one day when I was out riding. When I returned, the queen informed me that she had sent Gigi home to her sister. Because I no longer needed a nursemaid. The queen herself would oversee my *instruction*." Issylte glanced down at her lap, trying to quell the shaking of her legs by rubbing her hands along the sides of her thighs.

"But in the *sighting,* I saw that the queen had ordered Gigi *killed.*" Issylte gazed desperately into

295

Ronan's intense eyes. His strong grip anchored her as she floundered in the waves of grief and terror.

"Just like in the Hazelwood Forest when the queen's royal guards killed *Tatie*, Bran, and Dee, they took Gigi into the woods. They dragged her off her horse…pinned her arms behind her back…and *slit her throat*." Issylte pulled her hand from Ronan's steady grip, covered her face, and sobbed. He stroked her back, his strong touch and soothing presence calming her like a frightened horse.

Her sobs subsided; she raised her face to his. Her voice filled with grief, Issylte choked, "The queen killed Gigi, the nurse who was like my mother." She swallowed a sob and spat, "She killed Maiwenn, my *Tatie* that I loved like a grandmother. She killed Bran, and Dee. She even tried to kill me—*twice!*" Issylte turned sideways to face him, her heart aflame with anguish.

"Ronan," she gasped, clutching his forearm, "I'm afraid she'll kill my father next." Issylte scooted closer to him. "I must *do* something. I'm a gifted healer—a *guérisseuse*. My father is very ill…The queen sent for a healer to treat him. But I had a vision of him, too. He was standing with the queen beside my bedridden father, who was covered with blood sucking leeches." She shuddered uncontrollably.

"They're weakening him. Killing him. The *healer* had dreadful yellow eyes. With slits like a snake. Evil slithering all over my sick father. By the Goddess, Ronan, I must do something. I must help him. Before the queen kills him, too!"

Inconsolable, she wept as Ronan pulled her against his chest, stroking her back and kissing her hair. When her anguished sobs finally lessened to whimpers, he lifted her chin and fixed her with intense green eyes.

"Issylte, you *cannot* go back to your father's castle. The queen knows that you live; she hunts you even now. If you were to return to Ireland, you would deliver yourself directly into her hands. She'd accomplish what she has tried to do twice before. *Kill you*! You absolutely cannot go back. You must remain here in Avalon. Where you are safe."

Ronan stood and began to pace in front of the fireplace. He turned back to meet Issylte's eyes, his rugged face distraught with pain.

"Eight years ago," he whispered, his voice hoarse, "my wife Yanna and I lived on an island to the east of here, with our infant son, Loïc." Issylte raised her eyebrows, surprised to learn that he had been married. She listened quietly as he struggled to continue. Ronan's voice hitched with emotion.

"I had a blacksmith shop there, on *l' Île Verte*—the Green Island—as I do here. I learned the trade from my father." He began pacing again, staring at his boots as he stomped before the hearth. A wild stallion caged in a stall.

"We lived in a stone cottage, in a village like Briac. We had horses, a garden, a new baby…We were very happy," he choked, shaking his long blond hair down his shoulders like a golden mane.

He peered at Issylte on the settee, his handsome face ravaged by grief. "Our island was attacked by two ships—marauders who knew the value of the weapons made by the Elves of Avalon. All of our warriors banded together to confront the assault."

Bitter with rage, Ronan's wounds were still raw as his tormented eyes tore into Issylte's.

"We repelled the invaders, triumphant in our victory. But when I returned home, I found my wife and son..." his voice quavered, his eyes dropping to the floor. "They'd been *slaughtered*...their bloodied bodies thrown on the floor of the cottage." Ronan dropped onto the settee beside Issylte. He leaned forward over his long legs, propping his head in his hands, elbows on his knees. He raked his fingers through his hair in anguish. *"I was not there to protect them!"*

Ronan rocked back and forth, engulfed in grief, as the fire snapped and crackled in the hearth. "There was another ship on the south side of the island. While we were all off fighting the two ships to the north, Yanna and Loïc were defenseless. They *died* because I was not there to protect them. And that guilt has tormented me every day of my life ever since."

Ronan stared into the flames, swallowing his grief with gulps of cider. He shook his hair to calm himself, fixing his gaze on Issylte, his deep green eyes blazing in the firelight.

"After the attack, many of the villagers rebuilt their lives. But I couldn't. I kept seeing my wife and son everywhere. The guilt smothered me. I left our island and sailed here. My father had come here after my mother's death—he'd become Viviane's lover. I'd heard that the Lady of the Lake had established a center of healing here on Avalon. When she commissioned my father to forge the sword Excalibur for King Arthur of Britain, he asked for my help. I settled on this island and have remained here ever since. After his death six years ago, I assumed his role as master blacksmith of the Avalonian Elves."

Ronan dropped to his knees before her, grasping both of her slender hands in his calloused ones. His passionate eyes beseeched hers. "You *cannot* go back to Ireland. You *must* remain here, so that I may protect you... as I failed to do for my wife and son." He kissed her hands repeatedly as he choked, his voice raw with pain, "Issylte, you *cannot leave!*"

She lifted his face in her cupped hands and kissed him gently. He stood, pulled her roughly into his arms, and kissed her face, hair, neck, and finally, her lips. Cradling her against his chest, he laid his head against the top of hers and whispered, "I cannot lose you, too."

As if to compose himself, Ronan stepped back from her and wiped his hands against the sides of his breeches. He collected the cups and returned them to the kitchen. Noting the approaching twilight, he said with a soft smile, "Come, I will take you back now. Perhaps tomorrow, we can go into the village together."

Issylte understood that he was vulnerable. He'd bared his soul to her and now needed some time alone. She nodded, smiling softly as she accepted his invitation. "That would be lovely, Ronan. I'd love to go to the village again."

When they said goodbye at the entrance to *Le Centre*, Issylte sensed the grief weighing heavily upon him. She gazed up into his clouded eyes and whispered, "Ronan, you must heed your own advice." He raised an eyebrow, perplexed.

"*Do not blame yourself for the evil of another,*" Issylte said softly. "You, Ronan, are not guilty of the death of your wife and son. The invaders who attacked your island are responsible, *not you.*" He turned away, grim and resolute. She put a finger under his chin and pulled his face gently towards her. "You and I both must learn to forgive ourselves. Perhaps together, we can."

She raised up onto her tiptoes and kissed him lightly on the lips. He said goodnight, and she watched him climb into the saddle and ride down the hill towards the forest. In her heart, Issylte prayed that, on this island of nurturing, she and her warrior Elf would find a way to help each other heal.

As the weeks passed, Ronan seemed to have put up a defensive barrier, a wall that hadn't been there before, keeping himself shut off. Although they spent many afternoons together, he didn't come to fetch her as frequently as before. And when he did, he seemed distant. Different. Alone.

She sensed that he felt awkward now, having exposed his vulnerability to her. He'd lived alone for so many years, perhaps he regretted how close the two of them had become. Perhaps he even regretted having a relationship with her at all. He was broken, suffering. Issylte knew intuitively that he needed her healing. So, one afternoon, when he hadn't come to see her in three weeks, she picked a basket of apples, borrowed a horse from *le Centre* and rode through the forest to his blacksmith shop.

He was bent over his forge, shirtless, covered with sweat—even though it was quite chilly outside. Hearing her horse, he looked up from his work and flashed her a smile, obviously happy to see her. The white wings of the dove in her heart fluttered with joy.

Ronan spoke to his journeymen and apprentices, grabbed his tunic, and came out to greet her. He smelled of fresh sweat, leather, and smoke from the forge. "What a nice surprise," he grinned up at her, astride the chestnut bay. His lips puckered as he whispered a friendly greeting to the horse, stroking the mare's muzzle with a practiced hand.

He gestured to the men inside his shop. The metal clash of hammers and anvils thundered over the blazing forge. Issylte could feel the heat even from outside—a hot furnace in the crisp October air.

"I was just finishing up some of the weapons for King Hoël's order," Ronan said, wiping his face on a linen cloth. Issylte's eyes lingered over his muscled chest—covered in dark blond hair, matted with sweat—his huge arms, his wide neck… Her mouth was dry; her legs were weak.

She sputtered, "I… brought some apples… for the horses." Dismounting, she handed the reins to the stable hand who took them, nodding at her politely as he murmured, "My lady."

Ronan, having wiped the sweat from his torso, donned his tunic and strode over to accept the basket of apples. "Let's go see Maëva and Marron," he said brightly, taking her hand in his. His touch made her stomach quiver as he led her to the fenced area where the horses were grazing. At Ronan's whistle, the two mares came trotting over, eager to have their muzzles stroked and to crunch on the crisp red apples.

"Come, let's go inside for some mulled wine. It will warm you up." At her nod of acceptance, he led Issylte into the cozy cottage, took her cloak, and sat her on the settee while he stoked the fire. Ronan went into the kitchen and poured some red wine and spices into a pan, warming it over the crackling flames. The inviting smells of cinnamon, honey and brandy mingled with the rich fruity scent of red wine as it simmered in the pan.

Ronan poured her a cup and one for himself, placing a cinnamon stick and a slice of orange peel into the pewter goblets as he sat down beside her before the hearth. Issylte sipped the warm, spicy beverage, savoring the taste of cinnamon and cloves sweetened with honey, citrus, and brandy. The earthy, plum richness of the mulled wine slid smoothly over her tongue and down her throat, a liquid warmth glowing like embers in her veins. She purred contentedly. "Mmmm, this is *delicious*. Thank you."

Searching for a topic of conversation, hoping to break the ice, Issylte said cheerfully, "Marron seems to be very healthy. When is her foal due?"

"In the spring—late March or early April." He sipped some of his mulled wine, gazing thoughtfully at the fire. "I'll remain here to be sure the foal is healthy, then head for *Bretagne* in May. I'll sail to Armorique again, to deliver the new order of weapons and armor to King Hoël."

"Will you be gone for several months?" she asked, trying to hide the disappointment in her voice.

"No, no longer than three months." Ronan took another sip of mulled wine, warming his hands on the cup. He smiled at her, his white teeth gleaming in the firelight. Issylte's breath caught in her throat.

"It takes a few days to sail from here to the mainland. After I deliver the king's order, I plan to stop in several local villages to sell some of the extra weapons and armor that I plan to bring with me, making the voyage as profitable as possible. I expect to be back in late July or early August. Will you miss me?" he asked with a sly grin. His deep green eyes twinkled with impish delight.

He set his mug down on the table, took her hand, and kissed it. A thrill of pleasure rippled up Issylte's arm and throughout her whole body. Wanting to touch him, yet hesitant, she pushed a strand of silvery blond hair from his forehead. At her touch, he turned his face and kissed the inside of her palm.

"I've missed you, Ronan," she whispered. She glanced up at him from lowered eyes, her voice hesitant. "You have seemed troubled lately." Although her pulse raced, she waited, trying to appear patient, allowing him time to respond. Inside, she held her breath, fearful and anxious. She didn't want him to push her away. She wanted him. And wanted him to want her. To need her as much as she needed him. She watched the flames dancing in the hearth.

He took another large swallow of wine, savoring the flavor as he licked his lips in appreciation. He sat back, took her hand, his deep green eyes locking hers. "Talking about my wife and son was incredibly difficult for me," he said gently. "I relived that anguish, and the guilt. But what has been troubling me most," he said, gazing fiercely into her eyes, "is the thought of you returning to Ireland."

He glanced down at her hand, cradled in his own. His voice choked with emotion, Ronan stammered, "I cannot bear the thought of losing you, Issylte." He raised her face to his with a curved, gentle finger. The intensity of his eyes bore into her soul.

"You *must* stay here in Avalon. Where I can protect you. Where you are safe. *With me.*"

As if a torrent had been released, he pulled her to him, crushing her in his arms. His mouth devoured hers; his hungry lips kissed her neck, her shoulders, her throat. He was famished, ravenous, starved.

He yanked down one shoulder of her gown to

expose a soft breast, his greedy lips devouring it as Issylte melted in his arms. A deep hollow ached within her, yearning to be filled. Her whole body quivered in his arms.

His pleading eyes met hers, asking permission to continue. She responded by taking his lips into her own, pouring her longing for him into a desperate kiss. He stood, raised her from the settee to stand before him, and lowered the other shoulder of her gown, reveling in the sight of her bare breasts. A guttural moan came from deep in his throat. He kissed and suckled first one, then the other, his warm lips and tongue making Issylte swoon. Ronan took her by the hand and led her into his bedroom, where he removed his tunic and turned to face her. His savage look was fierce with longing.

She touched the dark blond hair on his chest, nuzzling it with her nose and mouth, breathing in the scent of him—smoke from the forge, a touch of leather from the cord in his hair, the hint of pine from the forest. She kissed his neck and shoulders, tasting the salty flavor of his fresh sweat. Liquid fire flowed in her loins.

He lifted her gown over her head, followed by her chemise, so that she stood nude before him. He raked his eyes over every inch of her. "By the Goddess, Issylte. You are *exquisite*."

He laid her down on the bed before him, reveling in her naked beauty. Lowering himself over her, he kissed her lips, neck, breasts, and finally, the womanly softness between her legs. His tongue caressed her tender skin, sending ripples of pleasure with each delicate stroke. He lifted himself back up onto his knees to face her as he licked his fingers and slid first one, then two, deep inside her.

He returned his mouth between her legs, his tongue flicking, as he thrust his fingers in and out in a slow, steady rhythm. Issylte moaned with desire, writhing under his touch, feeling her body tightening in a pleasure so intense it was nearly painful. When she could bear no more, Ronan increased the pace of his caresses, until her body released, convulsing with pleasure, contracting on his fingers, quivering into his mouth.

When her trembling subsided, he stood and removed his breeches. Issylte gasped at the enormity of the warrior whose desire stood boldly and magnificently before her. Pushing her legs apart with his strong knees, he lowered himself to her, prodding the entrance he sought. Tilting her hips up with his powerful hands, Ronan thrust deeply into her, moaning, increasing his pulsing movements until he, too, collapsed onto her, contorting with pleasure, filling her to the brim with his seed.

He laid down beside her, cradling her in his arms, and whispered, "I have not lain with a woman since the death of my wife." He kissed the top of her head, nestled on his chest. "I had forgotten the intensity of the pleasure…and the joy."

Issylte kissed the thick blond hair on his chest and murmured contentedly, "I have never lain with a man before. I had no idea it could be so … *wonderful*."

Twilight was falling, so they returned to *Le Centre,* making plans to spend time together as the Yuletide season approached. The weeks passed, their lovemaking frequent and intense. On days when Ronan needed to work and was unable to visit, Issylte often went into Briac to deliver herbal remedies, to treat illnesses or injuries, or to procure supplies needed by the priestesses.

One afternoon, she went into a silversmith shop to deliver an elixir. She asked the shopkeeper if he could craft a pendant for an amber gemstone that she'd brought with her. The smith examined the stone and assured her that he could encase the crystal in a simple silver bezel and bale. She left the gem there, with plans to retrieve it in two weeks.

The pine boughs, garlands of holly and mistletoe decorations brought cheer to both patients and healers at *Le Centre* with the arrival of the Yuletide season. Many of the local villagers brought baskets of gifts to support the center for healing and to thank Viviane and her priestesses for the exceptional care they'd received. Meals in the dining hall often featured some of the delicious tartes and fruit preserves that had been offered to *Le Centre* as gifts. Mellow music from flutes filled the conservatory with seasonal joy as heartfelt gratitude reflected on the faces of patients and priestesses alike.

Ronan and Issylte decorated his cottage with boughs of fir and pine from the forest, adorning the mantle above the fireplace with fragrant Yuletide greenery. Clumps of holly with bright red berries cheered the cozy cottage, and garlands of fragrant white hellebore blossoms perfumed the air. A cluster of mistletoe, sacred plant of the Druids, hung over the entrance door, offering the blessing of the Goddess for a prosperous new year.

This afternoon, the setting sun streaked the sky a brilliant pink as Ronan and Issylte sat before his blazing hearth, enjoying the warmth of the fire and the sweet spice of mulled wine. He offered her his Yuletide gift, carefully wrapped in white linen and tied with a dark green ribbon. The sight of the emerald silk strand flooded her with memories of her father's wedding and the attendants plaiting her hair. Issylte swallowed a lump in her throat, focusing instead on the joy of the season with Ronan as she unwrapped his gift. His Elven eyes sparkled in the firelight. The sweet flavors of honey and brandied wine warmed her as much as the joy which blazed in his forest green eyes.

Issylte gasped in delight at the deep green hooded cloak, made of finest wool and lined with soft white rabbit fur. Her hand caressed the emerald fabric and the decadent fur, tears filling her eyes at the thoughtfulness and beauty of his precious gift.

She stood, wrapped the cloak around her shoulders, as Ronan rose to his feet and fastened it beneath her chin. He wrapped his strong arms around her, rocking her gently back and forth. With a luscious kiss and a smile that melted her heart, he grinned, "This will keep you warm throughout the winter. And replace the green cloak you had to sacrifice when we first set sail for Avalon."

She remembered the couple they'd met in the woods. The woman who had exchanged cloaks with her, enabling Issylte to escape. And now, here she sat with her Avalonian Elf, sipping spiced mulled wine before a roaring Yuletide fire. The joy in her heart glowed as she flashed Ronan a brilliant smile.

"Thank you so much. It is absolutely beautiful, and I will treasure it always." She kissed him softly, his warm lips sending a tingle up her spine. She stood, removed the cloak, and folded it neatly over her arm. She smiled at him, scurrying into the kitchen to place it on the oak table. Inside her bag was a small parcel, wrapped in green cloth that she'd embroidered with gold thread. It sparkled in the firelight. Quickly tiptoeing back to the settee before the hearth, Issylte offered Ronan his

Yuletide gift.

His rugged face lit up like a child's as he took the gift from her trembling hands. Carefully unwrapping the embroidered green cloth, he discovered the amber crystal that she'd had the silversmith craft into a pendant. She'd suspended the golden gem from a brown leather cord that she'd braided for him to wear around his muscled neck.

"I selected that amber stone because of the star pattern of the crystal formation," Issylte whispered, pointing to the center of the gem. "It reminds me of *la Grotte de l' Étoile,* where you showed me the sacred spring in the hidden sea cave." His dark green eyes glowed like deep emeralds. The white winged dove fluttered in her chest.

She rose onto her knees behind him on the settee, tying the cord behind his neck, as she inhaled his pine and leather scent deep into her lungs. Her verdant magic thrummed in response. Still kneeling behind him, she kissed the side of his face and whispered into his pointed ear. "Amber has many healing properties which will protect you. And I will be with you every time you wear it." She buried her nose in his hair, eliciting moans of pleasure from him as she sucked the back of his neck and gripped him tightly with her thighs.

Ronan turned to face her, pulling her into his arms with a passionate kiss that led to a memorable Yuletide thank you in his large, comfortable bed. And the promise of many more over the next few months before he had to leave again for Bretagne.

Issylte was careful to take herbs to prevent pregnancy, as did many of the other priestesses who had romantic relationships with local villagers or Avalonian Elves. Cléo remarked one day, as Issylte prepared her contraceptive tea, "You are most fortunate to share Ronan's bed. Many of the priestesses have tried and failed." With a soft smile, she added, "Including me." Issylte, at a loss for words, responded with a shy smile.

Spring returned, and with it, a profusion of white flowers as the apple trees, *aubépines,* and water lilies bloomed on the island of healing. Although the priestesses often treated injured soldiers at *Le Centre,* Issylte had noticed that in the past few weeks, there seemed to be a steadier stream of wounded warriors seeking care.

As they now applied a poultice to a serious wound, Issylte inquired of Viviane, "Why has there been such an increase in the number of injured soldiers lately? We are treating many more than ever before."

Viviane administered the healing ointment to the wounded man, wiping her hands on a clean cloth as she led Issylte outside to sit near the fountain. "We are indeed treating more injured warriors than ever before. Our priestesses and the Elves have been traveling throughout the realm to fetch the seriously wounded, bringing them here to Avalon."

Issylte searched the sorrowful eyes of the Lady of the Lake. "There have been dozens more arriving each week. Waves of them. But why?"

Viviane smoothed her white robe, staring at the folds of fabric as if the words she needed might be found there. "The Black Knight of Ireland—the one they call the Morholt—has been attacking the coast of Cornwall in southern Britain."

Issylte stared into the waters of the fountain as if across the Celtic Sea.

"The Black Knight has established a Viking

stronghold in the seaport of Dubh Linn, where he launches slave expeditions which have vastly weakened the Cornish king. The Morholt's warships bring invaders who pillage, burn, and destroy... and capture hundreds of slaves to take back to Ireland."

Issylte shuddered at the memory of the enormous Viking whose fiery beard was braided like the fangs of a massive beast. Whose black armor blazed with the flames of a golden dragon. Whose plumed helmet sizzled with slithering snakes. She shivered from head to toe.

"The injured we are treating...are the survivors of those attacks." Viviane turned to Issylte, her eyes glimmering. "Sadly, there will be many more. For the gold—and especially the slaves—have vastly enriched the Irish queen."

Issylte swallowed a lump of terror. The Irish queen! A tingling numbness crept up her arms, her stepmother's icy grip draining her strength. She rubbed her arms rigorously to dispel the memory.

Issylte rose to her feet and began pacing in front of the fountain. "These poor victims we are treating...the brutal attacks, the burns, the lost limbs, the orphaned children. Viviane, I *must* help my father. He would never allow this. The queen and her *healer* have weakened him. So that the Morholt can capture slaves."

Issylte dropped onto the bench beside the Lady of the Lake and buried her face in her hands. When she lifted her tear-stained face, her eyes desperately implored Viviane. "If I could get to my father, I could cure him. He could reclaim his kingdom—- and *stop the evil queen*!"

Viviane grasped Issylte's shaking hands and studied them before responding. Her voice was calm, stern,

solemn. Her deep blue eyes washed Issylte with the
tranquil waves of the lily strewn lake.

"Lilée, even if you *could* infiltrate your father's
castle and steal into his royal chambers without being
apprehended by the queen—who would certainly have
you *killed instantly*—there is no way of knowing how
long you would need to heal him. Or, for that matter, if
his recovery is even possible."

Patient, maternal eyes gazed into hers. "Even if you
brought with you all the herbs, crystals, and sacred
waters needed for his treatment, it might take weeks.
Even months. How would you stay hidden from the
queen?" Viviane placed her hand on top of Issylte's,
squeezing it lovingly. Her gaze became soft. Gentle.
Apologetic.

"Have you ever considered that if, despite all odds,
you were successful in healing your father...that he
might still be so smitten with his queen that he would
defend her...and not you?"

Issylte remembered her father's lovestruck face as
he beheld his exquisite bride. His giddy manner, his
flushed cheeks, the way he couldn't tear his eyes from
her. He would choose her. Of course he would. Issylte's
heart plummeted with her dashed hopes.

Viviane added, as gently as possible, "Lilée, while
your father lives, you have no claim to the Irish throne.
Even if you were to amass a powerful army, sail to
Ireland and challenge the queen, the kingdom is still *his*.
And the queen rules while he is ill."

Viviane fixed her resolute stare on Issylte. "You
cannot go to the castle, for she would *kill you*. As
difficult as it is to accept, there is nothing you can do to
intervene." Issylte dropped her tearful gaze to her feet,

gulping air into her constricted throat.

Then, as if to soften the impact of her words, the Lady of the Lake whispered, "You must be patient, Lilée, knowing that the Goddess has a fate for you which has yet to be revealed."

****

As the weather warmed, Issylte and Ronan visited the seashore frequently, stopping to enjoy the seafood delicacies in the inn at Rochefort, procuring supplies in the village shops, and returning to his cottage to make love before the fire. Since Ronan had worn the amulet she had given him as they shared an especially passionate, memorable afternoon, each time she now saw the amber gem around his neck, it reminded her of the bliss they shared together beside the glowing flames.

One afternoon, Issylte made a *tarte aux mirabelles* for Ronan in his cottage while he tended to the horses. He loved it as much as she had loved her *Tatie*'s pies. When Marron delivered a healthy foal at the beginning of April, Ronan brought Issylte to see the newborn filly, who was the same rich chestnut brown as her mother. Standing behind her as she admired Marron and the newborn foal, Ronan wrapped his arms around Issylte and kissed the back of her neck. His voice tender with emotion, he whispered into her good ear, "I've named the foal *Noisette*—Hazelnut—the fruit of the trees in your beloved Hazelwood Forest."

She whirled around to face him. He grasped her hands in his and brought them to his lips. "She is *yours*."

Her heart bursting with joy, Issylte blustered, "She's *mine*?"

With a huge grin, he nodded and drew her into his powerful arms. Holding her against his chest, he murmured, "I know how much you loved your horse, Luna." Kissing her hair, he said gently, "Now you'll have a horse of your own again. Happy Birthday, my princess."

The front of his shirt was damp as she wept in gratitude. Turning to *her* little foal, she cooed, "I love you, Noisette. I will take such good care of you!" With a fresh carrot in her trembling hand, she crooned to the mare, "And you, Marron. You're *such* a good mother!"

They watched the newborn foal and her loving mother for a long time, the warm spring sun gentle on their backs as they leaned against the fence. Then, Ronan and Issylte went inside the stone cottage to make love, as they often did, taking advantage of every afternoon they had left together before his departure for Bretagne.

****

The water was cold and sweet, fed from the same underground spring as *la Fontaine de Jouvence* in the courtyard of *Le Centre.* Today, as Ronan sat on a blanket under a canopy of oak leaves in the forest near the beach, Issylte was quenching her thirst at the base of a small waterfall. As she watched the ripples cascade down over the smooth rocks and collect in the pool, she remembered bathing in the stream near Maiwenn's cottage. A fist clenched around her heart. She turned to face Ronan. His steadfast gaze eased the painful grip in her chest.

She stared at the pool, feeling her senses slip into the water. Magic hummed in her veins as darkness enfolded her. An eerie stillness engulfed her as visions appeared on the rippling surface.

She saw her father, bedridden as before—but now with a trio in black beside him. A small man with dark, wrinkled skin was speaking to the tall wizard and the queen standing beside him. As the vision unfolded, Issylte saw the wizard place a small vial into the hand of the queen, who poured the contents into a silver chalice.

As the dwarf and the wizard watched, the queen lifted her husband's head and made him drink the contents of the goblet. The king convulsed, his face contorted with agony, then stilled as the three figures waited beside the royal bed. At that moment, as if he sensed her watching, the dark wizard's yellow reptilian eyes met Issylte's, sending a wave of terror and nausea through her body.

She became aware of Ronan calling her name, as if from afar. As she slowly came back to her senses, his arms were around her, cradling and rocking her, as he called her name. "Issylte… Issylte… Wake up, Issylte!"

Gasping, she clutched Ronan tightly and laid her face against his pounding chest. Shaking, her stomach roiling, she shivered in his arms until she was finally able to speak. Her tongue thick and dry, her heart pounding furiously, she told him of the horror she'd witnessed in the vision.

"The queen is poisoning my father," she gasped, struggling to catch her breath. Frantic, Issylte stood up and began pacing by the pool. Ronan stood and extended his arms to hold her, but she pushed them away, too overwrought to be contained.

"I saw the tall man in black—the same one I saw in the vision on the lake. The one with yellow eyes slit like a snake." She tore at her hair. Impotent rage burned in her ravaged soul.

"My father was bedridden. The dark wizard was beside the bed. With my stepmother, the queen. And a small, wrinkled man with brown, withered skin." Issylte searched Ronan's eyes. "They were conferring... then the dark wizard handed a vial to the queen. I saw her pour it into a cup. She made my father drink it." Her whole body shook.

She grasped Ronan's strong hand. "My father convulsed, his face grimaced in terrible pain. They watched, Ronan. Waiting for him to die. I *must* do something! I *must* save my father. Before it's too late!"

Her Elf held Issylte in his arms, stroking her hair, until she quieted. Lifting the blanket and shaking out the leaves, he folded it, retrieved their things, and said calmly, "Let's return to the cottage. We can discuss this further."

Settled now on the settee, wrapped in a blanket to calm her shivering limbs, Ronan offered her a cup of mulled wine and sat down beside her. He held her against his chest, encircling her in the safety of his thickly corded arms.

Issylte sat up suddenly, decisively, and turned to face him. "Ronan, you once said that the weapons and armor you forge are unparalleled in performance." She set down her cup and inched closer to him on the edge of the settee. "Viviane told me how she brought her son, Lancelot, here to Avalon to train with the Elves. Because you are the fiercest warriors in the entire realm."

She took his hand in hers, raising her eyes to search his rugged face.

"Ronan—will *you* be my champion? Will you lead an army of Avalonian Elves to sail with me to Ireland? So that I may challenge Queen Morag... and save my father?"

****

Ronan was lost in her desperate eyes. He gazed at

the quivering lips he longed to kiss. The long blond hair he loved to touch. The woman who held his barely healed heart in her pale, fragile hands.

She'd asked him for the impossible. He couldn't bear to face her. He'd do *anything* for her. Fight to defend her. *Die* defending her. But this request was beyond his power. He had to reach her—make her understand. His powerful legs were trembling next to hers.

"Issylte," he began, taking her hands in his. "You know that the Elves of Avalon have an extended life span." She nodded, puzzled, searching for meaning in his eyes. His heart hammered in his chest.

"We live two or three hundred of your human years." He released one of her hands and gently touched her imploring face. "But our longevity is directly linked to *la Fontaine de Jouvence*—the Fountain of Youth— here in Avalon." Her emerald eyes, filled with grief, searched his face as he broke the unbearable news.

"We may travel extensively throughout all of the islands of our realm. But," he said, kissing her hand to soften the impact of his words, "if we Elves leave Avalon for a period of longer than four months…the curative effects of the Fountain of Youth disappear. And we perish of old age in the domain of humans."

He lifted her chin to gaze into her forlorn eyes, his heart breaking to say the words she couldn't bear to hear. "Even if I could muster enough of an army for you to challenge the queen…we Elves would die before the battle could *even be fought*."

She stood abruptly, wanting to flee, but he caught her hand and stood to hold her. "The voyage to Ireland would take a month, with the return trip of equal length.

That would leave only two months to wage war against the Black Knight in the Viking stronghold he has established in Dubh Linn." Issylte struggled to break free of his hold, but he needed her to listen.

"He has dozens of warships…and hundreds—if not thousands—of knights in the seaport of Dubh Linn. And, my princess, we would need to launch a second attack in the north, to secure your father's castle." He released her, and she stared at her feet as tears fell down her cheeks.

"We would have to divide our forces, with half sailing to Sligeach. With warriors, weapons, armor, and horses. Then, assuming we could even dock in the port, we would need to ride for a full day to reach your father's castle, where we would establish a siege."

He reached for her hand and tugged it so that she would look at him. Grief dulled her brilliant eyes.

"But Issylte, the Elves would die of old age… before the war could *even be waged.*" He pulled her into an embrace and whispered into her rose-scented hair. "I am so terribly sorry, my princess, but it is an *impossible* request."

Angry, frustrated, and hurt, Issylte frapped her fists upon his chest. "If you cannot lead my army, Ronan, then I must find another way. I can't just *do nothing* while my father is being poisoned!"

Ronan was frustrated and angry, too. She couldn't challenge the powerful queen. And the Morholt—*the Scourge of the Celtic Sea.* An invincible Viking with an army of thousands. With a fleet of hundreds of *drakaar* warships. Issylte had no army—or even the means of raising one. And, while her father still lived, she had no claim to the throne. He had to convince her to abandon this outrageous plan.

"Issylte, you cannot simply sail to Ireland and challenge the queen. You have no army. Princess, you cannot do this. Please, Issylte…stay here where you are *safe*. Stay in Avalon… *with me*."

She shook with emotion. "I am tired of being told I must keep myself *safe*. That I must remain *hidden*, while the queen unleashes *evil*! Ronan, she has killed everyone I love. She has taken everything from me. And now, she is *poisoning my father*!"

She tore at her hair in frustration. "We've been treating the victims of the Morholt's attacks. The women with empty souls, brutally raped by the Viking beasts. The orphans whose parents were killed before their very eyes. The men who tried to defend their families and lost an arm, a leg, or an eye…"

Turning to face him, she lashed out, "Ronan, the same invaders who killed Yanna and Loïc are now killing hundreds of others. And *capturing slaves*! I *must* do something. How can I save my father and stop the evil queen?"

Again, Ronan tried to reason with her. "I know you grieve for the victims, as do I. But you cannot just sail to Ireland and challenge the queen! If you were to claim that you are the Princess Issylte, the rightful heir to the throne of Ireland, she would declare you an imposter. The entire country believes that you died years ago. The queen would have you imprisoned and executed for treason. Please stop this insanity."

He took her in his arms and kissed the top of her head. He held her as she sobbed, rocking her gently, his deep voice soothing. "There is nothing you can do, my princess. Without an army… without a claim to the throne… you can't challenge the queen. You *must* stay here in Avalon. *With me.*"

He lowered his lips to hers, pushing aside the torment which engulfed her, channeling it into the flames of passion. He carried her to his bed, where he lavished her entire body with all the love in his heart. When at last she lay quivering with pleasure, content in his arms, he prayed to the Goddess that she would listen.

****

Three days later, Ronan kissed Issylte goodbye and set sail for Bretagne to deliver the weapons and armor he had forged for King Hoël of Armorique.

Her eyes brimming, she kissed the amulet he wore—the pendant she had given him for protection during his travels—as she wished him a safe voyage and quick return. She watched his ship sail away, then went back inside *Le Centre* to care for her patients, unable to shake the premonition of dread which hovered above. An ominous, dark cloud, obscuring her path.

Two weeks after Ronan's departure, news of the death of King Donnchadh of Ireland reached the island of Avalon.

Issylte was buried anew in grief. She—the forest fairy with verdant healing magic—had been unable to save her father. Visions of his frail, leech-covered body tormented her. Choked her. The evil queen and her vile viper forcing her bedridden father to drink the poisoned brew. His body convulsing in agony.

She hid in her room, unable to face anyone, drowning in sorrow. Her wicked stepmother had killed everyone Issylte loved. Impotent rage sickened her soul.

She kept to her room, visited frequently by Nyda, Cléo and Viviane. They tried to coax her to eat, to come sit by the fountain, to gallop across the plains or ride

319

through the forest. Issylte couldn't bear to leave her darkened room. Guilt and grief consumed her.

But, as the weeks passed, with more and more critically wounded soldiers and ravaged victims washing like waves upon the shores of the healing island of Avalon, Issylte forced herself back to work, caring for those who so desperately needed her. Every one of the twelve rooms in *Le Centre* now housed four patients instead of one. The conservatory had been converted into a hospital room where twelve more critically wounded soldiers writhed in agony. The acolytes' residence had become a second hospital, and the young priestesses now shared two rooms that had been part of Viviane's private quarters in the main building of *Le Centre*. Everywhere—in corridors, the library, the storage room of sacred stones—victims of the Black Knight languished in pain.

Some of the patients Issylte treated had come to Avalon from Ireland, escaping starvation and misery. She learned that her stepmother the queen had raised taxes repeatedly over the past few years in order to fund the construction of hundreds of *drakaar* warships for the Black Knight's merciless slave raids. Issylte heard horrid tales of young women given as spoils of war to the Viking brutes who enjoyed their nubile bodies and reaped the rewards of additional slaves when the victims bore children as a result. Captured young men were forced to row the Viking warships as they pummeled the coast of Cornwall to weaken the Cornish king. Many slaves were forced to till fields and harvest crops to feed the voracious Viking soldiers while the people of Ireland starved, staggering under the weight of additional taxes to fund the Morholt's insatiable army.

As a result of the continuous increase of victims of the ruthless Viking slave raids, Viviane ordered the construction of a Women's Center and a Home for Orphans on the island of Avalon. Villagers from Briac and Rochefort banded together with the Avalonian Elves and the *Little Folk*—proficient in woodworking and carpentry—to build the two shelters for victims ravaged and ruined by the vicious Viking assaults. Many of the women who had lost their families to the Morholt's army now helped care for the poor children who had seen their parents slaughtered. On the island of healing, victims bonded together as they weathered the tumultuous storm of the relentless Viking tempest.

Ronan returned in autumn, as the apple trees were laden with ripe red fruit. Issylte rode with him to his cottage, feeding the horses the tart, delicious treats, sipping on mulled wine before the crackling hearth, deeply grateful to be reunited at last.

She found solace in his protective arms, unburdening the profound grief at the loss of her father. Ronan's warm lips, skilled tongue and *otherworldly* Elven body helped her escape the horrors of war, her guilt and despair. Riding her beautiful blond stallion was more exhilarating than anything she'd ever experienced in the saddle, and Issylte cherished every precious day they spent together.

Sometimes, when she had a savory rabbit stew simmering on Ronan's hearth, the familiar scents of garlic, rosemary and sage filled Issylte with nostalgic memories of Maiwenn's cozy kitchen. And, even as her heart was gripped in the tight vice of loss, *Tatie's* love flowed into everything she did. In many ways, Issylte had become her *Tatie*.

Her verdant magic—wielding the curative essence of the forest—flowed through her veins, into the bodies of the severely wounded patients she healed at *Le Centre*. Her gentle touch, kind manner and soothing voice comforted the desperate orphans, drowning in the same grief of loss that Issylte knew so well. On days when she and Ronan could be together, she baked fresh bread, harvested and cooked seafood delicacies, and made *tarte aux mirabelles* in his cottage, just as *Tatie* had always done in the beloved Hazelwood Forest. Pouring love into everything she did helped keep the guilt and grief at bay.

Issylte often found herself watching Ronan when he was bent over his forge, his light golden skin glistening with sweat, his powerful arm hammering the Elven weapons for the king of Armorique. She watched him care for little Noisette, giving her foal an extra carrot as he lovingly groomed the magnificent horses in his stables. She often dreamed of the beautiful Elven children they would have. The silvery blond hair, pointed ears, and *otherworldly* power of their father. The verdant, healing magic of their forest fairy mother. She and Ronan would raise horses and children. She'd heal the sick; he'd craft inimitable Elven weapons. They'd make passionate love in the cozy stone cottage. Her Elf would protect their little family. And she'd be safe from the wicked queen with the icy grip of wolfsbane. The evil stepmother who still wanted her dead. And hunted her like a ravenous predator.

Yet, despite the love in Ronan's arms, the bliss they shared in his enormous bed, the happiness he gave her every single day—her stepmother's evil gnawed at her insides like the sharp, pointed teeth of hungry rodents. As she cared for the soldiers with missing limbs, the burn victims screaming in pain, the agony of warriors with bloody, infested sockets of a missing eye—the hot coals of impotent rage burned in her soul.

Her wicked stepmother had killed her beloved father, Gigi, *Tatie*, Bran and Dee. And now, the merciless Black Knight was pummeling the coast of Cornwall, leaving countless victims in his wake. Capturing hundreds as slaves for his wretched Irish queen. Issylte's own kingdom was at the mercy of the evil queen and her dreadful snake. Issylte was compelled to stop her. But how?

As Ronan said, she had no army. She couldn't simply sail to Ireland and naively demand the right to her father's crown. The wicked queen had the full power of the Irish throne. And the might of the Morholt, the *Scourge of the Celtic Sea*. With his invincible, voracious Viking army. Devouring her impoverished country. Destroying the weakened kingdom of Cornwall.

It was killing her. There was absolutely nothing she could do. Her entire country was suffering—in misery, starvation, poverty. And the Morholt was planning a massive invasion of Cornwall. Which meant even more victims, suffering, and death. Frustration and anguish gnawed mercilessly at her grieving gut.

****

Another Yuletide season passed. She and Ronan decorated his cottage with holly and fragrant pine boughs. When Cléo and Nyda cared for her patients, allowing Issylte time to come to Ronan's cottage, she often cooked delicious meals that they shared in the quaint kitchen. She and her Elf would ride across the grassy plains, through the dense forest, to the seashore where the crashing waves and lull of the ocean soothed her aching heart. They'd return to his hearth and make love before the roaring fire, nestled among furs on a pile of soft blankets.

This year, she had a cobbler in the village of Rochefort craft a fine pair of leather boots from the softest deerskin she'd ever touched. Large enough for his enormous Elven feet. And Ronan gave her dark green woolen gloves lined with rabbit fur, to match her lovely cloak. They sipped mulled wine before the fire and shared their Yuletide joy in his enormous bed. Yet the happiness she savored with Ronan sickened her with guilt amid the misery and suffering of her patients and the constant, nagging worry about the evil queen.

Issylte—who now wore the dark blue robes of a full-fledged Priestess of Avalon, having earned the distinction of *guérisseue celtique*—worked alongside Viviane, Nyda and Cléo to decorate the newly completed Women's Center and Home for Children with Yuletide cheer. The priestesses and women of the village roasted duck and pheasant, celebrated with fruit pies and homemade toys for the children that many of the *Little Folk* had crafted from smooth wood or soft fabric. And, although the recovering patients grieved for the families they'd lost at this most joyous time of year, bonding with one another on Avalon was helping everyone heal.

Spring returned with a profusion of white flowers on the beautiful island of healing. The fragrance of jasmine, apple blossoms and *aubépines* filled the crisp cool air as Issylte stood on the sandy shore, watching Ronan and his Elves load up the weapons and armor they'd been crafting for months for King Hoël of Armorique. Sea gulls cawed in the soft blue sky; the tangy salt spray of ocean waves filled her nose as her handsome Elf walked across the white sand to kiss her goodbye.

"I'll be gone three months. Not long, my princess," he crooned into her good ear as he wrapped his loving arms around her. He pulled her against his broad chest and bent her backwards to plant a luscious kiss upon her soft lips, parting them gently with the tip of his skilled tongue. A warm glow stirred in her loins as she remembered the delicious goodbye they'd shared just a few hours ago.

"We'll sail to Armorique and deliver this order. Sell to a few other nobles in Bretagne who want to buy weapons and armor. There are rumors that the Morholt and his Viking army are eyeing the coasts of France, so many want to be prepared." Ronan's grin spread from ear to ear, lighting up his rugged face. "It will be a most profitable trip."

Issylte stroked the dark blond stubble on his cheek, inhaling the familiar smell of pine, leather, and smoke as she buried her nose into the tuft of hair at the base of his throat. She breathed deeply, bringing the scent of him down into her lungs, trapping his essence inside her. To tide her over until his return.

"Hurry back to me, my Elf. I will miss you desperately." Her eyes glistened as she gazed up into his.

"I will, my princess. You hold my heart in your beautiful hands. I love you, Issylte."

"And I love you, Ronan." She kissed the amber amulet at his throat. "May this protective talisman guide you safely back to me."

He jogged briskly to the dock, where his Elven crew was hoisting the sail, preparing to depart. Ronan climbed aboard and turned to wave with a bright smile as she wiped the tears from her adoring eyes. And, as the warm

May sun kissed her cheeks and the salty breeze caressed her long blond hair, the Emerald Princess waved goodbye to her beloved Avalonian Elf.

Chapter 25

The Morholt

The twenty Knights of the Round Table, each leading a troop of a hundred men at arms, rode hard across the forest of southern Britain, arriving in Cornwall to find King Marke's knights heavily engaged in battle with hundreds of Viking warriors who were still disembarking on the beach in front of the castle of Tintagel. Red and white striped sails of sleek *drakaar* warships—oars protruding from the bellies of the loathsome vessels with fearsome dragons blazing at the prow—littered the beaches as heavily armed Viking warriors stormed the Atlantic shore. Blood soaked the white sand as the clash of metal swords and the shrieks of dying men rent the salt strewn air.

Sir Bedivere, King Arthur's marshal, strategically divided the riders from Camelot, dispatching them to reinforce Gorvenal and the beleaguered knights of Cornwall, staggering under the Viking assault. Tristan, Lancelot and Indulf were among the group sent to the south shore, where the defending army was facing the thickest onslaught of invaders. The horned helmets, braided beards and heavy chain mail armor of the Viking army were a relentless wave crashing upon the craggy coast of Cornwall.

Lancelot, in his white armor atop his white

warhorse, blazed through the Vikings surging towards the castle, felling three warriors with ease. Tristan, atop his destrier, slew two attackers, driving his blade into the exposed throat of one Viking and the groin of another. Indulf impaled a third, penetrating the Nordic mail with the sharp, narrow tip of his *estoc.*

While most of the invading army was on foot, many Vikings were riding the same destriers as the knights from Camelot. As the deafening roar of battle continued in full force all around him, Tristan glimpsed an enormous warrior, clad in black armor astride a black warhorse, facing him in challenge. *The Morholt—indomitable and undefeated in battle.*

The Viking's bushy red hair extended past his shoulders, braided into two sections like large horns. An equally long red beard was divided and braided as well, like two enormous fangs extending from his massive jaw. A large black plume rose from his intricately carved headpiece, and the golden dragon upon the warrior's black armor glistened with the congealed blood of the opponents he had slain. The Morholt raised his sword in challenge, spurred his horse, and galloped directly toward Tristan.

For a split second, Tristan was a trembling eight-year-old boy again, watching helplessly as the massive arm of the Viking dropped like an axe. His body shook; his mouth went dry. He was light-headed, woozy.

The sea raven ring throbbed on his finger inside the gauntlet. Years of impotent rage flooded him. The Viking who beheaded his father. The monsters who brutalized his innocent sister, her piercing shrieks scraping up his spine. His beautiful mother, struggling vainly against the beasts who restrained her. The bloody blade which tore open her fragile white throat.

Fury fueled his sword as Tristan galloped toward the oncoming enemy. With a vicious slice, the Morholt slashed the foreleg of Tristan's horse, throwing him forward onto the sandy beach. Sweat stung his eyes as he shook the sand from his face.

He quickly recovered his footing and turned to prepare for the Black Knight's next assault. As the Viking charged, Tristan deftly toppled him as well. The two warriors were now engaged in hand-to-hand combat.

The Viking's arms were as thick as tree trunks. The force of each blow against Tristan's shield caused him to stagger nearly to the ground. It finally shattered, splintering apart with the impact of the Morholt's massive sword. The Viking, his victory imminent, roared in laughter—the bellow of a mighty beast.

The Black Knight stank with sweat and filth. The blood of Tristan's Cornish brothers—who had died defending their king, his uncle Marke. The last remaining member of his slaughtered family. Rage flared in Tristan's gut as he crouched into the stance Lancelot had taught him.

The months of training at *la Joyeuse Garde* had prepared him. *The otherworldly* maneuvers of the Avalonian Elves he'd mastered. The ferocity and tenacity of the Tribe of Dana which flowed in his veins. With a sudden surge of adrenaline, Tristan perfectly executed a maneuver that Lancelot had taught him, cleaving the Morholt's headpiece in two, deeply embedding his hefted blade into the Viking's vile skull.

Yet, in a simultaneous move, his opponent's deadly weapon carved through Tristan's armor, slicing him across the abdomen, as the Viking fell to his knees and collapsed face first into the sand.

Tristan removed his sword *Tahlfir* from the Morholt's headpiece. A section of the blade had broken off and was still embedded in the Viking's skull. As he lifted his sword and straightened his back, Tristan's wound began to burn savagely. His mouth went numb; his tongue swelled in his throat. Icy tingling crept up his limbs; he wobbled unsteadily on his feet. The last thing Tristan saw was Lancelot charging toward him as he lost consciousness and darkness overtook him.

****

Lancelot had seen Tristan kill the Morholt, flawlessly executing the Elven technique he'd learned last summer. But he'd also seen the potentially fatal blow inflicted by the Viking in his dying move. He called two of his men to carry Tristan to the nearby dock where King Marke's ships were anchored. The Morholt had the reputation of wielding a poisoned sword, so Lancelot wrapped the Viking blade in a blanket from the back of a nearby fallen horse. Tucking the Black Knight's sword under his arm, Lancelot rushed to join his injured friend, now aboard the boat, flanked by the knights who had carried him, awaiting Lancelot's orders.

He summoned a few of the crew members stationed inside the boathouse, ordering them to sail south to Bretagne with utmost speed. Lancelot glanced back at the bloody battlefield in front of Tintagel as the ship left port. The Viking ships were also departing, the invading army in retreat now that the Morholt had been slain and two thousand men from Camelot had arrived to aid King Marke. The reinforcements sent by King Arthur to defend Cornwall had been the decisive factor in the successful defense of the castle of Tintagel. The Irish invasion had failed, the indomitable Morholt defeated. Lancelot heaved a sigh of relief and turned his attention to his critically injured friend.

He packed a compress of clean cloth against Tristan's abdomen, for the slice was deep, and he was losing a great deal of blood. Lancelot removed Tristan's armor and dressed the wounded knight in his own, hoping that the spells of protection that his mother—the Fairy Viviane—had imbued within it would keep Tristan alive until they reached Avalon. Where he prayed the Goddess would heal him.

Chapter 26

The Black Widow Queen

Morag stood near a gilded chair in her royal antechamber where embroidered floral tapestries adorned the stone walls of Castle Connaught. She gazed through the aqua silk draperies of the enormous windows to the dense forest below, the fragrant scent of pine wafting in upon the early summer breeze. Two harried messengers stood at attention behind her, waiting for permission to speak. With a heavy heart, she ducked her chin, swallowed, and turned reluctantly to face them.

"This is the sword, my queen. Of Sir Tristan of Lyonesse. The Blue Knight of Cornwall. The knave who slew the valiant Morholt." The royal messenger, his eyes humbly lowered, held a broken, bloodied sword in his shaking hands. His companion, equally distressed at bearing the bad news to the icy queen, kept his eyes fixed firmly on the carved legs of her gilded chair.

Morag glowered at the abhorrent blade. Stained with his blood. Crusted with his dark red hair. A large section near the tip of the sword broken off. Embedded in his skull. She swallowed the lump in her throat. "Over there." She nodded to a table against the far wall. The messengers complied and returned to face her, their heads lowered deferentially before their aggrieved queen. "Leave me," she hissed, her eyes glued to the bloody blade. The two men scurried off, grateful to escape with their lives.

She crept hesitantly to the table. With trembling fingers, she gingerly touched her beloved Black Knight's hair, removing a strand to hold against her heart. Tears of rage stung her eyes as she glimpsed his blood upon the broken blade. The blade which had split his plumed helmet. And cloven his skull. She shuddered from head to toe. *I will avenge you, my Beloved Black Knight. This odious Blue Knight of Cornwall will die a most gruesome death.*

Morag's attendants followed her into the royal chambers where they dressed the grieving queen in black to properly mourn the Morholt. Servants poured a goblet of fine French wine and left the bottle on the table, quietly slipping from the room as ordered.

A thick haze clouded her thoughts. She sat at the table and drained the goblet. Poured another. Her eyes roamed over the bed where her virile Viking had driven her wild with his amorous assaults. His massive chest covered with dark red hair. His powerful thighs that thrust his mighty sword deep into her with infinite skill. His clever lips and wicked tongue. Hot tears streamed down her frozen, pallid face.

Morag downed the rest of her wine. Lay down upon her lavender scented bed. And sobbed mournfully into her downy soft, elaborately embroidered pillow.

She ate little over the next few weeks. Word of the failed invasion spread like wildfire throughout the ravaged kingdom. The remainder of the vanquished Viking fleet returned dishonorably to the seaport of Dubh Linn, where the Morholt had left behind a few capable commanders. The staggering loss of hundreds of soldiers and dozens of prized warships was an irreparable blow to the naval forces of Ireland. An insurmountable, humiliating defeat.

When Voldurk returned from Cornwall, Morag received him in her private chambers. Royal servants left a bottle of wine and a platter of food, which the queen barely touched. The loss of her Black Knight had wounded her most unexpectedly. She had believed him indomitable. Invincible. Infallible. And now he was gone. Her heart and body ached for him.

"My deepest condolences on the loss of your personal guard, my queen. I know that you were very fond of the Black Knight. A tremendous loss for Ireland." Voldurk poured her a goblet of wine, which she gratefully accepted and quickly drained. She raised black obsidian eyes to search his.

"My trip to Cornwall, however, was most profitable." He refilled her chalice and flashed her a cunning smile. She lifted an eyebrow, intrigued.

"The dwarf Frocin has agreed to our request. Now that he is aware of the Princess Issylte, he will be watching to see when she uses her *gift*." Voldurk took a large swallow of wine and observed her over the rim of his goblet.

"When a fairy uses the power of *sight*, it leaves a trail of magic that Frocin can trace. With his unique gift of clairvoyance." He grinned wickedly at her, his golden eyes smoldering with molten flames. "The dwarf will track her for us. And his merciless mercenary knights will eliminate her." Voldurk traced a finger seductively across Morag's white shoulder, his scorching touch enflaming her frosty skin.

"Meeting Frocin was most fortuitous, my queen.

Not only will he rid us of your damnably elusive stepdaughter. But he also introduced me to another most powerful ally." Voldurk's forked tongue flicked against her swanlike neck.

"The sworn enemy of the accursed Blue Knight of Cornwall." Morag widened her eyes in delightful surprise as her breath hitched. "Sir Indulf of Hame."

She wiped damp palms along the sides of her black gown. Voldurk kissed the back of her neck, his breath hot in her ear.

"Sir Indulf is a knight of Tintagel anxious to denounce—and replace—Sir Tristan of Lyonesse as King Marke's champion. A knight with powerful allies throughout the kingdom of Cornwall. A knight who will help us avenge the Morholt. And capture the Cornish crown."

Her pulse quickened as Voldurk's lips caressed her shoulder, nuzzling the crook of her neck where his finger had sizzled her skin.

He circled in front of her and retrieved a small flask from his pocket. She searched his gleaming, golden eyes. The eyes of a dragon that smoldered with passion. Liquid fire flowed through her loins.

He handed her the small black stoppered vial. It pulsed with power in her hand.

"What *is* this?" she gasped with a quick intake of breath. Her heart quivered in her breast.

"Your future, my *Black Widow Queen*." He leaned forward to take the vial, placing it on the table at her side. "The key to the throne of Cornwall."

Morag locked eyes with her golden dragon. Her mouth went dry.

Voldurk raised her to her feet, a sly grin spreading

across his darkly handsome face. His seductive voice slithered into the shell of her ear.

"Wolfsbane."

Her heart fluttered wildly as he planted a lush kiss upon her eager lips. Morag melted into his arms as her legs gave out. Power was a potent aphrodisiac.

He carried her across the room. Stripped off her black garments of mourning. His wicked lips scorching her icy bare skin, the golden dragon laid his queen's nude, quivering body upon the lavender scented bed. And engulfed her lovely, lonely loins in the blazing flames of *dragonfire*.

Chapter 27

La Fatalité

With Ronan gone, Issylte lost herself in her work, keeping her inner demons at bay as she battled festering wounds, soothed severely burned skin and amputated gangrenous limbs. She cradled traumatized women and children, easing her own agony by helping to alleviate theirs. Comforting herself as she consoled others. But the inability to stop the wicked queen and her murderous Morholt sickened Issylte's soul.

One of her patients, Gwennol, was especially dependent on Issylte, having lost her husband and three sons, captured in a Viking slave raid in Cornwall. Too old to bear more children, who would become slaves themselves, Gwennol was left behind, worthless to the Viking invaders. The poor woman found comfort in the tender care of the young blond priestess with empathetic green eyes, soothing voice, and gentle hands.

Many victims found refuge in the Women's Center and Home for Children that Viviane had built near *Le Centre*. Some of the women who had survived the Viking attacks now nurtured the homeless orphans, forging new families to help them all heal. Issylte struggled to remain stoic, but as more and more victims arrived on Avalon, their bodies battered, their souls shattered, heartache was her constant companion.

Despite the best efforts of the priestesses, many patients succumbed to illness or injury. A funeral pyre burned—a blaze of grief amidst the beauty of apple trees and white hawthorn blossoms on the healing island of Avalon. The same flames engulfed her soul. The loss of her father. Gigi. *Tatie.* Bran and Dee. Luna. Her life at the castle. Her life in the Hazelwood Forest. And now, missing Ronan terribly and surrounded by suffering victims of the horrific Viking slave raids…it was all she could do to bury herself in her work and not drown in despair.

Today, Issylte, Viviane, Cléo and two acolytes were gathering herbs at the edge of the forest near the eastern coast of the island. The weather was warm, and the women had walked down onto the beach to gaze out at the sea and enjoy the fresh air and sunshine before heading back to *Le Centre*. The roar of the waves and the salty tang of the ocean reminded her of Ronan. She forcefully swallowed her unbearable longing for her beloved Elf.

Issylte knelt to collect a shell, remembering the day they had strolled together along the beach not far from here. Where she'd found the enormous scallop shell as large as her palm. Where Ronan had tied up the hem of her gown so that she could feel the waves caress her bare feet. His familiar scent of woodsmoke, pine and leather stirred her soul.

She stared at the turquoise blue of the ocean, lulled by the rhythmic rocking of the waves. The sun was warm upon her face, the squawks of sea gulls a song to her heart. Without warning, darkness enveloped her with an *otherworldly* stillness as images began to appear on the surface of the sea.

Viking warships with carved dragons on the prow and red striped sails were sliding upon the shore of a kingdom she did not recognize. Heavily armed soldiers were disembarking onto a beach in front of a castle built high on a cliff, engaging in battle with knights defending against the onslaught. The clash of metal and the screams of dying men pierced the skies as the raiders advanced. Pools of blood and mutilated bodies were strewn along the water's edge.

In the distance, a white knight with extraordinary skill fell several Vikings, his powerful sword infallible, his white horse magnificent. Nearby, a knight in a white surcoat with the head of a black bird on a sea of blue captured her attention, her breath catching involuntarily in her throat. Inexplicably, Issylte was drawn to the dark-haired warrior.

He was very tall—nearly a head taller than his fellow knights—and enormously built. His armor gleamed in the sunlight, waves of dark brown hair extending below his helmet. Atop his fearsome warhorse, exuding power and emanating strength, Issylte was captivated by the mysterious knight.

Another image flashed, and she glimpsed a ring, with the head of the same black bird as on the warrior's surcoat. The eye of the bird was a sparkling blue stone, and Issylte intuitively sensed a connection between the warrior and the sea. Her magic thrummed in response.

As the *sighting* unfolded, the warrior's brilliant blue eyes met hers. Transfixing her with the intensity of his stare. In his gaze, the earth moved beneath her. Inexorably, their fates were entwined.

More images flashed, and suddenly, the Morholt— the wicked queen's Black Knight that Issylte had met the day of her father's betrothal—emerged from the sea of invaders to challenge the blue-eyed warrior.

The Viking's long red braids hung down below his helmet, his burly beard braided into two forks. The massive Morholt sized up his opponent, gnashing his teeth like a beast of prey. Issylte's mouth went dry.

Breathless, her body quivering, Issylte felt as if *she* were the one engaging in battle against the Morholt. As if *she* were wearing the surcoat with the black seabird. As if *she* now sat atop the destrier, ready to charge the Viking with his enormous, black-plumed headpiece and blood-soaked sword glinting in the sun.

The young warrior spurred his horse, and Issylte was galloping with him towards the Morholt, whose monstrous sword was poised to strike, his black warhorse charging at full speed. With a powerful slash to the front leg, the Black Knight felled the warrior's horse, throwing him to the ground. With fluid movement, the young knight regained his footing and, as the Morholt charged again, the Black Knight was thrown from his destrier, leaving the two opponents in hand-to-hand combat on the bloodied beach. A golden dragon, dripping with blood, blazed on the Morholt's black armor. Issylte's pulse raced in her throat.

The blue-eyed warrior struggled to block the Viking's savage strikes, sinking under the impact to his knees in the bloodied sand. When the shield finally splintered under a staggering blow, the Morholt roared like the beastly dragon on his gore-splattered breastplate. Issylte's eyes widened and her heart stopped as the warrior—in a sudden burst of agility and finesse—swirled in a dance of death, burying his sword into the skull of the Black Knight, cleaving the ostrich plumed helmet in two.

Her stomach quavering, her legs trembling, Issylte watched in horror as the Viking simultaneously slashed his own sword across the warrior's abdomen. The razor-sharp blade sliced through the chain mail armor and carved into the muscled flesh. Deep red blood spurted from the vicious gash.

Issylte screamed, doubling over in agony, desperately clutching her own stomach. The burning, searing pain tore through her, as if her own abdomen had been sliced. Her vision blurred; her mouth went dry. Her tongue swelled in her throat. The chilling numbness of her stepmother's hand crept up her arms and legs, her extremities tingling like shards of ice. Issylte's last conscious thought was *poison. Wolfsbane!*

When her eyelids fluttered open, Issylte glimpsed a white room alit with candles, fragrant with the smell of burning sage, yarrow, and beeswax. She was on her back, in a bed, with several priestesses nearby. Viviane's face came into focus above her. "Lilée, you are awake! Praise the Goddess—you have returned to us!"

Her head lifted by the High Priestess, cool water touched her lips as Viviane held a cup for her to drink. "This is the holy water from our fountain, with some sacred herbs to stabilize you. Drink, Lilée."

She swallowed two gulps, then lay back against the soft pillow. Cléo and Nyda were at her side, relief apparent on their faces as they smiled reassuringly. After a few more sips of water, she was revived a bit, able to raise herself onto an elbow. She locked eyes Viviane. "Why am I here?"

At the Lady of the Lake's nod, Nyda and Cléo left the room. Viviane sat down on the bed beside Issylte and took her trembling hand.

"The day we were on the beach, you stared off into the ocean. Your eyes clouded over, as if you were experiencing a *sighting*. Suddenly, you screamed. You bent over and clutched your stomach, as if in horrible pain. We brought you here, to *Le Centre*, so that we could care for you." The Lady of the Lake wiped Issylte's brow with a cool cloth.

"You have been unconscious for three days, Lilée."

Issylte's mouth dropped open. She gaped at Viviane in disbelief.

"Do you remember the vision?"

Issylte described the *sighting*—the invasion of Viking warships, the warriors engaging in battle on the beach before a castle high on a cliff. At the mention of the magnificent white knight on a white horse, Viviane's head turned quickly, her face conveying recognition.

She told Viviane of the blue-eyed knight in a white surcoat bearing the head of a black bird. Of the warrior's ring—the same black bird, but with a dazzling blue stone as its eye. How the warrior battled the Morholt, the Black Knight of Ireland she'd met at her father's betrothal. She tried to explain the intense bond she'd experienced with the knight, as if she herself had been the one in battle against the Viking. How, when the blue-eyed knight slew the Morholt, and was in turn struck by the Viking sword, Issylte had felt the slice across her own abdomen as the warrior was critically wounded in the vision.

"What does it mean, Viviane? Never before has it seemed as if *I* were in the vision. In my other *sightings*, I was a spectator—merely observing. But this time, it was as if *I were there*—as if *I were the blue-eyed knight*!"

The Lady of the Lake stared into the distance,

pensive and reflective. "I have never witnessed it before with humans... But you do wield the verdant magic of a forest fairy." Viviane's deep blue eyes bore into Issylte's. In the fairy realm, an *otherworldly* connection such as you experienced in this *sighting* only occurs between *mates."*

Viviane rose to her feet and walked to the window to gaze at the moonlight shimmering on the rippling waters of the fountain. The High Priestess turned to face Issylte, her face luminous and ethereal.

"The *mating bond* is the joining of two beings across all planes—spiritual, emotional, physical. When one mate is seriously injured, the other experiences the pain, as you did when this warrior was wounded."

The Lady of the Lake smiled softly. "Like the swans on *le Lac Diane*, mates are bound for life. When they first meet, an *otherworldly* bond forms when they look into each other's eyes. Their souls entwine, their spirits merge." The Blue Fairy held Issylte's rapt gaze.

"When mates share physical love and become one, the *mating bond* is finalized. Rendered unbreakable."

Viviane stared at the moonlight waters of *la Fontaine de Jouvence*. "When mates join together, it is *celestial*—the physical pleasure and spiritual bliss fill you with unimaginable energy, love, and joy." Her eyes glistening, Viviane whispered, "That, dear princess, is the essence of life... a precious gift from the Goddess...to be treasured above all else."

A sage smile spread across Viviane's lovely face. "It would seem, Lilée, that the fate you have been awaiting for so long—*la fatalité*—has finally been revealed."

She sat back down on the bed beside Issylte and took hold of her hand. "This blue-eyed warrior is not only your destiny. He is *your mate*."

Chapter 28

The Sea Raven and the White Dove

Issylte recovered physically from the effects of her
unnerving vision. She returned to caring for her patients,
collecting herbs, preparing remedies. But the *sighting* of
the blue-eyed warrior and the bloody battle against the
Morholt had shaken her very core. An ominous cloud of
foreboding shadowed her every step.

Viviane's description of the *mating bond* haunted
her. Issylte had indeed bonded with the warrior through
her gift of the *sight*. She'd been on the beach with him.
In the saddle charging towards the enemy. She'd hefted
the mighty sword, embedding it deep into the Morholt's
skull. And doubled over in agony as the poisoned blade
tore into flesh.

Her gift had carried her through the sacred waters of
the Goddess to the battlefield, entwining her essence
with his. She'd sensed the tingling numbness of
wolfsbane. The poison in the Viking blade. Her fate was
finally revealed, Viviane said. The blue-eyed warrior
was her destiny. But how?

Guilt tormented her. She loved Ronan. Her beautiful
blond stallion. She missed him achingly. Thought about
him constantly. How could a stranger in a vision be her
mate? It was unfathomable. Yet undeniable. She'd
bonded with the blue-eyed warrior. The pulse of her

magic was proof.

Issylte delved into her work. Caring for her patients—soldiers missing an eye or limb, women brutalized by Viking invaders, homeless orphans traumatized by loss—stoked the flames of rage which burned her insides like sizzling hot coals.

All were victims of the Morholt. The Black Knight of Ireland. The queen's rabid wolf.

Now that her father had passed away, Issylte was the rightful heir to his throne. The rightful Queen of Ireland. She could claim her father's crown. And stop the evil queen from destroying her kingdom.

But not without an army.

Impotent rage engulfed her. And the blue-eyed sea raven hovered on her horizon.

Two weeks after the *sighting*, Issylte was tending to a patient when there was a great commotion at *Le Centre*. Sir Lancelot, Viviane's son, had just arrived in Avalon on a Cornish ship, bringing with him a seriously wounded knight. Several priestesses were quickly preparing a room to receive the injured soldier, who was being transported by four knights bearing Lancelot's coat of arms. Viviane directed the porters to the prepared room and was now listening to Lancelot as Issylte approached.

"He's Tristan of Lyonesse. The Blue Knight of Cornwall. Nephew and heir to King Marke of Tintagel. He slew the Morholt in battle. But the Black Knight's sword sliced open his belly. A potentially mortal wound."

Lancelot carefully unwrapped a blanket cradled in his arms, revealing an enormous sword caked with dried blood. "This is the Morholt's weapon. A poisoned sword. I brought it here for you to identify the toxin. And hopefully administer the antidote."

Lancelot held out the blade to Viviane, who sniffed it. Despair dimmed her eyes as she shook her head with regret.

"I don't recognize the poison," Viviane whispered.

"Nor do I," said another. None of the priestesses were able to identify the poison on the enemy sword.

A tingling numbness crept up Issylte's limbs. She sniffed the bloodied blade, immediately recognizing the damp, dark, woodsy scent of wolfsbane. "I recognize it. Wolfsbane. I have a tincture that will counteract it."

She raced to her supply of herbs, rummaged through her remedies, and retrieved the infusion of foxglove. Her magic would tell her how much to give him. She had to trust it. Issylte scurried back down the hall.

The porters laid the patient on a bed in the hastily prepared room. The injured knight was dressed in white armor, which confused Issylte. In the *sighting*, the blue-eyed warrior had been wearing a surcoat with the image of a black bird. She glanced at the ring on his hand. The blue topaz gem—the eye of the sea raven—winked in the sunlight. Her magic thrummed. It was his sacred stone. She would use it to heal him.

Lancelot entered the room, carrying the warrior's bloodied armor and surcoat. With the head of the sea raven. On a background of blue waves. Issylte's verdant magic pulsed with power.

"I exchanged armor with him," Lancelot explained as Viviane entered the room. "You enchanted mine with spells of protection, so I dressed him in it. Hoping it would keep him alive until we reached Avalon."

Issylte and Viviane removed Lancelot's white armor

to cleanse the gore from the injured knight's body with calendula soap and water from the sacred spring. The Lady of the Lake murmured to Lancelot, "It's a good thing you did, son. For he would have died otherwise."

The warrior's pulse was barely perceptible. His heart was faltering. Issylte needed to administer the infusion immediately. But how many drops? Too much would be fatal. Yet too little would not counteract the wolfsbane. Three drops would kill him, she was sure. Two might as well. But he was enormous—at least double her weight. She held the vial, letting her magic delve into its essence and guide her. Two. He needed two drops to accelerate and strengthen his heart. Her legs trembled under her dark blue gown.

He was unconscious, so he couldn't drink. Issylte carefully lifted his tongue and placed two drops of the foxglove infusion so that it could be absorbed directly into his body without the need to swallow. His muscular chest was covered with dark hair, dampened by sweat from his raging fever. She would tend to that later. For now, she had to prevent the wolfsbane from stopping his heart.

Placing her two hands upon his chest, Issylte fueled her healing magic into his body as she whispered spells she'd learned from *Tatie* deep in the Hazelwood Forest. Verdant magic flowed through her, summoning the essence of foxglove coursing through the warrior's body. Forest fairy fingers pulsed power into his heart, which began to pound furiously. She prayed the two drops had not been too much. Enchantment whispered from her lips, channeling the divine power of the Goddess through her to heal him. She desperately wanted him to live.

After a few minutes, his heart rate stabilized into a

strong, steady rhythm. He became restless, and Issylte managed to get two swallows of water from *la Fontaine de Jouvence* into him before he lost consciousness again. Now that she'd regulated his heart rate and counteracted the wolfsbane, she needed to address his life-threatening wound. She was compelled to save this blue-eyed warrior. Intuitively, she knew her fate was entwined with his.

Issylte meticulously washed the blood and grime from his naked body and examined the wound across his abdomen. The slice was deep, but no vital organs had been punctured. It had begun to fester; a noxious yellow ooze emitted a rank, putrid odor. He was burning up, shaking violently with a raging fever. The skin around the wound was blackened with decay; streaks of red radiated from the gash. She would need to cut away the diseased flesh, flush out the wound, and drain the toxins with an herbal poultice. Adrenaline raced up her spine.

She burned sage to purify the air and sent two priestesses to fetch the herbs she would need. Comfrey, yarrow, red clover, burdock root, elderflower, willow bark, raw honey. As they hurried off to the herbal storage room, the brilliant star of the sacred spring flashed before her eyes. The hidden sea cave where Ronan had taken her. Where a bed of brilliant crystals reflected the celestial light of the Goddess at the base of the effervescent fountain. Her magic surged with power. She needed this stone to heal the warrior. She needed it *now.*

Lancelot was sitting in a chair outside Tristan's room, his head in his hands. Issylte rushed to his side. "I need your help. To save him. Will you please come with me?"

He jumped to his feet. "Of course. Where to?"

"*La Grotte de l' Étoile.* I'll take you there."

Issylte motioned to Viviane, Nyda and Cléo. "Please watch over him until we return. Lancelot and I must obtain a sacred gem for his cure. We'll be back in less than an hour."

The priestesses agreed, and Issylte grabbed two mallets and a knife. She turned to Lancelot, her heart pounding, her magic aflame. "Do you have a sharp dagger?" He nodded, patting a knife sheathed at his waist. "Good. We'll need it to cut some of the crystals on the floor of the sea cave. It's on the north side of the island. I'll show you. Follow me."

They sprinted down the hall and out to the stables. A groom promptly readied two horses, and Lancelot and Issylte vaulted into the saddles. They tore off down the hill, through the forest, to the cliff at the edge of the beach. The afternoon sun dipped low in the sky; they had perhaps an hour of daylight left at most.

They tethered the horses and flew down the narrow path from the forested ledge to the flat sandy shore. Issylte dashed around the jagged rocky cliff, with Lancelot close behind, until they came to the hidden sea cave. *La Grotte de l' Étoile*. The Cave of the Fallen Star.

The turquoise water of the sacred spring surged with life, sunlight reflecting from the mouth of the cave into five jet sprays of a radiant star. The roar of the fountain was deafening, the light from the crystal bed blinding. Issylte pointed to the sparkling gems beneath the effervescent water as she handed Lancelot a mallet.

"We need five crystals cut from this bed. To represent the five points of this star. The celestial power I need to heal him." She kicked off her boots and folded the hem of her gown, tucking it up around her waist. She

350

waded knee-deep into the cold water and chiseled a portion of rough crystal from the bed under the sacred spring.

Lancelot yanked off his boots, splashed into the water, and quickly carved three pieces of the clear crystal. Issylte yelped as she gouged her thumb with the tip of the knife but managed to chisel the final raw crystal. Five radiant gems. The five points of the sacred star. With a nod to Lancelot, she emerged from the water onto the dry floor of the cave, unfolded her gown so that it fell to her feet, and pulled on her leather boots.

He jumped out of the water and handed her the three precious crystals he'd cut. As he pulled on his boots, she tucked the five astral gems into her bodice, near her heart. The two quickly exited the sea cave, dashed back across the beach and up the steep path to the top of the forested cliff where the two horses were grazing. They jumped into the saddles, gasping for breath, and raced back through the forest and up the cobbled stone path as twilight descended on *Le Centre*.

Lancelot went directly to Tristan's room to inform the priestesses that they'd returned while Issylte searched the shelves where the sacred stones were kept. She deftly selected the gems she would need—sacred *merlinite* stones, the warrior's blue topaz gems, and her own emeralds. Gathering the crystals and the ancient scrolls with spells for healing, the gifted *guérisseuse* rushed down the hall to her patient's room where the scent of yarrow from the burning candle and the cleansing herbal fragrance of sage filled the air. She laid her array of healing tools upon the table and turned to face Viviane, Nyda and Cléo.

"I must heal him. But I need to be alone. To focus.

To channel my verdant magic into him." Emerald fire sparked in her veins. "Please bring water from *la Fontaine de Jouvence*. I will need it to bathe him and for him to drink."

With a tilt of her head, Viviane sent Nyda and Cléo from the room. The deep blue eyes of the Lady of the Lake washed Issylte in the healing waters of Avalon.

"I'll leave a fresh supply of our sacred water just outside the door," Viviane said. "And bring meals for you to keep up your strength." The Lady of the Lake motioned to a cot beside the bed. "You can sleep here. And one of us will always be right outside, should you need anything."

Viviane kissed her forehead and whispered, "Heal him, Lilée. Use all your knowledge and skill as a *guérisseuse*. Maiwenn's love that fills your heart. The verdant magic of a forest fairy. Wield the divine power of the Goddess that flows in your veins. *Guéris-le.* Heal him."

With the hint of a smile and a bow of her head, Viviane slipped from the room.

Issylte gazed at the warrior whose life lay in her hands. His ravaged body shook with fever, the stench of sickness assailing her nostrils. But his heart beat strong. And his limbs were lined with corded muscles. Rippled with youthful strength. Verdant power surged in her healing hands.

She made three crystal grids around the warrior's bed, channeling the energy of the earth into his wounded body. The merlinite stones formed the outer circle around his room as she applied her *guérisseuse* training, whispering spells from the ancient manuscripts transcribed by *Morgane la Fée*. The White Fairy of the

Sacred Stones, one of the trio of fairies who had learned from the master wizard himself.

For the second layer of protective crystals, Issylte alternated the blue topaz gems of the sea raven warrior with her own deep green emeralds, guiding the curative essence of water and the healing magic of the forest through the sacred stones into her unconscious patient.

Five points of a star outlined the warrior's body for the innermost crystal grid in his bed. A raw gem from *la Grotte de l' Étoile* lay at his head and each of his four limbs, channeling the celestial healing power of the stars into his critically injured body.

With a triple layer of enchantment, Issylte wielded her magic. The three sacred elements of the Goddess— the healing herbs of the forest, the curative waters of Avalon, and the protective crystals of sacred stones. To save the wounded sea raven warrior whose fate was inexorably entwined with her own.

Issylte held the sharp blade of her knife into the purifying flame of the candle. She meticulously cut away the diseased flesh, removing the blackened skin to expose healthy pink skin. The wound bled profusely, washing out the rank yellow ooze. She staunched the bleeding with a poultice of yarrow, absorbing the toxins with a blend of calendula, turmeric, and thistle.

He stirred again, so she was able to get him to swallow more of *la Fontaine de Jouvence,* mixed with the blood cleansing herbs of burdock root, milk thistle, nettles, and red clover.

For several hours, Issylte sponged the wound, applying poultices to absorb the toxins, coaxing swallows of herb infused water from the sacred fountain into his cracked lips. When the wound was finally clean,

Issylte held a needle in the candle flame, soaked thread in cleansing herbs, then painstakingly stitched closed the vicious slice across his abdomen. She smoothed raw honey over the puckered wound and covered it with clean linens, whispering spells of enchantment she'd learned from *Tatie,* verdant magic flowing through her healing touch.

Throughout the night, each time the warrior stirred, she helped him to swallow a few gulps of the healing waters of Avalon, laced with sacred herbs to purify his blood, wiping his hot brow with a cool cloth to reduce his fever. As dawn began to break, she dozed in a chair beside his bed and awakened to change his dressing as the rising sun shone through the window where the fragrant white blossoms of *aubépines,* apple trees, and jasmine vines scented the early summer breeze.

Viviane, Nyda and Cléo brought her fresh water and clean linens, along with some oats and honey for her simple meal. She ate quickly and returned to focus on her patient, coaxing him to drink more of the herbal water as he became semiconscious. For three days, she stayed by his side, cleansing his wound, changing the bandages, anointing him in antiseptic ointments and poultices. She murmured spells that she'd learned in the Hazelwood Forest, channeling the divine energy of her magic through the three-layered grid of sacred stones, summoning the healing properties of the herbs in the warrior's body, calling upon the curative essence of the waters of Avalon to heal him.

With all her verdant magic as a forest fairy, the Emerald Princess poured her spirit as a *guérisseuse celtique* into healing the wounded warrior from Cornwall.

Finally, on the fourth day, when the morning sun glistened in the sparkling waters of the fountain, Tristan's eyelids fluttered. Issylte leaned over him, his brow cool now that the fever had broken. He opened the brilliant blue eyes that she'd seen in the vision.

As she gazed into them, the earth tilted. Her heart raced; her bearings were lost. In the depths of his eyes, she glimpsed a fountain in a forest. The turquoise waters of the ocean. An underground well encased by sacred stones. She, the forest fairy, was immersed in the blue waters of the warrior's eyes, the waves emanating from him flowing through her, cleansing her. Beckoning her.

In Tristan's eyes, Issylte glimpsed a black bird—a sea raven—soaring over an open sea, hovering now before her. A small dove fluttered in her breast, called forth from her soul. White wings unfurled as she took flight, rising into the azure sky alongside the black seabird—-floating together through the diaphanous clouds scattered over the vast ocean.

In the breadth of an instant, Issylte was bound to this warrior, the Blue Knight of Cornwall, as if fate had indeed entwined them. Through the windows of his eyes, she peered into his soul, her own blending with his, as if they were the forest and the ocean, encircled now within the three layers of protective stones, the holy trinity of sacred elements of the Goddess.

The warrior gazed into her eyes, smiled weakly and whispered, "Goddess…" before falling back into restorative sleep. Sweet relief washed over her, knowing he would recover. Issylte whispered a prayer of gratitude for the divine guidance in healing the mysterious Blue Knight of Cornwall.

When a priestess brought her next meal, Issylte sent

word that Tristan was recuperating well, but that his visitors would be limited so that he could rest. Lancelot poked his head through the doorway, and she slipped out into the hall to speak with him while Tristan slept. Viviane was at his side, as eager as her son to hear about the warrior's miraculous recovery.

"Thank the Goddess you were able to heal him," Lancelot choked, taking Issylte's hands into his and showering them with kisses. "You alone knew the poison. And the antidote." He raised his head to smile at her, his grateful eyes conveying the depth of his friendship for the Blue Knight.

Viviane nodded in earnest agreement. "You learned from Maiwenn—*la Fée Verte de la Forêt.* The Green Fairy of the Forest." The Lady of the Lake turned to her son. "The Morholt came from Ireland, where he'd obtained the poison for his sword. We are most fortunate that Lilée, a healer trained in the Hazelwood Forest of Ireland, was with us in Avalon, to recognize that poison—and know the antidote."

Issylte accepted the praise with humility and returned to care for her patient. Lancelot promised to check in on him later that day as Issylte, *la guérisseuse celtique,* went back into Tristan's room to stay by his side.

He slept peacefully, his handsome face serene. Issylte took advantage of the opportunity to observe him as a man rather than patient. His dark brown hair was wavy and thick, extending to the tops of his wide shoulders. His forehead was broad; dark, thick brows arched over equally dark, thick lashes. Her eyes traced the strong jawline, covered in stubble. She spotted a scar on his left cheekbone, the vestige of one of his many battles as a warrior.

His bare torso was heavily muscled, with dark hair across his chest, extending down his abdomen to the stitches in his wound. The knight's arms were thickly corded with the same muscles that rippled throughout his body; Issylte found that he compared to Ronan in size and apparent strength. At thought of her Elf, she chided herself. Here she was, admiring the masculine form of Tristan while Ronan was returning to Avalon in a few short weeks. While part of her longed to welcome her Elf with open arms, another part, newly awakened, yearned to discover more about this sea raven warrior.

As if he sensed Issylte's attention, Tristan awoke and smiled at her. His deep voice was hoarse and gruff. "The first thing I saw was your green eyes. And your face—illuminated with golden light." He sipped the water that she offered from a cup and murmured, "I didn't know if I were still in this realm or if I had passed into the next. But I knew I was in the hands of the *Goddess*." He locked eyes with her, his voice reverent and hushed. "*You* are the vision I saw. I owe you my life." He took her hand and kissed it gently. "Thank you, my *green golden goddess*."

A surge of emotions flooded her—gratitude, joy, relief, wonder—as she gazed into the pools of his eyes. As he held her hand, his touch thrilled her, sending pulses of sensation into her body. Again, she thought of Ronan and withdrew her hand in a sudden flash of guilt. Her palms were damp, her mouth dry. Her magic pulsed with power.

Lancelot and Viviane entered the room, both smiling broadly to see the patient in such good spirits. Issylte stood to greet them, and Lancelot joked to his friend, "Tristan, it's great to see you've recovered. Ready to battle more Vikings?"

Tristan laughed, then winced and clutched his stomach. "I think I need a bit more time in the care of this most capable healer." He smiled at Issylte, his brilliant blue eyes gleaming with gratitude. "I don't even know your name, beautiful priestess."

She replied, her voice hushed, "My name is Issylte. But here in Avalon, I am called Lilée."

At the warrior's raised eyebrow, Viviane explained. "Issylte is the only child of the late King Donnchadh of Ireland. The rightful heir to his throne. She was sent here for her protection when Queen Morag, Issylte's stepmother, tried to kill her. *Twice*."

Tristan's eyes darted to Issylte, who nodded in agreement. "The Lady Viviane chose the name Lilée to hide my identity while I'm here in Avalon. She named me for the water lilies on *le Lac Diane*. The beautiful lake near *Le Centre*."

The corners of Tristan's mouth curved softly. "A lovely name… for a lovely priestess."

Lancelot flashed his boyish grin. "Tristan slew the Morholt—the Black Knight. Previously undefeated in battle." He grinned at his bed-ridden friend. "And he's also the *only* knight to have *ever* disarmed the great Lancelot of the Lake!"

Grasping Tristan's arm in a friendly squeeze, the First Knight of Camelot said affectionately, "Thank the Goddess you survived. I saw the Morholt slice you open. I brought you here, to the island of healing." Lancelot took Issylte's hand and kissed it as he had earlier in the day. "Thank you, Princess Issylte, Priestess of Avalon. For saving Tristan's life."

Lancelot turned his attention back to Tristan. "I borrowed one of King Marke's ships to bring you here. I'll sail on the morrow to return it to Cornwall." He glanced at his mother. "I shall also bring a ship from Avalon, so that I may return here from Tintagel." Viviane nodded, granting his request for the Avalonian vessel.

The White Knight addressed Tristan once again, his tone guarded and serious. "We repelled the Viking invasion, but I need to speak to Gorvenal about King Marke's losses. Ascertain that the Knights of the Round Table successfully returned to Camelot."

Lancelot leaned down to grip Tristan's shoulder. "I'll be gone for six to eight weeks, but I'll return as soon as possible. In the meantime," he drawled, grinning slyly at Issylte. "I'll leave you in the very capable hands of our lovely priestess Lilée."

Kissing Issylte's hand once again, then Viviane's cheek, the First Knight of Camelot bid them all farewell as he prepared to depart for Cornwall.

When a priestess delivered some broth for Tristan, Viviane said good night and left Issylte to care for her patient. She helped him elevate his torso a bit so that he could eat, spoon feeding him the vegetable broth, which he devoured. "Could I please have more? I'm famished." Issylte grinned at his request, quickly dashed to the kitchen, and returned with twice the amount as before, which he consumed with relish. The white dove fluttered in her grateful heart.

After he finished his meal, Issylte changed his bandage, applying more of the antiseptic salve to his stitches before placing a clean dressing on the wound. She promised to return in an hour or so, placed the chamber pot within his reach and left to care for her other patients.

Vibrant shades of pink and violet streaked the summer sky with the last rays of the setting sun. Issylte strolled through the jasmine scented gates of *Le Centre,* past the fragrant *aubépines* and apple blossoms, down the cobbled stone path to the new Women's Center where Gwennol's warm, smiling face greeted her approach. With an affectionate hug, her former patient whispered, "Thank you for the tender care you've given me, Lilée."

Gwennol gestured to the women around her, bustling with activity. Near the hearth in the large kitchen, some were chopping fresh vegetables from the garden while others added savory herbs and freshly plucked poultry to the simmering stew. The familiar aromas of garlic and rosemary wafted through the cheerful residence where children scurried under foot, squealing with glee as they chased each other madly out the front door.

"Many of us are settling into new homes here," Gwennol explained, hugging a little girl who bumped into her as the child raced to catch up to her friends. "And in the villages of Rochefort and Briac." She took Issylte's hand, her eyes brimming with tears.

"I must believe that my husband and sons are still alive. Even if they are slaves," she choked. "I cling to the hope that the Goddess reunites us one day."

Gwennol gazed out the window of the large eating area to the spacious grassy plain where little ones frolicked in front of the adjacent Children's Center. "Unlike these poor children, who have lost everyone." Her eyes glimmering, she whispered to Issylte, "I am sure that in your experience, Lilée, you know that the best way to heal oneself is to care for others."

She hugged Issylte warmly, then turned to greet a small boy who had wrapped his arms around her knees before dashing off to play again. "Caring for these children—and each other—is helping all of us to heal." With another affectionate hug and a warm goodbye, Issylte returned to Tristan, her heart filled with hope.

Over the next few days, Issylte helped him stand and, with the aid of a walking stick, stroll down the hall of *Le Centre* to the conservatory. When he spotted the harp, Tristan glanced at her and raised his eyebrows, asking permission to play. With a bright smile and a nod, she watched as he eased himself carefully onto the bench and began to strum the golden harp. To her delight, he was quite skilled, and soon Viviane, Nyda, Cléo and a small crowd pf patients gathered to enjoy the lilting, lyrical notes pouring from his gifted hands. As she listened to the ethereal music, her spirit soared as visions floated on the melody.

She danced with him in a ballroom of a gleaming white castle, crystal chandeliers glowing in the candlelight, windowed doors opening onto a courtyard filled with fragrant blooms upon an ivy-covered trellis. A pair of white swans swam upon a dark lake, rippling waves glinting in the moonlight under a starry night sky. Viviane's words returned to her. *"As it is with swans, the beautiful white birds on le Lac Diane, mates are bound for life."*

Issylte took in the smiling face of the Lady of the Lake, remembering how the High Priestess had once said she hoped someone would one day grace *Le Centre* with the beautiful music of the untouched harp. She met

Viviane's gaze, recognizing the gratitude she found in her mentor's glistening eyes.

****

Tristan was anxious to resume his physical training, but Issylte insisted he wait another three weeks until his injury was more fully healed. As she cleansed his wound to change the dressing, she was very aware of how he was responding to her touch. She murmured, "It is a good sign that your body is returning to normal. You are nearly healed."

He responded in a husky voice, "It is your touch, Issylte." His hungry eyes locked with hers. "I long for *more*."

Inexplicably drawn to him, she inhaled his earthy scent, uneasy at her body's awakening. Thoughts of Ronan flooded her with guilt. Unsure how to respond, she replied, "Come, let me show you where you can bathe. The natural spring which feeds the fountain flows into a waterfall that forms a wide pool. It's perfect for bathing."

He was now more adept at standing and walking, no longer needing the cane. They sauntered past the fountain to the bathing area for patients, enclosed by a stone wall covered in fragrant jasmine blooms. Placing the soap, towel, and clean clothing that she had brought for him on a nearby stone, Issylte prepared to leave, to offer him privacy. But he said instead, "Will you join me? I might need some…assistance." His beckoning smile made her heart flutter.

Her legs went weak as she envisioned joining him in the pool, but she recovered enough to respond. "It wouldn't be appropriate for a healer to bathe with her patient. I'll wait for you on the other side of the wall. Just call for me when you've finished."

A while later, when she heard him call her name, she came around the wall to see him emerge from the pool and stand in front of her, his magnificent body naked and proud as her eyes absorbed every inch of him. As she stood awestruck by the sight of him, he grinned as his body, responding to her attention, flustered her even more. Swallowing with difficulty, she helped him dry off and don his clean clothing so they could return to his room.

Once he was settled at the table, his midday meal in front of him, Issylte left to care for her other patients, promising to take him for a walk in the nearby woods when she returned. Later that afternoon, they strolled into the forest near the lake, enjoying the warm summer breeze and the heady fragrance of the jasmine flowers and *aubépines* in bloom. The thick canopy of trees sheltered them from the hot summer sun as their footsteps fell softly onto the pine needles strewn across the forested earth.

Tristan told her of his childhood at the *Château d'Or* in Lyonesse, where he and his sister Talwyn—as royal children preparing for their future as monarchs—had studied astronomy, geography, music, literature, and French. They'd learned to play the harp, dance with finesse, recite poetry, manage servants and household accounts, become proficient in equestrian skills. He shared with Issylte how he'd been a squire in his father's castle the fateful day he and the knight Goron had returned from their hunt to find *le Château d' Or* under attack.

How an enormous Viking—much like the Morholt he'd killed in the battle of Tintagel—had executed his father and slaughtered both his mother and sister, as Tristan was forced to endure their screams. He shared his guilt and impotent rage at being too young to defend his family, the shame of being the sole survivor, sent to the castle of his uncle Marke, the king of Cornwall, to complete his training as a knight. He told her of the Tournament of Champions, where the sea raven ring gifted by his uncle had led to his triumph. How he'd been dubbed the Blue Knight of Cornwall, training with Lancelot to become a Knight of the Round Table of King Arthur's Camelot.

He showed her the ring upon his left hand, the blue topaz eye of the sea raven sparkling in the dappled light. Issylte took his hand and touched the brilliant gem. "I saw this ring. In a vision I had of you."

Reliving the bond on the battlefield, she murmured, stroking the jewel with her thumb, "I saw you. Wearing the surcoat with this same black bird." She lifted her head and looked up at him.

"I saw your intense blue eyes." His breath brushed her face. Issylte's stomach quivered. "I saw the Morholt charge you. You clove his skull in two. And Tristan…" she said, locking his gaze, "I *felt* the slice of his sword *across my own abdomen* as he wounded you." Her voice wavering, she whispered, "I was unconscious *for three days.* Just as you were. When you were brought here to Avalon."

Tristan's voice was husky and deep. "When I awoke, I saw golden light, illuminating your face." He stroked her cheek softly. "In your eyes, I saw a forest…plants and vines… small pink flowers." He lifted her hand to his lips and whispered, "The Goddess herself…" as he kissed it softly.

Issylte withdrew her hand gently. "We should return now. You need to rest." He grinned as she led him back to *Le Centre*, glancing at her sideways as she walked beside him through the fragrant pines. She escorted him back to his room, applied a healing herbal salve to his stitches, and covered the wound with a fresh bandage. With a smile, she left him in bed, promising to return in the morning for his continued care.

Tristan began to train his body once again, slowly easing into a less strenuous version of the routine he'd done as one of Lancelot's knights. One day, when Issylte came into his room and found it empty, she glimpsed him through the open window, exercising on the grassy area of the courtyard outside *Le Centre*. As she paused to watch, he caught her staring, and flashed her a brilliant smile which took her breath away. Quickly returning to care for her patients, she thrilled at the memory of his bare chest, glistening with sweat, rippled with strength. Tristan of Cornwall was the most handsome man she'd ever seen. An enormous wave of guilt washed over her as she thought of her beautiful blond stallion. Well, Tristan would be leaving soon with Lancelot. The sooner the better. She swallowed forcibly and resumed her work.

Thoughts of Ronan flooded her. She was guilty and ashamed of her undeniable interest in Tristan. It was foolish to feel attracted to a man who would be leaving Avalon soon, sailing back to Camelot once Lancelot returned. Ronan would be home soon. Returning to her. But Issylte wasn't just attracted to Tristan. Her spirit stirred in his presence. Her magic sang when he was near. The kaleidoscope of images she'd seen in his eyes floated back to her. She'd soared as a white dove with his sea raven over an open ocean. Glimpsed a well in an enchanted forest, a white castle with swans swimming on a lake beneath flowered vines. She'd been with him on the battlefield, her limbs going numb from the wolfsbane poison in the Viking blade that had wounded him. Intuitively, she knew her fate was entwined with his. But how?

Ronan's return filled her with unease, so very different from the excited anticipation she'd experienced when he'd last gone to Bretagne. She missed him terribly yet feared his return. Conflicted and confused, Issylte remembered Viviane's prophecy.

"This blue-eyed warrior is not only your destiny— he is *your mate*." How could Tristan be her mate when she was romantically involved with Ronan? And how could he be her destiny if he were returning to Britain with Lancelot? None of it made any sense. Issylte decided that in the meantime, she would concentrate on her work.

Fortunately, the number of patients coming into *Le Centre* had diminished, since the death of the Morholt had halted his slaving expeditions and the subsequent victims of Viking attacks. Most of the injured soldiers treated by the priestesses of Avalon had either returned to their domains or relocated to the villages among the islands. All the orphans had been adopted by families in the villages of Rochefort and Briac or by women victims, forming new families united by shared grief. The newcomers were learning valuable skills—fishing, farming, building, weaving, and spinning wool. Children were eager to learn to care for the many animals, such as sheep, hens, and horses, delighted to run and play in the forest and on the seashore of the island of healing. For the first time in many months, hope bloomed among the beautiful white flowers of Avalon.

Tristan insisted on returning to horseback riding; he and Issylte rode frequently through the lush forest as he regained his strength. One day, he stopped his horse and dismounted to pick several wild roses, which he grouped into a small bouquet. "These are the pink flowers I saw in your eyes," he said, caressing the petals. His eyes aglow, he offered Issylte his floral gift.

She dismounted from her horse to accept the wild roses, inhaling the sweet fragrance so dear to her heart. "In Ireland," she whispered, her breath caught in her throat, "the forest fairies left a trail of these to lead me to *Tatie's* cottage." Issylte gazed up into Tristan's handsome face, his deep blue eyes fixed on hers. "She named me Églantine, as these wild roses are called in *Bretagne*, her native land. They will always be a part of me. And they will always remind me of her." Tears welled as *Tatie's* soft crinkled cheeks and enormous brown eyes twinkled in the trees. Her forest fairy grandmother's protective embrace. Issylte's verdant heart was full.

Tristan said softly, "That's why I saw them in your eyes. They're a part of your soul. Your spirit. Your essence." He kissed her hand, his eyes the brilliant blue of the sea raven ring. "They will always remind me of you, *Églantine*."

They walked through the dense oaks back to the horses. Issylte heard a woodland bird's beautiful song, and to her delight, Tristan imitated the call. As she watched in amazement, a nightingale came to rest on his finger. Tristan seemed to communicate with the bird, who flew off, returning with an *églantine* in its beak. The

Blue Knight grinned, took the flower from the bird, and handed it to Issylte, whose mouth was agape in amazement. The *rossignol* perched on Tristan's finger, eyeing her with interest.

"The nightingale wished to thank you for healing me." He grinned, his face alit with delight.

Issylte's magic fluttered, the wings of a white dove in her breast. "How did you do that?" she asked, breathless with wonder.

Tristan spoke wordlessly to the bird, who flew back to the highest branch of an oak and resumed his melodic song. "This is the mark of the Tribe of Dana," Tristan explained, pointing to the tattoo on his inner wrist which she'd noticed when bathing him. "A brotherhood of warriors who defend the sacred elements of the Goddess."

Issylte gazed into his deep blue eyes. A bubbling fountain surged from an underground well in a dark hidden forest. Verdant magic stirred in her soul.

"When I became a member of the Tribe," Tristan said, his deep voice hushed with reverence, "I was given a gift of Druidic magic—*l'herbe d'or.*" Chills shivered down her spine. "It allows me to communicate with birds." He looked up at the *rossignol* whose lilting song floated through the forest. "I asked the nightingale to bring you this flower, as a special thanks for healing me." Issylte lifted the *églantine* to her nose, inhaling the sweet wild rose scent. Her forest fairy magic soared in response.

They returned to *Le Centre*, Issylte marveling at the wonder of this extraordinary sea raven warrior. The Blue Knight of Cornwall. Whose destiny was inexplicably entwined with her own.

Chapter 29

Return from Cornwall

The centers that Viviane had established for the victims of the Viking slave raids were prospering. Many of the surviving women now worked collaboratively to cultivate large fruit and vegetable gardens, care for the orphaned children they'd adopted, tend to animals, and complete household tasks, such as cooking, cleaning, and laundry. Issylte often worked with Nyda and Cléo alongside the women, now that there were fewer patients at *Le Centre.* Sometimes, a sick child needed an herbal tincture for ear pain or a tonic for a stomach ailment. A few wounded soldiers were still recovering, including Tristan. But the priestesses were able to harvest crops, collect eggs from the hens, shear the sheep—whatever was necessary to help the women and children recover.

Today, Issylte delivered a healthy baby boy to one of the young women who, having lost her husband in a slave raid, had come to Avalon pregnant and alone. Both baby and mother were doing well, and Issylte was delighted to have welcomed a new life into the Women's Center on the nurturing island of healing.

Walking now with Gwennol, who had become the resident supervisor of the Women's Center, Issylte chatted about the new mother and baby, and the overall prosperity and positivity that the center had brought into so many lives. Gwennol, one of the oldest women, had become a mother figure to them all, showering the victims with love as she healed her own broken heart.

Issylte and Gwennol strolled along the edge of the forest where a stream irrigated the gardens and watered the many animals. The source of the stream was a natural underground spring, which flowed into a large pool, where the children loved to swim and frolic. Nearby was the well which served as the source of drinking water for the residents of the two new centers, which had been built upon an open, grassy plain, surrounded by forest, nourished by the sacred waters of Avalon.

The two women sat down upon one of the stone benches to rest in the shade of a large oak tree, gazing at the turquoise spring which bubbled from the depths of the pool. Dense foliage provided cool shade from the late July sun, the lulling sound of the gurgling spring restful and restorative. Two white butterflies fluttered in the soft breeze, flitting upon the fragrant jasmine blossoms which perfumed the sweet air. It was quiet and peaceful, for no one was swimming, and Issylte was content to enjoy Gwennol's company for a brief respite from work amid the idyllic natural surroundings.

Gwennol told Issylte how she'd come from the southwestern coast of Britain in Cornwall, the kingdom of Tristan's uncle, where she and her husband Paol, a commercial fisherman, had established a small seafood market. Gwennol had worked in the kitchen of the castle of Tintagel, adding to the meager income they earned from their shop. She and Paol were raising three teenage sons, avid fishermen and boatsmen like their father. When her husband and sons were captured as slaves in the Viking attack on their village, Gwennol had been beaten and left for dead. Fortunately, she'd been found by the local healer, who had arranged for Gwennol to be brought to Avalon, where Issylte had healed her wounds many months ago. And had now become her friend.

"Mara will be such a good mother," Gwennol mused, referring to the young woman who had just given birth. "And the babe is nursing well already."

Issylte smiled fondly. "Yes... he is a big, healthy boy. And the birth was relatively easy, so Mara will recover quickly. Be on her feet again in no time." Seated companionably upon the stone bench, the two women enjoyed the warm weather and the cool, fresh breeze coming from the underground spring.

As she gazed into the turquoise depths of the pool, the aura of a *sighting* came upon her. Suddenly surrounded by stillness, enshrouded in darkness, her spirit delved into the gurgling waters of the spring as visions began to emerge.

Issylte glimpsed a dark forest—intuiting that it was sacred—where a fountain sprayed from an underground well, encased in stones, at the base of a tall pine tree. She sensed Tristan there, for she felt his spirit. This was the fountain she'd seen in his eyes when he'd first regained consciousness after his battle with the Morholt. Her pulse quickened and her limbs trembled.

As the vision unfolded, a magnificent lake beckoned, its surface as smooth as glass. *A mirrored lake.* Something *sacred* was hidden in its dark depths. Something she had to protect. Magic danced in her veins.

A small, dark creature—*a dwarf* —emerged suddenly from the forest. A scavenger. A predator. A hunter. He was searching for the sacred object, his intent evil. Issylte had to prevent the dwarf from obtaining it, for the object was magic. Her own verdant magic. It sang to her from the murky depths of the mirrored lake.

A different vision came into focus. A trio of figures clad in black. The sinister wizard with yellow eyes of a python. Her stepmother the wicked queen. And another dwarf—the same one she'd seen in the vision of her father being poisoned.

The three figures stood in a semicircle around a bedridden king. A monarch Issylte had never seen. Transfixed with terror, she watched the wizard once again give a small vial to the queen, who poured it into a chalice, forcing the ill king to drink. Mortified, Issylte saw the wizened dwarf raise his head from the king's bedside to pierce her with penetrating black eyes. *He sees me*! Nausea surged as her stomach clenched and her bowels loosened.

Another image emerged onto the surface of the gurgling spring. Issylte saw a young pregnant woman imprisoned in the tower of a castle, nestled deep in a forest. The same dwarf that Issylte had just seen standing with the wizard and the queen entered the prisoner's chamber. Again, the dwarf looked up, his malevolent gaze locked onto Issylte. The black eyes of a lethal predator hunting her. Lurking in the shadows. Waiting. She swooned, her head spinning, her stomach roiling. Saliva flooded her mouth.

Gwennol's voice echoed in the distance. "Lilée! Lilée! Are you ill? Please answer me!" Issylte came back to her senses. Warm hands on her shoulders, gently shaking her awake. Shade from the oak trees, the gurgling bubbles of the spring. Woozy, disoriented and shaken, Issylte rushed to the edge of the forest and retched, ridding her body of the horrific visions.

When her heaving subsided, she walked unsteadily back to the spring and cupped a hand in the cool waters to rinse out her mouth. Gwennol crouched at her side, concern in her loving hazel eyes. Issylte drank from the cool spring, the curative waters of Avalon calming and refreshing her spirit and body. Returning to the stone bench, Issylte told her friend about the haunting visions.

"That's Frocin." Gwennol shuddered, rubbing her arms as if to ward off an ill chill. "He is a powerful dwarf who lives in a fortress—with a tower—in the dark Forest of Morois. On the outskirts of Cornwall." Gwennol smoothed Issylte's hair, her calming touch soothing.

"Frocin practices dark magic. He can read the stars and conjure evil spells. Whenever a wealthy lord wants to get revenge… or wants someone to *disappear*—he hires Frocin." Gwennol's eyes filled with foreboding. "He must be working for the wicked queen." Icy numbness crept up Issylte's arms. Wolfsbane. Her stepmother would poison another king. Issylte had to stop her. But how?

Gwennol met Issylte's troubled eyes. "Let's get you back to *Le Centre*. You can tell the Lady Viviane about your visions. Perhaps she'll know what to do." The older woman glanced across the plain to the Children's Center. "It's nearly time for the evening meal. I must return to prepare supper for the children. Shall we walk back now?"

Issylte nodded, wiping her damp palms on her dark blue gown. "Yes, that's a good idea. But I'm fine. You go on ahead to fix the meal for the children. I'll catch Viviane on my way."

With a kiss on each cheek—*la bise* that always reminded her of *Tatie*—the two friends bid each other a fond goodbye. Issylte headed up the path towards *Le Centre,* still shaken from the visions. Gwennol returned to the residence for the orphaned children who rushed up to hug her skirts and welcome her home. Passing the vines bursting with fragrant jasmine blossoms, amid the *aubépines* that the Lady of the Lake loved so well, Issylte spotted the High Priestess coming to greet her. Viviane's lovely face beamed, her moonstone necklace glistening in the late afternoon sun.

"Lilée, I was hoping to see you! How was Mara's birth? Did everything go well?" Viviane, a native to *Bretagne* like her beloved *Tatie,* kissed Issylte on each cheek in the familiar French greeting. It warmed Issylte's heart as she returned the embrace.

"Yes, everything went perfectly. Both mother and baby are doing well. He's a big, beautiful boy!" Smiling, arm in arm, the two women walked to *Le Centre* to wash for supper. Now that most of their patients had recovered, the acolytes had returned to rooms in their residence. And Issylte, a full priestess now like Nyda, Cléo and Viviane, had her own individual quarters in *Le Centre.*

Viviane sat in Issylte's new room at the table which overlooked the fountain, just as it had in her bedroom in the acolyte's residence. The Lady of the Lake noticed the lovely collection of seashells, picking one up to examine more closely. Issylte smiled, remembering the day on the beach with Ronan when they'd collected the shells. "Isn't that one beautiful? Ronan brought it back for me on his last voyage to Armorique." Guilt gripped her heart. Tristan would be leaving soon. And Ronan would return. All would get back to normal after the sea raven warrior left. Then why didn't she want him to go?

Issylte washed her face and hands with the fragrant jasmine soap, then turned to Viviane. "Ronan should be returning soon. He's been gone nearly three months." Anticipation, sadness, and guilt flickered in her heart as she dried her hands on a clean cloth, sat down beside Viviane, and gazed at the fountain from her window.

Issylte told Viviane about the visions. The hidden object in a mirrored lake that she needed to protect. The wicked queen, snake wizard and wizened dwarf forcing an unfamiliar king to drink from a poisoned chalice. A pregnant woman held prisoner in a high tower hidden deep in a dark forest. The penetrating black eyes of the hideous dwarf transfixing her with terror as he pierced her soul.

"Who is this king? And the pregnant woman? The dwarf with malevolent black eyes, staring right through me. What do these visions mean? I don't understand."

Viviane replied, "Neither do I, Lilée. But I will send messages through the woodland creatures to see what information can be gathered. Perhaps we can discover who they are." Viviane moved to stand up, but Issylte caught her hand, as if begging her to stay.

"Viviane, I am confused about what you said. That Tristan is my *mate*." Issylte searched the profound depths of Viviane's eyes, blue as *le Lac Diane*.

"Tristan will be leaving soon. To return to Cornwall and his uncle King Marke. Or back to Camelot, with Lancelot and the Knights of the Round Table." She held Viviane's hand as her pulse raced and her mouth went dry.

"How can Tristan possibly be *my mate*—his fate entwined with mine—when he is *leaving*?" Issylte noticed the shell Viviane had been admiring. Her thoughts flooded with images of the handsome blond Elf returning to Avalon. She raised her eyes to implore the Lady of the Lake. "How can Tristan be *my mate*—when I have been so romantically involved with Ronan?"

Viviane gazed at the fountain in the center of the courtyard, illuminated by the pink and orange glow of the setting sun. Contemplating the glorious colors, immersed in reflection, Viviane murmured pensively, "Ronan obviously plays a very important role in your destiny."

Directing her *otherworldly* gaze to Issylte, the Lady of the Lake whispered, "The Goddess works in mysterious ways. I do not know *how* Ronan will affect your future. But it is clear that he will."

Viviane stared into the depths of Issylte's eyes, as if peering into her forest fairy soul. "And it is also clear that Tristan is indeed your *mate*."

Pausing for her words to reach Issylte, the Lady of the Lake murmured, "Have you not felt the truth of this when you look into his eyes? Can you not sense a spiritual bond between your soul and his? Do you not long for him—not just physically—but across *all realms*?"

Issylte nodded, swallowing a surge of emotions. "Yes, I have sensed a spiritual bond with him that is unmistakable." Knowing that the guilt she felt in her heart must be written plainly across her face, Issylte confessed, "But I also long for Ronan. He and I have been lovers. Our relationship has been *wonderful*."

Her eyes fixed on the Lady of the Lake. "Viviane— If Tristan is leaving Avalon, and Ronan is coming back to me, how can Tristan possibly be my *mate*?"

Quietly, reverently, Viviane replied, "The Goddess

will reveal the path you must follow, Lilée. We must be patient and trust in Her divine wisdom."

The Lady of the Lake rose to her feet and smoothed her long white robe. "Come, let us go to the dining area. Your patient, Tristan, has been training with some of the injured warriors as part of their recuperation. His encouragement and praise have been very good for them." With a warm smile, she linked Issylte's elbow with her own. "I saw him near the fountain a little while ago. I am sure he'll be eager to tell you about their progress at supper."

****

For the past few weeks, as Tristan gained more and more strength, he and Issylte had been riding through the forest, sometimes heading into the villages of Rochefort and Briac to obtain supplies or check in on her former patients. To her delight, he loved seafood as much as she did, and they often brought back harvested shellfish and fresh catch for the cooks to use in preparing dishes for the priestesses and patients of *Le Centre*.

Now that he was nearly recovered, Tristan had been taking meals in the dining area, where most of the remaining patients also ate along with the priestesses and acolytes. Tonight, as she and Tristan were finishing their evening meal of *omelette aux fines herbes,* Issylte glimpsed Lancelot through the windowed doors. He had apparently just returned from Cornwall and was now striding briskly past the fountain towards the dining area. He approached their table, and by his countenance, Issylte could tell that the news he brought from Tintagel was anything but good.

Tristan stood to greet his friend, clasping him on the shoulders in a friendly embrace and offering to fetch him some food, which Lancelot heartily accepted. When Tristan returned with a heaping plate, he sat back down at the table and anxiously awaited Lancelot's report.

It seemed the Knight of Camelot did not wish to discuss Cornwall just yet, for he commented on Tristan's apparent good health and remarkable recovery. "You are looking very well, my friend," he beamed, as he devoured the *omelette* and fresh vegetables that Tristan had served. "How soon can you resume your training?"

"I've already begun," Tristan smirked. "You know me. I am not one to sit idle for long, am I?"

Chuckling, Lancelot agreed and finished off another mouthful. Turning to Issylte, he asked with his charming boyish grin, "And you, beautiful Princess of Ireland, how do you fare?"

She smiled warmly at his weary, handsome face. "I am doing very well indeed, Sir Lancelot. I am most pleased with the rapid recovery of my diligent patient." Tristan's gaze washed her in a wave of blue.

****

Once Lancelot had finished eating, they returned to Tristan's room, where the three of them sat at his table. Tristan, sensing the imminent bad news, blurted, "Out with it, Lance. Tell me."

Lancelot raked his dark brown hair with his fingers. "It's bad, Tristan." His eyes glazed with grief. Tristan's stomach sank and his mouth went dry. What had happened?

"Indulf claims to be the victor who defeated the Morholt." Tristan shot Lancelot an incredulous look. "He offers the split headpiece as proof. He brags that it was *his sword* that clove the Black Knight's skull in two."

Tristan leapt to his feet and slammed his hands down on the table. Fury pounded in his temples. "The *bloody bastard*! *I* slew the Morholt!! And he claims MY victory!"

Lancelot stood and turned to face him, his expression grave. "There's more. And it gets worse." The White Knight began pacing the length of the wall near the window. Tristan followed him with furious eyes.

"Indulf claims that you fled the battlefield, cowered by the Morholt. He denounces you as a traitor for abandoning your country. In a stolen ship. While the rest of the army faced the onslaught of the Viking assault." Lancelot lowered his eyes and sat down on the edge of the bed, his elbows on his knees. He placed his head in his hands and said quietly, "They claim that I pursued you, tried to reason with you, and when that failed, I returned the ship—without you—to Tintagel."

As if to minimize the blow of his words, Lancelot softened his voice. "Indulf, in alliance with the dwarf Frocin—and backed by Vaughan and Connor, who claim to be witnesses—have convinced your uncle Marke to banish you from Cornwall as a traitor, a thief, and a coward—thereby stripping you of your status as heir to his throne."

Tristan staggered, the words a painful physical blow.

"King Marke has agreed to the banishment. He's rescinded you as his heir... and has proclaimed Indulf the new champion of Cornwall."

Tristan stormed back and forth along the wall, his head pounding, his stomach roiling with rage. He couldn't breathe. This was impossible. His uncle would never banish him. Or replace him with Indulf!

Lancelot said gently, his eyes wary, "There is more, Tristan. You should sit down to hear the rest. It gets worse."

Tristan shot Lancelot a glance of utter disbelief. "*Worse*? What could *possibly* be worse?"

Lancelot stared at his feet, his voice barely audible. "The dwarf Frocin—and his close friend Indulf—have suggested to King Marke that an alliance with Ireland is in the best interest of Cornwall. They have suggested a *royal wedding*. Between King Marke of Cornwall, and…" his eyes rose to meet Issylte's.

"Queen Morag of Ireland."

Issylte shot to her feet, her hands clasped over her mouth. "The queen who *poisoned my father*?" She turned to Tristan, her eyes ablaze. "This dwarf Frocin. I have seen him. In my *visions.*"

She walked to the window and stared at the spray of the fountain in the courtyard, as if its healing waters calmed her ragged nerves. She faced the two knights whose eyes locked with her own. "Just before my father died, I had a *sighting*. My stepmother and a dark wizard with the yellow eyes of a snake were standing beside my bedridden father." She shuddered as the icy numbness of wolfsbane shivered up her limbs.

Issylte turned to Tristan, seated at the table, and Lancelot, sitting on the edge of the bed. "In the vision, I saw them poison my father." Her voice hoarse with grief, she spat, "And two weeks later, we received word that the king of Ireland was dead."

Shaking, pacing, she recounted her most recent *sighting.* "A few days ago, when I was with one of my former patients, I had another vision." She wiped her hands on her dress to calm their trembling. "Of a hideous dwarf with piercing black eyes." The memory sent a wave of nausea rolling through her.

"He was with the dark wizard and the queen, hovering over a bed-ridden king. Just like when I saw them beside my father's bed in the earlier vision. But this king I did not recognize."

Issylte wrung her hands, her heart racing. "The wizard gave the queen a vial. She added drops to a chalice. and made the king drink, just as she had done to my father." She locked eyes with Tristan, seated before her. "This king… Could it be *your uncle*, Tristan? Could the wicked queen who murdered my father now be poisoning King Marke of Cornwall?"

Lancelot and Tristan exchanged quick glances, then looked back at Issylte, who sat down at the table and whispered, "I saw the same dwarf in a *second vision*." The atmosphere in Tristan's room shifted, Frocin's dark presence hovering, lurking in shadows.

"He held a prisoner—a pregnant woman—high in a tower, hidden in a dark forest. She was desperate to escape, peering out a window above the trees, as if she wanted to jump." Issylte rubbed her arms, warding off an evil frost. "The dwarf entered the woman's room. She recoiled in terror. He stared directly at me. *He could see me watching him.* His black eyes were empty, cold… *evil*." Issylte buried her face in her hands, shivering uncontrollably.

She looked up, her eyes widened with fright. "I told Gwennol—the woman I was with—about the vision. She said it must be Frocin, for he has a fortress with a tower. And it's hidden, deep in the Forest of Morois. On the outskirts of Cornwall, where she is from." Issylte turned to Tristan. "This must be the same dwarf that is allied with Indulf, the knight who denounced you. And claimed your victory."

Nodding, his face livid, Tristan turned to Lancelot. "There is more," the White Knight said gravely, standing to face Tristan and Issylte, who exchanged quick, uneasy glances.

"A royal wedding between Cornwall and Ireland will take place in the castle of Tintagel after a year," he announced with a smirk, "allowing a sufficient *period of mourning* for the widowed queen. And, as King Marke's new champion, Indulf has received a title of nobility, becoming the new Earl of Dubh Linn. With the dwarf Frocin as his loyal ally."

Lancelot spat, "They plan to resume the slave expeditions that had been so prosperous to the Irish crown before the death of the Morholt."

Issylte shuddered with horror.

The White Knight turned to Tristan. "But now, with the queen betrothed to King Marke of Cornwall, the attacks will focus on the coast of France. They'll assault Bretagne, Armorique, Normandy. Even Anjou and Aquitaine."

Tristan's jaw clenched with rage. Lancelot sat down to face him, his voice scarcely above a whisper. "A second wedding will also take place at the castle of Tintagel, with the blessing of King Marke."

At this, Tristan raised an eyebrow. Lancelot's voice was barely audible. "Indulf, the new Earl of Dubh Linn, will marry Elowenn, Vaughan's younger sister."

Lancelot sighed, shaking his head in disbelief. "Her family is delighted to be elevated to a position of royalty. Which they'd hoped to achieve in marrying Elowenn to *you.*"

His lip raised in scorn, the White Knight smirked, "Needless to say, everyone is *thrilled* with Indulf's new title of nobility and the appointed lands. They look forward to both weddings with great anticipation and celebration."

Tristan was on his feet again, pacing with impotent rage. "I am *banished* from Cornwall. My name is *ruined*, and my uncle is *blind* to the truth. Lancelot, what on earth can I do?"

At that moment, Viviane entered through the open door, her smile disappearing as she absorbed the tension in the atmosphere and the distraught faces of her son and his companions, who were deep in conversation. "I am sorry to intrude," she said quietly, "I simply wanted to welcome Lancelot back and say hello." She met her son's anguished eyes. "Is there anything I can do?"

Lancelot stood to kiss his mother's cheeks, offering her his chair. "I bring bad news from Cornwall." After seating Viviane, Lancelot leaned against the wall and shared with her what he'd just told Tristan and Issylte.

Issylte explained how she'd described her most recent *sighting*—the poisoning of a king, a pregnant woman held hostage in a tower, the penetrating black eyes of the dwarf. How Gwennol had named the infamous dwarf Frocin.

Viviane listened intently, pensively, yet remained quiet, as the three resumed their discussion. Tristan began pacing anew.

"Indulf. And Frocin. Those two have plotted against me ever since the Tournament of Champions." He glared at Lancelot, exhaled with disgust, and plopped down on the edge of his bead. "Their first attempt failed, but now… they've succeeded. They've *destroyed* me."

Issylte looked inquisitively at Lancelot. He pulled up the sleeve of his tunic to reveal the same tattoo on his inner wrist that Tristan had shown her when the nightingale had fetched the *églantine.*

"This is the mark of the Tribe of Dana," the White Knight began, tracing the tattoo with his finger. "A band of warriors sworn to defend the sacred elements of the Goddess. And the entire Celtic realm."

Issylte remembered the little bird with the wild rose in its beak. "Yes," she replied, "Tristan told me about the Tribe, and his gift—*l'herbe d'or*—which allows him to speak to birds." She smiled at the sea raven warrior.

Lancelot nodded, his dark brown waves tumbling into his face. He pushed them back with calloused hands, locking eyes with hers. "It also allows him to communicate with *wolves.*" Issylte widened her eyes in surprise. She glanced at Viviane, who appeared equally intrigued.

"One afternoon, in Camelot, we Knights of the Round Table were competing in a hunt," he explained, glancing at his friend. "In the forest, a wolf appeared to Tristan, warning him that Frocin and Indulf were waiting just up ahead in the trees. Ready to ambush him."

"Fortunately," Tristan interjected, "Lancelot led our group of hunters in the opposite direction. A few minutes later, we heard snarling and growling. Horrific screaming. A pack of wolves had attacked and killed a man—one of Frocin's mercenaries. Identified by the dwarf's coat of arms on the victim's shield."

From his seat on the bed opposite Issylte's chair, Tristan said softly, "I was most grateful for the golden herb that day. The wolves of Morois saved my life."

Tristan looked back at Lancelot and smirked,

"Indulf and Frocin failed that day in the forest, but they've succeeded now." He leaned forward on the bed, raking his fingers through his hair. "I'm banished by my uncle—*my king.* I'm stripped of my title as Champion of Cornwall. I'm no longer heir to King Marke's crown. I've lost *everything.*" Lowering his face in grief, Tristan tore at his thick, chestnut locks, rocking on the edge of the bed in frustration and rage. He fixed his gaze on Lancelot, leaning against the wall. "Since I cannot return to Cornwall, I must return with you to Camelot."

Lancelot cast sorrowful eyes at Tristan, then his mother, and finally Issylte. "That is impossible." At everyone's obvious bewilderment, Lancelot lowered his head in shame. "You and I are both banished from King Arthur's court." The White Knight dropped onto the bed beside Tristan, placing his elbows on his knees, his head in his hands.

Tristan stared at his friend in disbelief. "What do you mean? Lance, *explain.*"

Lancelot's bleak face revealed despair, loss, and regret. "Frocin and Indulf have not only destroyed you, my friend. They have also destroyed *me.*"

The White Knight smiled sadly. "They have spread lies about my relationship with Queen Guinevere, claiming that I dishonor her with adulterous love in my heart." His anguished eyes spoke volumes. "To prevent any harm to the queen's reputation, Arthur has banished me from his kingdom."

And, as if gathering strength to deliver the final, bitter blow, he sighed, "Out of respect for his ally, King Marke of Cornwall, who has accused you of treason and stripped you of all titles—King Arthur has banished *you* from Camelot as well."

Bitter laughter erupted from Tristan. "What a pair of sorry bastards we are, eh, Lance?" he scoffed as he slapped his friend on the back. "Banished from our kingdoms. Homeless knights. Outlaws on the run." Shaking his head in despair and rage, Tristan spat, "What the hell do we do now?"

Viviane spoke at last. Rising to her feet, she walked to the window and gazed up at the stars which were just beginning to wink in the darkening sky. Moonlight glimmered in the sacred waters of the effervescent fountain. "The Goddess has brought you all together for a reason," she began, her voice ethereal and *otherworldly*. Turning to Issylte, she said, "You were the *only* priestess capable of healing Tristan, poisoned by the Black Knight's blade, because you had been trained by Maiwenn—in Ireland, home of the Morholt."

Facing Tristan, she continued. "And *you* were brought here, to Avalon—to the only priestess in the entire realm who could heal you." She cast her gaze at Lancelot. "And you, my son—trained by the Avalonian Elves--taught Tristan how to defeat the infallible Morholt."

Her limpid eyes glowed with preternatural wisdom. "And, because you had lived in Avalon, you were able to return to this Island of Healing—so that Tristan *would live*."

The Lady of the Lake sat down at the table to address all three. "The Princess Issylte has wanted for years to challenge Queen Morag." Viviane gazed at Issylte, who nodded in agreement, her breath hitching with rapt attention.

"While her father lived, Issylte had no claim to the throne. Later, after his death, she had no army to challenge the wicked queen who ordered her death and usurped her rightful claim to the crown."

The High Priestess turned to Tristan. "The Goddess brought *you*, the Blue Knight of Cornwall, here to Avalon—to meet Princess Issylte."

Tristan and Issylte met each other's gaze as they listened to the *otherworldly* Lady of the Lake.

"You, Sir Tristan, are the champion she needs to lead her army. The only warrior capable of defeating the formidable Morholt. And the *only* knight to have ever defeated *my indomitable son*."

Viviane spoke softly to the two knights seated before her. "You both belong to a fierce Tribe of warriors who defend the sacred realm." The weight of her prophesy hung in the air. "The Goddess Dana is finally revealing the fate—*la fatalité*—which entwines *you three*."

Issylte was awed by the fierce, determined faces of the two warriors before her. *My destiny lies with them.*

The Lady of the Lake met Issylte's gaze, her expression becoming grave. "Frocin is very powerful and extremely dangerous. He is the leader of the dwarves—*otherworldly* beings, like the forest fairies. But, while the Little Folk defend the sacred forests of the Goddess and protect those with a pure heart," she explained, glancing at Tristan and Lancelot, "the dwarves delve in dark magic, and seek to harm others with their malevolence." Viviane took Issylte's hands into her own. "Frocin *locked eyes* with you in the *sighting*. He knew that you were *watching*."

Issylte nodded fearfully, remembering the dwarf's penetrating stare.

"Frocin is *clairvoyant*. Capable of reading the stars.

But he also has a most unique gift." The waters of Viviane's deep blue eyes rippled with warning. "When a fairy uses her *sight*, it leaves a trail of magic. A trail that Frocin can trace." Icy numbness rippled up Issylte's arms. "The dwarf has undoubtedly tracked you here."

Issylte's stomach lurched *For the wretched stepmother who still hunts me. The wicked, relentless Black Widow Queen.*

The Lady of the Lake rose to her feet. "It is no longer safe for you to remain here. You *must leave* Avalon."

Flustered and shaken, Issylte stammered, "But…Avalon is enchanted with spells of protection. I'm not safe here?"

Viviane looked out the window to the sacred fountain, shimmering in the starlight. "I have enshrouded the islands of Avalon with mists that keep us hidden from intruders. But Frocin, a powerful dwarf, allied with a dark wizard whose powers are unknown to me…" Viviane turned to Issylte, her serene face contorted with dread. "No, you are no longer safe here. You must leave. Before the queen, her dark wizard, and evil dwarf come for you here in Avalon."

Issylte was lost, her world turned upside down. She needed to flee the wicked queen. Again. The stepmother who'd already tried to kill her. *Twice*. The wretched queen who forced her to leave her father's castle. Then *Tatie's* cottage. And now Viviane's Island of Healing. The Black Widow who poisoned Issylte's father. Who murdered Gigi, *Tatie,* Bran and Dee. Who unleashed the Morholt and his Viking invaders upon the innocent victims of the slave raids. By the Goddess, she needed to stop her evil stepmother! But *how*?

She couldn't breathe. Where could she go? Her

limbs were shaking. "But *where*? Where can I go to escape the dwarf, the wizard, and the evil queen?"

Lancelot jumped to his feet. "To *la Joyeuse Garde!*" The White Knight beamed at Tristan, his radiant smile a beacon in the dark. He was at once rejuvenated, renewed, refreshed. "Tristan, we'll bring her—*with us!*"

The White Knight seemed to gain momentum as he spoke. "You can't return to Cornwall. I can't go back to Camelot. And she must flee Avalon."

With his boyish grin, he offered the perfect solution. "We'll bring her to *my castle!*"

His brain seemed to be churning, his strategy forming. "Tristan can train with my knights at *la Joyeuse Garde* until he regains his full strength." Lancelot's brilliant blue eyes gleamed with inviting challenge.

"Issylte will be safe with us. I'll invite Esclados and Laudine—and a few other nobles, potential allies—to my *château.* So we can plan how to challenge the queen!"

Lancelot gripped his friend's shoulder, his voice filled with hope. "Perhaps we can save your uncle— before it's too late. And find a way to clear your name."

Taking Issylte's hands in his, Lancelot knelt before her, gazing into her eyes with his blue ones that so resembled Tristan's. "The Tribe of Dana can summon the army you need to defeat this evil queen that threatens us all." He kissed her hand tenderly, his eyes meeting hers. "You, my Emerald Princess, are the rightful Queen of Ireland. May the Goddess grant Tristan and me the strength to help you reclaim your throne."

Tristan knelt before her, next to Lancelot. He took her other hand and kissed it reverently, too. "I will be your champion, Issylte. I will fight for you—beside you—as we challenge this wicked queen. Together, united, we'll defeat her. We'll save my uncle, reclaim both of our crowns. We'll restore the good names of the White Knight of Avalon and the Blue Knight of Cornwall. We'll regain the respect of our kings. And establish peace throughout the Celtic realm. Together, we'll prevail."

She was swept up in a torrent of emotions. Thrilled at the prospect of finally challenging her wretched stepmother. Terrified at confronting the trio of evil—the dwarf Frocin, the dark wizard, and the Black Widow queen—which threatened them all.

She needed to flee Avalon—her refuge, her haven—as she'd been forced to flee her father's castle, then *Tatie's* cottage. And Ronan was returning to her!

Yet, Issylte was empowered by the chance to summon an army. To have Lancelot and Tristan—the most powerful knights in the realm—lead the warriors of the fearsome Tribe of Dana. To fight for her right to the throne. To save King Marke from the queen's poisoned touch, which she had been unable to do for her beloved father.

Perhaps they could prevent Queen Morag and the dark wizard from poisoning King Marke and seizing the kingdoms of Cornwall and Lyonesse—Tristan's inheritance and birthright. Perhaps they could prevent Indulf and Frocin from resuming the slave expeditions which decimated kingdoms and left countless helpless victims. Perhaps they could restore Tristan's good name, enlighten King Marke, and reunite the royal uncle with his nephew. Perhaps King Arthur would be so impressed with Lancelot's valor that he would proclaim him First Knight of Camelot once more. And perhaps, after six long years, the Goddess had finally revealed her destiny.

In the breadth of a few seconds, processing all these conflicting emotions, Issylte determined that no matter where this path led, she must find the courage to follow it, with Tristan and Lancelot at her side. Rising to her feet, she raised the two knights who knelt before her. Her eyes brimming, she whispered, "Yes. We must go... *together*."

Lancelot smiled proudly, grateful that she'd accepted his proposal. "We'll depart for Bretagne in three days. I'll send word ahead that we'll be arriving soon. In the meantime, Tristan," he said, addressing the knight beside him, "let's dispatch invitations for potential allies to join us at *la Joyeuse Garde*. I can think of several whom I'd like to recruit."

He glanced at his mother and suggested, "Tristan has been training many of the injured warriors, helping with their convalescence. Encourage them to continue—and even train with the Avalonian Elves. Perhaps the victims will fight with us, as allies, anxious to claim vengeance for the lives lost to the Viking slave trade. They could be a most valuable asset to our knights."

As they bid each other goodnight, amid kisses, tears, and hugs, the Emerald Princess, the Blue Knight of Cornwall, and the White Knight of Avalon looked forward to embarking on the journey and embracing *la fatalité*—the destiny—in which the Goddess had entwined them all.

Chapter 30

The Golden Hawk

Aqua silk draped the enormous windows where rays
of the setting summer sun cast a golden halo around
Morag, seated imperially atop the gilded chair of her
royal antechamber. Her golden dragon, Lord Voldurk,
stood before her with two allies from Cornwall who,
having just arrived, wished to pay their respects to the
powerful Irish queen. In her black silk gown, the
fragrance of lavender perfuming the air, Morag assessed
the wizened creature and blond knight as they knelt at
her satin slippered feet.

The dwarf Frocin was elegantly dressed, a wealthy
noble in rich velvet, brocade, and leather. Yet his
blackened skin was hideous—wrinkled and withered
like the rotting, gnarled roots of a dying tree. Thick, wiry
hair was greasy and unkempt, poking out around his
grotesque face like wayward switches of a disintegrating
broom. Rotten stench of evil oozed from his every pore.
A slimy slug wrapped up in finest frippery. Morag
suppressed a gag of revulsion, daintily dabbing her nose
with lavender scented lace.

"You may rise," she said regally, eyeing the
impressive blond knight at Voldurk's side. Tall and
muscular—not quite as magnificent as her Morholt had
been, but wiry and lanky. With eyes as sharp as a falcon

and a prominent aquiline nose. Many would consider him ugly. Yet, a thick blond beard covered most of the pockmark scars on his savage face, and the curved beak gave him the appearance of a ravenous, rapacious predator. A fierce, formidable fighter. A hawk among doves. Morag's full mouth curved upward in a satisfied smirk at the obvious lust in the knight's eagle eyes.

"My queen, allow me to present Sir Indulf of Hame, knight of Cornwall and champion of King Marke of Tintagel, whom you have appointed Earl of Dubh Linn." Voldurk's golden eyes gleamed in the gilded light. "Sir Indulf has recently arrived in Ireland, establishing residence at the castle. He now reports to you as his sovereign queen."

Indulf bowed before her, his blond head bare, armored helmet in his scarred hand tucked under a superbly chiseled arm. His finely crafted chain mail glinted in the sunlight. A knight in shining armor like the enchanting legends of old.

"Good day, Lord Indulf. Welcome to Castle Connaught. It is a pleasure to meet you at last," Morag crooned, extending her slender white hand for the knight to kiss as he locked his eagle eyes with hers. A thrill rippled up her arm at his rough touch and bold, daring stare. "I am most grateful to you for arranging my betrothal to King Marke of Cornwall. In return, I am pleased to award you the prestigious position as the Earl of Dubh Linn." Indulf rose to his full height, standing at military attention before her scrutinizing gaze, his dark eyes dancing with desire.

"I trust that, given time and additional funds, you will resume the lucrative slave raids of the inimitable Morholt, *Scourge of the Celtic Sea*." She flashed him her most seductive smile.

To her delight, the knight grinned ferally, a dangerous spark in his predatory eye. "My queen, I am pleased to report that I have already ordered my Viking commanders to construct hundreds of *drakaar* warships to refurbish our ravaged fleet. I am anxious to resume the profitable pillaging that the Black Knight established in the seaport that I now proudly call home." He bowed his golden head, meeting her eyes once again. A shiver of wicked pleasure slithered up her spine.

"My queen, since your betrothed is the King of Cornwall, our new slave expeditions will target the coast of France rather than Britain. Our stealthy ships will sail right up the Seine into Paris and sack *la Sainte-Chapelle*, where gold icons and precious jewels are ripe for the taking. Our Viking vessels will float up the Loire and siege *le Duc d' Anjou* in his *château-fort*. Pillage the port of La Rochelle. Assault the fertile shores of Aquitaine. And make you the wealthiest queen in all of Europe." His dark brown eyes gleamed like ripe, rich chestnuts. Morag positively salivated at the tantalizing taste of power.

Voldurk's deep voice interrupted her sumptuous reverie. "Your Majesty, may I present Frocin, leader of an innumerable legion of dwarves who inhabit the dense forests of the entire Celtic realm. A powerful sorcerer whose dark magic has traced your elusive stepdaughter, the Princess Issylte. An invaluable ally whose mercenary knights will eliminate her and any possible threat she may pose to your claim to the Irish crown."

The dwarf spoke, his voice the creak of toad. "The Princess Issylte has used her gift of *sight*, leaving a trail of verdant magic which I have easily traced. Your stepdaughter hides on the island of Avalon, off the northern coast of Bretagne. Where Sir Tristan of Lyonesse, the Blue Knight of Cornwall, was taken, mortally injured by the poisoned sword of the Morholt."

Frocin's wicked grin revealed the pointed yellow fangs of vile vermin amid blackened stumps of rotted teeth. The dwarf's putrid beath fouled the lavender scented air.

"My knights will entrap them both, my queen. Eliminate the sole threat to your throne. And avenge the valiant Morholt, slain by the ignoble Blue Knight of Cornwall." He grinned wickedly, his black eyes glowing with malice.

"But alas, my queen," he faltered, lowering his sinister gaze. "We cannot touch them on Avalon. The Lady of the Lake has enchanted all seven of the islands of the Avalonian Elves with powerful wards of protection that neither my dwarves nor mercenary knights can penetrate." His beady black eyes rose to meet hers. A slug slithered up Morag's spine.

"But when either the Emerald Princess or the disgraced Knight of Tintagel leaves Avalon, we shall be ready, my queen." Blackened stumps and pointed yellow fangs grinned sickeningly as a wave of nausea washed over the revolted queen. "I, Frocin, never fail." The dwarf's cryptic laugh was the sharp hiss of a snake.

Lord Voldurk gallantly interrupted the foreboding atmosphere. "My queen, Frocin has graciously offered us lodging within his spacious tower in the Forest of Morois in western Cornwall. I propose we spend this year—a respectable period of mourning for your late husband, King Donnchadh—to refurbish our Viking fleet. Elevate taxes to fortify our army. Prepare the Royal

Triumvirate—our Seneschal, Marshal, and Steward—to govern Castle Connaught when we sail to Cornwall next summer. For you to be officially presented to your betrothed, King Marke of Cornwall." The golden dragon's gaze blazed in the setting sun, his white teeth lustrous as pearls.

Morag's eyes returned to the blond knight whose stare devoured her like a man starved. She leaned forward to adjust her satin slipper, feasting him on her delicious *décolletage*, then turned to address her Royal Advisor.

"Thank you, Lord Voldurk. I am eternally grateful for your unswerving loyalty and infallible guidance. We shall indeed elevate taxes, fortify our army, and refurbish our fleet of Viking warships. To support the most promising new Earl of Dubh Linn." She blinded the blond knight with her most dazzling smile. "And prepare the Royal Triumvirate to govern when we depart for Cornwall next summer." She addressed the vile but inordinately valuable dwarf. "I thank you most sincerely, Lord Frocin, for the generous offer of hospitality, which we gratefully accept. And for the promise to rid me of both painful thorns in my royal side." The dwarf grinned wickedly and bowed his slimy head.

With smug satisfaction, Morag announced, "You both have my leave. But Lord Indulf," she drawled, her voice soft as velvet, "I should like to speak more of your plans to restore the Viking stronghold of Dubh Linn." The queen motioned to her servants, who placed a silver platter replete with wine and fresh fruit upon the lace covered table at her side. As Voldurk and Frocin bowed and slipped humbly from the royal antechamber, Morag smiled enticingly at the bold blond knight. "Come, let us share some fine French wine and discuss this matter further."

A goblet of heady, fruity wine in her slender white hand, Morag slid from her gilded chair and approached the golden hawk with ravenous eyes. He accepted the proffered chalice and drank deeply, his dark eagle eyes never leaving hers. She stood before him, luxuriating in the barely bridled lust that choked him. Throttled him. Weakened him. Seductive power sizzled in her veins.

She led him by the hand into her adjacent royal chambers, where a bouquet of deep purple lilacs scented the sweet air. Pink and lavender rays of the setting sun gilded her mauve velvet draperies as she took the armored helmet from his trembling hand and laid it gently upon the table under the violet-streaked sky. Shaking with desire, yet immobile and above reproach as a dutiful, reverent knight, Indulf stood transfixed before her sultry, shimmering silk. A tensely coiled spring aching for release.

Morag raked her long fingers through his thick blond waves, the sharp tang of his desire empowering her. Enflaming her. Engulfing her. She pulled his eager lips to her own as the torrent of his passion burst like the unstoppable current of a swift flowing river.

And, amid the seductive perfume of lilacs, Morag moaned as the rapacious beak of her ravenous golden hawk ravished her elegant swanlike neck. And swept her up in powerful wings like prized prey, swooping swiftly and surely to nest in the lavender scented bed.

Chapter 31

Return from Armorique

The seagulls were squawking, diving for the entrails tossed by the fishermen filleting the fresh catch just harvested from the sea as Ronan's ship approached the mist-shrouded coast of Avalon. White clouds sailed across the late summer sky as the salty tang of ocean breeze welcomed the Elf home.

The trip had been most profitable, for King Hoël and his son Kaherdin, who had ordered supplies for two hundred knights, were delighted with the quality of the weaponry and armor that Ronan had forged in his blacksmith shop in Avalon and delivered to them in Armorique.

In fact, they had been so impressed with the Avalonian craftsmanship that the king had requested twice the amount as he placed a new order, with half to be delivered in the spring, and the remainder the following winter solstice. To keep up with the increased demand for his wares, Ronan planned to open a second forge when he arrived in Avalon, hiring additional strikers, journeymen, and apprentices, to fulfill the new order. Yes, the voyage had been lucrative indeed. He couldn't wait to share his success with Issylte.

King Hoël had insisted that Ronan remain as guest of honor for a full two weeks in his castle, *Le Château*

Rose, where he'd hosted a feast and ball in the Elf's honor—a celebration that had also enabled the king and his son to don the magnificent royal armor just delivered from Avalon. Ronan had accepted the invitation, of course, and had been very much the pampered guest for the duration of his stay. As his vessel now approached the enchanted shores of Avalon, Ronan reminisced about his prosperous trip.

Le Château Rose had been named for the pink granite—abundant in Armorique—from which the imposing fortress was constructed. Perched high upon a cliff, overlooking the sea and tidal bay, the castle was accessible only from the south, where it connected to the mainland by a narrow stone bridge. The cliff face of the curved peninsula upon which the fortress was built was steep enough to provide an impenetrable defense from the north, east, and west. The stone bridge, to the south, was the only entrance to the *château*, spanning a deep saltwater moat, fed by the tumultuous waves of the sea, encased by treacherous rocks and jagged peaks.

Despite its rugged, fortified exterior, the interior of the castle had been most elegant, richly appointed, warm and inviting. A wide, expansive corridor, with luminous chandeliers, marble floors, and gleaming hardwood tables adorned with bouquets of fragrant summer blooms, opened onto an enormous ballroom and banquet hall, which boasted a magnificent view of the granite cliffs and turbulent ocean. The enormous kitchen abutted the banquet hall, sheltered behind the spiral staircase leading to the bedrooms and guest quarters on the second floor, where Ronan had stayed, and up to the royal chambers on the uppermost level, overlooking the magnificent pink granite coast of Armorique.

As the royal guest of honor, Ronan had been expected to chat amicably with the noble lords and ladies of King Hoël's court as they dined in the spacious banquet room on sumptuous seafood and imbibed in fine French wine. During the ball, while the royal musicians entertained the court with lively fiddles and melodious harps, Ronan had politely danced with the king's daughter, Blanchine—called the Maid of the White Hands, for her long, delicate fingers and skill as a healer. Tall, thin, with black hair and icy blue eyes, Blanchine was regal, yet Ronan had found her detached and cold. Although she danced with him as the guest of honor, fulfilling her duty as the king's daughter, she spoke little, her eyes flitting across the ballroom, nervous and suspicious, as she watched the distant revelry which surrounded them with haughty disdain.

Kaherdin, on the contrary, was amicable and jovial. Tall and dark-haired, like his sister, but broad in the shoulders, he exuded the rugged strength of a well-honed soldier. Ronan had liked him immediately, finding he much preferred the company of the warm prince to his chilly sister. Kaherdin's guest, the Lady Gargeolaine, was a vibrant beauty with golden auburn hair, a voluptuous figure, and expressive amber eyes. Judging by the love light which shone in his eyes, it was apparent that Prince Kaherdin was truly besotted.

King Hoël, although past his prime in his mid-fifties, had still displayed the regal bearing of a warrior king. His children had inherited his tall stature and dark hair, now heavily streaked with gray, like his neatly trimmed beard. Ronan had enjoyed the king's youthful mirth and keen sense of humor, making him feel a most welcome guest.

During the ball, while seated at the monarch's table, King Hoël had addressed his guest of honor amid the gaiety of music and dancing. "Sir Ronan," he'd beamed, "I am most pleased with the exceptional quality of the royal armor you crafted for my son and me." The king had nodded to his daughter Blanchine, who'd placed a small but ornate jewelry box on the table before her father.

The carved wooden box had been painted white and adorned with delicate pink roses. Opening the small treasure chest, Hoël had displayed the dazzling contents to Ronan. "Perhaps your lady might fancy one of my late queen's baubles," he'd offered with a generous smile.

As Ronan had surveyed the sparkling gems, an exquisite emerald ring had caught his eye. He'd picked it up to admire the deep green oval gem, brilliant in clarity and surrounded by a halo of flawless diamonds. *Perfect for my Emerald Princess,* he'd mused, gratefully accepting King Hoël's generous bonus.

Tapping the pocket of his tunic, where he now held the exquisite jewel for Issylte, Ronan cast aside the memories of his voyage and focused on the sandy beach and forested cliff as his cog ship docked at the shore of Avalon. After three months at sea, he was eager to return. And he couldn't wait to surprise Issylte with his gift.

The fishermen, recognizing his ship, waved in greeting as the nearby stable hands joined in docking Ronan's vessel alongside the wharf. His crew, as eager to return home as the Elf himself, leapt onto the wooden dock, strapped their belongings upon the backs of the horses provided by the grooms, and rode off to rejoin their families.

After greeting several of the workers and stable

hands, Ronan decided he would go home first to bathe before venturing to *Le Centre,* for he did not want to crush Issylte into his arms, reeking like a fishmonger.

The men in his forge welcomed him back, as did his own grooms, who had been caring for the horses and animals during his absence. Noz, his beautiful black stallion, was anxious to greet him—and grateful for the crunchy carrot—as was Maëva, Marron, and the pretty little foal, Noisette. *She is now old enough for Issylte to ride. I can't wait for us to be together, back in the saddle again!*

Ronan rushed to the pool—a small lake—in the woods near his cottage, where he bathed, washing the brine from his hair with some of the soap he'd once purchased in the village with Issylte. The fragrant smell of yarrow reminded him of her soft body, and the longing he felt for her stirred painfully in his loins.

He rinsed the soap from his hair, emerged from the pool and dried off, donning a new tunic, fresh pair of breeches, and clean boots. He refastened the amulet that Issylte had made for him around his neck, knowing that she'd be pleased to see him wearing it. He carefully placed the exquisite emerald ring in his pocket. *Pray the Goddess she says yes!*

Saddling Noz and Maëva—for he planned to bring his princess back to the cottage—he envisioned the warm welcome she would give him. She'd tantalize him with her scent, devour his lips, welcome him into her body, then—drunk with love, sated in his arms, filled with his seed—he would give her the ring. *Easy now, or you won't be able to ride,* he laughed to himself. Quickly packing the supplies he'd procured for Viviane, the Elf mounted his horse, grasped Maëva's reins, and rode off to find Issylte.

When he arrived at *Le Centre*, he handed the horses' reins to the groom who approached, retrieved the supplies from his pack, and headed towards Viviane's quarters. Since she was not in her room, he placed the parcel on her table and walked down the hall toward the exit door leading onto the courtyard and fountain. As he approached, he spotted Viviane entering a patient's room. Ronan poked his head through the open door, and was surprised to see Issylte, Lancelot, and another knight with dark hair in the room with Viviane. *He must be a patient, and Issylte was his healer. But why is Lancelot here?* Unease crept up his spine.

Glancing up to see who had come in, Lancelot shouted heartily, "Ronan! It's good to see you again, my friend!" The knight clasped the Elf's shoulders, warmly greeting the warrior who had trained him so well.

"I heard that you had gone to Armorique," Lancelot chortled, delighted to see his former mentor. "How was your voyage?"

Taking in the sight of Issylte assembling supplies, the dark-haired knight packing a bag, Viviane gathering herbal medicines and soaps, Ronan assumed that Lancelot and his companion were preparing for their departure. *Good,* he thought, feeling inexplicably suspicious and threatened by the unknown knight.

"It was a most prosperous voyage, Lancelot," Ronan replied, eyeing Tristan warily. "King Hoël and Kaherdin were so impressed with the quality of the goods, they doubled the order." Looking at Issylte, he added, "I'll be forging weapons and armor for four hundred knights—to be delivered next spring and the following winter solstice." Turning his attention back to Lancelot, he said grimly, "Hoël wants to be prepared. There are rumors that the Vikings plan to attack Armorique." When Ronan glanced at Tristan, Lancelot took the opportunity to introduce his friend.

With his famous boyish grin, the White Knight beamed, "Ronan, I'd like you to meet Tristan of Lyonesse, the Blue Knight of Cornwall. He is the nephew…" Lancelot glanced awkwardly at Tristan, then recovered quickly, "…and heir to King Mark of Tintagel."

As Ronan and Tristan shook hands, Lancelot added, "Tristan was one of the ten winners of the Tournament of Champions who trained with me at Camelot. He was dubbed a Knight of the Round Table this past summer."

"Congratulations," Ronan muttered, trying to shake the feeling that this knight somehow posed a threat.

Tristan, his face aglow with admiration for the famed Avalonian Elf who had trained Sir Lancelot of the Lake, shook Ronan's hand vigorously as he effused, "It is a pleasure to meet you, Sir Ronan. Lancelot has told me all about your extraordinary skill as a warrior."

As he continued to size Tristan up, Ronan noted that the knight was exceptionally tall for a human—only an inch or so shorter than himself—and every bit as wide and broad as he. Something about this young warrior irked Ronan; he was challenged, ready to fight, despite the lack of provocation.

Lancelot continued bragging about the prowess of his friend, the Blue Knight of Cornwall. "Tristan is the warrior who slew the Morholt!" he exclaimed, grinning proudly at his companion. Looking back at Ronan, he added with a hearty chuckle, "And the *only knight* to have ever *defeated me*."

Ronan raised an eyebrow, impressed. Issylte said softly, "Tristan was seriously wounded in the battle against the Morholt." Her luminous green eyes gazed at the knight, and Ronan seethed beneath the surface. What was going on here? Something was definitely wrong. His pulse quickened as his temper flared.

"The Black Knight's sword was poisoned," she continued, "and Lancelot brought him here to be healed." She smiled warmly at the White Knight, while Ronan wondered how the three of them had become so close in his absence. *She healed the wounded one, and Lancelot is the knight's friend. They are leaving soon, to return to the Round Table. Relax—there is no reason for concern about this friendship.* Still, unease and doubt nagged at him.

"We are preparing to depart for Bretagne on the morrow," Lancelot explained. Grinning at the princess, he added, "Issylte will be joining Tristan and me as we sail for *la Joyeuse Garde.*"

Ronan's eyes flashed to Issylte, who was avoiding his gaze. He turned to Viviane—who knew of their romantic involvement—for an explanation. "*What?*" he cried incredulously. His eyes darting back to Issylte, he sputtered, his voice increasing in volume as his anger increased in intensity, "You cannot be serious. You are *leaving Avalon*? To sail to *Bretagne*? With two men you *barely know?*"

The Lady of the Lake attempted to calm him. "The princess must flee Avalon, Ronan. It is no longer safe for her here." Ronan glared at Issylte, his eyes filled with fury.

Viviane continued, "Issylte has had *two sightings* in which the dwarf Frocin locked eyes with her. Aware that she could see him. "

Ronan could not comprehend what was happening. *Issylte was leaving? With this knight? NO!*

"Frocin is clairvoyant, Ronan. He has the gift to track the use of *sight* and has undoubtedly traced her here." Viviane fixed her deep blue gaze upon him. "With Frocin's dark magic, an evil wizard, and the wicked, powerful queen—Issylte must leave. *Immediately."*

Quickly, he rebutted. "But Viviane—you have *enchanted* Avalon. We are well protected here. The Elves will defend her. *I will defend her!*"

Ronan was shouting, shaking with anger, imploring Issylte with desperate eyes. "Issylte, may I please speak with you... *privately?*"

She replied quietly, "Of course." Addressing the two knights and the High Priestess, Issylte said, "Please excuse me. I shall return soon."

Shall return soon? What? This was not at all the welcome he envisioned. He needed to dissuade her—quickly—for he simply could not allow her to leave.

Outside, twilight was settling; the stars were just beginning to wink in the darkening sky. Two patients hurried by, as if not wanting to intrude upon an obviously private conversation.

Pulling her into the darkness of a recessed corner, among the jasmine resplendent vines, Ronan crushed her in his arms and kissed her. "Issylte, I missed you so much!" Breathless, he devoured her mouth, neck, shoulders. The delicate swell of her breasts.

Issylte seemed to panic in his strong embrace, her breath coming in short gasps. "Ronan, please..." she stammered, resisting his advances and squirming in his arms.

Grasping her hips, he pulled her to him so that she could feel his urgent need for her. "Come with me to the cottage, Issylte. I have brought Maëva for you to ride…" His hands roamed over her, his mouth searching, his body hard and insistent. "Or we could go to your room. It's closer…" he rasped hoarsely, his breath ragged. Pinning her against the wall, he sucked on her neck as he began lifting her dress, his other hand holding her hips firmly in place as he pressed his hardness against her.

"Ronan, please stop. Ronan, I must talk to you. Please listen! Ronan, *stop!*" Issylte wailed, desperately struggling against him.

"I believe the lady has asked you to *stop*." At the sound of Tristan's voice, Ronan backed away from Issylte, who quickly lowered her dress and straightened her bodice.

Ronan snarled, "It is no concern of yours, Knight of Cornwall. *Go back inside.*"

Tristan replied firmly, "I swore an oath of chivalry to defend a lady." His deep voice exuded calm and power. "And I will defend *that* lady," he proclaimed, glancing at Issylte, then back at him, "*with my life.*"

Ronan barked out a bitter laugh and growled, "*You* would challenge *me*? *You*? An injured knight, not yet fully recovered from your wound? Do you even know *who I am*?"

Tristan, his eyes never leaving Ronan's, responded quietly, "I do." He squared his shoulders, raising himself to his full height, and declared, "And I will not allow you to assault the princess."

"*Assault the princess*?" Ronan scoffed—-the realization dawning upon him, hitting him like a blow to the gut. *He is defending her… against me! What is*

407

happening? How can this be? This is not at all the way I planned!

Rebuked and contrite, Ronan lowered his eyes to the ground. Then, his arms bent at the elbow, he raised his hands, palms extending outward in a gesture of peace. He stared Tristan in the eye and promised, "I will not harm her, Knight from Cornwall. You have *my word.*"

Tristan seemed to assess Ronan's more controlled demeanor. Ducking his chin, he glanced at Issylte, who nodded to him in return.

She whispered, "It is all right, Tristan. Thank you."

He bowed his head and said simply, "I am just inside, should you need me." Glaring at Ronan, his eyes aflame with challenge, Tristan backed away and returned to his room.

Ronan rushed forward to take her hands as he sputtered, "I am sorry, Issylte. I let my passion for you... *consume* me." Kissing her palms, he whispered, "This is not at all how I envisioned my *welcome home.*" His desperate eyes begged for forgiveness. "Please come with me to the cottage. Let me show you how much I have *missed you.*" He approached her slowly, gently placing his hands on her slender waist, drawing her to him tenderly. Cautiously. Reverently.

Issylte touched the stubble on his face. Her eyes focused on the amber talisman around his neck—the Yuletide gift she'd offered him. He was glad he'd worn it tonight.

Her determined voice jolted his fond reverie. "I am leaving in the morning, Ronan. Sailing to *la Joyeuse Garde* with Lancelot and Tristan."

His temper flared again. "You cannot be serious, Issylte." He stormed away from her, then turned abruptly to face her, livid with fury. "You would throw away everything we have shared—the life we have built together—to sail off with two men you *barely know*?" He shook his glorious golden mane and stomped his foot. "*I forbid it*! You will stay here with me. Where I can *keep you safe*."

Issylte retorted, "You *forbid* it? You *forbid* it? Ronan, you do not *own me!*" Her emerald eyes blazed at him in the starlight.

Ronan realized he had to try a different approach. "Issylte, I *want* you to stay with me. Every day, in Armorique, I thought of you. *Longed* for you." He approached her again, took her hands in his and showered them with kisses. He drew her gently towards him, lifted her chin and kissed her sweet lips softly. He wanted to devour her. To worship her body as he'd done so many times in his cottage. He wanted to claim her— to make her *his* once again. He could not let her leave. Losing her would kill him.

He took the emerald ring from his pocket and held it out it to her, the diamonds sparkling in the starlight, the emerald glimmering in the moonlight.

Gazing into her deep green eyes, he whispered, "I love you, Issylte. I want you to *be my wife*." He placed the ring on her delicate finger—*King Hoël's wife must have had long, slender fingers, too,* he mused idly, for the fit was perfect. "We have everything we need here in Avalon, my princess."

He kissed her hand and murmured, "We can raise children, Issylte. And horses…" He raised her chin as his lips met hers. "I have my shop… you can heal the villagers. We'll be *happy together*, here in Avalon. Do not leave me, Issylte. Stay here, where I can protect you.

And *keep you safe*." He pulled her to his chest and kissed her softly, enveloping her with his strong arms. "Say yes. Stay here with me. *Marry me*, Issylte. *I love you*."

Tears streamed down her face as she struggled to speak. "I love you too, Ronan." Her eyes glistened, filled with sadness, as she met his gaze. "But I cannot marry you. I *cannot* stay here."

She placed a trembling hand against his pounding chest. "Not only is it no longer safe for me in Avalon, with the threat of the dwarf Frocin... But I now have the chance to lead an army. And *stop the evil queen*." Gaining momentum, Issylte's words seemed to flow more freely. "For years, Ronan, I was told to *be patient*. To wait and see what fate the Goddess had in store for me." She searched his eyes and pleaded, "Don't you see? *This is the fate which She has finally revealed*!"

He lowered his gaze, shaking his head, refusing her words.

Issylte persisted. "I was the *only priestess* who recognized the Black Knight's poison. Because I had been trained in Ireland, home of the Morholt." She began pacing, animated, as if to convince him. "*Tatie* always said she believed the Goddess had brought me to her doorstep so that she could help me find a way to reclaim my throne." She turned back to him, her face alight, her voice alive. "Lancelot brought Tristan here, *for me to heal him*." At the mention of the knight's name, he snarled and shook his head. But Issylte persisted. "I know you cannot lead my army, Ronan. I understand that you cannot leave Avalon." She walked up to him and took his calloused hand in hers. Her pleading eyes looked up to meet his gaze. "*But I must*." Issylte kissed his gnarled warrior's fist. "I *must stop the wicked queen*."

Ronan stared out at *la Fontaine de Jouvence*, the source of the sacred water which bound him—and all Elves—to Avalon. He couldn't live with her in the human realm. She was unwilling to stay here with him. Compelled to challenge the queen, to save her kingdom, to restore peace. How could he possibly keep her here? It would be like trying to stop the tide, to extinguish the stars, to stifle the wind.

"Tristan and Lancelot are members of a band of warriors," she murmured. "The Tribe of Dana—sworn to protect the sacred elements of the Goddess. To defend the entire Celtic realm." She brushed aside a long lock of his blond hair. "They will be *my allies* and lead my army. As I fight to reclaim the throne of Ireland. *My father's crown.*"

Her eyes were filled with pain, yet brimming with hope as she held his gaze and whispered, "I cannot stay here with you and decide my future as a *woman*, Ronan." Issylte placed her flat palm over his galloping heart, her emerald eyes brimming with tears. "I must follow my destiny. *And decide as a queen.*"

She took his hand and gently placed the beautiful emerald ring back in his palm. Closing his fingers around the precious gem, she murmured the words which pierced his Elven heart like a swift, sharp sword. "I cannot accept this, Ronan. I am so terribly sorry."

She rose onto her tiptoes to kiss him softly and whispered, her voice choking, her lip quavering, "Please take good care of Noisette for me." With a guttural sob, she quickly turned from him and dashed away, as if desperate to regain the shelter of her room.

Ronan bellowed in pain like a wounded beast.

"Issylte! *Issylte…*"

****

In the dark, she threw herself on the bed, her breath heaving, the pain of loss smothering. Stifling. Suffocating. All night long, she wept for her beloved Elf. And the impossible future they could never share.

When morning dawned bright and clear, Issylte said goodbye to her patients, the priestesses, the villagers. Everyone was told that Lilée was sailing home to her native Anjou, a necessary lie which would thwart the dwarf and queen, in the event they did trace her to Avalon.

As she tearfully hugged Gwennol and the children in the Women's Center, giving a special kiss to Mara and her newborn son, Issylte spotted Cléo and walked over to the priestess.

"We will all miss you, Lilée," her dark-haired friend whispered as she kissed Issylte goodbye.

Issylte took Cléo's hands, and said, her voice barely audible, her eyes brimming with unshed tears, "Please take good care of Ronan for me. He will be so alone…"

For a moment, she imagined riding swiftly to his cottage, throwing herself into his arms, making love before the fireplace. She could feel herself welcoming him into her body, envision the blond children they would have—the beautiful Elven babies she'd dreamed about. She could see Maëva, Marron, the sweet little foal Noisette. *He even named her after the forest in Ireland that I loved so much.*

She pictured herself turning her back on Queen Morag, casting her horrid stepmother out of her life once and for all—becoming Ronan's wife, staying here in Avalon. With him. Her beautiful blond stallion.

He had a prosperous blacksmith shop; she was a gifted healer. She could cure illness, treat countless patients. They could raise horses! Lots of beautiful horses…like Noisette, the gift that had melted her heart. She truly *loved* Ronan, and he was so strong. He could defend her against a dwarf!

And yet, her stepmother wanted her dead. At any cost. The wicked queen now had a powerful wizard and a dwarf with dark magic as her allies. A Viking army and *drakaar* warships. If they were to descend upon Avalon, then all the patients here who had so courageously recovered from the horrific Viking slave raids would fall victim to another unified assault of evil. Issylte couldn't subject the people she had come to love to that. She *had* to leave. So that they would be safe.

And King Marke… *Would you turn your back on him, too? Do nothing to prevent his death, as you did nothing to prevent your father's?* If Issylte did nothing to stop the queen, the slave raids would begin anew. *How many hundreds—perhaps even thousands—of victims will suffer and die if you turn your back and do nothing?* And her kingdom. The people of Ireland were drowning in taxes, starving—unable to feed their families because the crops were needed for the Viking amies and the dreaded slave expeditions. *Would you turn your back on the country you were born to lead?*

If she took no action, she would be complicit in the death of King Marke, just as she was guilty of doing nothing to prevent the death of her own father. If she stayed here with Ronan, basking in his love, forsaking everything else, thinking only of her own happiness— then her father, Gigi, *Tatie*, Bran and Dee—had all died in vain.

If she tolerated evil, accepted it, did nothing to prevent it when the opportunity was finally laid out right before her—she was culpable of the death and suffering of every victim of the wretched queen's wrath.

You could never live with yourself, Issylte. Do not be a coward, hiding in the darkness. Find the courage to lead—to be the light. Stop the evil queen, avenge the ones you love, and bring peace, prosperity, and tranquility to the Celtic realm. Embrace your fate… and become the queen you were born to be.

Resolute, Issylte finished her farewells and rode with Viviane to the dock, where she joined Lancelot and Tristan, who were loading supplies onto the ship along with the crew.

The Lady of the Lake took her hands. "I will miss you dearly," she whispered, kissing each cheek to bid her goodbye. Viviane gently wiped the tears from Issylte's face. "My son and Sir Tristan will protect you. And lead your army. May the Goddess help you all in your noble quest." The High Priestess pushed back a strand of blond hair from Issylte's crumpled face. "Remember…you may always return to Avalon, now that you have lived among us." Viviane kissed her forehead and said, her voice hushed and hopeful, "Perhaps our paths will cross again."

Forcing a smile, Issylte nodded and turned to the crew members who helped her board the ship sailing for *Bretagne*. Once everything was properly stored below deck, Tristan and Lancelot climbed aboard as the vessel unfurled its white sails into the brisk breeze. Waving arms dotted the island shore as the ship left port under a brilliant summer sky and headed out to the open sea.

****

Ronan stood on the cliff near the sandy beach at the edge of the forest, watching the ship depart for Bretagne, carrying away the woman he loved with all his heart. When at last it disappeared on the horizon, he returned home to his forge, driving his body to exhaustion with his heavy hammer and bellows over a furious flame. Angry, empty, and broken, his Elven soul would never find solace from this suffocating grief. He would love Issylte until the day he died.

****

The square sail of the cog ship billowed in the strong wind, propelling Issylte, Tristan, and Lancelot south to the craggy coast of Bretagne. As they embarked on the journey to *la Joyeuse Garde,* Issylte watched the island of Avalon disappear into the mist, crying for the Elf she loved and another life she was forced to leave behind.

She wept for the future they would have had, the love they would have shared, the years they would have spent together, raising children and horses. Her throat constricted. The physical pain of loss overwhelming, she retreated to her quarters below deck to grieve alone, unable to face anyone in her miserable state.

Yet, between bouts of retching and sobbing, seasick and heartsick—a glimmer of hope flickered in Issylte's fragile heart.

In Bretagne, she would soon meet the Tribe of Dana. A band of warriors as fierce as the Elves of Avalon. Committed to helping her eradicate the evil of her wicked stepmother, the dark wizard, and the diabolical dwarves.

The long-awaited army she needed to challenge the Black Widow Queen.

With Tristan and Lancelot at her side. Two

unparalleled knights. The finest in the entire Celtic realm. Warriors of the Tribe of Dana.

Together, they would prevent King Marke's death.

Restore the knights' good standing with their respective monarchs.

And finally, after six long years of waiting, the Emerald Princess could at last embrace her fate.

And become the Emerald Queen.

A word about the author...

Jennifer Ivy Walker has an MA in French literature and is a professor of French at a state college in Florida. Her debut novel, "The Wild Rose and the Sea Raven," is a dark fantasy, paranormal romance retelling of the medieval French legend of "Tristan et Yseult," blended with elements of Arthurian myth, fairy tales, and folklore from the enchanted Forest of Brocéliande.

Be sure to follow "The Wild Rose and the Sea Raven" trilogy with book two, "The Lady of the Mirrored Lake," and the thrilling conclusion, "The Emerald Fairy and the Dragon Knight," both published by The Wild Rose Press.

Please visit her at the following websites:

https://jenniferivywalker.com/

https://jenniferivywalker.blogspot.com/

https://twitter.com/bohemienneivy

Thank you for purchasing
this publication of The Wild Rose Press, Inc.

For questions or more information
contact us at
info@thewildrosepress.com.

The Wild Rose Press, Inc.
www.thewildrosepress.com